Michael Moorcock was born in London in 1939 and published his first novel in 1962. From 1964 to 1980 he edited the seminal imaginative fiction magazine *New Worlds*. He has written for and performed with the rock groups Hawkwind and Blue Oyster Cult, scripted films and an interactive live-action computer game. Of his many novels *Behold The Man* won the Nebula Award, *Gloriana* won the World Fantasy Award, *The Condition of Muzak* won the Guardian Fiction Prize and *Mother London* was shortlisted for the Whitbread Prize. He and his wife Linda divide their time between Austin, Texas, London and the Mediterranean.

D1394400

By the same author

For further information about Michael
Moorcock and his work please send
SAE to The Nomads of the Time Streams,
18 Laurel Bank, Truss Hill Road, South
Ascot, Berks, UK, or PO Box 5201,
Pinehurst, North Carolina, 28374, USA.

†In preparation (Cape)

Michael Moorcock

THE PRINCE
WITH THE
SILVER HAND

MILLENNIUM

Orion Paperbacks
A Millennium Book
This edition first published in Great Britain
by Millennium in 1993
This paperback edition published in 1997 by
Orion Books Ltd,
Orion House, 5 Upper St Martin's Lane,
London WC2H 9EA

A CIP catalogue record for this book
is available from the British Library.

ISBN: 0 75280 877 X

Typeset at Spartan Press Ltd,
Lymington, Hants
Printed and bound in Great Britain by
Clays Ltd, St Ives plc

Dear Reader,

This second Corum sequence was perhaps even more influenced by Celtic myth than the first and draws on images and ideas inspired by the Cuchulain stories and other Irish tales, of a time when the dark Gods of Ireland were still abroad, threatening all we hold dear . . .

It seems to me that there is a common thread of romance linking the old stories of gods and heroes with modern fantasy – satisfying the identical needs we share with our remote ancestors. In the old days, when we had less of a handle on the truth, we didn't bother too much about what was fiction and what was not, so long as it didn't involve us directly. We enjoyed the stories for their own sake, perhaps as readers of today's popular newspapers and magazines enjoy unlikely tales of the rich and famous. The main difference appears to be that people tended to wait until their subjects were safely dead or on the other side of an ocean before telling their stories – or else making sure that their version was a very flattering one.

I suppose it's presumptious of me to wander into territory explored with far greater talent and profundity by half the great writers of Dublin, but the Corum stories are my acknowledgement of the huge debt I have to both the mythology and the modern literature of Ireland, especially Yeats.

An almost forgotten Irish writer who gave me enormous pleasure as a boy was Charles Lever, who had much of Dickens' zest, his taste for the extraordinary, his talent for melodrama and extravagant comedy. A lively writer in the main, he wrote a three volume comedy in 1864, *Cornelius O'Dowd*, which is no longer very funny since it touches mainly on forgotten issues. His *Dodd Family Abroad*, however, written in 1854 with illustrations by Phiz, is still a minor comic masterpiece and far superior in my view to his tales of army life with *Harry Lorrequer* or *Charles O'Malley, the Irish Dragoon*, which made him famous and immensely popular in his day.

I read Lever around the same time I was reading Harrison Ainsworth, whose tales of Dick Turpin and the Tower of London were also huge best-sellers once and established the form of the historical romance we know today. These led me to darker stories by Lewis and LeFanu and Maturin's *Melmoth the Wanderer*, perhaps the greatest of all Gothic extravaganzas. Oscar Wilde, when he left prison in 1897, took the name of Melmoth when he left to live abroad.

We owe much that is good in imaginative literature to Irish writers – Swift, of course, being one, and Lord Dunsany, who gave us those marvellously witty fantasies like *The Gods of Pagana* and *The Sword of Welleran*, which were also part of my youthful reading and which, together with the stories of James Branch Cabell and Fritz Leiber, made me realize that heroic fantasy could be both witty, elegant and intelligent.

This heroic fantasy, a somewhat rougher beast than Dunsany's, is dedicated to all those old hippies with whom I shared an honest track or two in a kind of golden Celtic afternoon some years ago – Nik Turner, Dave Brock, Terry Ollis, Huw Lloyd Langton, Harvey Bainbridge, Simon House, Simon King, Pete Pavli, Graham Charnock, Bob Calvert, Adrian Shaw, Steve Gilmore, Lang Jones, Martin Griffin, Barnie Bubbles, Martin Stone and many others – when gods and heroes still knew how to have a damned good time.

Yours,
Michael Moorcock

The Bull and the Spear

FOR MARIANNE

Prologue

In those days there were oceans of light and cities in the skies and wild flying beasts of bronze. There were herds of crimson cattle that roared and were taller than castles. There were shrill, viridian things that haunted bleak rivers. It was a time of gods, manifesting themselves upon our world in all her aspects; a time of giants who walked on water; of mindless sprites and misshapen creatures who could be summoned by an ill-considered thought but driven away only on pain of some fearful sacrifice; of magics, phantasms, unstable nature, impossible events, insane paradoxes, dreams come true, dreams gone awry; of nightmares assuming reality.

It was a rich time and a dark time. The time of the Sword Rulers. The time when the Vadhagh and the Nhadragh, age-old enemies, were dying. The time when Man, the slave of fear, was emerging, unaware that much of the terror he experienced was the result of nothing else but the fact that he, himself, had come into existence. It was one of many ironies connected with Man (who, in those days, called his race Mabden).

The Mabden lived brief lives and bred prodigiously. Within a few centuries they rose to dominate the westerly continent on which they had evolved. Superstition stopped them from sending many of their ships towards Vadhagh and Nhadragh lands for another century or two, but gradually they gained courage when no resistance was offered. They began to feel jealous of the older races; they began to feel malicious.

The Vadhagh and the Nhadragh were not aware of this.

They had dwelt a million or more years upon the planet which now, at last, seemed at rest. They knew of the Mabden, but considered them not greatly different from other beasts. Though continuing to indulge their traditional hatreds of one another, the Vadhagh and the Nhadragh spent their long hours in considering abstractions, in the creation of works of art and the like. Rational, sophisticated, at one with themselves, these older races were unable to believe in the changes that had come. Thus, as it almost always is, they ignored the signs.

There was no exchange of knowledge between the two ancient enemies, even though they had fought their last battle many centuries before.

The Vadhagh lived in family groups occupying isolated castles scattered across a continent called by them Bro-an-Vadhagh. There was scarcely any communication between these families, for the Vadhagh had long since lost the impulse to travel. The Nhadragh lived in their cities built on the islands in the seas to the north-west of Bro-an-Vadhagh. They, also, had little contact, even with their closest kin. Both races reckoned themselves invulnerable. Both were wrong.

Upstart Man was beginning to breed and spread like a pestilence across the world. This pestilence struck down the old races wherever it touched them. And it was not only death that Man brought, but terror, too. Wilfully, he made of the older world nothing but ruins and bones. Unwittingly, he brought psychic and supernatural disruption of a magnitude which even the Great Old Gods failed to comprehend.

And the Great Old Gods began to know fear.

And Man, slave of fear, arrogant in his ignorance, continued his stumbling progress. He was blind to the huge disruptions aroused by his apparently petty ambitions. As well, Man was deficient in sensitivity, had no awareness of the multitude of dimensions that filled the universe, each plane intersecting with several others. Not so the Vadhagh or the Nhadragh, who had known what it was to move at will between the dimensions they termed the Five Planes. They had glimpsed and understood the nature of many planes, other than the Five, through which the Earth moved.

Therefore it seemed a dreadful injustice that these wise races should perish at the hands of creatures who were still little more than animals. It was as if vultures feasted on and squabbled over the paralysed body of the youthful poet who could only stare at them with puzzled eyes as they slowly robbed him of an exquisite existence they would never appreciate, never know they were taking.

'If they valued what they stole, if they knew what they were destroying,' says the old Vadhagh in the story *Now The Clouds Have Meaning*, 'then I would be consoled.'

It was unjust.

By creating Man, the universe had betrayed the old races.

But it was a perpetual and familiar injustice. The sentient may perceive and love the universe, but the universe cannot perceive and love the sentient. The universe sees no distinction between the multitude of creatures and elements which comprise it. All are equal. None is favoured. The universe, equipped with nothing but the materials and the power of creation, continues to create: something of this, something of that. It cannot control what it creates and it cannot, it seems, be controlled by its creations (though a few might deceive themselves otherwise). Those who curse the workings of the universe curse that which is deaf. Those who strike out at those workings fight that which is inviolate. Those who shake their fists, shake their fists at blind stars.

But this does not mean that there are not some who will try to do battle with and destroy the invulnerable. There will always be such beings, sometimes beings of great wisdom, who cannot bear to believe in an insouciant universe.

Prince Corum Jhaelen Irsei was one of these. Perhaps the last of the Vadhagh race, he was sometimes known as the Prince in the Scarlet Robe.

This is the second chronicle, concerning his adventures.

The first chronicle, known as 'The Books of Corum', told how the Mabden followers of Earl Glandyth-a-Krae killed Prince Corum's relatives and his nearest kin and thus taught the Prince in the Scarlet Robe how to hate, how to kill, and how to desire vengeance. We have heard how Earl Glandyth tortured Prince Corum and took away a hand and an eye and how Corum was rescued by the Giant of Laahr and taken to the castle of the Margravine Rhalina – a castle set upon a mount surrounded by the sea. Though Rhalina was a Mabden woman (of the gentler folk of Lwym-an-Esh), Corum and she fell in love. When Glandyth roused the Pony Tribes, the forest barbarians, to attack the Margravine's castle, she and Corum sought supernatural aid and thus fell into the hands of the sorcerer Shool, whose domain was the island called Svi-an-Fanla-Brool – Home of the Gorged God. And now Corum had direct experience of the morbid, unfamiliar powers at work in the world. Shool spoke of dreams and realities ('I see you are beginning to argue in Mabden terms,' he told Corum. 'It is just as well for you, if you wish to survive in this Mabden dream.' – 'It is a dream . . .?' said Corum – 'Of sorts. Real enough. It is what you might call the dream of a god. Then again you might say that it is a dream that a god has allowed to become reality. I refer of course to the Knight of the Swords, who rules the Five Planes . . .').

With Rhalina his prisoner, Shool could make a bargain with Corum. He gave him two gifts – the Hand of Kwll and the Eye of Rhynn – to replace his own missing organs. These jewelled and alien things were once the property of two brother gods known as the Lost Gods since they mysteriously vanished.

Armed with these Corum began his great quest, which was to take him against all three Sword Rulers – the Knight, the Queen and the King of the Swords – the mighty Lords of Chaos. And Corum discovered much concerning these gods, the nature of reality and the nature of his own identity. He learned that he was the Champion Eternal, that, in a thousand other guises, in a thousand other ages, it was his lot to struggle against those forces which attacked reason, logic and justice, no matter what form they took. And, at long last, he was able to overwhelm (with the help of a mysterious ally) those forces and banish gods from his world.

Peace came to Bro-an-Vadhagh and Corum took his mortal bride to his ancient castle which stood on a cliff overlooking a bay. And meanwhile the few surviving Vadhagh and Nhadragh turned again to their own devices, and the golden land of Lwym-an-Esh flourished and became the centre of the Mabden world – famous for its scholars, its bards, its artists, its builders and its warriors. A great age dawned for the Mabden folk; they flourished. And Corum was pleased that his wife's folk flourished. On the few occasions when Mabden travellers passed near Castle Erorn he would feast them well and be filled with gladness when he heard of the beauties of Halwyg-nan-Vake, capital city of Lwym-an-Esh, whose walls bloomed with flowers all year round. And the travellers would tell Corum and Rhalina of the new ships which brought great prosperity to the land, so that none in Lwym-an-Esh knew hunger. They would tell of the new laws which gave all a voice in the affairs of that country. And Corum listened and was proud of Rhalina's race.

To one such traveller he offered an opinion: 'When the last of the Vadhagh and the Nhadragh have disappeared from this world,' he said, 'the Mabden will emerge as a greater race than ever were we.'

'But we shall never have your powers of sorcery,' answered the traveller, and he caused Corum to laugh heartily.

'We had no sorcery at all! We had no conception of it. Our "sorcery" was merely our observation and manipulation of certain natural laws, as well as our perception of other planes of the multiverse, which we have now all but lost. It is the Mabden who imagine such things as sorcery – who would always rather invent the miraculous than investigate the ordinary (and find the miraculous therein). Such imaginations will make your race the most

7

exceptional this Earth has yet known, but those imaginations could also destroy you!'

'Did we invent the Sword Rulers whom you so heroically fought?'

'Aye,' answered Corum, 'I suspect that you did! And I suspect that you might invent others again.'

'Invent phantoms? Fabulous beasts? Powerful gods? Whole cosmologies?' queried the astonished traveller. 'Are all these things, then, unreal?'

'They're real enough,' Corum replied. 'Reality, after all, is the easiest thing in the world to create. It is partly a question of need, partly a question of time, partly a question of circumstance . . .'

Corum had felt sorry for confounding his guest and he laughed again and passed on to other topics.

And so the years went by and Rhalina began to show signs of age while Corum, near-immortal, showed none. Yet still they loved each other – perhaps with greater intensity as they realized that the day drew near when death would part her from him.

Their life was sweet; their love was strong. They needed little but each other's company.

And then she died.

And Corum mourned for her. He mourned without the sadness which mortals have (which is, in part, sadness for themselves and fear of their own death).

Some seventy years had passed since the Sword Rulers fell, and the travellers grew fewer and fewer as Corum of the Vadhagh people became more of a legend in Lwym-an-Esh than he was remembered as a creature of ordinary flesh. He had been amused when he had heard that in some country areas of that land there were now shrines to him and crude images of him to which folk prayed as they had prayed to their gods. It had not taken them long to find new gods and it was ironic that they should make one of the person who had helped rid them of their old ones. They magnified his feats and, in so doing, simplified him as an individual. They attributed magical powers to him; they told stories of him which they had once told of their previous gods. Why was the truth never enough for the Mabden? Why must they forever embellish and obscure it? What a paradoxical people they were!

Corum recalled his parting with his friend, Jhary-a-Conel, self-styled Companion to Champions, and the last words he had spoken to him – 'New gods can always be created,' he had said. Yet he had never guessed, then, from what at least one of those gods would be created.

And, because he had become divine to so many, the people of Lwym-an-Esh took to avoiding the headland on which stood ancient Castle Erorn, for they knew that gods had no time to listen to the silly talk of mortals.

Thus Corum grew lonelier still; he became reluctant to travel in Mabden lands, for this attitude of the folk made him uncomfortable.

In Lwym-an-Esh those who had known him well, known that, save for his longer lifespan, he was as vulnerable as themselves, were now all dead, too. So there were none to deny the legends.

And, likewise, because he had grown used to Mabden ways and Mabden people about him, he found that he could not find much pleasure in the company of his own race, for they retained their remoteness, their inability to understand their situation, and would continue to do so until the Vadhagh race perished for good. Corum envied them their lack of concern, for, though he took no part in the affairs of the world, he still felt involved enough to speculate about the possible destiny of the various races.

A kind of chess, which the Vadhagh played, took up much of his time (he played against himself, using the pieces like arguments, testing one strain of logic against another). Brooding upon his various past conflicts, he doubted, sometimes, if they had ever taken place at all. He wondered if the portals to the Fifteen Planes were closed forever now, even to the Vadhagh and the Nhadragh, who had once moved in and out of them so freely. If this were so, did it mean that, effectively, those other planes no longer existed. And thus his dangers, his fears, his discoveries, slowly took on the quality of little more than

9

abstractions; they became factors in an argument concerning the nature of time and identity and, after a while, the argument itself ceased to interest Corum.

Some eighty years were to pass since the fall of the Sword Rulers before Corum's interest was to be re-awakened in matters concerning the Mabden folk and their gods.

THE CHRONICLE OF CORUM AND THE SILVER HAND

BOOK ONE

*In which Prince Corum
finds himself dreaming an
unlikely and unwelcome
dream . . .*

CHAPTER ONE

Fearing the Future
as the Past Grows Dim

Rhalina, ninety-six years old, and handsome, had died, Corum had wept for her. Now, seven years later, he still missed her and he contemplated his own lifespan of perhaps another thousand years and envied the race of Mabden its brief years, yet shunned the company of that race, because he was reminded of her.

Dwelling again in their isolated castles – whose forms so mirrored the natural rock that many Mabden passing by could not see them for buildings at all but mistook them for outcrops of granite, limestone and basalt – were his own race, the Vadhagh. These he shunned because he had grown, while Rhalina lived, to prefer Mabden company. It was an irony about which he would write poetry, or paint pictures, or compose music in the several halls of Castle Erorn set aside for the purpose.

And thus he grew strange, in Castle Erorn by the sea.

He grew remote. His retainers (all Vadhagh now) wondered how to express to him their view that perhaps he should take a Vadhagh wife, by whom he might have children and through whom he might discover a renewed interest in the present and the future. But there was no way they could find to approach their lord, Corum Jhaelen Irsei, Prince of the Scarlet Robe, who had helped conquer the most powerful gods and rid this world of much that it had feared.

The retainers began to know fear. They grew to fear Corum, that lonely figure, with an eye-patch covering an empty socket, with his variety of artificial right hands, each one of exquisite craftsmanship (made by Corum for his own use), that silent strider in midnight halls, that moody rider through the winter woods.

And Corum knew fear, too. He felt a fear of empty days, of lonely years, waiting through the slow-turning centuries for death.

He contemplated ending his life, but somehow he felt that such an action would be an insult to Rhalina's memory. He considered embarking upon a quest, but there were no lands to explore in this bland, this warm, this tranquil world. Even the bestial Mabden of King Lyr-a-Brode had returned to their original pursuits, becoming farmers, merchants, fishermen, miners. No enemies threatened, no injustice was evident. Freed from gods, the Mabden had become content, kindly and wise.

Corum recalled the old pursuits of his youth. He had hunted. But now he had lost any relish he had ever had for the chase. He had been hunted too frequently during his battle with the Sword Rulers to feel anything now but anguish for the pursued. He had ridden. He had relished the lush and lovely countryside landward of Castle Erorn. But his relish for life had waned. He still rode, however.

He would ride through the broadleaf forests which skirted the promontory on which Castle Erorn was raised. Sometimes he would venture as far as the deep, green moor beyond with its thick gorse, its hawks, its skies and its silence. Sometimes he would take the coast road back to Castle Erorn, riding dangerously close to the crumbling cliff edge. Far below, the high, white surf would rear against the rocks, hissing and growling. Sometimes tendrils of spray would strike Corum's face, but he would hardly feel them. Once such sensations had made him grin with pleasure.

On most days Corum would not venture out. Neither sun, nor wind, nor rattling rain would lure him from the gloomy rooms which had, in the days when his family occupied them and, later, when Rhalina occupied them, been replete with love and light and laughter. Sometimes he would not move, even, from his chair. His tall, slender body would sprawl upon the cushions, he would rest his beautiful, tapering head upon his fleshly fist and his almond-shaped yellow and purple eye would stare into the past, a past which grew dimmer all the time and increased his desperation as he strove to remember every detail of his life with Rhalina. A prince of the great Vadhagh folk, grieving for a mortal woman. There had never been ghosts in Castle Erorn before the Mabden came.

And sometimes, when he did not yearn for Rhalina, he would wish that Jhary-a-Conel had not decided to leave this plane, for Jhary, like him, was apparently immortal. The self-styled Companion to Heroes seemed able to move at will through all the Fifteen Planes of existence, acting as a guide, a foil, a counsellor to one whom, in Jhary's opinion, was Corum in several different guises. It had been Jhary-a-Conel who had said that he and Corum could be 'aspects of a greater hero', just as, in the tower of Voilodion Ghagnasdiak, he had met two other aspects of that hero, Erekosë and Elric. Jhary had claimed that those two were Corum in other incarnations and it was Erek-osë's particular doom to be aware of most of those incarnations. Intellectually, Corum could accept such an idea, but emotionally he rejected it. He was Corum. And that was his doom.

Corum had a collection of Jhary's paintings (most of them self-portraits, but some were of Rhalina and of Corum and of the small black and white winged cat which Jhary took everywhere with him, as he took his hat). Corum, in his most morbid moments, would study the portraits, recalling the old days, but slowly even the portraits came to be those of strangers. He would make efforts to consider the future, to make plans regarding his own destiny, but all his intentions came to nothing. There was no plan, no matter how detailed, how reasonable, which lasted more than a day or so. Castle Erorn was littered with unfinished poems, unfinished prose, un-finished music, unfinished painting. The world had turned a man of peace into a warrior and then left him with nothing to fight. That was Corum's fate. He had no reason to work the land, for Vadhagh food was grown within the castle walls. There was no shortage of meat or wine. Castle Erorn provided all its few inhabitants needed. Corum had spent many years working on a variety of artificial hands, based on what he had seen at the doctor's house in the world of Lady Jane Pentallyon. Now he had a selection of hands, all perfect, which worked as well for him as any hand of flesh had done. His favourite, which he wore most of the time, was one which resembled a finely-wrought gauntlet in filigreed silver, an exact match to the hand which Earl Glandyth-a-Krae had cut off nearly a century before. This was the hand he could have used to hold his sword or his lance or his bow, had there been any call for him to use his weapons now. Tiny movements of the muscles in the stump of his original wrist would make it do everything an ordinary hand could do, and more, for the grip was stronger. Secondly, he had become ambidextrous, able to use his left hand as well as he had used his right hand. Yet all his skill could not make him a new eye and he had to be content with a simple patch, covered in scarlet silk and worked with Rhalina's fine needle into an intricate pattern. It was his unconscious habit, now, to run the fingers of his left hand frequently over the needlework as he sat brooding in his chair.

Corum began to realize that his taciturnity was turning to madness when, in his bed at night, he began to hear voices. They were distant voices, a chanting chorus which called a name which might be his in a language which resembled the Vadhagh tongue and yet which was unlike it. Try as he might, he could not drive the voices out, just as he could not, however much he strained his ears to listen, understand more than a few words of what they said. After several nights of these voices, he began to shout for them to stop. He would groan. He would roll in his silks and his furs and try to stuff his ears. And in the days he would try to laugh at himself, would go for long rides to tire himself so that he would sleep heavily. Yet still the voices would come to him. And, later, there were dreams. Shadowy figures stood in a grove in a thick wood. Their hands were linked in a circle, apparently surrounding him. In his dreams he would speak to them, saying that he could not hear them, that he did not know what they wanted. He asked them to stop. But they continued to chant. Their eyes were closed, their heads were flung back. They swayed.

'Corum. Corum. Corum. Corum.'

'What do you want?'

'Corum. Help us. Corum.'

He would break through their circle and run into the forest and then he would awake. He knew what had happened to him. His mind had turned in on itself. Not properly occupied it had begun to invent phantoms. He had never heard of such a thing happening to a Vadhagh, though it happened frequently enough to Mabden people. Did he, as Shool had once told him, still live in a Mabden dream? Was the dream of the Vadhagh and the Nhadragh completely over? And did he therefore dream one dream within another?

But these thoughts did not help his sanity. He tried to drive them away. He began to feel the need for advice, yet there was none to advise him. The Lords of Law and Chaos no longer ruled here, no longer had servants here to whom they imparted at least some of their knowledge. Corum knew more of philosophical matters than did anyone else. Yet there were wise Vadhagh who had come here from Gwlās-cor-Gwrys, the City in the Pyramid, who knew something of these matters.

He determined that, if the dreams and the voices continued, then he would set off on a journey to one of the other castles where the Vadhagh lived and there seek help. At least, he reasoned, there was a good chance that the voices would not follow him from Castle Erorn.

His rides grew wilder and he tired all his horses. He went further and further away from Castle Erorn, as if he hoped to find something. But he found nothing but the sea to his west and the moors and the forests to his east, south and north. No Mabden villages were here, no farms or even the huts of charcoal-burners or foresters, for the Mabden had no desire to settle in Vadhagh lands, not since the fall of King Lyr-a-Brode. And was that really what he sought?

Corum wondered. Mabden company? Did his voices and his dreams represent his desire to share adventures with mortals again? The thought was painful to him. He saw Rhalina clearly for a moment, as she had been in her youth, radiant, proud and strong.

With his sword he slashed at the stems of ferns. With his lance he drove at the boles of trees. With his bow he shot at rocks. A parody of battle. Sometimes he would fall upon the grass and sob.

And still the voices called him:

'Corum! Corum! Help us!'

'Help you?' he screamed back. 'It is Corum who needs help!'

'Corum. Corum. Corum . . .'

Had he ever heard those voices before? Been in a situation like this one before?

It seemed to Corum that he had, yet, as he recalled all the events in his life, he knew that it could not be true. He had never heard those voices, dreamed those dreams. And still he was sure that he remembered them from another time. Perhaps from another incarnation? Was he truly the Champion Eternal?

Weary, sometimes ragged, sometimes without his weapons, sometimes leading a limping horse, Corum would return to Castle Erorn by the sea, and the pounding of the waves in the caves below Erorn would be like the pounding of his own heart.

His servants would try to comfort him, to restrain him, to ask him what ailed him. He would not reply. He was civil, but he would tell them nothing of his torment. He had no way of telling them and he knew that they would not understand, even if he could find a way.

And then, one day, as he stumbled across the threshold of the castle courtyard, barely able to keep himself from falling, the servants told him that a visitor had come to Castle Erorn and that he waited for Corum in one of the music chambers which Corum had had closed for some years, for the sweetness of the music had reminded him too much of Rhalina, whose favourite chamber it had been.

'His name?' Corum muttered. 'Is he Mabden or Vadhagh? His purpose here?'

'He would tell us nothing, master, save that he was either your friend or your enemy – that you would know that.'

'Friend or enemy? A riddler? An entertainer? He'll have hard work here . . .'

Yet Corum was curious, almost grateful for the mystery. Before he went to the music room he washed himself and put on fresh clothes and drank a little wine until he felt revived enough to face the stranger.

The harps and the organs and the crystals in the music chamber had begun their symphony. He heard the faint notes of a familiar tune drifting up to his apartments. At once he felt overwhelmed by depression and determined that he would not do the stranger the courtesy of receiving him. But something in Corum wanted to listen to that music. He had composed it himself, one year, for Rhalina's birthday. It expressed much of the tenderness he had felt towards her. She had then been ninety years old, with her mind and body as sound as they had ever been. 'You keep me young, Corum,' she had said.

Tears came into Corum's single eye. He brushed them away, cursing the visitor who had revived such memories. The man was a boor, coming uninvited to Castle Erorn, opening up a deliberately closed chamber. How could he justify such actions?

And then Corum wondered if this were a Nhadragh, for the Nhadragh, he had heard, still hated him. Those who had remained alive after King Lyr-a-Brode's conquests had degenerated into semi-sentience. Had one of them remembered just enough of his hatred to seek out Corum to slay him? Corum felt something close to elation at this thought. He would relish a fight.

And so he strapped on his silver hand and his slender sword before he went down the ramp to the music chamber.

As he neared the chamber the music grew louder and louder, more complex and more exquisite. Corum had to struggle against it as he might struggle against a strong wind.

He entered the room. Its colours swirled and danced with the music. It was so bright that Corum was momentarily blinded. Blinking, he peered around the chamber, seeking his visitor.

Corum saw the man at last. He was sitting in the shadows, absorbed in the music. Corum went amongst the huge harps, the organs and the crystals, touching them and quieting them until, at last, there was complete silence. The colours faded from the room. The man rose from his corner and began to approach. He was small of stature and walked with a distinct swagger. He had a wide-brimmed hat upon his head and a deformity on his right shoulder, perhaps a hump. His face was entirely obscured by the brim of the hat, yet Corum began to suspect that he knew the man.

Corum recognized the cat first. It sat upon the man's shoulder. It was what Corum had at first mistaken for a hump. Its round eyes stared at him. It purred. The man's head lifted and there was the smiling face of Jhary-a-Conel.

So astonished was Corum, so used was he to living with ghosts, that at first he did not respond.

'Jhary?'

'Good morrow, Prince Corum. I hope you did not mind me listening to your music. I don't believe I have heard that piece before.'

'No. I wrote it long after you left.' Even to his own ears, Corum's voice was distant.

'I upset you, playing it?' Jhary became concerned.

'Yes. But you were not to blame. I wrote it for Rhalina and now . . .'

'Rhalina is dead. I heard she lived a good life. A happy life.'

'Aye. And a short life.' Corum's tone was bitter.

'Longer than most mortals, Corum.' Jhary changed the subject. 'You do not look well. Have you been ill?'

'In my head, perhaps. I still mourn for Rhalina,

Jhary-a-Conel. I still grieve for her, you see. I wish she . . .'
Corum offered Jhary a somewhat bleak smile. 'But I must
not consider the impossible.'

'Are there impossibilities?' Jhary gave his attention to
his cat, stroking its fur-covered wings.

'There are in this world.'

'There are in most. Yet what is impossible in one is
possible in another. That is the pleasure one has in
travelling between the worlds, as I do.'

'You went to seek gods. Did you find them?'

'A few. And some heroes whom I could accompany. I
have seen a new world born and an old one destroyed,
since we last talked. I have seen many strange forms of life
and heard many peculiar opinions regarding the nature of
the universe and its inhabitants. Life comes and goes, you
know. There is no tragedy in death, Corum.'

'There is a tragedy here,' Corum pointed out. 'When one
has to live for centuries before rejoining the object of one's
love – and then only joining her in oblivion.'

'This is morbid, silly talk. It is unworthy of a hero.' Jhary
laughed. 'It is unintelligent, to say the least, my friend.
Come now, Corum – I'll regret paying you this visit if
you've become as dull as that.'

And at last Corum smiled. 'You are right. It is what
happens to men who avoid the company of their fellows, I
fear. Their wits grow stale.'

'It is for that reason that I have always, by and large,
preferred the life of the city,' Jhary told him.

'Does the city not rob you of your spirit? The Nhadragh
lived in cities and they grew degenerate.'

'The spirit can be nurtured almost anywhere. The mind
needs stimuli. It is a question of finding the balance. It also
depends upon one's temperament, too, I suppose. Well,
temperamentally I am a dweller in cities. The larger, the
dirtier, the more densely populated, the better! And I have
seen some cities so black with grime, so packed with life, so
vast, that you would not believe me if I told you the details!
Ah, beautiful!'

Corum laughed. 'I am pleased that you have come back,

Jhary-a-Conel, with your hat and your cat and your irony!'
And then they embraced each other and they laughed
together.

CHAPTER TWO

The Invocation of a Dead Demigod

That night they feasted and Corum's heart lightened and he enjoyed his meat and wine for the first time in seven years.

'You know, of course, of the famous von Beks,' Jhary told him. Jhary had been recounting his deeds for nearly two hours. 'You're closely related, but I think even you would find this tale a strange one . . .' And for another hour he told the tale of von Bek and his arrangement with the Original Insect.

There were other tales to follow, he promised, if Corum wished to hear them. There were tales of Elric and Erekosë, whom Corum had met, of Kane and Cornelius and Carnelian, of Glogauer and Bastable and many more. All aspects, Jhary swore, of the same champion and all his friends (if not himself). And he spoke of such weighty matters with so much humour, with so many joking asides, that Corum's spirits rose still higher, until he was helpless with laughter and quite drunk on the wine.

Then, in the early morning, Corum confided to Jhary his secret – that he feared that he had gone mad.

'I hear voices, dream dreams – always the same. They call for me. They beg me to join them. Do I pretend to myself that this is Rhalina who calls me? Nothing I do will rid me of them, Jhary. That is why I was out again today – hoping to tire myself so much that I would not dream.'

And Jhary's face became serious as he listened. And when Corum had finished, the little man put a hand on his friend's shoulder, saying, 'Fear not. Perhaps you have been mad, these past seven years, but it was a quieter madness altogether. You did hear voices. And the people you saw in your dream were real people. They were summoning – or trying to summon – their champion. They were trying to bring you to them. They have been trying for many days now.'

Again Corum had difficulty in understanding Jhary. 'Their champion . . .?' he said vaguely.

'In their age you are a legend,' Jhary told him. 'A demigod, at very least. You are Corum Llaw Ereint to them – Corum of the Silver Hand. A great warrior. A great champion of his people. There are whole cycles of tales concerning your exploits and proving your divinity!' Jhary smiled a little sardonically. 'As with most gods and heroes you have a legend attached to your name, which says that you will return at the time of your people's greatest need. Now their need is great indeed.'

'Who are these people that they should be "mine"?'

'They are the descendants of the folk of Lwym-an-Esh – Rhalina's people.'

'Rhalina's . . . ?'

'They are a fine folk, Corum. I know them.'

'You come from them now?'

'Not exactly.'

'You cannot make them stop this chanting? You cannot make them cease appearing in my dreams?'

'Their strength weakens daily. Soon they will trouble you no longer. You will sleep tranquilly again.'

'Are you sure?'

'Oh, I am certain. They can survive for only a little while more, before the Cold Folk overwhelm them. Before the People of the Pines enslave or slay what remains of their race.'

'Well,' said Corum, 'as you say, these things come and go . . .'

'Aye,' said Jhary. 'But it will be sad to see the last of that golden folk go down beneath the dark and savage invaders who now sweep across their land, bringing terror where there was peace, bringing fear where there was joy . . .'

'It sounds familiar,' said Corum dryly. 'So the world turns, and turns again.' He was now fairly well satisfied that he understood why Jhary was harping upon this particular subject.

'And turns again,' agreed Jhary.

'And even if I would, I could not help them, Jhary. I am no longer able to travel between the planes. I cannot even see through to other planes. Besides, how could one warrior help this folk of which you speak?'

'One warrior could help greatly. And it is their invocation which would bring you to them, if you would let it. But they are weak. They cannot summon you against your will. You resist them. It does not take much resistance. Their numbers grow small, their power fades. They were once a great people. Even their name derives from your name. They call themselves Tuha-na-Cremm Croich.'

'Cremm?'

'Or Corum, sometimes. It is an older form. It means simply "Lord" to them – Lord of the Mound. They worship you in the form of a stone slab erected on a mound. You are supposed to live beneath that mound and hear their prayers.'

'These are superstitious people.'

'A little. But they are not god-ridden. They worship Man above all else. And all their gods are really nothing more than dead heroes. Some folk make gods of the sun, the moon, the storms, of the beasts and so on. But this folk deifies only what is noble in Man and loves what is beautiful in nature. You would be proud of your wife's descendants, Corum.'

'Aye,' said Corum, narrowing his eye and giving Jhary a sideways look. There was a faint smile on his lips. 'Is this mound in a forest. An oak forest?'

'An oak forest, yes.'

'It is the same that I saw in my dream. And why is this folk attacked?'

'A race from beyond the sea (some say from beneath the sea) comes from the east. The whole land which used to be named Bro-an-Mabden has either gone under the waves or lies beneath a perpetual cloak of winter. Ice covers all – brought by the eastern folk. It has also been said that this is a folk that once conquered this land and was driven back. Others suggest that it is a mixture of two old races, or more, banded together to destroy the ancestors of the Mabden of Lwym-an-Esh. There is no talk of Law or Chaos there. If this folk has power it comes from themselves. They can produce phantasms. Their spells are powerful. They can destroy either by means of fire or by means of ice. And they have other powers, too. They are called the Fhoi Myore and they control the North Wind. They are called the Cold Folk and they can make the northern and the eastern seas answer their bidding. They are called the People of the Pines and can command black wolves as their servants. They are a brutal people, born, some say, of Chaos and Old Night. Perhaps they are the last vestiges of Chaos upon this plane, Corum.'

Corum was smiling openly now. 'And you urge me to go against such a folk? On behalf of another folk which is not my own?'

'Your own by adoption. Your wife's folk.'

'I have already fought in one conflict that was not my own,' said Corum, turning away and pouring himself more wine.

'Not your own? All such conflicts are yours, Corum. It is your fate.'

'And what if I resist that fate?'

'You cannot resist it for any great time. I know that. It is better to accept your destiny with good grace – with humour, even.'

'Humour?' Corum swallowed the wine and wiped his lips. 'That is not easy, Jhary.'

'No. But it is what makes the whole thing bearable.'

'And what do I risk if I answer this call and help that folk?'

'Many things. Your life.'

'That is worth little. What else?'

'Your soul, perhaps.'

'And what is that?'

'You could discover the answer to that question if you embark upon this enterprise.'

Corum frowned. 'My spirit is not my own, Jhary-a-Conel. You have told me that.'

'I did not. Your spirit is your own. Perhaps your actions are dictated by other forces, which is another question altogether . . .'

Corum's frown changed as he smiled. 'You sound like one of those priests of Arkyn who used to thrive in Lwym-an-Esh. I think the morality is somewhat doubtful. However, I was ever pragmatic. The Vadhagh race is a pragmatic race.'

Jhary raised his eyebrows, but said nothing. 'Will you allow yourself to be called by the People of Cremm Croich?'

'I will consider it.'

'Speak to them, at least.'

'I have tried. They do not hear.'

'Perhaps they do. Or perhaps you must be in a certain frame of mind to answer so that they can hear.'

'Very well. I will try. And what if I do allow myself to be borne into this future time, Jhary? Will you be there?'

'Possibly.'

'You cannot be more certain?'

'I am no more master of my fate than are you, Champion Eternal.'

'I would be grateful,' said Corum, 'if you will not use that title. I find it discomforting.'

Jhary laughed. 'I cannot say that I blame you, Corum Jhaelen Irsei!'

Corum rose and stretched his arms. The firelight touched his silver hand and made it gleam red, as if suddenly suffused with blood. He looked at the hand, turning it this way and that in the light as if he had never properly seen it before. 'Corum of the Silver Hand,' he said musingly. 'They think the hand of supernatural origin, I take it.'

'They have more experience of the supernatural than what you would call "science". Do not despise them for that. Where they live there are strange things happening. Natural laws are sometimes the creation of human ideas.'

'I have often contemplated that theory, but how does one find evidence for it, Jhary?'

'Evidence, too, can be created. You are doubtless wise to encourage your own pragmatism. I believe everything, just as I believe nothing.'

Corum yawned and nodded. 'It is the best attitude to have, I think. Well, I'll to my bed. Whatever comes of all this, know that your coming has improved my spirits considerably, Jhary. I'll speak with you again in the morning. First I must see how this night passes.'

Jhary stroked his cat under its chin. 'You could benefit greatly from helping those who call to you.' It was almost as if he had addressed the cat.

Corum paused as he walked towards the door. 'You have already hinted as much. Can you tell me in what way I would benefit?'

'I said "could", Corum. I cannot say more. It would be foolish of me, and irresponsible. Perhaps it is already true that I have said too much. For now I puzzle you.'

'I'll dismiss the question from my mind – and bid you good night, old friend.'

'Good night, Corum, may your dreams be clear.'

Corum left the room and began to climb the ramp to his own bedchamber. This would be the first night in many months that he looked forward to sleep less with fear than with curiosity.

He fell asleep almost immediately. And, almost immediately, the voices began. Instead of resisting them, he relaxed and listened.

'Corum! Cremm Croich. Your people need you.'

For all its strange accent, the voice was quite clear. But Corum saw nothing of the chorus, nothing of the circle with linked hands which stood about a mound in an oak grove.

'Lord of the Mound. Lord of the Silver Hand. Only you can save us.'

And Corum found himself replying:

'How can I save you?'

The answering voice sounded excited. 'You answer at last! Come to us, Corum of the Silver Hand. Come to us, Prince in the Scarlet Robe. Save us as you have saved us in the past.'

'How can I save you?'

'You can find for us the Bull and the Spear and lead us against the Fhoi Myore. Show us how to fight them, for they do not fight as we fight.'

Corum stirred. Now he could see them. They were tall and good-looking young men and women whose bronzed bodies glinted with warm gold, the colour of autumn corn, and the gold was woven into intricate and pleasing designs. Armlets, anklets, collars and circlets, all of gold. Their flowing clothes were of linen dyed in light reds, blues and yellows. There were sandals upon their feet. They had fair hair or hair as red as rowan berries. They were, indeed, the same race as the folk of Lwym-an-Esh. They stood in the oak grove, hands joined, eyes closed, and they spoke as one.

'Come to us, Lord Corum. Come to us.'

'I will consider it,' said Corum, making his tone a kindly one, 'for it is long since I have fought and I have forgotten the arts of war.'

'Tomorrow?'

'If I come, I will come tomorrow.'

The scene faded, the voices faded. And Corum slept peacefully until morning.

When he awoke he knew that there was nothing to debate. While he slept he had decided, if possible, to answer the call of the people of the oak grove. His life at Castle Erorn was not only miserable, it served no-one, not even himself. He would go to them, crossing the planes, moving through time, and he would go to them willingly, proudly.

Jhary found him in the armoury. He had selected for himself the silver byrnie and the conical helm of silvered steel with his full name engraved above the peak. He had

29

found greaves of gilded brass and he had laid out his surcoat of scarlet silk, his shirt of blue samite. A long-hafted Vadhagh war-axe stood against a bench and beside it was a sword manufactured in a place other than the Earth, with a hilt of red and black onyx; a lance whose shaft was carved from top to bottom with miniature hunting scenes comprising more than a hundred tiny figures, all depicted in considerable detail; a good bow and a quiver of well-fletched arrows. Resting against these was a round war-board, a shield made of a number of layers of timber, leather, brass and silver and covered all over with the fine, strong hide of the white rhinoceros which had once lived in the northern forests of Corum's land.

'When do you go to them?' said Jhary, inspecting the array.

'Tonight.' Corum weighed the lance in his hand. 'If their Summoning is successful. I shall go mounted, on my red horse. I shall ride to them.'

Jhary did not ask how Corum would reach them and Corum himself had not considered that problem, either. Certain peculiar laws would be involved and that was all they knew or cared to know. And much depended on the power of invocation of the group who waited in the oak grove.

Together, they broke their fast and then they went up to the battlements of the castle. From those battlements they could see the wide ocean to the west and the great forests and moors to the east. The sun was bright and the sky was wide and clear and blue. It was a good, peaceful day. They talked of the old times, recalling dead friends and dead or banished gods, of Kwll who had been more powerful than either the Lords of Law or the Lords of Chaos, who had seemed to fear nothing. They wondered where Kwll and his brother Rhynn had gone, whether there were other worlds beyond the Fifteen Planes of Earth and if those worlds resembled Earth in any way.

'And then, of course,' said Jhary, 'there is the question concerning the Conjunction of the Million Spheres and what follows when that conjunction is over. Is it over yet, do you think?'

'New laws are established after the Conjunction. But established by what? And by whom?' Corum leaned against the battlements, looking out across the narrow bay. 'I suspect that it is we who make those laws. And yet we do so unknowingly. We are not even sure what is good and what is evil – or, indeed, if anything is either. Kwll had no such beliefs and I envied him. How pitiful we are! How pitiful am I that I cannot bear to live without loyalties! Is it strength which makes me decide to go to these people? Or is it weakness?'

'You speak of good and evil and say you know not what they are – it is the same with strength and weakness. The terms are meaningless.' Jhary shrugged. 'Love means something to me, and so does hate. Physical strength is given to some of us – I can see it. And some are physically weak. But why equate the elements in a man's character with such attributes? And, if we do not condemn a man because, through luck, he is not physically strong, why condemn him if, for instance, his resolve is not strong? Such instincts are the instincts of the beasts and, for beasts, they are satisfactory instincts. But men are not beasts. They are men. That is all.'

Corum's smile had some bitterness in it. 'And they are not gods, Jhary.'

'Not gods – or devils, either. Just men and women. How much happier would we be if we accepted that!' And Jhary threw back his head and laughed suddenly. 'But perhaps we should be more boring, too! We are both of us beginning to sound too pious, my friend. We are warriors, not holy men!'

Corum repeated a question of the previous night. 'You know this land, where I have decided to go. Shall you go there, too – tonight?'

'I am not my own master.' Jhary began to pace the flagstones. 'You know that, Corum.'

'I hope that you do.'

'You have many manifestations in the fifteen planes,

Corum. It could be that another Corum somewhere needs a companion and that I shall have to go with him.'

'But you are not sure?'

'I am not sure.'

Corum shrugged. 'If what you say is true – and I suppose I must accept that it is – then perhaps I shall meet another aspect of you, one who does not know his fate?'

'My memory often fails me, as I have told you before. Just as yours fails you in this incarnation.'

'I hope that we shall meet on this new plane and that we shall recognize one another.'

'This is my hope, also, Corum.'

They played chess that evening and spoke little and Corum went early to his bed.

When the voices came, he spoke to them slowly:

'I shall come in armour and I shall be armed. I shall ride upon a red horse. You must call me with all your powers. I give you time to rest now. Gather your strength and in two hours begin the invocation.'

In one hour Corum rose and went down to put his armour on, to dress himself in silk and samite, to have his ostler lead his horse into the courtyard. And when he was ready, with his reins in his gloved left hand and his silver hand upon the pommel of a poignard, he spoke to his retainers and told them that he rode upon a quest and that if he did not return they should throw open Castle Erorn to any traveller who needed shelter and that they should feast such travellers well, in Corum's name. Then he rode through the gates and down the slope and into the great wood, as he had ridden nearly a century before when his father and his mother and his sisters had been alive. But then he had ridden through the morning. Now he rode into the night, beneath the moon.

Of all those in Castle Erorn, only Jhary-a-Conel had not bid goodbye to Corum.

Now the voices grew louder in Corum's ears as he rode through the dark, ancient forest.

'Corum! Corum!'

Strangely, his body began to feel light. He touched spurs to the flanks of his horse and it broke into a gallop.

'Corum! Corum!'

'I am coming!' The stallion galloped harder, its hooves pounding the soft turf, plunging deeper and deeper into the dark wood.

'Corum!'

Corum leaned forward in his saddle, ducking as branches brushed his face.

'I come!'

He saw the shadowy group in the grove. They surrounded him, yet still he rode and his speed grew even faster. He began to feel dizzy.

'Corum!'

And it seemed to Corum that he had ridden like this before, that he had been called in this way before and that was why he had known what to do.

The trees blurred, he rode with such speed.

'Corum!'

White mist began to boil all around him. Now the faces of the chanting group could be seen in sharper detail. The voices grew faint, then loud, then faint again. Corum spurred the snorting horse on into the mist. That mist was history. It was legend. It was time. He glimpsed sights of buildings, the like of which he had never seen, rising hundreds and thousands of feet into the air. He saw armies of millions, he saw weapons of terrifying power. He saw flying machines and he saw dragons. He saw creatures of every shape, size and form. All seemed to cry out to him as he rode by.

And he saw Rhalina.

He saw Rhalina as a girl, as a boy, as a man, as an old woman. He saw her alive and he saw her dead.

And it was that sight that made him scream and it was why he was still screaming as he rode suddenly into a forest clearing, bursting through a circle of men and women who had stood with hands linked around a mound, and who chanted as with a single voice.

He was still screaming as he drew his bright sword and

raised it high in his silver hand as he reined his horse to a halt on top of the mound.

'Corum!' cried the folk in the clearing.

And Corum ceased to scream and lowered his head, though his sword was still raised.

The red Vadhagh horse in all its silken trappings pawed at the grass of the mound and again it snorted.

Then Corum said in a deep, quiet voice, 'I am Corum and I will help you. But remember, in this land, in this age, I am a virgin.'

'Corum,' they said. 'Corum Llaw Ereint.' And they pointed out his silver hand to each other and their faces were joyful.

'I am Corum,' he said. 'You must tell me why I have been summoned.'

A man older than the others, his red beard veined with white, a great gold collar about his neck, stepped forward.

'Corum,' he said. 'We called you because you *are* Corum.'

CHAPTER THREE

The Tuha-na-Cremm Croich

Corum's mind was clouded. For all that he could smell the night air, see the people around him, feel the horse beneath him, it still seemed that he dreamed. Slowly he rode back down the mound. A light wind caught the folds of his scarlet robe and lifted them, swirling them about his head. He tried to realize that somehow he was now separated from his own world by at least a millennium. Or could it be, he wondered, that he really did still dream? He felt the detachment that he sometimes felt when he was dreaming. As he reached the bottom of the grassy mound the tall Mabden folk stood back respectfully. By the expressions on their well-formed features it seemed plain that they, too, were dazed by this event, as if they had not really expected their invocation to be successful. Corum felt sympathy with them. These were not the superstitious barbarians he had first suspected he would find. There was intelligence in those faces, a clarity about their gaze, a dignity about the way in which they held themselves, even though they thought they were in the presence of a supernatural being. These, it seemed, were the true descendants of the best of his wife's folk. At that moment he felt no regret that he had answered their summons.

He wondered if they felt the cold, as he did. The air was sharp and yet they wore only thin cloaks which left their arms, chests and legs bare, save for the gold ornaments, leather straps and high sandals which all – men and women – had.

The older man who had first spoken to Corum was powerfully built and as tall as the Vadhagh himself.

Corum reined his horse before this man and he dismounted. They stared at each other for some moments. Then Corum spoke distantly:

'My head is empty,' he said. 'You must fill it.'

The man stared thoughtfully at the ground and then raised his head, saying:

'I am Mannach, a king.' He smiled faintly. 'A wizard, I, of sorts. Druid, some call me, though I've few of the Druids' skills – nor much of their wisdom. But I am the best we have now, for we have forgotten most of the old lore. Which is perhaps why we are now in this predicament.' He added, almost with embarrassment, 'We had no need of it, we thought, until the Fhoi Myore came back.' He looked curiously at Corum's face as if he disbelieved in the power of his own invocation.

Corum had decided almost at once that he liked this King Mannach. Corum approved of the man's scepticism (if that was what it was). Plainly the invocation had been weak because Mannach and probably the others had only half-believed in it.

'You summoned me when all else failed?' said Corum.

'Aye. The Fhoi Myore beat us in battle after battle, for they do not fight as we fight. At last we had nothing left but our legends.' Mannach hesitated and then admitted: 'I did not believe much in those legends before now.'

Corum smiled. 'Perhaps there was no truth in them before now.'

Mannach frowned. 'You speak more like a man than a god – or even a great hero. I mean no disrespect.'

'It is other folk who make gods and heroes of men like myself, my friend.' Corum looked at the rest of the gathering. 'You must tell me what you expect of me, for I have no mystic powers.'

It was Mannach who smiled now. 'Perhaps you had none before.'

Corum raised his silver hand. 'This? It is of earthly manufacture. With the right skills and knowledge any man might make one.'

'You have gifts,' said King Mannach. 'The gifts of your

race, your experience, your wisdom - aye, and your skills, Lord of the Mound. The legends say that you fought mighty gods before the Dawn of the World.'

'I fought gods.'

'Well, we have great need of a fighter of gods. These Fhoi Myore are gods. They conquer our land. They steal our Holy things. They capture our people. Even now our High King is their prisoner. Our Great Places fall to them – Caer Llud and Craig Dôn among them. They divide our land and so separate our folk. Separated, it becomes harder for us to join in battle against the Fhoi Myore.'

'They must be numerous, these Fhoi Myore,' said Corum.

'There are seven.'

Corum said nothing, allowing the astonishment, which he had been unable to hide, to serve in place of words.

'Seven,' said King Mannach. 'Come with us now, Corum of the Mound, to our fort at Caer Mahlod, there to take meat and mead with us while we tell you why we called for you.'

And Corum remounted his horse and allowed the people to lead it through the frost-rimed oak wood and up a hill which overlooked the sea upon which a moon cast a leprous light. Stone walls rose high around the crown of the hill and there was only one small gate, really a tunnel which went down then up again, through which a visitor could pass in order to enter the city. These stones were white, too. It was as if the whole world were frozen and all its scenery carved from ice.

Within, the city of Caer Mahlod reminded Corum of the stone cities of Lyr-a-Brode, though some attempts had been made to finish the granite of the houses' walls, to paint scenes upon the walls, to carve gables. Much more fortress than town, the place had a gloomy aspect Corum could not equate with the people who had summoned him.

'These are old forts,' King Mannach explained. 'We were driven from our great cities and forced to find homes here, where our ancestors were said to dwell. They are strong, at least, settlements like Caer Mahlod, and during the day it is possible to see many miles in all directions.' He ducked beneath a portal as he led Corum into one of the big buildings which was lit with rush torches and oil lamps. The others who had been with Mannach in the oak wood followed them in.

At last they all stood in a low-roofed hall furnished with heavy wooden benches and tables. On these tables, however, was some of the finest gold, silver and bronze plate Corum had ever seen. Each bowl, each platter, each cup, was exquisite and, if anything, of even finer workmanship than the ornaments the people wore. For all that the walls were of rough stone, the hall danced with glittering light as the flames of the brands were reflected in the tableware and the ornaments of the People of Cremm Croich.

'This is all that is left of our treasure,' said King Mannach, and he shrugged. 'And the meat we serve is poor fare now, for game grows scarce, running before the Hounds of Kerenos which hunt the whole land as soon as the sun has set and do not cease hunting until the sun rises. One day, we fear, the sun will not rise again at all and soon the only life in all the world will be those hounds and the huntsmen who are their masters. And ice and snow will prevail over all – everlasting Samhain.'

Corum recognized this last word for it was like the word the folk of Lwym-an-Esh had used to describe the darkest and bleakest days of winter. He understood King Mannach's meaning.

They seated themselves at the long wooden table and servants brought the meat. It was an unappetising meal and again King Mannach apologized for it. Yet there was little gloom in that hall this night as harpists played merry tunes and sang of the old glories of the Tuha-na-Cremm Croich and made up new songs describing how Corum Jhaelen Irsei would lead them against their enemies and destroy those enemies and bring back the summer to their land. Corum noticed with pleasure that men and women were on terms of complete equality here and he was told by King Mannach that the women fought beside the men in their battles, being particularly adept in the use of the battle-snare, the weighted thong which could be hurled through the air to encircle the throats of the enemy and strangle them or snap their necks or limbs.

'These are all things which we have had to learn again in the past few years,' Mannach told Corum, pouring him frothy mead into a large golden cup. 'The arts of battle had become little more than exercise, games of skill with which we entertained each other at festivals.'

'When did the Fhoi Myore come?' Corum asked.

'Some three years ago. We were unprepared. They arrived on the eastern shores during the winter and did not make their presence known. Then, when spring did not come in those parts, people began to investigate the causes. We did not believe it at first, when we heard what had happened from the folk of Caer Llud. Since then the Fhoi Myore have extended their rule until now the whole of the eastern half of this land, from top to bottom, has become their undisputed domain. Gradually they move westward. First come the Hounds of Kerenos, then come the Fhoi Myore.'

'The seven? Seven men?'

'Seven misshapen giants, one of which is female. And they have strange powers, controlling forces of nature, beasts and, perhaps, even demons.'

'They come from the east. Where in the east?'

'Some say from across the sea, from a great mysterious continent of which we know little, a continent now bereft of life and entirely covered in snow. Others say that they come from beneath the sea itself, from a land where only they can live. Both these lands were called by our ancestors Anwyn, but I do not think this is a Fhoi Myore name.'

'And Lwym-an-Esh? Do you know aught of that land?'

'It is where, in legend, our folk came from. But in ancient times, in the misty past, there was a battle between the Fhoi Myore and the folk of Lwym-an-Esh and Lwym-an-Esh was drawn beneath the sea to become part of the land of the Fhoi Myore. Now only a few islands remain and on those islands are a few ruins, I have heard, speaking for the truth of the legends. After this disaster our people defeated the Fhoi Myore – with magical help in the form of a sword, a spear, a cauldron, a stallion, a ram, an oak tree and other things. These things were kept at Caer Llud in the care of our High King, who had rule over all the different peoples of this land and who, once a year at midsummer, would mete out justice in any disputes thought to be too complicated for kings such as myself. But now our magical treasures are scattered – some say lost forever – and our High King is a slave of the Fhoi Myore. That is why, in desperation, we recalled the legend of Corum and begged you for your help.'

'You speak of mystical things,' said Corum, 'and I was never one to understand magic and the like, but I will try to help.'

'It is strange, what has happened to us,' mused King Mannach, 'for here I sit eating with a demigod, and discover that in spite of the evidence of his own existence, he is as unconvinced by the supernatural as was I!' He shook his head. 'Well, Prince Corum of the Silver Hand, we must both learn to believe in the supernatural now. The Fhoi Myore have powers which prove that it exists.'

'And so have you, it seems,' added Corum. 'For I was brought here by an invocation distinctly magical in character!'

A tall red-haired warrior leaned across the table, raising a wine-cup high to toast Corum. 'Now we shall defeat the Fhoi Myore. Now their devil dogs shall run! Hail to Prince Corum!'

And all rose then, echoing the toast.

'Hail to Prince Corum!'

And Prince Corum acknowledged the toast and replied to it with:

'Hail to the Tuha-na-Cremm Croich!'

But in his heart he was disturbed. Where had he heard a similar toast? Not during his own life. Therefore he must recall another life, another time when he was hero and saviour to a people not unlike these in some ways. Why did he feel a sense of dread, then? Had he betrayed them? Try as he might, he could not rid himself of these feelings.

A woman left her place on the bench and swayed a little as she approached him. She put a soft, strong arm about him and kissed his right cheek. 'Hail to thee, hero,' she murmured. 'Now you shall bring us back our bull. Now you shall lead us into battle with the spear Bryionak. Now you will restore to us our lost treasures and our Great Places. And will you sire us sons, Corum? Heroes?' And she kissed him again.

Corum smiled a bitter smile. 'I will do all else, if it is in my power, lady. But one thing, the last thing, I cannot do, for Vadhagh cannot sire Mabden children.'

She did not seem distressed. 'There is magic for that, too, I think,' she said. For the third time she kissed him before returning to her place. And Corum felt desire for her and this sense of desire reminded him of Rhalina and then he became sad again and his thoughts turned inwards.

'Do we tire you?' King Mannach asked a little later.

Corum shrugged. 'I have been sleeping for too long, King Mannach. I have stored up my energy. I should not be tired.'

'Sleeping? Sleeping in the mound?'

'Perhaps,' answered Corum dreamily. 'I thought not, but perhaps it was in the mound. I lived in a castle overlooking the sea, wasting my days in regret and despair. And then you called. At first I would not listen, then an old friend came and told me to answer your call. So I came. But possibly that was the dream . . .' Corum began to think he had quaffed too much of the sweet mead. It was strong. His vision was cloudy and he was filled with a peculiar mixture of melancholy and euphoria. 'Is it important to you, King Mannach, my place of origin?'

'No. What is important is that you are here at Caer Mahlod, that our people see you and take heart.'

'Tell me more of the Fhoi Myore and how you were defeated.'

'Of the Fhoi Myore I can tell you little, save that it is said they were not always united against us – that they are not all of the same blood. They do not make war as we once made war. It was our way to choose champions from the ranks of the contesting armies. Those champions would fight for us, man to man, matching skills until one was beaten. Then his life would be spared, if he had not sustained bad injuries from his fight. Often no weapons at all would be used – bard would match bard, composing satires against their enemies until the best satirist sent the others slinking away in shame. But the Fhoi Myore had no such notion of battle when they came against us. That is why we were defeated so easily. We are not killers, but that folk are killers. They want Death – crave for Death – follow Death – cry after Him to turn and face them. That folk, the Cold Folk, are like that. Those People of the Pines, they ride willy-nilly in pursuit of Death and herald the Reign of Death, of the Winter Lord, across all the land you ancients called Bro-an-Mabden, the Land in the West. This land. Now we have people in the north, the south and the west. Only in the east have we no people left, for they are cold now, fallen before the People of the Pines . . .'

King Mannach's voice began to take on the aspects of a dirge, a lament for his people in their defeat. 'O Corum, do not judge us by what you see now. I know that we were once a great folk with many powers, but we became poor after our first fights with the Fhoi Myore, then they took away the land of Lwym-an-Esh and all our books and lore with it . . .'

'This sounds like a legend to explain a natural disaster,' Corum said gently.

'So thought I until now,' King Mannach told him and Corum was bound to accept this.

'Though we are poor,' continued the king, 'and though much of our control over the inanimate world is lost, for all this, we are still the same folk. Our minds are the same. We do not lack intelligence, Prince Corum.'

Corum had not considered that they had. Indeed, he had been astonished at the king's clear thinking, having expected to meet a race much more primitive in its ideas.

And though this people had come to accept magic and wizardry as a fact, they were not otherwise superstitious.

'Yours is a proud and noble people, King Mannach,' he said sincerely. 'And I will serve them as best I can. But it is for you to tell me how to serve, for I have less knowledge of the Fhoi Myore than have you.'

'The Fhoi Myore have great fear of our old magical treasures,' King Mannach said. 'To us they had become little more than objects of interesting antiquity, but now we believe that they mean more – that they do have powers, that they represent a danger to the Fhoi Myore. And all here will agree on one thing, that the Bull of Crinanass has been seen in these parts.'

'This bull has been mentioned before.'

'Aye. A giant black bull which will kill any who seek to capture it, save one.'

'And is that one called Corum?' asked Corum with a smile.

'His name is not mentioned in the old texts. All the texts say is that he will bear the spear called Bryionak, clutched in a fist which shines like the moon.'

'And what is the spear Bryionak?'

'A magical spear, made by the Sidhi smith, Goffanon, and now again in his possession. You see, Prince Corum, after the Fhoi Myore came to Caer Llud and captured the High King, a warrior called Onragh, whose duty had been to protect the ancient treasures, fled with them in a chariot. But as he fled the treasures fell, one by one, from the chariot. Some were captured by pursuing Fhoi Myore, we heard. Others were found by Mabden. And the rest, if the rumours are to be trusted, were found by folk older than the Mabden or the Fhoi Myore – the Sidhi, whose gifts to us they originally were. We cast many runes and our wizards sought many oracles before we learned that the spear called Bryionak was once again in the possession of this mysterious Sidhi, the smith Goffanon.'

'And do you know where this smith dwells?'

'He is thought to dwell in a place called Hy-Breasail, a mysterious island of enchantment lying south of our eastern shores. Our Druids believe that Hy-Breasail is all that remains of Lwym-an-Esh.'

'But the Fhoi Myore rule there, do they not?'

'They avoid the island. I know not why.'

'The danger must be great if they deserted a land that was once theirs.'

'My thinking also,' King Mannach agreed. 'But was the danger only apparent to the Fhoi Myore? No Mabden has ever returned from Hy-Breasail. The Sidhi are said to be blood relations to the Vadhagh. Of the same stock, many say. Perhaps only a Vadhagh could go to Hy-Breasail and return?'

Corum laughed aloud. 'Perhaps. Very well, King Mannach, I will go there and look for your magical spear.'

'You could go to your death.'

'Death is not what I fear, king.'

Soberly, King Mannach nodded. 'Aye. I believe I understand you, Prince Corum. And be reminded that there is much more to fear than death in these dark days of ours.'

The flames of the brands were burning low, guttering. The merry-making was now subdued. A single harpist played a soulful tune and sang a song of doomed lovers which Corum, in his drunkenness, identified with his own story, the story of himself and Rhalina. And it seemed to him, in the half-light, that the girl who had spoken to him earlier looked much like Rhalina. He stared at her as, unconscious of his gaze, she talked and laughed with one of the young warriors. And he began to hope. He hoped that somewhere in this world Rhalina had been reincarnated, that he would find her somewhere and, though she would not know him, she would fall in love with him as she had done before.

The girl turned her head and saw that he stared. She smiled at him, bowing slightly.

He raised his wine-cup, shouting somewhat wildly as he got to his feet, 'Sing on, bard, for I drink to my lost love Rhalina. And I pray that I shall find her in this grim world.'

And then he lowered his head, feeling that he had become foolish. The girl, seen properly, looked very little like Rhalina. But her eyes remained fixed on his as he sank back into his seat and, again, he stared at her with curiosity.

'I see you find my daughter worthy of your attention, Lord of the Mound,' came King Mannach's voice from beside Corum. The king spoke a little sardonically.

'Your daughter?'

'She is called Medhbh. Is she fair?'

'She is fair. She is fine, King Mannach.'

'She is my consort, since her mother was killed in our first fight with the Fhoi Myore. She is my right hand, my wisdom. A great battle-leader is Medhbh and our finest shot with battle-snare and the sling and tathlum.'

'What is the tathlum?'

'A hard ball, made from the ground-up brains and bones of our enemies. The Fhoi Myore fear it. That is why we use it. The brains and bones are mixed with lime and the lime sets hard. It seems an effective weapon against the invaders – and few weapons are effective, for their magic is strong.'

Corum said softly, as he sipped still more mead, 'Before I set off to find your spear for you, I should like very much to see the nature of our enemies.'

King Mannach smiled. 'It is a request we can easily grant, for two of the Fhoi Myore and their hunting packs have been seen not far from here. Our scouts believe that they head towards Caer Mahlod to attack our fort. They should be here by tomorrow's sunset.'

'You expect to beat them? You seem unconcerned.'

'We shall not beat them. Attacks such as this are, we think, more in the nature of a diversion for the Fhoi Myore. On some occasions they have succeeded in destroying one of our forts, but mainly they do this simply to unnerve us.'

'Then you will let me guest here until tomorrow's sunset?'

'Aye. If you promise to flee and seek Hy-Breasail if the fort begins to fall.'

'I promise,' said Corum.

Again he found himself glancing at King Mannach's daughter. She was laughing, flinging back her thick, red hair as she drained her mead-cup. He looked at her smooth limbs with their golden bangles, her firm, well-proportioned figure. She was the very picture of a warrior-princess, yet there was something else about her manner that made him think she was more than that. There was a fine intelligence in her eyes, and a sense of humour. Or did he imagine it all, wanting so desperately to find Rhalina in any Mabden woman?

At length he forced himself to leave the hall, to be escorted by King Mannach to the room set aside for him; a simple room, plainly furnished, with a wooden bed sprung with hide ropes, a straw mattress and furs to cover him against the cold. And he slept well in that bed and he did not dream at all.

BOOK TWO

*New foes, new friends,
new enigmas*

CHAPTER ONE

Shapes in the Mist

And the first morning dawned, and Corum saw the land.

Through the window, filled with oiled parchment to admit light and allow a shadowy view of the world outside, Corum saw that the walls and roofs of rocky Caer Mahlod sparkled with bright frost. Frost clung to grey granite stones. Frost hardened on the ground and frost made the trees, in the nearby forest below, bright and sharp and dead.

A log fire had burned in the low-roofed room Corum had been given, but now it was little more than warm ash. Corum shivered as he washed and donned his clothes.

And this, Corum thought, was spring in a place where once spring had been early and golden and winter barely noticed, an interval between the mellow days of autumn and the fresh mornings of the springtime.

Corum thought he recognized the landscape. He was not, in fact, far from the promontory on which Castle Erorn stood. The view through the oiled parchment window was further obscured by a suggestion of sea-mist rising from the other side of the fortress town, but far away could just be seen the outline of a crag which was almost certainly one of the crags close to Erorn. He conceived a wish to go to that point and see if Castle Erorn still stood and, if it did stand, if it was occupied by one who might know something of the castle's history. Before he left this part of the country he promised himself he would visit Castle Erorn, if only to witness a symbol of his own mortality.

Corum remembered the proud, laughing girl in the hall

on the previous night. It was no betrayal of Rhalina, surely, if he admitted that he was attracted to the girl. And there had been little doubt that she had been attracted to him. Yet why did he feel so reluctant to admit the fact? Because he was afraid? How many women could he love and watch grow old and perish before his own long life was over? How many times could he feel the anguish of loss? Or would he begin to grow cynical, taking the women for a short while and leaving them before he could grow to love them too much? For their sake and for his, that might be the best solution to his profoundly tragic situation.

With a certain effort of will he dismissed the problem and the image of the red-haired daughter of the king. If today were a day for the making of war, then he had best concentrate on that matter before any other, lest the enemy silence his conscience when they silenced his breathing. He smiled, recalling King Mannach's words. The Fhoi Myore followed Death, Mannach had said. They courted Death. Well, was not the same true of Corum? And, if it were true, did that not make him the best enemy of the Fhoi Myore?

He left his chamber, ducking through the doorway, and walked through a series of small, round rooms until he reached the hall where he had dined the previous night. The hall was empty. Now the plate had been stored away and faint, grey light came reluctantly through the narrow windows to illuminate the hall. It was a cold place, and a stern one. A place, Corum thought, where men might kneel alone and purify their minds for battle. He flexed his silver hand, stretching the silver fingers, bending the silver knuckles, looking at the silver palm which was so detailed that every line of a natural hand was reproduced. The hand was attached by pins to the wrist-bone. Corum had performed the necessary operation himself, using his other hand to drive the drill through the bone. Well might anyone believe it to be a magic hand, so perfect a copy of the fleshly one was it. With a sudden gesture of distaste Corum let the hand fall to his side. It was the only thing he had created in two-thirds of a century. The only work he had finished since the end of the adventure of the Sword Rulers.

He felt self-disgust and could not analyse the reason for the emotion. He began to pace back and forth over the great flagstones, sniffing at the cold, damp air like a hound impatient to begin the chase. Or was he so impatient to begin? Perhaps he was, instead, escaping from something. From the knowledge of his own, inevitable doom? The doom which Elric and Erekosë had both hinted at?

'Oh, by my ancestors, let the battle come and let it be a mighty one!' he shouted aloud. And, with a tense movement, he drew his battle-blade and whirled it, testing its temper, gauging its balance, before resheathing it with a crash which echoed through the hall.

'And let it be a successful one for Caer Mahlod, Sir Champion.' The voice was the sweet, amused voice of Medhbh, King Mannach's daughter, leaning in the doorway, a hand on her hip. Around her waist was a heavy belt bearing a sheathed dagger and broadsword. Her hair was tied back and she wore a sort of leather toga as her only armour. In her free hand she held a light helmet not unlike a Vadhagh helmet in design but made of brass.

Rarely given to bombastics and embarrassed at being discovered declaiming his confusion, Corum turned away, unable to look into her face. His humour left him momentarily. 'I fear you have very little of a hero in me, lady,' he said coldly.

'And a mournful god, Lord of the Mound. We hesitated, many of us, before summoning you to us. Many thought that, if you existed at all, you would be some dark and awful being of the Fhoi Myore kind, that we should release something horrible upon ourselves. But, no, we brought to us instead a man. And a man is much more complicated a being than a mere god. And our responsibilities, it seems, are different altogether – subtler and harder to accomplish. You are angry because I saw that you were fearful . . .'

'Perhaps it was not fear, lady.'

'But perhaps it was. You support our cause because you chose to. We have no claim on you. We have no power over you, as we thought we might have. You help us in spite of your fear and your self-doubt. That is worth much more than the help of some barely sensate supernatural creature such as the Fhoi Myore use. And the Fhoi Myore fear your legend. Remember that, Prince Corum.'

Still Corum would not turn. Her kindness was unmistakable. Her sympathy real. Her intelligence was as great as her beauty. How could he turn, when to turn would be to see her and to see her would be to love her helplessly, to love her as he had loved Rhalina?

Controlling his voice he said: 'I thank you for your kindness, lady. I will do what I can in the service of your folk, but I warn you to expect no spectacular aid from me.'

He did not turn for he did not trust himself. Did he see something of Rhalina in this girl because he needed Rhalina so much? And if that were the case what right had he to love Medhbh, herself, if he loved in her only qualities he imagined he saw?

Silver hand covered embroidered eye-patch, the cold and unfeeling fingers plucking at the fabric Rhalina had sewn. He almost shouted at her:

'And what of the Fhoi Myore? Do they come?'

'Not yet. Only the mist grows thicker. A sure sign of their presence somewhere near.'

'Does mist follow them?'

'Mist precedes them. Ice and snow follow. And the East Wind often signals their coming, bearing hailstones large as gulls' eggs. Ah, the earth dies and the trees bow when the Fhoi Myore march.' She spoke distantly.

The tension in the hall was increasing.

And then she said: 'You do not have to love me, lord.'

That was when he turned.

But she had gone.

Again he stared down at his metal hand, using the soft one, the one of flesh, to brush the tear from his single eye.

Faintly, from another, distant, part of the fortress, he thought he heard the strains of a Mabden harp playing music sweeter than any he had heard at Castle Erorn, and it was sad, the sound of that harp.

'You have a harpist of great genius in your Court, King Mannach.'

Corum and the king stood together on the outer walls of Caer Mahlod, looking to the east.

'You heard the harp, too?' King Mannach frowned. He was dressed in a breastplate of bronze with a bronze helmet upon his greying head. His handsome face was grim and his eyes puzzled. 'Some thought that you played it, Lord of the Mound.'

Corum held up his silver hand. 'This could not pluck such a strain as that.' He looked at the sky. 'It was a Mabden harpist I heard.'

'I think not,' said Mannach. 'At least, prince, it was no harpist of my Court we heard. The bards of Caer Mahlod prepare themselves for the fight. When they play, it will be martial songs we shall hear, not music like that which sounded this morning.'

'You did not recognize the tune?'

'I have heard it once before. In the grove of the mound, the first night that we came to call to you to help us. It was what encouraged us to believe that there might be truth in the legend. If that harp had not played, we should not have continued.'

Corum drew his brows together. 'Mysteries were never to my taste,' he said.

'Then life itself cannot be to your taste, lord.'

Corum smiled. 'I take your meaning, King Mannach. Nonetheless, I am suspicious of such things as ghostly harps.'

There was no more to say on the matter. King Mannach pointed towards the thick oak forest. Heavy mist clung to the topmost branches. Even as they watched, the mist seemed to grow denser, descending towards the ground until few of the frost-rimed trees could be seen. The sun

53

was up, but its light was pale, for thin clouds were beginning to drift across it.

The day was still.

No birds sang in the forest. Even the movements of the warriors inside the fort were muted. When a man did shout, the sound seemed magnified and clear as a bell's note for a second before it was absorbed into the silence. All along the battlements had been stacked weapons – spears, arrows, bows, large stones and the round tathlum balls which would be flung from slings. Now the warriors began to take their places on the walls. Caer Mahlod was not a large settlement, but it was strong and heavy, squatting on the top of a hill whose sides had been smoothed so that it seemed like a man-made cone of enormous proportions. To the south and north stood several other cones like it and on two of these could be seen the ruins of other fortresses, suggesting that once Caer Mahlod had been part of a much larger settlement.

Corum turned to look towards the sea. There the mist had gone and the water was calm, blue and sparkling, as if the weather which touched the land did not extend across the ocean. And now Corum could see that he had been right in judging Castle Erorn nearby. Two or three miles to the south was the familiar outline of the promontory and what might be the remains of a tower.

'Do you know that place, King Mannach?' asked Corum, pointing.

'It is called Castle Owyn by us, for it resembles a castle when seen from the distance, but really it is a natural formation. Some legends are attached to it concerning its occupation by supernatural beings – by the Sidhi, by Cremm Croich. But the only architect of Castle Owyn was the wind and the only mason the sea.'

'Yet I should like to go there,' said Corum. 'When I can.'

'If both of us survive the raid of the Fhoi Myore – indeed, if the Fhoi Myore decide not to attack us – then I will take you. But there is nothing to see, Prince Corum. The place is best observed from this distance.'

'I suspect,' said Corum, 'that you are right, king.'

Now, as they spoke, the mist grew thicker still and obscured all sight of the sea. Mist fell upon Caer Mahlod and filled her narrow streets. Mist moved upon the fortress from all sides save the west.

Even the small sounds in the fort died as the occupants waited to discover what the mist had brought with it.

It had become dark, almost like evening. It had become cold so that Corum, more warmly clothed than any of the others, shivered and drew his scarlet robe more tightly about him.

And there came the howling of a hound from out of the mist. A savage, desolate howling which was taken up by other canine throats until it filled the air on all sides of the fortress called Caer Mahlod.

Peering through his single eye, Corum tried to see the hounds themselves. For an instant he thought he saw a pale, slinking shape at the bottom of the hill, below the walls. Then the shape had gone. Corum carefully strung his long, bone bow and nocked a slender arrow to the string. Grasping the shaft of the bow with his metal hand, he used his fleshly hand to draw back the string to his cheek and he waited until he saw another faint shape appear before he let fly.

The arrow pierced the mist and vanished.

A scream rose high and horrible and became a snarl, a growl. Then a shape was running up the hill towards the fort. It ran very fast and very straight. Two yellow eyes glared directly into Corum's face as if the beast recognized instinctively the source of its wound. Its long, feathery tail waved as it ran and at first it seemed it had another tail, rigid and thin, but then Corum realized that it was his arrow, sticking from the animal's side, which he saw. He nocked another arrow to his bowstring. He drew the string back and glared, himself, into the beast's blazing eyes. A red mouth gaped and yellow fangs dripped saliva. The hair was coarse and shaggy and, as the dog approached, Corum realized it was as large as a small pony.

The sound of its snarling filled his ears and still he did

not let fly, for it was sometimes hard to see against the background of mist.

Corum had not expected the hound to be white. A glowing whiteness which was somehow disgusting to look upon. Only the ears of the hound were darker than the rest of its body and these ears were a glistening red, the colour of fresh blood.

Higher and higher up the hill raced the white hound, the first arrow bouncing apparently unnoticed in its side, and its howl seemed almost to be a howl of obscene laughter as it anticipated sinking its fangs into Corum's throat. There was glee in the yellow eyes.

Corum could wait no longer. He released the arrow.

The shaft seemed to travel very slowly towards the white hound. The beast saw the arrow and tried to side-step, but it had been running too fast, too purposefully, its movements were not properly coordinated and as it ducked to save its right eye, its legs tangled and it received the arrow in its left eye with such an impact that the tip of the arrow burst through the other side of the skull.

The hound opened its great jaws as it collapsed, but no further sound escaped that frightful throat. It fell, rolled a short way down the hill, and was still.

Corum let out a sigh and turned to speak to King Mannach.

But King Mannach was already flinging back his arm, aiming a spear into the mist where at least a hundred pale shadows skulked and slavered and wailed their determination to be revenged upon the slayers of their sibling.

CHAPTER TWO

The Fight at Caer Mahlod

'Oh, there are many!'

King Mannach's expression was troubled as he took up a second spear and flung that after the first. 'More than any I have seen before.' He glanced round to see how his men fared. Now all were active against the hounds. They whirled slings, shot arrows and threw spears. The hounds surrounded Caer Mahlod. 'There are many. Perhaps the Fhoi Myore have already heard that you have come to us, Prince Corum. Perhaps they have determined to destroy you.'

Corum made no reply, for he had seen a huge white hound slinking at the very foot of the wall, sniffing the entranceway which had been blocked with a large boulder. Leaning out over the battlements Corum let fly with one of his last arrows, striking the beast in the back of its skull. It moaned and ran off into the mist. Corum could not see if he had killed it. They were hard to kill, these hounds, and hard to see in the mist and the frost, save for their blood-red ears, their yellow eyes.

Even had they been darker it would have been difficult to fight them. The mist grew thicker still. It attacked the throats and the eyes of the defenders so that they were constantly wiping the stuff from their faces, spitting over the walls at the hounds as they tried to free their lungs of the cold and clogging dampness. Yet they were brave. They did not falter. Spear after spear darted down. Arrow after arrow arced into the ranks of those sinister dogs. Only the piles of tathlum balls were not used and Corum was curious to know why, for King Mannach had not had time to tell him. But spears and arrows and rocks were already running low and only a few of the pale dogs were dead.

Kerenos, whoever he might be, had well-stocked kennels, thought Corum as he shot the last of his arrows, dropped his bow and pulled his sword from its scabbard.

And their howling brought tension to every nerve so that one had to fight one's own cringing muscles as well as the dogs themselves.

King Mannach ran along the battlements encouraging his warriors. So far none had fallen. Only when the missiles were no more would they be forced to defend themselves with their blades, with their axes and their pikes. That time was almost upon them.

Corum paused to draw a breath and try to take account of their situation. There were something less than a hundred hounds below. There were something more than a hundred men on the battlements. The hounds would have to make enormous leaps to get a foothold on the walls. That they were capable of making such leaps, Corum was in no doubt.

Even as he considered this he saw a white beast come flying towards him, its forelegs outstretched, its jaws snapping, its hot, yellow eyes glaring. If he had not already unsheathed his blade he would have been slain there and then. But now he brought the sword up, stabbing out at the hound even as it flew through the air towards him. He caught it in the belly and he nearly lost his footing as the thing impaled itself upon the point of his sword, grunted as if in mild surprise, growled as it understood its fate, and made one feeble, futile snap at him before it went tumbling backwards to fall directly upon the spine of one of its fellows.

For a little while Corum thought that the Hounds of Kerenos had had enough of battle for that day, for they seemed to retreat. But their growlings, their mutterings, their occasional howlings, made it plain that they were simply resting, biding their time, preparing for the next attack. Perhaps they were taking instructions from an unseen master – perhaps Kerenos himself. Corum would have given much for a glimpse of the Fhoi Myore. He wanted to see at least one, if only to form his own opinion of what they were and from where they derived their powers. A little earlier he had seen a darker shape in the mist, a shape which was taller than the hounds and had seemed to walk on two legs, but the mist was shifting so rapidly all the time (though never dispersing) that he might have been deceived. If he had actually seen the outline of a Fhoi Myore, then there was no doubt that they were considerably taller than Man and probably not of the same race at all. Yet where could others, not Vadhagh, Nhadragh or Mabden, have come from? This had puzzled Corum ever since his first conversation with King Mannach.

'The hounds! 'Ware the hounds!'

A warrior shouted as he was borne backward by a gleaming white shape which had flown silently at him from out of the mist. Hound and man went together off the walls and fell with a terrific crack into the street below.

Only the hound got up, its jaws full of the warrior's flesh. It grinned, turned and loped into the street. Barely thinking, Corum flung his sword at it and struck it in the side. It shrieked and tried to snap at the sword protruding between its ribs, just as a puppy might chase its own tail. Four or five rotations the great hound made before it understood that it was dead.

Corum bounded down the steps to the street to retrieve his sword. He had never seen such monstrous dogs before, neither could he understand their strange colouring, which was like nothing else in nature he had ever seen. With distaste he tugged his blade free from the massive carcass, wiping the blood on the pale, coarse fur. Then he ran back up the steps to take his place on the wall.

For the first time he noticed the stink. It was definitely a canine stink, like the smell of wet, dirty hair, but for a few seconds at a time it could be almost overpowering. With the mist attacking eyes and mouths and the stink of the hounds attacking their nostrils, the defenders were being hard-pressed to accomplish their work. Dogs were on the walls now in several places and four warriors lay with their throats torn out, while two of the Hounds of Kerenos were also dead, one with its head hacked clean off.

Corum was beginning to tire and judged that the others must also be wearying. In an ordinary battle they would have had every right to be exhausted by now, but here they did not fight men but beasts and the allies of the beasts were the elements themselves.

Corum leaped to one side as a hound – one of the largest he had so far seen – cleared the battlements behind him and landed on the platform beyond, hissing and panting, its eyes rolling, its tongue lolling, its fangs dripping. The smell choked Corum. It issued from the mouth of the beast, a fetid unhealthy smell. Growling softly, the hound gathered itself to attack Corum, the strange red ears lying flat against the tapering skull.

Corum shouted something, grabbed up his own long-hafted war-axe from where he had kept it by the wall, and whirling this weapon ran at the hound.

The hound cringed perceptibly as the blade flashed over its white head. Its tail began to sink between its legs before it realized that it was considerably heavier and stronger than Corum and drew back its lips in a snarl exposing teeth some twelve inches long.

Bringing the war-axe round for a second swing, Corum was caught off-balance and the hound charged before the axe could come back. Corum had to take three rapid paces away from the beast as it flung itself at him, to allow the axe to continue its swing and thud into the hound's hind-leg, crippling it but not stopping it. Corum was close to the edge and knew that a leap might break his legs at the very least. One more step backwards would be enough to send him falling into the street. There was only one thing he could do. As the hound charged at him, he sidestepped and ducked and the dog went sailing past him and smashed head-first on to the cobbles, breaking its neck.

Now the noise of battle came from every part of the fortress, for several Hounds of Kerenos had gained access to the streets and were roaming those, sniffing for the old women and children who huddled behind the barricaded doors.

Medhbh, King Mannach's daughter, had been in charge of the streets and Corum glimpsed her running at the head of a handful of warriors, charging upon two of the hounds who had found themselves trapped in a street with no exit. Some of her red hair had come loose from her helmet and it flew as she ran. Her lithe figure, the speed and control of her movements, her evident courage, astonished Corum. He had never known a woman like this Medhbh – or, indeed, other women here who fought with their men and who shared equal duties with them. Such beautiful women, too, thought Corum; and then he cursed himself for his lack of attention, for another beast came leaping and snapping and howling at him and he whirled his war-axe and he shouted his Vadhagh war-cry and he smashed the blade deep into the hound's skull, between its red, tufted ears, and he wished that the fight would end, for he was so weary that he could not believe he could slay another of the dogs.

The baying of those dreadful beasts seemed to grow louder and louder, the stink of their breath made Corum wish for the harshness of the mist in his lungs, and still the white bodies flew through the air and landed upon the battlements, still the great fangs snapped and the yellow eyes blazed, still men died as the jaws ripped flesh, sinew and bone. And Corum leaned against the wall and panted and knew that the next dog to attack him would kill him. He had no intention of resisting. He was finished. He would die here and all problems would be solved in an instant. Caer Mahlod would fall. The Fhoi Myore would rule.

Something made him look down into the street again.

There was Medhbh, standing alone, sword in hand, while a massive hound rushed at her. The rest of her party were all down. Their torn corpses could be seen strewn across the cobbles. Only Medhbh remained and she would perish soon.

Corum had jumped before he knew that he had made up his mind. His booted feet landed full on the rump of the great hound, bringing its hind parts to the ground. The war-axe whistled now and crunched through the bone of the huge dog's vertebrae, almost chopping the beast in two. And Corum, carried forward by his own momentum, fell across the corpse, slipped in the beast's blood, struck his skull against its broken spine and fell over on to his back, desperately trying to regain his footing. Even Medhbh had not realized what had happened, for she had struck at one of the dog's eyes with her sword, not realizing that the creature was already dead, before she saw Corum.

She grinned as he got to his feet and began to tug his war-axe from the corpse.

'So you would not see me dead, then, my elfin prince.'

'Lady,' said Corum, gasping for breath, 'I would not.'

He freed his axe and staggered back up the steps to the battlements where weary warriors did their best to meet the attacks of seemingly innumerable hounds.

Corum forced himself forward, to help a warrior who was about to go down before one of the dogs. His axe was becoming blunt with all the slaughter and this time his blow only stunned the dog which recovered almost immediately and turned on him. But a pike took it in the belly and the worst Corum got was the thing's thick and ill-smelling blood pouring over his breastplate.

He stumbled away, peering through the mist beyond the walls. And this time he did see a looming shape – a gigantic figure of a man, apparently with antlered horns growing from the sides of its head, its face all misshapen, its body all warped, raising something to its lips, as if to drink.

And then came a sound which made all the hounds stop dead in their tracks and caused the surviving warriors to drop their weapons and cover their ears.

It was a sound full of horror, part laughter, part

screaming, part agonized wail, part triumphant shout. It was the sound of the Horn of Kerenos, calling back his hounds.

Corum glimpsed the figure again as it disappeared into the mist. The hounds which remained alive instantly began to dive over the walls and run back down the hill until there was not a single living dog remaining in Caer Mahlod.

Then the mist began to lift, rushing back towards the forest as if drawn behind Kerenos like a cloak.

Once more the Horn sounded.

Some men were vomiting, so terrible was the sound. Some men screamed, while others sobbed.

Yet it was plain that Kerenos and his pack had had enough sport for that day. They had shown the people of Caer Mahlod a little of their power. It was all they had wanted to do. Corum could almost understand that the Fhoi Myore might see the battle in terms of a friendly passage of arms before the main fight began.

The fight at Caer Mahlod had brought about the deaths of some four and thirty hounds.

Fifty warriors had died, men and women both.

'Quickly, Medhbh, the tathlum!' King Mannach, wounded in the shoulder and bleeding still, cried to his daughter. She had put one of the round balls of brains and lime into her sling and was whirling it.

She let fly into the mist, after Kerenos himself.

King Mannach knew she had not hit the Fhoi Myore.

'It is one of the few things they believe will kill them, the tathlum,' he said.

Quietly they left the walls of Caer Mahlod and went to mourn their dead.

'Tomorrow,' said Corum, 'I will set off upon this quest to find your spear Bryionak for you and bring it to you, clutched in my silver hand. I will do all that I can to save the folk of Caer Mahlod from the likes of Kerenos and his hounds. I will go.'

King Mannach, aided down the steps by his daughter, merely nodded his head, for he was very faint.

'But I must go to this place you call Castle Owyn,' said Corum. 'That I must do first, before I leave.'

'I will take you there this evening,' said Medhbh.

And Corum did not refuse.

CHAPTER THREE

A Moment in the Ruins

Now that it was late afternoon and the cloud had dropped away from the face of the sun which had melted the frost a little and warmed the day and brought traces of the odour of spring to the landscape, Corum and the warrior princess Medhbh, nicknamed 'of the Long Arm' for her skill with snare and tathlum, rode horses out to the place which Corum called Erorn and she called Owyn.

Though it was spring, there was no foliage on the trees and barely any grass growing upon the ground. It was a stark world, this world. Life was fleeing it. Corum remembered how lush it had been, even when he had left. It depressed him to think what so much of the country must look like after the Fhoi Myore, their hounds and their servants, had visited it.

They reined their horses near the edge of the cliff and looked at the sea muttering and gasping on the shingle of the tiny bay.

Tall black cliffs – old and crumbling – rose out of the water and the cliffs were full of caves, as Corum had known them at least a millennium before.

The promontory, however, had changed. Part of it had fallen at the centre, collapsing into the sea in a tumble of rotting granite, and now Corum knew why little of Castle Erorn remained.

'There is what they call the Sidhi Tower – or Cremm's Tower – see.' Medhbh showed him what she meant. It lay on the other side of the chasm created by the falling rock. 'It looks man-made from a distance, but it is really nature's work.'

But Corum knew better. He recognized the worn lines. True they seemed the work of nature, for Vadhagh building had always tended to blend into the landscape. That was why, in his own time, some travellers even failed to realize that Castle Erorn was there.

'It is the work of my folk,' he said quietly. 'That is the remains of Vadhagh architecture, though none would believe it, I know.'

She was surprised. She laughed. 'So the legend has truth in it. It *is* your tower!'

'I was born there,' said Corum. He sighed. 'And, I suppose, I died there, too,' he added. Leaving his horse he walked to the edge of the cliff and looked down. The sea had made a narrow channel through the gap. He looked across at the remains of the tower. He remembered Rhalina and he remembered his family, his father Prince Khlonskey, his mother the Princess Colatalarna, his sisters Ilastru and Pholhinra, his uncle Prince Rhanan, his cousin Sertreda. All dead now, Rhalina at least had lived her natural lifespan, but the others had been brutally slain by Glandyth-a-Krae and his murderers. Now none remembered them save Corum. For a moment he envied them, for too many remembered Corum.

'But you live,' she said simply.

'Do I? I wonder if perhaps I am no more than a shade, a figment of your folk's desires. Already my memories of my past life grow dim. I can barely remember how my family looked.'

'You have a family – where you come from?'

'I know that the legend says that I slept in the mound until I was needed, but that is not true. I was brought here from my own time – when Castle Erorn stood where ruins stand now. Ah, there have been so many ruins in my life . . .'

'And your family is there? You left it to help us?'

Corum shook his head and turned to look at her, smiling a bitter smile.

'No, lady, I would not have done that. My family was

66

slain by your race – by Mabden. My wife died.' He hesitated.

'Slain, too?'

'Of old age.'

'She was older than you?'

'No.'

'You are truly immortal, then?' She looked down at the distant sea.

'As far as it matters, yes. That is why I fear to love, you see.'

'I would not fear that.'

'Neither did the Margravine Rhalina, my bride. And I think I did not fear it, for I could not experience it until it happened. But when I experienced the loss of her I thought I could never bear that emotion again.'

A single gull appeared from nowhere and perched on a nearby spur of rock. There had been many gulls here once.

'You will never feel that exact emotion again, Corum.'

'True. And yet . . .'

'You love corpses?'

He was offended. 'That is cruel . . .'

'What is left of dead people is the corpse. And if you do not love corpses, then you must find someone living to love.'

He shook his head. 'Is it so simple to you, lovely Medhbh?'

'I did not think that I said something simple, Lord Corum of the Mound.'

He made an impatient gesture with his silver hand. 'I am not of the Mound. I do not like the implications of that title. You speak of corpses – that title makes me feel like a corpse that has been resurrected. I can smell the mould on my clothes when you speak of "the Lord of the Mound".'

'The other legends said you drank blood. There were sacrifices on the mound during the darker times.'

'I have no taste for blood.' His mood was lifting. The experience of the fight with the Hounds of Kerenos had helped rid him of some of his gloomy thoughts and replaced them with more practical considerations.

And now he was reaching out to touch her face, to trace, with his hand of flesh, the line of her lips, her neck, her shoulder.

And now they were embracing and he was weeping and full of joy.

They kissed. They made love near the ruins of Castle Erorn while the sea pounded in the bay below. And then they lay in the last of the sunshine, looking out to sea.

'Listen,' Medhbh raised her head, her hair floating about her face.

He heard it. He had heard it a little while before she mentioned it, but he had not wanted to hear it.

'A harp,' she said. 'What sweet music it plays. How melancholy it is, that music. Do you hear it?'

'Yes.'

'It is familiar . . .'

'Perhaps you heard it this morning, just before the attack?' He spoke reluctantly, distantly.

'Perhaps. And in the grove of the mound.'

'I know – just before your folk tried to summon me for the first time.'

'Who is the harpist? What is the music?'

Corum was looking across the gulf at the ruined tower that was all that remained of Castle Erorn. Even to his eyes it did not look mortal-built. Perhaps, after all, the wind and the sea had carved the tower and his memories were false.

He was afraid.

She, too, now stared at the tower.

'That is where the music comes from,' he said. 'The harp plays the music of time.'

CHAPTER FOUR

The World Turned White

Garbed in fur, Corum set forth.

He wore a white fur robe over his own clothes and there was a huge hood on the robe to cover his helmet, all made from the soft pelt of the winter marten. Even the horse they had given him had a coat of fur-trimmed doeskin embroidered with scenes of a valiant past. They gave him fur-lined boots and gauntlets of doeskin, also embroidered, and a high saddle and saddle panniers and soft cases for his bow, his lances and the blade of his war-axe. He wore one of the gauntlets on his silver hand, so that no casual eye would know him. And he kissed Medhbh and he saluted the folk of Caer Mahlod as they stood regarding him with grave and hopeful eyes upon the walls of the fortress town and was kissed upon his forehead by King Mannach.

'Bring us back our spear Bryionak,' said King Mannach, 'so that we may tame the bull, the Black Bull of Crinanass, so that we may defeat our enemies and make our land green again.'

'I will seek it,' promised Prince Corum Jhaelen Irsei, and his single eye shone brightly, with tears or with confidence, none could tell. And he mounted his great horse, the huge and heavy warhorse of the Tuha-na-Cremm Croich, and he placed his feet in the stirrups he had had them make for him (for they had forgotten the use of stirrups) and he put his tall lance in the stirrup rest, though he did not unfurl his banner, stitched for him all the previous night by the maidens of Caer Mahlod.

'You look a great war-knight, my lord,' murmured

Medhbh and he reached down to stroke her red-gold hair and touch her soft cheek.

He said: 'I will return, Medhbh.'

He had ridden south-east for two days and the riding had not been difficult, for he had come this way more than once and time had not destroyed many of the landmarks that had been familiar to him. Perhaps because he had found so little and yet so much at Castle Erorn he now headed for Moidel's Mount where Rhalina's castle had stood. It was easy to justify this goal in terms of his quest, for Moidel's Mount had been the last outpost of Lwym-an-Esh and now the last of Lwym-an-Esh was Hy-Breasail. He would lose neither time nor direction by seeking out Moidel's Mount, if that had not, too, sunk when Lwym-an-Esh sank.

South and east he rode and the world grew colder and showers of bright, bouncing hailstones capered on the hard earth, pattered on his armoured shoulders and his horse's neck and withers. Many times his road across the great, wild moor was obscured by sheets of this frozen rain and sometimes it grew so bad that he was forced to take shelter where he could, usually behind a boulder, for there were few trees on the moor, save some gorse and stunted birch, and all the bracken and heather, which should have been flourishing at this season, was either completely dead or feebly alive. Once deer and pheasant had been everywhere but now Corum saw no pheasant and had seen only one wary stag, thin, mad-eyed, on the whole of his journey. And the further east he rode, the worse the prospect of the land became, and soon there was heavy frost sparkling on every piece of vegetation, and coverings of snow on every hill-top, on every boulder. The land rose higher and the air grew thinner and colder and Corum was glad of the heavy robe his friends had given him, for slowly the frost gave way to snow and every way he looked the world was white and its whiteness reminded him of the colour of the Hounds of Kerenos, and now his horse waded through snow up to its hocks and Corum knew that, if attacked, he would have difficulty in fleeing any danger and almost as much in manoeuvring to face it. But at least the skies remained blue and sharp and clear and the sun, though giving little heat, was bright. It was the mist which made Corum wary, for he knew that with the mist might come the devil hounds and their masters.

And now he began to discover the shallow valleys of the moors and in the valleys the hamlets, villages and towns where once Mabden folk had lived. And every settlement was deserted.

Corum took to using these deserted places for his night camps. Hesitant to build a fire lest the smoke be seen by enemies or potential enemies, he found that he could burn peat on the flagstones of empty cottages in a manner which would let the smoke disperse before it could be detected from even a close distance. Thus he was able to keep both his horse and himself warm and cook hot food. Without these comforts his ride would have been miserable indeed.

What saddened him was that the cottages still contained the furniture, ornaments and little trinkets of the folk who had lived in them. There had been no looting for, Corum imagined, the Fhoi Myore had no interest in Mabden artefacts, but in some of the villages, the most easterly, there were signs that the Hounds of Kerenos had come a-hunting and found no shortage of prey. Doubtless that was why so many had fled and sought safety in the old, disued hill-forts like Caer Mahlod.

Corum could tell that a complex and reasonably sophisticated culture had flourished here, a rich, agricultural people who had had time to develop their artistic gifts. In the abandoned settlements he found books as well as paintings, musical instruments as well as elegant metalwork and pottery. It saddened him to see it all. Had his battle against the Sword Rulers been pointless, then? Lwym-an-Esh, which he had fought for as much as he had fought for his own folk, was gone and what had followed it was now destroyed.

After a while he began to avoid the villages and seek

out caves where he would not be reminded of the Mabden tragedy.

But then, one morning, after he had been riding for little more than an hour, he came to a broad depression in the moor, in the centre of which was a frozen tarn. To the north-east of the tarn he saw what he at first took to be standing stones, all about the height of a man, but there were several hundred whereas most stone circles were usually made up of hardly more than a score of granite slabs. As with everywhere else on this moor, snow was thick and snow covered the stones.

Corum's path took him the other side of the tarn and he was about to avoid the monuments (for such he judged them) when he thought he caught a movement of something black against the universal whiteness. A crow? He shaded his eyes to peer among the stones. No, something larger. A wolf, possibly. If it were a deer, he had need of meat. He drew the cover off his bow and strung it, swinging his lance behind him to give him a clear shot as he fitted an arrow to the string. Then, with his heels, he urged his horse forward.

As he drew closer he began to realize that these standing stones were not typical. The carving on them was much more detailed, so much so that they resembled the finest Vadhagh statuary. And that was what they were – statues of men and women poised as if in battle. Who had made them and for what purpose?

Again Corum saw the movement of a dark shape. Then it was hidden again by the statues. Corum found something familiar about the statues. Had he seen work like them before?

Then he recalled his adventure in Arioch's castle and slowly the truth came. Corum resisted the truth. He did not want to know it.

But now he was close to the nearest of the statues and he could not avoid the evidence.

These were not statues at all.

These were the corpses of folk very much like the tall, fair folk of Tuha-na-Cremm Croich; corpses frozen as they prepared to do battle against an enemy. Corum could see their expressions, their attitudes. He saw the look of resolute courage on every face – men, women, quite young boys and girls – the javelins, axes, swords, bows, slings and knives still clutched in their hands. They had come to do battle with the Fhoi Myore and the Fhoi Myore had answered their courage with this – this expression of contempt for their power and their nobility. Not even the Hounds of Kerenos had come against this sad army; perhaps the Fhoi Myore themselves had refused to appear, sending only a coldness – a sudden, awful coldness which had worked instantly and turned warm flesh into ice.

Corum turned away from the sight, the bow forgotten in his hands. The horse was nervous and was only too glad to bear him away around the banks of the frozen tarn where still, dead reeds stood like stalagmites, like a travesty of the dead folk nearby. And Corum saw two who had been wading in the water and they too were frozen, appearing to be chopped off at the waist by the flat ice, their arms raised in attitudes of terror. A boy and a girl, both probably little older than sixteen years.

The landscape was dead. The landscape was silent. The plodding of the horse's hooves sounded to Corum like the tolling of a death-knell. He fell forward across his saddle-pommel, refusing to look, unable even to weep, so horror-struck was he by the images he had seen.

Then he heard a moan which at first he thought was his own. He lifted his head, drawing cold air into his lungs, and he heard the sound again. He turned. He forced himself to glance back at the frozen host, judging that to be the direction from where the moan had come.

A black shape was clearly visible now among the white ones. A black cloak flapped like the broken wing of a raven.

'Who are you?' Corum cried, 'that you weep for these?'

The figure was kneeling. As Corum called out, it rose to its feet, but no face or even limbs could be seen emerging from the tattered cloak.

'Who are you?' Corum turned his horse.

'Take me, too, Fhoi Myore vassal!' The voice was weary and it was old. 'I know you and I know your cause.'

'I think that you do not know me, then,' said Corum kindly. 'Now, say who you are, old woman.'

'I am Ieveen, mother of some of these, wife of one of these, and I deserve to die. If you be enemy, slay me. If you be friend, then slay me, friend, and prove thyself a good friend to Ieveen. I would go, now, where my lost ones go. I want no more of this world and its cruelties. I want no more visions and terrors and truths. I am Ieveen and I prophesied all that you see and that is why I fled when they would not listen to me. And when I came back, I found that I had been right. And this is why I weep – but not for these. I weep for myself and my betrayal of my folk. I am Ieveen the Seeress, but now I have none to see for, none to respect me, least of all myself. The Fhoi Myore came and they struck them down. The Fhoi Myore left, in their clouds, with their dogs, hunting more satisfactory game than my poor clan who were so brave, who believed that the Fhoi Myore, no matter how depraved, how wicked, would respect them enough to offer them a fair fight. I warned them of what would befall them. I begged them to flee as I fled. They were reasonable. They told me I could go but they wished to stay, that a folk must keep its pride or perish in different ways, each one dying within themselves. I did not understand them. Now I understand them. So slay me, sir.'

Now the thin arms were raised imploringly, the black rags falling away from flesh that was blue with cold and with age. Now the head-covering dropped and the wrinkled face with its thin, grey hair was revealed, and Corum saw the eyes and wondered if, in all his travels, he had ever seen such misery as that which he saw in the eyes of Ieveen the Seeress.

'Slay me, sir!'

'I cannot,' said Corum. 'If I had more courage I would do what you ask, but I have no courage of that sort, lady.' He pointed westward with his bow which was still strung. 'Go that way and try to reach Caer Mahlod, where your folk still resist the Fhoi Myore. Tell them of this. Warn them of this. And thus you will redeem yourself in your own eyes. You are already redeemed in mine.'

'Caer Mahlod? You come from there? From Cremms-mound and the coast?'

'I am upon a quest. I seek a spear.'

'The spear Bryionak?' Her voice now had a peculiar gasp in it. The tone was higher. And her eyes were now looking out beyond Corum as she swayed a little. 'Bry-ionak and the Bull of Crinanass. Silver hand. Cremm Croich shall come. Cremm Croich shall come. Cremm Croich shall come.' The voice had changed again to a soft chant. The lines seemed to leave her old face and a certain beauty was there now. 'Cremm Croich shall come and he shall be called – called – called . . . And his name shall not be his name.'

Corum had been about to speak but now he listened in fascination as the old seeress continued to chant.

'Corum Llaw Ereint. Silver hand and scarlet robe. Corum is thy name and ye shall be slain by a brother . . .'

Corum had begun to believe in the old woman's powers but now he found himself smiling. 'Slain I might be, old woman, but not by a brother. I have no brother.'

'Ye have many brothers, prince. I see them all. Proud champions all. Great heroes.'

Corum felt his heart begin to beat faster and there was a tightness in his stomach. He said hastily: 'No brothers, old woman. None.' Why did he fear what she said? What did she know that he refused to know?

'You are afraid,' she said. 'I can see that I speak truth. But do not fear. You have only three things to fear. The first is the brother, of which I spoke. The second is a harp. And the third is beauty. Fear those three things, Corum Llaw Ereint, but nothing else.'

'Beauty? The other two are at least tangible – but why fear beauty?'

'And the third is beauty,' she said again. 'Fear those three things.'

'I'll listen to this nonsense no more. You have my

75

sympathy, old woman. Your ordeal has turned your mind. Go, as I said, to Caer Mahlod and there they will look after you. There you can atone for what makes you guilty, though I say again that you should not feel guilt. Now I must continue my quest for the spear of Bryionak.'

'Bryionak, Sir Champion, will be yours. But first you will make a bargain.'

'A bargain? With whom?'

'I know not. I take your advice. If I live, I will tell the folk of Caer Mahlod of what I have seen here. But you must take my advice, also, Corum Jhaelen Irsei. Do not dismiss my advice. I am Ieveen the Seeress and what I see is always true. It is only the consequences of my own actions that I cannot foresee. That is my fate.'

'And it is my fate, I think,' said Corum as he rode away from her, 'to flee from truth. At least,' he added, 'I think I prefer small truths to larger ones. Farewell, old woman.'

Surrounded by her frozen sons, her ragged cloak fluttering about her old, thin body, her voice high and faint, she called once more to him:

'Fear only those three things, Corum of the Silver Hand. Brother, harp and beauty.'

Corum wished that the harp had not been mentioned. The other two things he could easily dismiss for a mad woman's ravings. But he had already heard the harp. And he already feared it.

CHAPTER FIVE

The Wizard Calatin

Bowed and broken by the weight of the snow, its trees without leaves, without berries, its animal inhabitants dead or fled, the forest had lost its strength.

Corum had known this forest. It was the Forest of Laahr where he had first awakened after being mutilated by Glandyth-a-Krae. Reflectively he looked at his left hand, the silver hand, and he touched his right eye, recalling the Brown Man of Laahr and the Giant of Laahr. Really the Giant of Laahr had begun all this, first by saving his life, then by . . . He dismissed the thoughts. On the far side of the Forest of Laahr was the westerly tip of this land and at that tip Moidel's Mount had stood.

He shook his head as he looked at the ruined forest. There would be no Pony Tribes living there now. No Mabden to plague him.

Again he recalled the evil Glandyth. Why did evil always come from the eastern shores? Was it some special doom that this land had to suffer, through cycle upon cycle of history?

And so, with such idle speculation consuming his thoughts, Corum rode into the snowy tangle of the forest.

Dark and bleak, the oaks, the alders, the elms and the quickens stretched on all sides of him now. And of the trees in the forest, only the yews seemed to be bearing the burden of the snow with any fortitude. Corum recalled the reference to the People of the Pines. Could it be true that the Fhoi Myore slew broadleaf trees and left only the conifers? What reason could they have for destroying mere trees? How could trees be a threat to them?

Shrugging, Corum continued his ride. It was not an easy ride. Huge drifts of snow had banked up everywhere, and elsewhere trees had cracked and fallen, one upon the other, so that he was forced to make wide circles around them, until he was in great danger of losing his way.

But he forced himself to continue, praying that beyond the forest, where the sea was, the weather would improve.

For two days Corum plunged on through the Forest of Laahr until he admitted to himself that he was completely lost.

The cold, it was true, seemed just a little less intense, but that was no real indication that he was heading west. It was quite possible that he had simply grown used to it.

But, warmer though it might be, the journey had become gruelling. At night he had to clear away the snow to sleep and he had long since forgotten his earlier caution concerning the lighting of fires. A big fire was the easiest way of melting the snow and he hoped that the snow-heavy tree boughs would disperse the smoke enough so that it would not be seen from the edge of the forest.

He camped one night in a small clearing, built his fire of dead branches, using melted snow to water his horse and searching beneath the snow for a few surviving blades of grass on which the beast might feed, and had begun to feel the benefit of the flames upon his frozen bones, when he thought he detected a familiar howling coming from the depths of the forest in what he took to be the north. Instantly he got up, hurling handfuls of snow upon the fire to extinguish it, and listening carefully for the sound to come again.

It came.

It was unmistakable. There were at least a dozen canine throats baying in unison, and the only throats which could make that particular sound belonged to the hunting dogs of the Fhoi Myore, the Hounds of Kerenos.

Corum got his bow and quiver of arrows from where he had stacked them with the rest of his gear when unsaddling his horse. The nearest tree to him was an ancient oak. It had not completely died and he guessed that its branches would probably support his weight. He tied his lances together with a cord, put the cord between his teeth, cleared snow as best he could from the lower branches and began to climb.

Slipping and almost falling twice he got as high as he could and, by carefully shaking the branches, managed to clear some of the snow so that he could see into the glade below without being easily seen himself.

He had hoped that the horse might try to escape when it scented the hounds, but it was too well trained. It waited trustingly for him, cropping the sparse grass. He heard the hounds come closer. He was now almost sure that they had detected him. He hung the quiver on a branch within easy reach of his hand and selected an arrow. He could hear the dogs, now, crashing through the forest. The horse snorted and flattened its ears, its eyes rolling as it looked this way and that for its master.

Now Corum saw mist beginning to form on the edges of the glade. He thought he detected a white, slinking shape. He began to draw back the bowstring, lying flat along the branch and bracing himself with his feet.

The first hound, its red tongue lolling, its red ears twitching, its yellow eyes hot with bloodlust, entered the glade. Corum sighted along the shaft of the arrow, aiming for the heart.

He released the string. There was a thud as the string struck his gauntleted wrist. A twang as the bow straightened. The arrow flew directly to his target. Corum saw the hound stagger and reel, staring at the arrow protruding from its side. Plainly, it had no idea from where the deadly missile had come. Its legs buckled. Corum reached for another arrow.

And then the bough snapped.

For a second Corum seemed suspended in the air as he realized what had happened. There was a dull cracking noise, a crash, and he was falling, trying futilely to grab at other branches as he went down, snow flying, making a terrible noise. The bow was wrenched from his hand; quiver and lances were still in the tree. He landed painfully on his left shoulder and thigh. If the snow had not been thick he would almost certainly have broken bones. As it was, the rest of his weapons were on the far side of the clearing and more of the Hounds of Kerenos were skulking in, having been momentarily surprised by the death of their brother and the sudden collapse of the tree branch.

Corum pulled himself to his feet and began to lope towards the bole against which his sword was leaning.

The horse whinnied and cantered towards him, blocking the path between him and his sword. Corum yelled at it, trying to force it out of the way. A long-drawn-out and triumphant howl came from behind him. Two huge paws struck his back and he went down. Hot, sticky saliva dripped on his neck. He tried to get up, but the giant dog pinned him, howling again to announce its victory. Corum had seen others of the hounds do the same thing. In a moment it would bare its fangs and rip his throat out.

But then Corum heard the horse's neighing, got an impression of flying hooves, and the dog's weight was off his body and he was rolling clear, seeing the great war-steed standing on its hind-legs and striking at the snarling hound with its iron-shod hooves. Half of the hound's head was caved in, but it still snapped at the horse. Then another hoof struck the skull and the dog collapsed with a groan.

Corum was already limping across the glade and then he had his silver hand on the scabbard, his fleshly hand on the hilt of the sword, and the blade was scraping free even as he turned back.

Tendrils of mist were sinuously entering the glade itself now, like searching, ghostly fingers. Already two more hounds were attacking the valiant warhorse which bled from two or three superficial bites but was still holding its own.

Then Corum saw a human figure appear from among the trees. Dressed all in leather, with a leather hood and heavy leather shoulder pads, it held a sword.

At first Corum thought the figure had come to aid him, for the face was as white as the bodies of the hounds and its eyes blazed red. He remembered the strange albino he had met at the Tower of Voilodian Ghagnasdiak. Was it Elric?

But no – the features were not the same. The features of this man were heavy, corrupt, and his body was thick, unlike the slim form of Elric of Melniboné. He began to lumber knee-deep through the snow, the sword raised to deliver a blow.

Corum crouched and waited.

His opponent brought his sword down in a clumsy blow which Corum easily parried and returned, stabbing upward with all his strength to pierce the leather and drive the point of his blade into the man's heart. A peculiar grunt escaped the white-faced warrior's lips and he took three steps backward until the sword was free of his body. Then he took his own sword in both hands and swung it again at Corum.

Corum ducked barely in time. He was horrified. His thrust had been clean and true and the man had not died. He hacked at his opponent's exposed left arm, inflicting a deep cut. No blood spurted from the wound. The man seemed oblivious of it, slashing again at Corum.

Elsewhere in the darkness more of the hounds were bounding into the glade. Some merely sat on their haunches and watched the fight between the two men. Others set upon the warhorse whose own breath steamed in the cold night air. It was tiring now, the horse, and would soon be dragged down by the frightful dogs.

Corum stared in astonishment at his foe's pale face, wondering what manner of creature this actually was. Not Kerenos himself, surely? Kerenos had been described as a giant. No, this was one of the Fhoi Myore minions, of whom he had heard. A hound-master, perhaps, to Kerenos's hunt. The man had a small hunting dirk at his belt and the blade that he bore was not unlike a flenching cutlass used for stripping meat and hacking at the bones of large prey.

The man's eyes did not seem to focus on Corum at all, but on some distant goal. That was possibly why his responses were sluggish. Nonetheless, Corum was still winded from his fall and, if he could not kill his opponent, then sooner or later one of those clumsy blows would strike true and Corum would be slain.

Implacably, swinging the great cutlass from side to side, the white-faced warrior advanced on Corum who was barely able to do more than parry the blows.

He was retreating slowly backwards, knowing that behind him, at the edge of the glade, waited the hounds. And the hounds were panting – panting in hot-breathed anticipation, their tongues lolling, as ordinary domestic dogs might pant when they anticipated food.

Corum could think of no worse fate, at that moment, than to become meat for the Hounds of Kerenos. He tried to rally, to carry the attack to his enemy, and then his left heel struck a hidden tree-root, his ankle twisted, and he fell, hearing the note of a horn from the forest – a horn that could only belong to the one considered the greatest of the Fhoi Myore, Kerenos. Now the dogs were up, moving in on him as he tried to struggle up, his sword raised to ward off the blows which the white-faced warrior rained upon him.

Again the horn sounded.

The warrior paused, cutlass raised, a dull expression of puzzlement appearing on his heavy features. The dogs, too, were hesitating, red ears cocked, unsure of what they were expected to do.

And the horn sounded for the third time.

Reluctantly the hounds began to slink back into the forest. The warrior turned his back on Corum and staggered, dropping his blade, covering his ears, moaning softly, as he, too, followed the dogs from the glade. Then, suddenly, he stopped. His arms dropped limply to his sides, blood suddenly began to spurt from the wounds Corum had inflicted.

The warrior fell upon the snow and was still.

Warily, uncertainly, Corum got to his feet. His warhorse plodded up to him and nuzzled him. Corum felt a pang of guilt that he had considered leaving the brave beast to its fate when he had climbed the tree. He rubbed its nose. Though bleeding from several bites, the horse was not seriously hurt, and three of the devil dogs lay dead in the glade, their heads and bodies smashed by the horse's hooves.

A quietness fell upon the glade then. Corum used what he considered only a pause in the attack to seek his fallen bow. He found it, near the broken branch. But the arrows and his two lances remained where he had hung them in the tree. He stood on tiptoe, reaching up with his bow to try to dislodge them, but they were too high.

Then he heard a movement behind him and turned, sword at the ready.

A tall figure had entered the glade. He wore a long, pleated surcoat of soft leather, dyed a deep, rich blue. There were jewels on his slender fingers, a golden, jewelled collar at his throat and, beneath the surcoat, could just be seen a samite robe, embroidered with mysterious designs. The face was handsome and old, framed by long, grey hair and a grey beard that ended just above the golden collar. In one of his hands the newcomer held a horn – a long horn bound with bands of silver and gold, each band fashioned in the shape of a beast of the forest.

Corum drew himself up, dropping the bow and taking his sword in both hands.

'I face you, Kerenos,' said the Prince in the Scarlet Robe, 'and I defy you.'

The tall man smiled. 'Few have ever faced Kerenos.' His voice was mellow, weary and wise. 'Even I have not faced him.'

'You are not Kerenos? Yet you have his horn. You must have called off those hounds. Do you serve him?'

'I serve only myself – and those who aid me. I am Calatin. I was famous once, when there were folk in these parts to speak of me. I am a wizard. Once I had twenty-seven sons and a grandson. Now there is only Calatin.'

'There are many now who mourn sons – and daughters, too,' said Corum, recalling the old woman he had seen some days since.

'Many,' agreed the wizard Calatin. 'But my sons and my grandson died not in battle against the Fhoi Myore. They died on my behalf, seeking something I require in my own feud with the Cold Folk. But who are you, warrior, who fights the Hounds of Kerenos so well, and who sports a silver hand like the hand of some legendary demigod?'

'I am pleased that you, at least, do not recognize me,' said Corum. 'I am called Corum Jhaelen Irsei. The Vadhagh are my folk.'

'Sidhi folk, then?' The tall old man's eyes became reflective. 'What do you on the mainland?'

'I am upon a quest. I seek something for a people who dwell now at Caer Mahlod. They are my friends.'

'So Sidhi befriend mortals now. Perhaps there are some advantages to the Fhoi Myore's coming.'

'Of advantages and disadvantages I know nought,' said Corum. 'I thank you, wizard, for calling off those dogs.'

Calatin shrugged and tucked the horn away in the folds of his blue robe. 'If Kerenos himself had hunted with his pack, I should not have been able to aid you. Instead he sent one of those.' Calatin nodded towards the dead creature whom Corum had fought.

'And what are those?' Corum asked. He crossed the glade to look down at the corpse. It had stopped bleeding now, but the blood had congealed in all its wounds. 'Why could I not kill it with my blade while you could kill it by the blast of a horn?'

'The third blast always slays the Ghoolegh,' said Calatin with a shrug. 'If "slay" is the proper word to use, for the Ghoolegh folk are half-dead already. That is why you doubtless found that one hard to slay. Normally they are bound to obey the first blast. A second blast will warn them and the third blast will kill them for failing to obey the first. They make good slaves, as a result. My horn-note, being subtly different to that of Kerenos's own horn, confused both dogs and Ghoolegh. But one thing the Ghoolegh knew – the third blast kills. So he died.'

'Who are the Ghoolegh?'

'The Fhoi Myore brought them with them from across the water to the east. They are a race bred to serve the Fhoi Myore. I know little else about them.'

'Do you know from where the Fhoi Myore came originally?' asked Corum. He began to move around the camp, finding sticks to build up the fire he had extinguished. He noted that the mist had disappeared entirely now.

'No. I have ideas, of course.'

All the while he had spoken, Calatin had not moved but had watched Corum through narrowed eyes. 'I would have thought,' he continued, 'that a Sidhi would know more than a mere mortal wizard.'

'I do not know what the Sidhi folk are like,' Corum said. 'I am a Vadhagh – and not of your time. I come from another age, an earlier age, or even an age which does not exist, as such, in your universe. I know no more than that.'

'Why did you choose to come here?' Calatin seemed to accept Corum's explanation without surprise.

'I did not choose. I was summoned.'

'An incantation?' Now Calatin was surprised. 'You know a folk with power to summon the Sidhi to their aid? In Caer Mahlod? It is hard to believe.'

'In that,' Corum told him, 'I had some choice. Their incantation was weak. It could not have brought me to them against my will.'

'Ah,' Calatin seemed satisfied. Corum wondered whether the wizard had been displeased when he thought there were mortals more powerful at sorcery than himself. He looked hard into Calatin's face. There was something most enigmatic about the wizard's eyes. Corum was not sure that he trusted the man very much, for all Calatin had saved his life.

At last the fire began to blaze and Calatin moved towards it, extending his hands to warm them.

'What if the hounds attack again?' Corum asked.

'Kerenos is nowhere near. It will take him some days to discover what happened here and then we shall be gone, I hope.'

'You wish to accompany me?' Corum asked.

'I was going to offer you the hospitality of my lodgings,' said Calatin with a smile. 'They are not far from here.'

'Why were you wandering the forest at night?'

Calatin drew his blue robe about him and seated himself on cleared ground near the fire. The light from the blaze stained his face and beard red, giving him a somewhat demonic appearance. He raised his eyebrows at Corum's question.

'I was looking for you,' he said.

'Then you did know of my presence?'

'No. I saw smoke a day or so ago and I came to investigate it. I wondered what mortal could be daring the dangers of Laahr. Happily I got to you before the hounds could dine off your corpse. Without my horn, I could not, myself, have survived in these parts. Oh, and I have one or two other small sorceries to help me remain alive,' Calatin smiled a thin smile. 'It is the day of the sorcerer in this world, again. Once, only a few years since, I was deemed eccentric because of my interests. I was thought mad by some, evil by others. Calatin, they said, escapes from the real world by studying occult matters. What use can such things be to our people?' He chuckled. It was not entirely a pleasant sound to Corum's ears. 'Well, I have found some uses for the old lore. And Calatin is the only one to remain alive in the whole of the peninsula.'

'You have used your knowledge for selfish ends alone, it seems,' said Corum. He drew a skin of wine from his pack and offered it to Calatin, who accepted it without suspicion and who seemed to experience no rancour at Corum's remark. Calatin raised the skin to his lips and drank deeply before replying.

'I am Calatin,' said the wizard. 'I had a family. I have had several wives. I had twenty-seven sons and a grandson. They were all I could care for. And now that they are dead, I care for Calatin. Oh, do not judge me too harshly, Sidhi, for I was mocked by my fellows for many years. I divined something of the Fhoi Myore's coming, but they ignored me. I offered my help, but they laughed, they rejected it. I have no cause to love mortals much. But I have less cause to hate the Fhoi Myore, I suppose.'

'What became of your twenty-seven sons and your grandson?'

'They died together or individually in different parts of the world.'

'Why did they die if they did not fight the Fhoi Myore?'

'The Fhoi Myore killed some of them. They were all upon quests seeking things I needed to continue my researches into certain aspects of mystic lore. One or two were successful and, dying of their wounds, brought me those things. But there are still several things I need and, I suppose, shall not have, now.'

Corum made no response to Calatin's statement. He felt faint. As the fire warmed his blood and brought pain to the minor wounds he had sustained, he began to realize the full extent of his tiredness. His eyes began to close.

'You see,' Calatin continued, 'I have been frank with you, Sidhi. And what quest are you upon?'

Corum yawned. 'I seek a spear.'

In the dim firelight Corum thought he saw Calatin's eyes narrow.

'A spear?'

'Aye.' Corum yawned again and stretched his body beside the fire.

'And where do you seek this spear?'

'A place that some doubt exists, where the race I call Mabden – your race – does not dare go, or cannot go on pain of death, or . . .' Corum shrugged. 'It is hard to separate one superstition from another in this world of yours.'

'Is this place you go to – this place which might not exist – an island?'

'An island, aye.'

'Called Hy-Breasail?'

'That is its name.' Corum forced sleep away, becoming a little more alert. 'So you know it?'

'I have heard it lies out to sea, to the west, and that the Fhoi Myore dare not visit it.'

'I have heard that also. Do you know why the Fhoi Myore cannot go there?'

'Some say that the air of Hy-Breasail, while beneficial to mortals, is deadly to the Fhoi Myore. But it is not the air of the island that endangers mortals – it is the enchantments of the place, they say, that bring death to ordinary men.'

'Enchantments . . .?' Corum could resist sleep no longer.

'Aye,' echoed the wizard Calatin thoughtfully, 'enchantments of fearful beauty, it is said.'

They were the last words Corum heard before he fell into a deep and dreamless slumber.

CHAPTER SIX

Over the Water to Hy-Breasail

In the morning Calatin led Corum from the forest and they stood beside the sea. Warm sun shone upon white beaches and blue water, yet behind them, still, the forest lay crushed by snow.

Corum was not riding his horse; he was reluctant to mount the brave beast until its wounds had healed, but he had gathered his gear, including his arrows and his lances, and laid it upon his mount's back where the load would not irritate the wounds it had sustained in the previous night's fight. Corum's own body was bruised and aching, but he forgot his discomfort as soon as he recognized the shore.

'So,' said Corum, 'I was merely a mile or two from the coast when those beasts attacked.' He smiled ironically. 'And there is Moidel's Mount.' He pointed along the shore to where the hill could be seen, rising from a deeper sea than when Corum had last visited it – but unmistakably the place where Rhalina's castle had stood, guarding the Margravate of Lwym-an-Esh. 'Moidel's Mount remains.'

'I do not know the name you speak,' said Calatin, stroking his beard and arranging his finery as if about to receive a distinguished visitor, 'but my house is built upon that tor. It is where I have always lived.'

Corum accepted this and began to walk on towards the mount. 'I have lived there, too,' he said. 'And I was happy.'

Calatin, with long strides, caught up with him. 'You lived there, Sidhi? I know nothing of that.'

'It was before Lwym-an-Esh was drowned,' Corum explained. 'Before this cycle of history began. Mortals and gods come and go, but nature remains.'

'It is all relative,' Calatin said. Corum thought his tone a little peevish, as if he resented hearing this truism.

Nearing the place, Corum saw that once the old causeway had been replaced by a bridge, but now that bridge was in ruins, deliberately destroyed, it seemed. He commented on this to Calatin.

The wizard nodded. 'I destroyed the bridge. The Fhoi Myore and the things of the Fhoi Myore are, like the Sidhi, reluctant to cross western water.'

'Why western water?'

'I have no understanding of their customs. Have you any fear of wading through the shallows to the island, Sir Sidhi?'

'None,' said Corum. 'I have made the same journey many times. And do not draw too many conclusions from that, wizard, for I am not of the Sidhi race, though you seem to insist otherwise.'

'You spoke of Vadhagh and that is an old name for the Sidhi.'

'Perhaps legend has confused the two races.'

'You have the Sidhi look, nonetheless,' Calatin said flatly. 'The tide is retreating. Soon it will be possible to cross. We shall make our way along what remains of the bridge and enter the water from there.'

Corum continued to lead his horse, following Calatin as he set foot on the stone bridge, and walked as far as he could until he reached crude steps which led down into the sea. 'It is shallow enough,' the wizard announced.

Corum looked at the green mount. There it was lush spring. He looked behind him. There it was cruel winter. How could nature be controlled so?

He had difficulty with the horse. Its hooves threatened to slip on the wet rocks. But eventually both man and horse were shoulder deep in the water and feeling with their feet for the remains of the old causeway below. Through the clear sea Corum could just make out the worn cobblestones that might have been the same ones he had stepped on a thousand or more years past. He remembered his first coming to Moidel's Mount. He remembered the hatred he had had, then, of all Mabden. And he had been betrayed by Mabden many times.

The wizard Calatin's cloak floated out behind him on the surface of the water as the tall old man led the way.

Slowly they began to emerge from the sea until they were two-thirds of the way across and the water was now only up to their shins. The horse snorted with pleasure. Evidently its soaking had soothed its wounds. It shook its mane and dilated its nostrils. Perhaps the sight of the good, green grass on the slopes of the tor also improved its spirits. Now there was no trace at all of Rhalina's castle. Instead, a villa had been built near the top – a villa two storeys high, made of white stone that sparkled in the sunshine. Its roof was of grey slate. A pleasant house, thought Corum, and not a typical one for a man who dabbled in the occult arts. He recalled his last sight of the old castle, burned by Glandyth in revenge.

Was that why he felt so suspicious of this Mabden, Calatin? Was there something of the Earl of Krae about him? Something in the eyes, the bearing, or, perhaps, the voice? It was foolish to make comparisons. Calatin did not have an agreeable manner, it was true, but it was possible that his motives were kindly. He had saved Corum's life, after all. It would not be fair to judge the wizard on his outward and seemingly very cynical comportment.

Now they began to climb the winding track to the top of the mount. Corum smelled the spring, the flowers and the rhododendrons, the grass and the budding trees. Sweet-scented moss covered the old rocks of the hill, birds nested in the larches and the alders and flew among the new, bright leaves. Corum had another reason now to be grateful to Calatin, for he had become profoundly weary of the deadness of the landscape.

And then they came to the house itself, Calatin showing Corum where he could stable his horse and then flinging open a door wide so that Corum could go first into the place. The ground floor consisted mainly of one large room whose wide windows were filled with glass and looked from one side to the open sea and from the other to the white and desolate land. Corum could observe how the clouds formed over the land but not over the sea. The clouds seemed to remain in one place as if forbidden to cross an invisible barrier.

Corum had observed little glass in any other part of this Mabden world. Calatin had found benefits, it appeared, in his studying of ancient lore. The roofs of the house were high and supported by stone beams, and the rooms of the house, as Calatin showed it to him, were filled with scrolls, books, tablets and experimental apparatus; truly a wizard's lair.

Yet there was nothing sinister, to Corum, in Calatin's possessions or, indeed, his obsessions. The man called himself a wizard, but Corum would have called him a philosopher, someone who enjoyed exploring and discovering the secrets of nature.

'Here,' Calatin told him, 'I have almost everything saved from Lwym-an-Esh's libraries before that golden civilization sank beneath the waves. Many mocked me and told me that I filled my head with nonsense, that my books were only the work of madmen who had preceded me and that they contained no more truth than my own work contained. They said that the histories were mere legends, that the grimoires were fantasies – fiction, that the talk of gods and demons and such was merely poetic, metaphorical. But I believed otherwise and I was proved correct.' Calatin smiled coldly. 'Their deaths proved me right.' The smile changed. 'Though I did not have very much satisfaction in knowing that all who might have apologized to me are now slain by the Hounds of Kerenos or frozen by the Fhoi Myore.'

'You have no pity for them, have you, wizard?' Corum said, seating himself upon a stool and staring through the window out to sea.

'Pity? No. It is not my character to know pity. Or guilt.

Or any of those other emotions which other mortals care so much for.'

'You do not feel guilty that you sent your twenty-seven sons and your grandson upon a fruitless series of quests?'

'They were not entirely fruitless. There is little more I seek now.'

'I meant that you must surely feel some remorse for the fact that they all died.'

'I do not know that all of them died. Some simply did not return. But, yes, most did die. It is a shame, I suppose. I would rather that they lived. But my interest is more in abstractions – pure knowledge – than the usual considerations which hold so many mortals in chains.'

Corum did not pursue the subject.

Calatin moved about the big room complaining of his wet clothes but making no effort to change them. They had dried before he next spoke to Corum.

'You go to Hy-Breasail, you said.'

'Aye. Do you know where the island lies?'

'If the island exists, yes. But all mortals who go close to the island, so it is said, are immediately put under a glamour – they see nothing, save perhaps a reef or cliffs impossible to scale. Only the Sidhi see Hy-Breasail as the island really looks. That, at least, is what I have read. None of my sons returned from Hy-Breasail.'

'They sought it and perished?'

'Losing several good boats into the bargain. Goffanon rules there, you see, and will have naught to do with mortals or Fhoi Myore. Some say he is the last of the Sidhi.' Calatin looked suddenly at Corum in suspicion. He drew back slightly. 'You are not . . .?'

'I am Corum,' Corum said. 'I told you that. No, I am not Goffanon, but Goffanon, if he exists, is the one I seek.'

'Goffanon! He is powerful.' Calatin was frowning. 'But perhaps it is true and you are the only one who can find him. Perhaps we could make a bargain, Prince Corum.'

'If it is to our mutal benefit, aye.'

Calatin became pensive, fingering his beard, muttering to himself. 'The only servants of the Fhoi Myore who do not fear the island and are not subject to its enchantments are the Hounds of Kerenos. Kerenos himself, even, fears Hy-Breasail – but not his hounds. Therefore you would be in danger, even there, of the dogs.' He looked up and looked hard at Corum. 'You might reach the island, but you probably would not live to find Goffanon.'

'If he exists.'

'Aye, aye – if he exists. I thought I guessed your quest when you spoke of the spear. That is Bryionak, I take it?'

'Bryionak is its name.'

'One of the treasures of Caer Llud, was it not?'

'I believe that is common knowledge amongst your folk.'

'And why do you seek it?'

'It will be useful to me against the Fhoi Myore. I can say no more.'

Calatin nodded. 'There is no more that needs saying. I will help you, Prince Corum. A boat? To go to Hy-Breasail? I have a boat you may borrow. And protection against the Hounds of Kerenos? You may borrow my horn.'

'And what must I do in return?'

'You must pledge me that you will bring me back something from Hy-Breasail. Something very valuable to me. Something which you can only get from the Sidhi smith, Goffanon.'

'A jewel? A charm?'

'No. Much more.' Calatin fumbled among his papers and his equipment until he found a little bag of smooth, soft leather. 'This is watertight,' he said. 'You must use this.'

'What do you want? Magic water from a well?'

'No,' said Calatin urgently, quietly. 'You must bring me some of the spittle belonging to the Sidhi smith, Goffanon. In this. Take it.' He reached inside his robes and drew out the beautiful horn he had used to drive away the Hounds of Kerenos. 'And take this. Blow it three times to drive them off. Blow it six times to set them upon an enemy.'

Corum fingered the ornate horn. 'It must be a powerful thing, indeed,' he murmured, 'if it can match that of Kerenos.'

'It was once a Sidhi horn,' Calatin told him.

An hour later Calatin had taken him to the far side of the mount where a little natural harbour still was. And in the harbour was a small sailing boat. Calatin gave Corum a chart and a lodestone. Corum carried the horn at his belt now and his own weapons were upon his back.

'Ah,' said the wizard Calatin, fingering his own noble skull with trembling fingers, 'perhaps at last I may have my ambition fulfilled. Do not fail, Prince Corum. For my sake, do not fail.'

'For the sake of the people of Caer Mahlod, for all the people who have not so far been slain by the Fhoi Myore, for the sake of a world in perpetual winter that might never see the spring again, I shall try not to fail, wizard.'

And then the sea-wind had caught the sail and the boat sped out over the sparkling water, heading west to where Lwym-an-Esh and her beautiful cities had once been.

And Corum fancied for a moment that he would find Lwym-an-Esh just as he had seen it last and that all the rest, all the events of the past weeks, would be a dream.

Moidel's Mount and the mainland were soon far behind, out of sight, and flat water lay all around him.

If Lwym-an-Esh had survived, he would have seen it by this time. But lovely Lwym-an-Esh was not there. The stories of her sinking beneath the waves were true. And would the stories be true of Hy-Breasail? Was it really all that was left of the land? And would he be subject to the same illusions suffered by previous voyagers?

He studied his charts. Soon he would know the answers. In another hour or so he would sight Hy-Breasail.

CHAPTER SEVEN

The Dwarf Goffanon

Was this the beauty against which the old woman had warned him?

Certainly it was beguiling. It could only be the island named Hy-Breasail. It was not what he had thought he would find for all that it bore resemblance to parts of Lwym-an-Esh. The breeze caught the sail of his boat and blew him closer to the coast.

Surely there could be no danger here?

Soft seas whispered on the white beaches and the light wind stirred the green branches of cypress trees, willows, poplars, oaks and strawberry trees. Gentle, rolling hills protected quiet valleys. Flowering rhododendron bushes bloomed with deep scarlets, purples and yellows. Warm, glowing light touched the landscape and gave it a faint, golden haze.

Corum, as he looked upon the island, was filled with a deep sense of peace. He knew that he could rest there forever, be content to lie beside the sparkling, winding rivers, to walk over the sweet-smelling lawns looking at the deer, the squirrels and the birds which teemed there.

Another Corum, a young Corum, would have accepted this vision without question. After all, there had once been Vadhagh estates which resembled this island. But that had been the Vadhagh dream and the Vadhagh dream was over. Now he inhabited the Mabden dream – perhaps even the Fhoi Myore dream which was overwhelming it. Was there a place in either of those dreams for the land of Hy-Breasail?

So it was with a certain caution that Corum beached his

boat upon the strand and then dragged it into the cover of some rhododendron bushes growing close to the shore. His weapons he adjusted in his harness so that they would be within easy reach and then he began to march inland, experiencing a certain guilt that so martial a figure as himself should be invading this peaceful place.

As he walked through groves and across meadows he passed small herds of deer which showed no fear of him and, indeed, other animals which showed open curiosity and came closer to investigate this stranger. It was possible, Corum thought, that he was under the spell of a powerful illusion, but it was hard to believe on anything but the most abstract of levels. Yet no Mabden had ever returned from the place and many voyagers denied finding it at all, while the Fhoi Myore, fearsome and cruel, were terrified of setting foot here, for all that legend said they had once conquered the whole land of which only this part remained. There were many mysteries, thought Corum, concerning Hy-Breasail, but there was no denying the fact that, to a weary mind and an exhausted body, there could be no more perfect a world.

He smiled as he saw the bright butterflies fluttering through the summer air, the peacocks and pheasants serene upon the green lawns. Even at its finest the landscape of Lwym-an-Esh could not have equalled this. Yet there was no sign of habitation. There were no ruins, no houses – not even a cave where a man might dwell. And perhaps that was what made him retain a shade of suspicion concerning this paradise. Yet one being, surely, did live here, and that was the smith Goffanon who protected his domain with enchantments and terrors which were said to bring death to any who dared invade it.

Subtle enchantments, indeed, thought Corum; and well-hidden terrors.

He paused to look at a small waterfall which flowed over limestone rocks. Rowan trees grew on the banks of the clear stream and in the stream were small trout and grayling. The sight of the fish, as well as the game he had seen earlier, began to make him feel hungry. He had eaten such poor fare since he had first gone to Caer Mahlod and he dearly wanted to unsling one of his lances and try to spear a fish. But something warned him against this action. It occurred to him – and it might have been a thought inspired by nothing more than superstition – that if he attacked even one of the denizens of the island then all the life of the island would turn against him. He determined to avoid killing as much as an irritating insect during his sojourn on Hy-Breasail and took, instead, a piece of dried meat from his pouch and began to gnaw on that as he walked. He was climbing uphill now, towards a great boulder which seemed perched on the very top of the slope.

The climb became steeper the nearer to the top he came, but at last he reached the boulder and paused, leaning against it and looking about him. He had expected to see the whole of the island from this eminence, for it was certainly the highest hill he had seen. But, strangely, he saw no sea at all in any direction.

A peculiar shimmering mist, blue and flecked with gold, was on every horizon. It seemed to Corum to follow, perhaps, the coastline of the island, for it was irregular. Yet why had he not seen it when he first landed? Was it this mist which kept the eyes of most travellers from sight of Hy-Breasail?

He shrugged. The day was warm and he was tired. He found a smaller rock in the shade of the great boulder and sat down on it, drawing a small flask of wine from his pouch and sipping it slowly as he let his gaze wander over the valleys, groves and streams of the island. Everywhere it was the same, as if carefully landscaped by a gardener of genius. He had already come to the conclusion that Hy-Breasail's countryside was not wholly natural in origin. It was more like a great park, such as the Vadhagh had created at the height of their culture. Perhaps that was why the animals were so tame, he thought. It could be that they all led protected lives and so trusted mortals like himself, having had no experience of danger at the hands of two-legged creatures. Yet he was again forced to remind himself of the Mabden who had not returned, of the Fhoi

Myore who had conquered the place and then fled, fearing ever to return.

He felt drowsy. He yawned and stretched hmself out on the grass. His eyes closed and his mind began to wander a little as sleep slowly overwhelmed him.

And he dreamed that he spoke to a youth whose flesh was all gold and from whom, in some odd way, a great harp grew. And the youth, who smiled without kindness, began to play upon his harp. And Medhbh the warrior princess listened to the music and her face became full of hatred for Corum and she found a shadowy figure who was Corum's enemy and directed him to slay Corum.

And Corum woke up, still hearing the strange music of the harp. But the music faded before he could determine whether he had actually heard it or whether it had lingered on from his dream.

The nightmare had been a cruel one and it had made him afraid. He had never dreamed such a dream before. It was possible, he thought, that he was beginning to understand something of the peculiar dangers of this island. Perhaps it was the nature of the island to turn men's minds in on themselves and let them create their own terrors – terrors far worse than any others which might be inflicted upon them. He would avoid sleep, if he could, from now on.

And then he wondered if he were not still dreaming, for there came in the distance the familiar sound of the baying of hounds, the Hounds of Kerenos. Had they followed him to the island, swimming across a score of miles of sea? Or had they come already to Hy-Breasail, to wait for him? He touched the ornate horn at his belt as their yapping and howling came closer. He scanned the land for sight of them, but all he could see was a startled herd of deer led by a great stag bounding across a meadow and into a forest. Did the hounds pursue the herd? No. The hounds did not appear.

He saw something else moving in a valley on the other side of the hill. He guessed that it was probably another deer, but then he realized that it ran on two legs in peculiar leaping bounds. It was heavy, tall, and it carried something which flashed whenever the sun's rays touched it. A man?

Corum saw a white hide in the trees some distance behind the man. Then he saw another. Then there burst from the grove a pack of some twelve great dogs with tufted, red-tipped ears. The hounds pursued what was for them more familiar quarry than deer.

The man – if man it was – began to leap up a rocky hillside, following the course of a big waterfall, but this did not deter the dogs who kept implacably upon his track. The hillside became almost sheer, but still the man climbed – and still the dogs followed. Corum was amazed at their agility. Again something bright flashed. Corum realized that the man had turned and that the bright thing was a weapon which he was wielding to ward off the attack. It was obvious to Corum that the dogs' victim would not last for long.

It was only then that he remembered the horn. Hastily he raised it to his lips and blew three long blasts in quick succession. The notes of the horn sounded out clear and sharp across the valley. The dogs turned and began to circle, as if scenting, though their quarry was in easy sight.

Then the Hounds of Kerenos began to lope away. Corum laughed in delight. For the first time he had won a victory over the hellish dogs.

At his laughter, it seemed, the man on the far side of the valley looked up. Corum waved to him but the man did not return the wave.

As soon as the Hounds of Kerenos had disappeared, Corum began to run down the hillside towards the one whom he had helped. It did not take him long to reach the bottom of the slope and begin to ascend the next. He recognized the waterfall and the shelf of rock where the man had turned to do battle with the hounds, but the man himself was nowhere to be seen. He had not climbed higher, that was certain, neither had he come down, Corum was sure, for he had had a fairly clear view of the waterfall as he ran.

'Ho, there!' shouted the Prince in the Scarlet Robe, brandishing his horn. 'Where are you hiding, comrade?'

He was answered only by the rattling of water upon rocks as the waterfall continued its progress down the cliff face. He stared about him, peering at every shadow, every rock and bush, but it was as if the man had actually become invisible.

'Where are you, stranger?'

There was a faint echo, but this was drowned quickly by the sound of the water hissing and slapping as it foamed over the crags.

Corum shrugged and turned away, thinking it ironic that the man should be more timid than the beasts on the island.

And then suddenly, from nowhere, he felt a heavy blow in the small of his back and he was tumbling forward on to the heather, arms outstretched to break his fall.

'Stranger, eh?' said a deep surly voice. 'Call me stranger, eh?'

Corum struck the ground and rolled over, trying to free his sword from its scabbard.

The man who had pushed him was massive. He must have stood eight feet high and was a good four feet broad at the shoulder. He wore a polished iron breastplate, polished iron greaves, inlaid with red gold, and an iron helm upon his shaggy, black-bearded head. In his monstrous hands was the largest war-axe Corum had ever seen.

Corum scrambled up, drawing his blade. He suspected that this was the one whom he had saved. But the huge creature appeared to feel no gratitude at all.

Corum managed to gasp: 'Whom do I fight?'

'You fight me. You fight the dwarf Goffanon,' said the giant.

CHAPTER EIGHT

The Spear Bryionak

In spite of his danger, Corum found himself grinning in disbelief. 'Dwarf?'

The Sidhi smith glared at him.

'Aye? What is funny?'

'I should be afraid to meet ordinary-sized men on this island!'

'I miss your point.' Goffanon's eyes narrowed as he readied his axe and took up a fighting stance.

It was only then that Corum realized that the eyes were the same as his own remaining single orb – almond-shaped, yellow and purple – and that the self-called dwarf's skull structure was more delicate than it had at first appeared due to the beard covering so much of it. His face was, in most particulars, a Vadhagh face. Yet in all other respects Goffanon did not resemble a member of Corum's own race.

'Are there others of your kind in Hy-Breasail?' Corum used the pure tongue of the Vadhagh, not the dialect spoken by most Mabden, and produced an expression of gaping-mouthed astonishment on Goffanon's features.

'I am the only one,' the smith replied in the same tongue. 'Or thought so. Yet if you be of my folk, why did you set your dogs upon me?'

'They are not my dogs. I am Corum Jhaelen Irsei, of the Vadhagh race.' With his left hand, his silver hand, Corum held up the horn. 'This is what controls the dogs. This horn. They think their master sounds it.'

Goffanon lowered his axe a fraction. 'So you are not some servant of the Fhoi Myore?'

'I hope that I am not. I battle the Fhoi Myore and all that they stand for. Those dogs have attacked me more than once. It was to save me from further attacks that I was loaned the horn by a Mabden wizard.' Corum decided that this was a judicious time to sheathe his sword and hope that the Sidhi smith did not take the opportunity to split his skull.

Goffanon frowned, sucking at his lips as he debated Corum's words.

'How long have the Hounds of Kerenos been on your island?' Corum asked.

'This time? A day – no more. But they have been before. They seem the only things unaffected by the madness which comes upon the rest of the denizens of this world when they set foot upon my shores. And since the Fhoi Myore have had an abiding hatred for Hy-Breasail, they do not rest in sending their minions to hunt me. Often I am able to anticipate their coming and take precautions, but this time I had grown too confident, not expecting them back so soon. I thought you to be some new creature, some huntsman like the Ghoolegh, of whom I have heard, who serve Kerenos. But it seems to me now that I once listened to a tale concerning a Vadhagh with a strange hand and only one eye, but that Vadhagh died, even before the Sidhi came.'

'You do not call yourself Vadhagh?'

'Sidhi, we are called.' Now Goffanon had lowered his axe completely. 'We are related to your folk. Some of your people visited us once, I know – and we visited you. But that was when access to the Fifteen Planes was possible, before the last Conjunction of the Million Spheres.'

'You are from another plane. Then how did you reach this one?'

'A disruption in the Wall Between the Realms. Thus came the Fhoi Myore, from the Cold Places, from Limbo. And thus we came – to help the folk of Lwym-an-Esh and their Vadhagh friends – and fought the Fhoi Myore. There was great slaying in those days, long ago, and huge wars, which sank Lwym-an-Esh, killing all the Vadhagh and most of the Mabden – also my folk, the Sidhi, were slain, for we could not return to our own plane, since the rupture swiftly mended. We thought all the Fhoi Myore destroyed, but lately they have returned.'

'And you do not fight them?'

'I am not strong enough, alone. This island is physically part of my own plane. Here I can live in peace, save for the dogs. I am old. I shall die in a few hundred years.'

'I am weak,' Corum said. 'Yet I fight the Fhoi Myore.'

Goffanon nodded. Then he shrugged. 'Only because you have not fought them before,' he said.

'Yet why can they not come to Hy-Breasail? Why do not Mabden return from the island?'

'I try to keep the Mabden away,' said Goffanon, 'but they are an intrepid little race. Their very courage brings about their dreadful deaths. But I will tell you more when we have eaten. Will you guest with me, cousin?'

'Gladly,' said Corum.

'Then come.'

Goffanon began to climb back up the rocks, worked his way around the ledge on which he had stood to fight the Hounds of Kerenos, and disappeared again. His head reappeared again almost instantly. 'This way. I have lived here since the dogs began to plague me.'

Corum climbed slowly after the Sidhi, reached the ledge and saw that it went around a slab of rock which hid an entrance to a cave. The slab could be moved in grooves to block the entrance and, as Corum stepped through, Goffanon put his gigantic shoulder to the slab and heaved it into place. Inside was light coming from well-made lamps set in niches in the walls. The furniture was plain but expertly carved and there were woven tapestries upon the floor. Save for the lack of a window, Goffanon's lair was more than comfortable.

While Corum rested in a chair Goffanon busied himself at his stove, preparing soup, vegetables and meat. The smell that arose from his pots was delicious and Corum congratulated himself for curbing his desire to spear fish from the stream. This meal promised to be much more appetising.

Goffanon, apologizing for the scarcity of his plate, for he had lived alone for hundreds of years, put a huge bowl of soup before Corum. The Vadhagh Prince ate gratefully.

Next followed meat and a variety of succulent vegetables which were, in turn, followed by the best-tasting fruit Corum had ever eaten. When, at last, he sank back in his chair it was with a feeling of well-being such as he had not experienced in years. He thanked Goffanon profusely and the self-styled dwarf's huge frame seemed to writhe in embarrassment. He apologized again and then seated himself in his own chair and put an object into his mouth which was like a small cup from which projected a long stalk which Goffanon sucked at, holding over the bowl of the little cup a piece of burning wood. Soon clouds of smoke issued from the bowl and from his mouth and he smiled with contentment, only noticing Corum's surprised expression some time later. 'A custom of my folk,' he explained. 'It is an aromatic herb which we burn in this way and inhale the smoke. It pleases us.'

The smoke did not smell particularly sweet to Corum, but he accepted the Sidhi's explanation, though he refused Goffanon's offer of a bowl of his own smoke.

'You asked,' said Goffanon slowly, half-closing his huge, almond-shaped eyes, 'why the Fhoi Myore feared this island and why the Mabden perished here. Well, neither is any deliberate doing of mine, though I am glad that the Fhoi Myore avoid me. Long ago, during the period of the first Fhoi Myore invasion, when we were called to help our Vadhagh cousins and their friends, we had great difficulty in breaching the Wall Between the Realms. Finally we did so, causing enormous disruptions in the world of our own plane, resulting in a great piece of land coming with us through the dimensions to your world. That piece of land settled, luckily, upon a relatively unpopulated part of the kingdom of Lwym-an-Esh. However, it retained the properties of our plane – it is, as it were, part of the Sidhi dream, rather than the Vadhagh, the

Mabden or the Fhoi Myore dreams; though, as you will have noticed, of course, the Vadhagh being closely related to the Sidhi have little difficulty in adapting themselves to it. The Mabden and the Fhoi Myore, on the other hand, cannot survive here at all. Madness overwhelms them as soon as they land. They enter a world of nightmare. All their fears multiply and become competely real for them and they are thus destroyed by their own terrors.'

'I guessed something of this,' Corum told Goffanon. 'For I had a hint of what might happen when I slept earlier today.'

'Exactly. Even the Vadhagh sometimes experience a little of what it means for a mortal Mabden to land on Hy-Breasail. I try to hide the island's outlines with a mist I am able to prepare, but it is not always possible to keep a sufficient supply of the mist in the air. That is when the Mabden find the island and suffer enormously as a result.'

'And where do the Fhoi Myore originate from? You spoke of the Cold Places.'

'The Cold Places, aye. Do you not know of them in Vadhagh lore? The places *between* the planes – a chaotic limbo which occasionally spawns intelligence of sorts. That is what the Fhoi Myore are – creatures of Limbo who fell through the breach in the Wall Between the Realms and arrived upon this plane, whereupon they embarked upon conquest of your world, planning to turn it into another limbo where they might best survive. They cannot live for much longer, the Fhoi Myore. Their own diseases destroy them. But they will live long enough, I fear, to bring freezing death to all but Hy-Breasail, to bring freezing death to Mabden and to all beasts, even the smallest sea-creature, on this world. It is inevitable. They will probably outlive me, some of them – Kerenos, anyway – but their plagues will slay them at last. Virtually all this world, save the land from which you have just come, has died under their rule. It happened quickly, I think. We thought them all dead, but they must have found hiding places – perhaps at the edge of the world where ice always may be found. Now their patience is rewarded, eh?'

Goffanon sighed. 'Well, well – there are other worlds – and those they cannot reach.'

'I wish to save this one,' said Corum quietly. 'I would save what is left, at least. I am sworn to that. Sworn to help the Mabden. Now I quest for their lost treasures. It was rumoured that you have one of those, something you made for the Mabden in their first fight with the Fhoi Myore, ages since.'

Goffanon nodded. 'You speak of the spear called Bryionak. I made it. Here it is only an ordinary spear, but in the Mabden dream and the Fhoi Myore dream it has great power.'

'So I heard.'

'It will tame, among other things, the Bull of Crinanass, which we brought with us when we came.'

'A Sidhi beast?'

'Aye. One of a great herd. He is the last.'

'Why did you seek the spear and carry it back to Hy-Breasail?'

'I have not left Hy-Breasail. That spear was brought here by one of the mortals who came exploring. I tried to comfort him as he died raving, but he could not be comforted. When he had died I took my spear. That is all. He had thought, it seemed, that Bryionak would protect him from the dangers of my island.'

'So you would not deny the Mabden its help again.'

Goffanon frowned. 'I do not know. I am fond of that spear. I should not like to lose it again. And it will not help the Mabden much, cousin. They are doomed. It is best to accept that. They are doomed. Why not let them die swiftly? To send them Bryionak would be to offer them a false hope.'

'It is in my nature to put my faith in hopes, no matter how false they seem,' Corum said quietly.

Goffanon looked at him sympathetically. 'Aye. I was told of Corum. Now I recall the tale. You are a sad one. A noble one. But what happens, happens. There is nothing you can do to stop it.'

'I must try, you see, Goffanon.'

'Aye.' Goffanon pulled his great bulk from the chair and went to one side of the cave which was in shadow.

He returned bearing a spear of very ordinary appearance. It had a well-worn wooden shaft, was bound in iron. Only its head had something odd about its manufacture. Like the blade of Goffanon's axe, it shone brighter than ordinary iron.

The Sidhi handled it with pride. 'My tribe was always the smallest of the Sidhi, both in numbers and in stature, but we had our skills. We could work metals in a way which you might describe as philosophical. We understood that metals had qualities beyond their obvious properties. And so we made weapons for the Mabden. We made several. Of them all, only this survives. I made it. The spear Bryionak.'

He held it out to Corum who, for some reason, accepted it with his left hand, the silver hand. It was beautifully weighted, a practical weapon of war, but, if Corum had expected to sense in it anything extraordinary, he was disappointed.

'A good, plain spear,' said Goffanon, 'Bryionak.'

Corum nodded. 'Save for the head, that is.'

'No more of that metal can be smelted,' Goffanon told him. 'A little of it came with us when we left our own plane. A few axe blades, a sword or two – and that spear – were all we could manufacture. Good, sharp metal. It does not dull or rust.'

'And it has magical properties?'

Goffanon laughed. 'Not to the Sidhi. But the Fhoi Myore think so. As do the Mabden. Therefore, of course, it has magical properties. Spectacular properties. Yes, I am glad to have my spear back.'

'You would not part with it again?'

'I think not.'

'But the Bull of Crinanass will obey the one who wields it. And the Bull will aid the people of Caer Mahlod against the Fhoi Myore – perhaps help them destroy the Fhoi Myore.'

'Neither bull nor spear is powerful enough to do that,' said Goffanon gravely. 'I know that you want the spear, Corum, but I repeat this – nothing can save the Mabden world. It is doomed to die, just as the Fhoi Myore are doomed, just as I am doomed – and you also, unless you have a means of returning to your own plane, for I take it you are not from this one.'

'I am doomed, too, I think,' said Corum quietly. 'But I would carry the spear Bryionak back to Caer Mahlod, for that was my oath, that is my quest.'

Goffanon sighed and took the spear from Corum's hand. 'No,' he said. 'When the Hounds of Kerenos come again I shall need all my weapons to destroy them. The pack which attacked me today is doubtless still upon the island. If I kill that pack there will come another pack. My spear and my axe, they are my only security. You have yon horn, after all.'

'It is only loaned to me.'

'By whom?'

'By a wizard. Calatin's his name.'

'Aha. I tried to turn three of his sons away from this shore. But they died, as the others died.'

'I know that many of his sons came here.'

'What did they seek?'

Corum laughed. 'They wanted you to spit upon them.' He recalled the little watertight bag Calatin had given him. He drew it from his pouch.

Goffanon frowned. Then his brow cleared and he shook his head, puffing at the little bowl of herbs which still burned near his mouth. Corum wondered where he had witnessed a similar custom, but his memory had become very hazy, of late, concerning his previous adventures. That was the price one paid, he guessed, for entering another dream, another plane.

Goffanon sniffed. 'Another of their superstitions, no doubt. What do they do with these things? Animals' blood drawn at midnight. Bones. Roots. How debased has Mabden knowledge become!'

'Would you grant the wizard his wish?' Corum asked. 'I

am pledged to ask you. He loaned me the horn on that understanding.'

Goffanon stroked his heavy beard. 'It has come to something when the Vadhagh must beg the Mabden for their help.'

'This is a Mabden world,' Corum said. 'You made that point yourself, Goffanon.'

'A Fhoi Myore world soon. And then no world at all. Ah, well, if it will help you, I will do what you want. I can lose nothing by it and I doubt if your wizard will gain anything either. Hand me the bag.'

Corum passed the bag to Goffanon who grunted, laughed again, shook his head again, and spat into the bag, handing it back to Corum who, somewhat fastidiously, replaced it in his pouch.

'But it was the spear I really sought,' said Corum quietly. He regretted his insistence, after Goffanon had taken his other request with such good humour and, as well, had offered him good hospitality.

'I know,' Goffanon lowered his head and stared at the floor. 'But if I help you save a few Mabden lives, I stand the chance of losing my own.'

'Have you forgotten the generosity which led you and your people to come here in the first place?'

'I was more generous in those days. Besides, it was our kin, the Vadhagh, who asked for that help.'

'I am your kin, then,' Corum pointed out. He felt a pang of guilt at playing on the Sidhi dwarf's better feelings. 'And I ask.'

'One Sidhi, one Vadhagh, seven Fhoi Myore and still a fair horde of the ever-breeding Mabden. Yet it is not much compared with what I saw when first I came to this world. And the land was lovely. It bloomed. Now it is harsh and nothing will grow. Let it die, Corum. Stay with me here in the fair island, in Hy-Breasail.'

'I made a bargain,' said Corum simply. 'Everything in me would force me to agree with you and to accept your offer, Goffanon – save for that one thing. I made a bargain.'

'But my bargain – the bargain the Sidhi made – that is over. And I owe you nothing, Corum.'

'I helped you when the devil dogs attacked you.'

'I helped you keep your bargain with the Mabden wizard. Have I not paid that debt?'

'Must all things be discussed in terms of bargains, of debts?'

'Yes,' said Goffanon seriously, 'for it is nearly the end of the world and there are only a few things left in the world. They must be bartered and a balance kept. I believe that, Corum. It is not an attitude inspired by venality – we Sidhi were rarely considered venal – but by a necessary conception of order. What have you to offer me more useful to me in so many ways than the spear Bryionak?'

'Nothing, I think.'

'Only the horn. The horn that will dismiss the dogs when they attack me. The horn is more valuable to me than the spear. And the spear – is that not more valuable to you than the horn?'

'I agree,' said Corum. 'But the horn is not mine, Goffanon. The horn is only lent to me – by Calatin.'

'I will not give you Bryionak,' Goffanon said heavily, almost reluctantly, 'unless you give me the horn. That is the only bargain I will strike with you, Vadhagh.'

'And it is the only one I have no right to make.'

'Is there nothing Calatin wants from you?'

'I have already made my bargain with Calatin.'

'You cannot make another.'

Corum drew his brows together and with his right hand he fingered his embroidered eye-patch, as he was wont to do when faced with a difficult problem. He owed Calatin his life. Calatin would owe Corum nothing until Corum returned from the island with the little bag of the Sidhi's spittle. Then neither would be in the other's debt.

Yet the spear was important. Even now Caer Mahlod might be under attack from the Fhoi Myore and the only thing which might save them would be the spear Bryionak and the Bull of Crinanass. And Corum had sworn that he would return with the spear. He plucked the horn from where it hung at his hip by the long thong looped over his shoulder. He looked at the fine, mottled bone, the ornamental bands, the silver mouthpiece. It was a hero's horn. Who had borne it before Calatin found it? Kerenos himself?

'I could blow this horn now and bring the dogs upon us both,' Corum said musingly. 'I could threaten you, Goffanon, and make you give me Bryionak in return for your life.'

'Would you do that, cousin?'

'No.' Corum let the horn fall. Then, without realizing that he had made a decision before he spoke, he said:

'Very well, Goffanon. I will give you the horn for the spear and try to make some other bargain with Calatin when I return to the mainland.'

'It is a sad bargain that we make,' said Goffanon, handing him the spear. 'Has it harmed our friendship?'

'I think that it has,' said Corum. 'I shall leave now, Goffanon.'

'You think me ungenerous?'

'No. I feel no rancour. I feel merely sad that we are all brought to this, that our nobility is somehow warped by our circumstances. You lose more than a spear, Goffanon. And I too lose something.'

Goffanon let out a mighty sigh. Corum gave him the horn that was not Corum's to give.

'I fear the consequences of this,' Corum said. 'I suspect that I shall face more than a Mabden wizard's wrath by giving you the horn.'

'Shadows fall across the world,' said Goffanon. 'And many strange things can hide in those shadows. Many things can be born, unseen and unsuspected. These are days for fearing shadows, Corum Jhaelen Irsei, and we should be fools if we did not fear them. Yes, we are brought low. Our pride diminishes. May I walk with you to the shore?'

'To the borders of your sanctuary? Why not come with me, Goffanon, to fight – to wield that great axe of yours against our foes? Would such an action not restore your pride?'

'I think not,' said Goffanon sadly. 'A little of the cold has come to Hy-Breasail, too, you see.'

BOOK THREE

*More bargains made while the
Fhoi Myore march*

CHAPTER ONE

What the Wizard Demanded

As Corum beached the boat in the small bay of Moidel's Mount he heard footsteps behind him. He turned, reaching for his sword. The transition from the peace and beauty of Hy-Breasail to the outside world had brought with it depression and a certain amount of fear. Moidel's Mount, which had seemed such a welcome sight when he had first seen it again, now looked faded and sinister and he wondered if the Fhoi Myore dream had begun to touch the tor at last or whether the place had merely seemed pleasanter in comparison with the dark and frozen forest in which he had originally met the wizard.

Calatin stood there, tall in his blue robe, white-haired and handsome. There was a hint of anxiety in his eyes.

'Did you find the Glamorous Isle?'

'I found it.'

'And the Sidhi smith?'

Corum picked the spear Bryionak from out of the boat. He showed it to Calatin.

'But what of my request?' Calatin seemed hardly interested at all in a spear which was one of the treasures of Caer Llud, a mystic weapon of legend.

Corum found it faintly amusing that Calatin should care so little for Bryionak and so much about a little sack of saliva. He drew the pouch out and handed it to the wizard who sighed with relief and grinned with pleasure.

'I am grateful to you, Corum. And I am glad that I was able to serve you. Did you encounter the hounds?'

'Once,' said Corum.

'The horn aided you?'

'It aided me. Aye.' Corum began to walk up the beach, Calatin following.

They reached the brow of the hill and looked towards the mainland where the world was cold and white and brooding grey cloud filled the sky.

'Will you stay the night with me?' Calatin said. 'And tell me of Hy-Breasail and what you discovered there?'

'No,' said Corum. 'Time grows short and I must ride back for Caer Mahlod, for I feel that the Fhoi Myore will attack that place. They must know, by now, that I aid their enemies.'

'It is likely. You will want your horse.'

'Aye,' said Corum.

There was a pause. Calatin began to say something and then changed his mind. He led Corum to the stable below the house and there was the warhorse, almost healed from its wounds. It snorted in recognition when it saw Corum. Corum stroked its nose and led it from the stable.

'My horn,' said Calatin. 'Where is that?'

'I left it,' Corum told him, 'in Hy-Breasail.' He looked directly into the wizard's eyes and saw those eyes heat with fear and anger.

'How?' Calatin almost screamed. 'How could you mislay it?'

'I did not mislay it.'

'You left it there deliberately? It was agreed that you should borrow it. That was all.'

'I gave it to Goffanon. In a way you could say that if I had not had the horn to give him I could not have got you what you want.'

'Goffanon? Goffanon has my horn?' Calatin's eyes became colder. They narrowed.

'Aye.'

There was no excuse Corum could make, so he said nothing further. He waited for Calatin to speak.

Then the wizard said:

'You are in my debt again, Vadhagh.'

'Aye.'

The wizard's tone was level now, calculating. He smiled

a quiet, unpleasant smile. 'You must give me something to replace my horn.'

'What do you want?' Corum was becoming tired of bargaining. He was anxious to ride away from Moidel's Mount, to return as siftly as possible to Caer Mahlod.

'I must have something,' said Calatin. 'You understand that, I trust?'

'Tell me what, wizard.'

Calatin looked Corum over as a farmer might look over a horse at market. Then he reached out and touched the surcoat Corum wore beneath the fur cloak the Mabden had given him. It was Corum's Vadhagh robe, red and light and made from the delicate skin of a beast which had dwelt once upon another plane and which had become extinct even there.

'Your robe, prince, is of great value, I think?'

'I have never considered its price. It is my Name-robe. Every Vadhagh has one.'

'Then is it not valuable to you?'

'Is this what you want, my robe? Will that satisfy you for the loss of the horn?' Corum spoke impatiently. His liking for the wizard had not increased. Yet he was morally in the wrong, he knew. And Calatin knew that, too.

'If you think it is a fair bargain.'

Corum flung off the fur robe and began to unbuckle his belt, to undo the pin which attached his robe to his shoulder. It would be strange to lose the garment he had worn for so long, but he attached no special sentiment to it. The other robe warmed him well enough. He did not need his scarlet one.

He handed the robe to Calatin. 'There you are, wizard. Now we are neither of us in the other's debt.'

'Just so,' said Calatin, watching as Corum buckled on his weapons and then climbed into the high saddle of the horse. 'I wish you a good journey, Prince Corum. And be wary of the Hounds of Kerenos. After all, there is no horn to save you now.'

'And none to save you,' said Corum. 'Will they attack you?'

'It is unlikely.' Calatin spoke mysteriously. 'It is unlikely.'

And then Corum rode down to the drowned causeway and entered the sea.

He did not look back at the wizard Calatin. He looked ahead, at the snow-buried land, not relishing the prospect of his journey back to Caer Mahlod, but glad to be leaving Moidel's Mount. He clutched the spear Bryionak in his silver hand, his left hand, and he guided his horse with his right, and soon he had reached the mainland, and his breath and the breath of his horse began to steam in the chill air. He headed north-west.

And, as he entered the bleak forest, he thought for a moment that he heard the sound of a wild and melancholy harp.

CHAPTER TWO

The Fhoi Myore March

The horseman rode a beast that was only a little like a horse. Both were coloured a strange, pale green. There were no other shades of colour in either. The snow was churned by the beast's hooves. The snow flew high on both sides of it. The horseman's pale green face was blank, as if the snow had frozen it. His pale green eyes were cool. And in his hand was a pale green sword. Not too far distant from Corum, who was drawing his own blade, the rider came to a sudden halt, crying out:

'Are you the one they think will save them? You seem more man than god to me!'

'Man I am,' said Corum evenly. 'And warrior. Do you challenge me?'

'Balahr challenges you. I am merely his instrument.'

'Balahr does not wish to fight me himself, then?'

'The Fhoi Myore do not fight hand to hand with mortals. Why should they?'

'The Fhoi Myore have much fear in them for a race so powerful. What is the matter with them? Do the diseases which eat at them, which will at last destroy them, weaken them?'

'I am Hew Argech, lately of the White Rocks, beyond Karnec. There was once a people, an army, a tribe. Now there is me. And I serve Balahr the One-eyed. What else can I do?'

'Serve your own folk, the Mabden.'

'The trees are my folk. The pines. They keep us both alive, my steed and me. The sap in my veins is nurtured not by meat and drink but by earth and rain. I am Hew Argech, brother to the pines.'

Corum could hardly believe the import of what this creature said. A man he must have been once, but now he had changed – been changed by Fhoi Myore sorcery. Corum's respect for Fhoi Myore power increased.

'Will you dismount, Hew Argech, and fight a manly fight, sword against sword in the snow?' Corum asked.

'I cannot. Once I fought so.' The voice was innocent, like the voice of a candid child. But the eyes remained blank, the face expressionless. 'Now I must fight with cunning, not honour.'

And Hew Argech was charging forward again, sword whirling as he bore down on Corum.

It had been a week since Corum had left Moidel's Mount; a week of bitter cold. His bones were stiff with it. His eye had blurred from looking at nothing but snow, so that it had been some time before he had seen the pale green rider on the pale green steed coming riding across the white moor.

So quick was Hew Argech's attack that Corum barely had time to bring his own sword up to block the first blow. Then Hew Argech had passed him and was turning his beast for a second assault. This time Corum charged and his sword nicked Hew Argech's arm, but Argech's sword clanged on Corum's breastplate and half-knocked the Vadhagh Prince from his saddle. Corum still clutched the spear Bryionak in his silver hand, and the silver hand also gripped the reins of his snorting warhorse as it lumbered round, up to its knees in thick snow, to face the next attack.

The two fought in this manner for some time, with neither managing to break the other's guard. Corum's breath issued from his mouth in great clouds, but no breath at all seemed to escape Hew Argech's lips and the pale green man showed no signs of tiring, while Corum was desperately weary, barely able to keep a grip on his sword.

It was obvious to Corum that Hew Argech knew he was

tiring and was merely waiting until he should become so dazed that a quick sword-thrust would finish him. Several times he managed to rally himself, but now Argech was circling him, thrusting, slicing, battering, and then his sword was knocked from his frozen fingers and there came from Hew Argech's mouth a peculiar, rustling laugh, like wind through leaves, and he bore down on Corum for the last time.

Swaying in his saddle, Corum brought up the spear Bryionak to defend himself and managed to block the next blow. As Hew Argech's sword struck the head of the spear it clanged with a musical, silvery note, which surprised both opponents. Argech had gone past Corum again, but was turning rapidly. Corum flung back his left arm and threw the spear with such force at the pale green warrior he fell forward over his horse's neck and had strength enough only to raise his head to see the Sidhi spear pierce Hew Argech's chest.

Hew Argech sighed and he fell from the back of his pale green beast, the spear protruding from him.

Then Corum saw something that amazed him. How it happened he could not be sure, but the spear left the body of the pale green man and flew back into the open palm of Corum's silver hand. The hand closed involuntarily around the shaft.

Corum blinked his eye, barely able to believe what had happened, though he could feel, as well as see, the spear, for its shaft rested partly against his leg.

He looked towards his fallen foe. The beast which Hew Argech had ridden had picked up the man in its mouth and was dragging him away.

It suddenly occurred to Corum that the beast rather than the rider was the true master. He could not explain why he felt this, save that for a second he had looked into the beast's eyes and seen what looked like irony there.

And as he was dragged, Hew Argech opened his mouth to call to Corum in that same ingenuous tone:

'The Fhoi Myore march,' he said. 'They know that the folk of Caer Mahlod called you. They march to destroy

Caer Mahlod before you return with the spear which slew me. Farewell, Corum of the Silver Hand. I go back now to my brothers, the pines.'

And soon beast and man had disappeared beyond a hill and Corum was alone, holding the spear which had saved his life, turning it this way and that in the grey light as if he thought that by inspecting it he would understand how it had come to return to his hand after it had aided him.

Then he shook his head, dismissed the mystery, and urged his horse to gallop faster through the clinging snow, still heading for Caer Mahlod. Heading there with even greater urgency than he had before.

The Fhoi Myore were still an enigma. Every description of them he had heard had somehow not explained how they could command creatures like Hew Argech, how they could work such strange enchantments, control the Hounds of Kerenos and their Ghoolegh huntsmen. Some saw the Fhoi Myore as insensate creatures, little more than beasts; others saw them as gods. They must have some kind of intelligence, surely, if they could create the likes of Hew Argech, brother of the trees?

At first he had wondered if the Fhoi Myore were related to the Chaos Lords whom he had fought so long in past times. But the Fhoi Myore were at once less manlike and more manlike than the Chaos Lords had been, and their aims seemed different. They had had no choice, it seemed, in coming to this plane. They had fallen through a gap in the fabric of the multiverse and had been unable to return to their own strange half-world between the planes. Now they sought to recreate Limbo on Earth. Corum found that he could feel a certain sympathy for their plight, even.

He wondered if Goffanon's prediction had been a true one, or whether the prediction had been the product of Goffanon's own sense of despair. Was the doom of the Mabden inevitable?

Looking across the bleak, snow-covered land, it was easy to believe that it was their fate – and his – to die, victims of the Fhoi Myore encroachment.

*

He camped less frequently now, sometimes riding wildly through the night, careless of the pitfalls, half-asleep in his saddle. And his warhorse galloped less readily through the snow.

Once, in the evening, he saw a line of figures in the distance. Mist swirled around the figures as they marched or rode in huge chariots. He almost hailed them before he realized that they were not Mabden. Were these the Fhoi Myore on the march to Caer Mahlod?

And several times during his ride he heard a distant howling and he guessed that the hunting packs, the Hounds of Kerenos, were seeking him. Doubtless Hew Argech had returned to his masters and told them of how he had fallen before the spear Bryionak, which had then wrenched itself from his body and settled back in Corum's silver hand.

Caer Mahlod still seemed very distant and the cold seemed to eat into Corum's body like a worm which fed on his very blood.

More snow had fallen since he had first ridden this way and the snow had succeeded in disguising many landmarks. This fact, coupled with his blurring eyesight, made it difficult for him to find his way at all. He prayed that the horse knew the route back to Caer Mahlod and he came to trust more and more in the beast's instincts.

As exhaustion overwhelmed him he began to know a deep despair. Why had he not listened to Goffanon and lived out his days in the tranquillity of Hy-Breasail? What did he owe to these Mabden? Had he not fought enough in Mabden battles? What had that folk ever given him?

And then he would remember. They had given him Rhalina.

And he remembered Medhbh, too, King Mannach's daughter. Red-haired Medhbh in her war-gear, with her sling and her tathlum, waiting for him to bring salvation back to Caer Mahlod.

They had given him hatred, the Mabden, when they slew his family, cut off his hand and tore out his eye. They had given him fear, terror and a thirst for vengeance.

But they had also given him love. They had given him Rhalina. Now they gave him Medhbh.

These thoughts would sustain him a little, even warm him a little, drive the despair to the edges of his mind, and he would ride on. Ride on for Caer Mahlod, the fortress on the hill, and those whose only hope he remained.

But Caer Mahlod seemed to grow further away. It seemed a year since he had seen the Fhoi Myore war-chariots on the horizon, heard the howling of the hounds. Perhaps Caer Mahlod had already fallen; perhaps he would find Medhbh frozen as those others had been frozen, in battle-posture, unaware that there would be no battle for them to fight, that they had already lost.

Another morning came. Corum's horse was slow now. It staggered sometimes as it caught its foot in a hidden furrow. It breathed with difficulty. Corum would have dismounted, if he could, and walked beside the horse to relieve its load, but he had neither the will nor the energy to get down. He began to regret that he had let Calatin have his scarlet robe. That small amount of extra heat might have saved his life, it now seemed. Had Calatin known this? Was that why Calatin had asked for the coat? An act of revenge?

He heard something. He raised his aching head and peered through his bloodshot, bleary eye. Figures blocking his way. Ghoolegh. He tried to straighten himself in the saddle, fumbling for his sword.

He urged his warhorse into a gallop, feebly waving the spear Bryionak, a croaking battle-cry breaking from his frost-bitten lips.

And then the horse's forelegs buckled under and it fell to the ground, pitching Corum over its head and leaving him exposed to the swords of his enemies.

But, thought Corum, as he sank into a coma, he would not feel the pain of their blades, at least, for a sense of warmth, of oblivion, was sweeping through him.

He smiled and let the darkness come.

CHAPTER THREE

The Ice Phantoms

He dreamed that he sailed a massive ship over an infinity of ice. The ship was raised on runners and had fifty sails. Whales inhabited the ice, and other strange creatures, too. Then he no longer sailed the ship, but rode in a chariot drawn by bears beneath a strange, dull sky. But the ice remained. Worlds bereft of heat. Old, dead worlds in the final stages of entropy. But everywhere was ice – harsh, gleaming ice. Ice which brought death to any who dared it. Ice which was the symbol of ultimate death, the death of the very universe itself. Corum groaned in his sleep.

'It is the one I heard of.' The voice was soft, yet intrusive.

'Llaw Ereint?' came another's voice.

'Aye. Who else could it be? There is the silver hand. And that is a Sidhi face, I'd swear, though I've never seen one.'

Corum opened his single eye and glared at the speaker.

'I am dead,' said Corum, 'and would be grateful if you would allow me to be dead in peace.'

'You live,' said the youth practically. He was a boy of about sixteen. Though his face and body were thin, starved, his eyes were bright and intelligent and, like most of the Mabden Corum had found here, he was well-formed. He had a great mop of blond hair, kept back from his eyes by a simple leather band. He had a fur cape over his shoulders and the familiar gold and silver collar and bangles on arms and ankles. 'I am Bran. This is my brother, Teyrnon. You are Cremm, the god.'

'God?' Corum began to realize that the people he had seen ahead of him had been Mabden, not Fhoi Myore. He smiled at the youth. 'Do gods fall so easily from exhaustion?'

Bran shrugged and ran his fingers through his hair. 'I know nothing of the customs of gods. Could you not have been in disguise? Pretending to be a mortal in order to test us?'

'That is a fine way of looking at a rather more ordinary fact,' said Corum. He turned to look at Teyrnon and then looked in surprise at Bran again. The two were virtually identical in features, though Bran's fur cloak was from a brown bear and Teyrnon's was from a tawny wolf. Corum looked up and realized that he saw the folds of a small tent in which he lay while Bran and Teyrnon crouched beside him.

'Who are you?' Corum asked. 'Where are you from? Do you know aught of the fate of Caer Mahlod?'

'We are the Tuha-na-Ana – or what is left of that folk,' the youth replied. 'We are from a land to the east of Gwyddneu Garanhir, which in turn lies due south of Cremm Croich, your land. When the Fhoi Myore began to come, some of us fought them and thus perished. The rest of us – youths and old people for the most part – set off for Caer Mahlod where we heard warriors resisted the Fhoi Myore. We lost our way and had to hide many times from the Fhoi Myore and their dogs, but now we are only a short distance from Caer Mahlod, which lies west of here.'

'Caer Mahlod is my destination, too,' said Corum, sitting up. 'I carry the spear Bryionak with me and would tame the Bull of Crinanass.'

'That Bull cannot be tamed,' said Teyrnon softly. 'We saw it less than two weeks since. We were hungry and hunted it for its meat, but it turned on our hunters and slew five of them with its sharp horns before it went away towards the west.'

'If the Bull cannot be tamed,' said Corum, accepting the mug of thin soup which Bran handed him and sipping it gratefully, 'then Caer Mahlod is lost and you would be wiser to seek some other sanctuary.'

'We are looking for Hy-Breasail,' Bran told him seriously. 'The Enchanted Isle beyond the sea. We thought we might be happy there and safe from the Fhoi Myore.'

'Safe from the Fhoi Myore you would be,' Corum said, 'but not from your own fears. Do not seek Hy-Breasail, Bran of the Tuha-na-Ana, for it means awful death to Mabden folk. No, we shall all go together to Caer Mahlod, if the Fhoi Myore do not find us first, and I will see if I can speak to the Bull of Crinanass and make him see our point of view.'

Bran shook his head sceptically. Teyrnon, his twin, echoed the gesture.

'We move on again in a few minutes,' Teyrnon told Corum. 'Will you be fit to ride again, then?'

'Is my horse still alive?'

'Alive and rested. We found a little grass for him.'

'Then I am fit to ride,' said Corum.

There were less than thirty people in the band which moved slowly across the snow, and of those thirty more than a score were old men and women. There were three other boys like Bran and his brother Teyrnon, and there were three girls, one of whom was less than ten years old. The younger children, it was learned, had perished in a sudden raid which the Hounds of Kerenos had made on the camp when the remnants of the tribe had first begun its trek to Caer Mahlod. Snow rimed the hair of all and made it sparkle. Corum joked that they were all kings and queens and wearing diamond crowns. They had been weaponless before he came and now he distributed his gear among them – a sword to one, a dirk to another, a lance each to two more, and his bow and arrows to Bran. He kept only the spear Bryionak as he rode at the head of the column, or walked beside his horse which would take two or three old people at a time, for few had eaten much in recent months and they were all light enough.

Bran had estimated that they were still two days from

Caer Mahlod, but the going began to get easier, the further west they travelled. Corum's spirits had begun to rise considerably and his horse's energy was increasing so that he was able to make short gallops ahead to spy out the land. Judging by the improvement in the weather, the Fhoi Myore had not yet reached the hill fortress.

The little party entered a valley late on the afternoon of what they hoped would be their last full day of travelling. It was not a particularly deep valley but it offered some shelter from the icy wind which occasionally blew across the moor, and they welcomed any shelter. Corum noticed that on the slopes of the hills on either side of them were gleaming formations of ice which had perhaps been formed from waterfalls blown by a wind coming from the east. They were some distance into the valley and had decided to make camp for the night, although the sun had not yet set, when Corum looked up from watching the youths erecting the tents and saw a movement. He had been sure that one of the ice-shapes had changed its position. He put this down to his own tired vision and the failing light.

And then more of the shapes were moving and it was unmistakable – they converged on the camp.

Corum shouted the alarm and began to run towards his horse. The shapes were like gleaming phantoms, darting down the slopes into the valley. Corum saw an old woman at the far end of the camp throw up her arms in horror and turn to escape, but a shimmering, ghostly figure seemed to absorb her and drag her back up the hill. Before hardly anyone was aware of it, two more old women were seized and dragged away.

Now the camp was in a furore. Bran shot two accurate shafts at the ice phantoms, but the arrows merely passed through them. Corum hurled the spear Bryionak at another and took it where its head might be, but Bryionak came sailing back to his hand without having harmed the phantom. However, it seemed that the things were timid for, once they had taken their prey, they faded back again into the hills. Corum heard Bran and Teyrnon shout and begin to run together up the steep slopes in pursuit of one of the phantoms. Corum called to them that the chase would be futile and would put them in even greater danger, but they would not listen. Corum paused for a moment and then followed.

The darkness was creeping in now. Shadows fell across the snow. The sky bore only a tinge of sunlight, a smear of blood in milk. At the best of times this was poor light for hunting – and the ice phantoms would be hard to see in the full brightness of noon.

Corum managed to keep Bran and Teyrnon in sight, but only just. Bran had paused to shoot a third arrow at what he thought to be an ice phantom. Teyrnon pointed and they ran off in another direction altogether, Corum still calling to them, though he feared to attract the attention of the strange creatures the two boys pursued.

It grew darker still.

'Bran!' shouted Corum. 'Teyrnon!'

And then he found them and they were kneeling in the snow and they were weeping. Corum looked and saw that they knelt beside what was probably the body of one of the old women.

'Is she dead?' he murmured.

'Aye,' said Bran, 'our mother is dead.'

Corum had not known that one of the women had been the youths' mother. He let out a deep, long sigh and turned away, and looked into the shadowy, grinning faces of three of the phantoms.

Corum cried out, raising Bryionak to stab at the things. Silently the phantoms moved upon him. He felt their tendrils touch his skin and his flesh began to freeze. This was how they paralysed their victim and this was how they fed, drawing his heat into their own bodies. Perhaps this was how those people he had seen before had died, beside the lake. Corum despaired of saving either his life or those of the two boys. There was no means of fighting such intangible foes.

And then the tip of the spear Bryionak began to glow a peculiar orange-red, and when the tip touched one of the ice phantoms the creature hissed and disappeared, becoming no more than a cloud of steam in the air; and then the steam dispersed. Corum did not question the power of the spear. He swung it at the other two phantoms, touching them lightly with the glowing tip, and they, too, vanished. It was as if the ice phantoms needed heat to live, but too much heat overloaded them and they perished.

'We must make fires,' Corum told the boys. 'Brands. That will keep them away. And we will not camp here. We will march – by torchlight. It does not matter if the Fhoi Myore or any of their servants see us. It would be best to reach Caer Mahlod as soon as possible, for we have no means of knowing what other creatures like these the Fhoi Myore command.'

Bran and Terynon picked up their mother's corpse between them and began to follow Corum down the hillside. The tip of the spear Bryionak now faded again until it looked as it had always looked – merely a well-made spearhead.

In the camp Corum told the others of his decision and all were agreed.

And so they moved on, the ice phantoms lurking just beyond the light which the torches cast, making small gasping sounds, little wet sounds, pleading sounds, until they had passed through the valley and were on the other side.

The phantoms did not follow them, but still they marched on, for the wind had turned for the moment and it brought the salty smell of the sea and they knew that they must surely be close to Caer Mahlod and sanctuary. But they knew, too, that the Fhoi Myore and all whom the Fhoi Myore commanded were nearby, and this gave even the oldest of the folk new energy and speed and all prayed that they would be spared until the morning when they must surely see Caer Mahlod ahead.

CHAPTER FOUR

The Cold Folk's Massing

The conical hill was there and the stone walls of the fortress were there and King Mannach's sea-beast banner was there and there was Medhbh, beautiful Medhbh, riding a horse from the gates of Caer Mahlod and waving to him and laughing, her red hair flying and her green-grey eyes all alight with joy, her horse's hooves sending up a flurry of frost as she cried out to him:

'Corum! Corum! Corum Llaw Ereint, do you bring the spear Bryionak?'

'Aye,' Corum called back, brandishing the spear, 'and I bring guests to Caer Mahlod. We are hasty, for the Fhoi Myore are not far behind.'

She reached his side and leaned over to fling an arm about his neck and kiss him full upon the lips so that all his earlier gloom left him suddenly and he was glad that he had not stayed in Hy-Breasail, that he had not been killed by Hew Argech, that he had not been drained of his body's heat by the ice phantoms.

'You are here, Corum,' she said.

'I am here, lovely Medhbh. And here is the spear Bryionak.'

She looked at it in wonder, but she would not touch it, even when he offered it to her. She drew back. She smiled strangely. 'It is not for me to hold. That is the spear Bryionak. That is the spear of Cremm Croich, of Llaw Ereint, of the Sidhi, of the gods and the demigods of our race. That is the spear Bryionak.'

He laughed at the serious expression which had come suddenly upon her face and he kissed her so that her eyes cleared and she laughed at him and then turned her chestnut mare to gallop ahead of the weary band, to lead the way through the narrow gate into the fortress town of Caer Mahlod.

And there, on the other side of the gate's passage, stood King Mannach, smiling in gratitude and respect at Corum, who had found one of the great treasures of Caer Llud, one of the lost treasures of the Mabden, the spear which could tame the last member of a herd of Sidhi cattle, the Black Bull of Crinanass.

'Greetings, Lord of the Mound,' said King Mannach without pomposity. 'Greetings, hero. Greetings, son.'

Corum swung down from the saddle, and again he stretched out the silver hand which held Bryionak. 'Here it is. Look at it. It is an ordinary spear, King Mannach – or seems so. Yet it has already saved my life twice upon my journey back to Caer Mahlod. Inspect it, and tell me if you think it an unusual spear.'

But King Mannach followed the example of his daughter and backed away from the spear. 'No, Prince Corum, only a hero may carry the spear Bryionak, for a lesser mortal would be cursed if he tried to hold it. It is a Sidhi weapon. Even when it was in our possession it was kept in a case and the spear itself was never touched.'

'Well,' said Corum, 'I'll respect your customs, though there is nothing at all to fear from the spear. Only our enemies should fear Bryionak.'

'As you say,' said King Mannach in a subdued tone. Then he smiled. 'Now we must eat. We caught fish today and there are several hares. Let all these people come with us to the hall and eat, too, for they look hungry indeed.'

Bran and Teyrnon spoke for their few surviving clansfolk. 'We accept your hospitality, great king, for we are fair famished. And we offer you our services, as warriors, to aid you in your fight against the fierce Fhoi Myore.'

King Mannach inclined his noble head. 'My hospitality is poor compared with your pride and your pledge, and I thank you, warriors, for your presence at our battlements.'

As King Mannach spoke the last word there came a shout from above and a girl who had been on guard above the gate called:

'White mist boiling on the north and south. The Cold Folk are massing. The Fhoi Myore come.'

King Mannach said, not without humour, 'I fear that the banquet will have to be postponed. Let us hope it will be a victory feast.' He smiled grimly. 'And that the fish is still fresh when we've finished our fight!'

King Mannach turned to Corum after directing more of his men to the walls. 'You must call the Bull of Crinanass, Corum. You must call it soon. If it does not come then we are over, the folk of Caer Mahlod.'

'I do not know how to call the Bull, King Mannach.'

'Medhbh knows. She will teach you.'

'I know,' said Medhbh.

Then she and Corum joined the warriors on the walls and looked eastward; and there were the Fhoi Myore with their mist and their minions.

'They do not come for sport this day,' said Medhbh.

With his right hand Corum took her left hand, holding it tightly.

About two miles distant, beyond the forest, they saw pale mist churning. It covered the whole horizon from north to south and it moved slowly but purposefully towards Caer Mahlod. Ahead of this mist were many packs of hounds, questing and scenting as ordinary dogs run ahead of a hunt. Behind the hounds were small figures whom Corum guessed were white-faced Ghoolegh huntsmen and behind these huntsmen were riders, pale green riders who, like Hew Argech, were doubtless brothers to the pines. But in the mist itself could be detected larger shapes, the shapes Corum had seen only once before. These were the dark outlines of monstrous war-chariots drawn by beasts which were certainly not horses. And there were seven of these chariots and in the chariots were seven riders of enormous size.

'A great massing,' said Medhbh, in a voice which succeeded in sounding brave. 'They send their whole strength against us. All seven of the Fhoi Myore come. They must respect us greatly, those gods.'

'We shall give them cause,' said Corum.

'Now we must leave Caer Mahlod,' Medhbh told him.

'Desert the city?'

'We have to go to call the Bull of Crinanass. There is a place. The only place to which the Bull will come.'

Corum was reluctant to go. 'In a few hours – perhaps in less time than that – the Fhoi Myore will attack.'

'We must try to return by that time. That is why it is urgent that we go now to the Sidhi Rock and seek the Bull.'

So they left Caer Mahlod quietly, on fresh horses, and rode along the cliffs above a sea which groaned and roared and rolled as if in anticipation of the coming struggle.

At last they stood upon yellow sand with the dark and jagged cliffs behind them and the uneasy sea before them and looked up at a strange rock which stood alone on the beach. It had begun to rain and the rain and the sea-spray lashed the rock and made it shine with a peculiar variety of soft colours which veined it. And in places the rock was opaque and in other places it was almost completely transparent so that other, warmer colours could be seen at its heart.

'The Sidhi Rock,' said Medhbh.

Corum nodded. What else could the rock be? It was not of this plane. Perhaps, like the island of Hy-Breasail, it had come with the Sidhi when they journeyed here to fight the Cold Folk. He had seen things like it before – objects which had no real place upon this plane, which had part of themselves in another plane altogether.

The wind blew the water against his face. It blew their hair and their cloaks about them and they had difficulty climbing the smooth, worn stone and standing at last on the top of the rock. Huge waves rolled down upon the coast. Great gusts threatened to blow them from their perch. Rain washed down them and cascaded over the rock so that small waterfalls were formed.

'Now take the spear Bryionak in your silver hand,' directed Medhbh. 'Raise it high.'

Corum obeyed her.

'Now you must translate what I tell you into your speech, the pure Vadhagh tongue, for that is the same tongue as the Sidhi.'

'I know,' said Corum. 'What must I say?'

'Before you speak you must think of the Bull, the Black Bull of Crinanass. He is as tall at the shoulder as you are at the head. He has a long coat of black hair. His horns are wider from tip to tip than you can stretch your arms, and they are sharp, those horns. Can you picture such a creature?'

'I think so.'

'Then speak this and speak it clearly:'

All around them the day was turning grey, save for the great rock on which they stood.

'*You shall pass through tall gates of stone, you, Black Bull.*
You shall come forth from where you dwell when Cremm Croich calls.
If you sleep, Black Bull, awaken now.
If you wake, Black Bull, then rise now.
If you rise, Black Bull, then walk. Shake the earth, Black Bull.
Come to the rock where you were sired, where you were born, Black Bull.
For he who holds the spear is master of your fate.
Bryionak, forged at Crinanass and mined from Sidhi stone,
Fights once more the dread Fhoi Myore, whom you must fight, Black Bull.
Come, Black Bull. Come, Black Bull. Come home.'

Medhbh had spoken this whole thing without drawing breath. Now her grey-green eyes looked anxiously into his single eye. 'Can you translate that into your own speech?'

'Aye,' said Corum. 'But why would a beast come to answer such chanting?'

'Do not question that, Corum.'

The Vadhagh shrugged.

'Do you still see the Bull in your mind's eye?'

He paused. Then he nodded. 'I do.'

'Then I will speak the lines again and you will repeat them in the Vadhagh tongue.'

And Corum obeyed, though the chant seemed a crude one to him and hardly Vadhagh in origin. Slowly he repeated what she told him and, as he chanted, he began to feel light-headed. The words began to trip from his lips. He declaimed them. He stood at his full height, clothing and hair blown this way and that by the grey wind, and he held the spear Bryionak high, and he called for the Bull of Crinanass. His voice grew louder and louder and sounded above the wind's snore.

'Come, Black Bull! Come, Black Bull! Come home!'

Speaking the words in his own tongue somehow seemed to give them more weight, though the language Medhbh spoke was scarcely different from the Vadhagh language.

When the words were finished, she put a hand on his arm and a finger to his lips and they listened through the howling wind and the thrashing sea and the cascading rain and heard a distant lowing from somewhere, and the Sidhi rock seemed to glow with richer colours and tremble a little.

The lowing came again, closer.

Mehdbh was grinning at him, holding his arm very tightly now.

'The Bull,' she whispered. 'The Bull comes.'

But still they could not tell from which direction the lowing reached their ears.

The rain fell in even heavier sheets until they could barely see beyond the rock at all and it was as if the sea had engulfed them.

But the sounds began to merge into one sound and that sound gradually became identified as the deep, reflective lowing of a bull. They peered from where they stood on the top of the Sidhi Rock and it seemed to them that they saw the great Bull bring its great, black bulk up out of the waters of the sea and stand shaking itself upon the shore, turning its huge, intelligent eyes from side to side as it sought the source of the chant which had brought it here.

'Black Bull!' cried Medhbh. 'Black Bull of Crinanass! Here stands Cremm Croich and the spear Bryionak. Here stands your destiny!'

And the monstrous Bull lowered its head with the sharp, wide-spaced horns, and it shook its shaggy black body, and it pawed at the sand with its heavy hooves. And they could smell its warm body; they could smell the comforting, familiar stink of cattle. But this was like no familiar farmyard beast. This was a war-beast, proud and confident, a beast which served not a master but an ideal.

It swung its black tufted tail from side to side as it stared up at the two people who stood side by side on the Sidhi Rock and who stared back at it in wonder.

'Now I know why the Fhoi Myore fear that beast,' said Corum.

CHAPTER FIVE

The Blood-harvesting

As Corum and Medhbh descended somewhat nervously from the Sidhi Rock, the Bull's eyes remained fixed on the spear which Corum carried. Now the animal stood very still, looming over them as they approached it, its head still slightly lowered. It seemed as suspicious of them as they were fearful of it, yet it was plain that it recognized Bryionak, and that it had respect for that spear.

'Bull,' said Corum, and he did not feel foolish for speaking to a beast in this way, 'will you come with us to Caer Mahlod?'

The rain had turned to sleet now and the sleet glistened on the Bull's black flanks. Further along the beach the horses were showing signs of fear. They were more than suspicious of the Black Bull of Crinanass: they were in stark terror of it. But the Bull ignored the horses. It shook its head, and droplets of moisture flew from the tips of its two sharp horns. Its nostrils quivered. Its hard, intelligent eyes glanced once at the horses and then returned to gaze upon the spear.

Although Corum had, in the past, been in the presence of much larger creatures, he had never confronted an animal which gave such a strong impression of power. It seemed to him at that moment that nothing on Earth could stand against the massive Bull.

Corum and Medhbh left the Bull watching them and crossed the wind-blown sand to calm their horses. They succeeded eventually in soothing them enough so that they could be ridden, but they were still skittish. Then, for there was naught else they could do, they began to ride up the cliff-paths, going back towards Caer Mahlod.

After a few minutes, when it remained stock-still, as if considering a problem, the Black Bull of Crinanass started to follow them, though it never came very close to them. Perhaps, thought Corum, such a beast as that disdained to keep intimate company with mortals as weak as themselves.

And the sleet soon turned to snow and the snow blew cold and fierce upon the cliffs of the west, and Corum and Medhbh knew that these were signs that the Fhoi Myore approached and might, even now, have reached the walls of Caer Mahlod.

It was indeed a horrid massing which had collected at the walls of the Mabden fortress as scum might collect around a proud ship's hull. The white mist was thick, almost viscous, but it still clung largely to the forest and usually in parts of the forest where there were conifers. Here hid the Fhoi Myore themselves, and the mist was necessary to them – it was a limbo-mist which sustained them; without it they would be ill at ease. Corum saw the seven dark shapes moving about in it. They had left their chariots and seemed to be conferring. Kerenos himself, Chief of the Fhoi Myore, must be there. And Balahr who, like Corum, had but one eye, but a deadly eye. And Goim, the female Fhoi Myore, with a taste for the manhood of mortals. And the others.

Corum and Medhbh reined in their horses and turned to see if the Black Bull still followed.

It did. It stopped when they stopped, its eyes still upon the spear Bryionak.

The fight had begun. The hounds of Kerenos leaped at the walls as they had leaped before. But the Ghoolegh ran against the Mabden, too, with bows and spears. And the pale green riders charged the gate, led by one who was unmistakably Hew Argech, whom Corum should have slain. Even from where they watched upon an eminence looking down upon Caer Mahlod, Corum and Medhbh could hear the cries of the defenders and the howlings of the dreadful dogs.

'How can we reach our folk now?' Medhbh said in despair.

'Even if we reached the gates they would be fools to open them to admit us,' Corum agreed. 'We must confine ourselves, I suppose, to attacking them from the rear until they realize that we are behind them.'

Medhbh nodded. She pointed. 'Let us ride over there, where the walls are almost breached. We might be able to give our folk time to repair the damage.'

Corum saw that her suggestion had sense in it. Without a word he spurred his horse down the hill, the spear Bryionak poised for a cast at the first of his foes that he should meet. He was almost certain that he and Medhbh would die, but at that moment he did not care. All he regretted was that he would not die in his Name-robe, the scarlet robe he had given to Calatin on the coast of Moidel's Mount.

As he rode nearer, he was able to see that the ice phantoms were not in this army. Perhaps those creatures were not the creations of the Fhoi Myore, after all? But the Ghoolegh were, that was certain. Being almost indestructible they were proving a hard enemy for the Mabden to cope with. And who led them into battle? A rider on a tall horse. A rider who was not pale green, like Hew Argech, yet still familiar. How many men were familiar to him in this world? Very few. The light caught the armour of the rider. In a moment it had changed from bright gold to dull silver, from scarlet to flickering blue.

And Corum knew he had seen that armour before and that he, himself, had sent its wearer to Limbo in a great fight at the camp of Queen Xiombarg's forces. To Limbo – where the Fhoi Myore, perhaps, were still secure, before the disruption of the fabric of the multiverse had sent them into this world to poison it. And had it sent that rider with them? It was a likely explanation. The dark yellow plume still nodded on the rider's helm which, as before, completely obscured the face. The breastplate was still engraved with the Arms of Chaos, the eight arrows radiating from a central hub. And in his glove of metal was a sword which also shone sometimes gold, sometimes silver, sometimes blue and scarlet.

'Gaynor,' said Corum, and he recalled the terror of Gaynor's death. 'It is Prince Gaynor the Damned.'

'You know that warrior?' she said.

'I slew him once,' said Corum grimly. 'Or, at least, I banished him – I thought from this world, at least. But there he is. My old enemy. Could he be the "brother", I wonder, of whom the old woman spoke?' This last question was addressed to himself. He had already drawn back his arm and flung Bryionak towards Prince Gaynor, who had once been a champion (perhaps the Champion Eternal himself) but was now pledged wholly to evil.

Bryionak went flying to its target and it struck Prince Gaynor's shoulder and made him stagger in his saddle. The faceless helm turned and watched as the spear flew back to Corum's hand. Gaynor had been directing his Ghoolegh against the weak parts of Caer Mahlod's walls. They ran through the snow which had been stained red by blood and black by mud; many were missing limbs, features and even innards, but still they worked. Corum gripped the spear Bryionak, and he knew that, as before, Gaynor was not easily beaten, even by magic.

He heard Gaynor's laughter from within the helm. Gaynor seemed almost pleased to see him, as if glad to see a familiar face whether it was friend's or foe's. 'Prince Corum, the Champion of the Mabden! We were speculating on your absence, thinking that you had sensibly fled, perhaps even returning to your own world. But here you are. How whimsical is Fate that she wills us to continue our silly squabble.'

Corum looked back for a moment and saw that the Bull of Crinanass still followed. He looked beyond Gaynor at the battered walls of Caer Mahlod. He saw many dead men on the battlements.

'Indeed she is,' he said. 'But would you fight me again, Prince Gaynor? Would you beg me for mercy again? Would you have me send you to Limbo again?'

Prince Gaynor laughed his bitter laugh and said:

'Ask the Fhoi Myore that last question. They would be only too pleased to return to their dreadful homeland. And if they left me and if I had no loyalties, now that Chaos and Law no longer war upon this plane, I should be pleased to join with you, Corum. As it is, as usual, we must battle.'

Corum remembered what he had seen on Gaynor's face the time he had opened the man's helm. He shuddered. Again he felt pity for Gaynor the Damned who was bound to live out many existences in many different planes, just as was Corum – though Gaynor was destined to serve the meanest, the most treacherous of masters. And now his soldiers were half-dead things. Previously they had been beast-things.

'The quality of your infantry seems up to standard,' said Corum.

Gaynor laughed again, his voice muffled from within his never-opened helm. 'Even better, in some respects, I'd say.'

'Would you not call them off and join with me, Gaynor? You know that I had little hatred for you at the end. We have more in common than any others here.'

'True,' said Gaynor. 'So why not side with me, Corum? After all, Fhoi Myore conquest is inevitable.'

'And will inevitably lead to death.'

'That is what I have been promised,' said Gaynor simply.

And Corum knew that Gaynor wanted death more than anything and that he could not argue with the Damned Prince unless he, Corum, could offer Gaynor a death that was still quicker.

'When the world dies,' Gaynor continued, 'shall not I die, too?'

Corum looked beyond Prince Gaynor the Damned, at the battlements of Caer Mahlod and the handful of Mabden fighting for their lives against half-dead Ghoolegh, snapping devil dogs and creatures who were more trees than men. 'It is possible, Gaynor,' he said thoughtfully, 'that it is your doom to be forever siding with evil in an effort to gain your ends, when if you achieved a noble deed your wishes would be granted.'

'A romantic view, I fear, Prince Corum.' Gaynor turned his horse away.

'What?' said Corum. 'You will not fight me?'

'Nay – nor your bovine friend,' said Gaynor. He rode back towards the cover of the mist. 'I wish to remain on this world until the finish. I'll not be sent back to Limbo again by you!' His tone was equable, even friendly, as he cried: 'But I'll return later to look upon your corpse, Corum.'

'You think it will be here?'

'We think that perhaps thirty of your folk are left alive and that before the evening our hounds will be feasting within your walls. Therefore – yes, I think your corpse will be here. Farewell, Corum.'

And Gaynor had gone; and Corum and Medhbh were riding on for the broken wall and now they heard the Black Bull of Crinanass snorting behind them. They thought at first it chased them for daring to summon it, but it veered off and charged at a knot of pale green riders who had sighted Corum and Medhbh and had intended to ride them down.

The Black Bull of Crinanass lowered its head and drove straight into the group of riders, scattered their beasts, tossing men high into the air and then charging onward, straight into a rank of Ghoolegh, trampling every one of them, turning, its tail high and its head nodding, to spike a devil dog on each horn.

It dominated the whole battlefield, that Black Bull of Crinanass. It shook off any weapons which might find a mark in its hide. It charged with fearful speed thrice around the walls of Caer Mahlod while Corum and Medhbh, forgotten by their enemies, looked on with stunned delight. And Corum held the spear Bryionak high into the air, and cheered the Black Bull of Crinanass until he saw that there was a gap in the ranks of the stunned besiegers and he lowered his head, bade Medhbh to follow him, and urged his horse towards Caer Mahlod, leaping it through the breach and stopping it, by chance, directly before a weary and much-wounded King Mannach who sat upon a rock trying to stop the blood flowing from his mouth while an old man tried to remove the arrow-head from his lung.

There were tears in King Mannach's eyes as he lifted his old, noble head to stare at Corum. 'But the Bull has come too late,' he said.

'Too late, perhaps,' said Corum, 'but at least you will see the Bull destroy those who have destroyed your folk.'

'No,' said King Mannach. 'I will not watch. I am tired of it.'

As Medhbh comforted her father, Corum went around the walls of Caer Mahlod, taking stock of their situation while the Bull of Crinanass occupied the enemy outside.

Prince Gaynor had been wrong. There were not thirty able-bodied men left on the walls, but forty. And outside were still many of the hounds, several squadrons of pale green riders and a fair number of Ghoolegh. Moreover the Fhoi Myore themselves had yet to move upon Caer Mahlod and any one of the Gods of Limbo probably had the power to destroy the city if he cared to leave his misty sanctuary for a few moments.

Corum climbed to the highest tower of the battlements, now partially in ruins. The Bull was chasing little groups of their enemies all over the muddy battlefield. Many were fleeing, heedless of the chilling, booming noises which came from the mist over the forest – the voices, no doubt, of the Fhoi Myore. And those who did not heed the voices were as doomed as those who paused, turned and were destroyed by the mighty Bull, for they did not run far before they fell dead, slain by their own masters.

The Fhoi Myore did not seem to care that they wasted their creatures so and did nothing to stop the carnage which the Black Bull of Crinanass was wreaking. Corum supposed that the Cold Folk knew that they could still crush Caer Mahlod and perhaps deal with the Bull, too.

And then it was over. Not a single Ghoolegh, not a single hound and not a single pale green rider remained alive. What mortal weapons could not slay, the Black Bull had slain.

It stood triumphant amongst the corpses of men, beasts and things that were like men. It pawed at the ground and its breath foamed from its nostrils. It raised its head and it bellowed and that bellow shook the walls of Caer Mahlod.

Yet still the Fhoi Myore had not moved from their mist.

None on the battlements cheered, for they knew that the main attack was still to come.

Now, save for the great Bull's triumphant lowing, there was a silence about the scene. Death was everywhere. Death hung over the battlefield; Death inhabited the fortress. And Death waited in the mist-shrouded forest. Corum remembered something King Mannach had told him – how the Fhoi Myore pursued Death. Did they, like Prince Gaynor, long for oblivion? Was this their main concern? If so, it made them an even more terrifying enemy.

The mist had begun to move. Corum cried out to the survivors to ready themselves. In his silver hand he held up the spear Bryionak, so that all could see.

'Here is the spear of the Sidhi! There is the last of the Sidhi war-cattle! And here stands Corum Llaw Ereint. Rally, men of Caer Mahlod, for the Fhoi Myore come against us now in all their strength. But we have strength. We have courage. And this is our land, our world, and we must defend it!'

Corum saw Medhbh. He saw her smile up at him and heard her cry out:

'If we die then let us die in a way that will make our legend great!'

Even King Mannach, leaning on the arm of a warrior who was, himself, wounded, seemed to recover from his depression. Sound men and wounded men, youths and maidens, the aged, now swarmed up to the walls of Caer Mahlod and steadied their hearts as they saw seven shadows in seven creaking battle-carts drawn by seven misshapen beasts reach the bottom of the hill upon which Caer Mahlod stood. And the mist surrounded them again, and the Black Bull of Crinanass was also engulfed in the pale, clinging stuff, and they no longer heard his lowing. It was as if the mist had poisoned him and perhaps that was what had happened.

Corum took aim at the first looming shade, aiming for what appeared to be the head, though the outline was much distorted. The creaking of the chariots grated on his bones and his body wanted to do little but curl in on itself, but he resisted the sensation and cast the spear Bryionak.

Slowly the spear seemed to sunder the mist as it passed through and went true to its target and produced, for an instant, a strange honk of pain. Then the spear returned to his hand and the honking continued. In other circumstances the sound might have been ludicrous, but here it was sinister and menacing. It was the voice of an insensate beast, of a stupid being, and Corum realized that the owner of that voice was a creature of little intelligence and monstrous will, of primitive will. That was what made the Fhoi Myore so dangerous. They were motivated by blind need, they could not understand their plight, they could think of no way to deal with it but to continue their conquests, continue them without malice, or hatred or any sense of vengeance. They used what they needed, they made use of whatever powers they had, of whoever would serve them, to seek an impossible goal. Yes, that was what made them almost impossible to defeat. They could not be bargained with, reasoned with. Fear was all that might stop them and it was plain that the one who had honked did fear the Sidhi spear. The advancing chariots began to slow as the Fhoi Myore grunted to each other.

A moment later a face appeared out of the mist. It was more like a wound than a face. It was red and there were lumps of raw flesh hanging on it and the mouth was distorted and appeared in the left cheek and there was but one eye – one eye with a great lid of dead flesh. And attached to that eyelid was a wire which ran over the skull and under the arm-pit and could be pulled by the two-fingered hand to open it.

The hand moved now, tugging at the wire. Corum was

filled with an instinctive feeling of danger and was already ducking behind the battlement as the eye opened. The eye was blue, like northern ice, and from it poured a radiance. Bitter cold gnawed at Corum's body, though he was not in the direct path of that radiance. And now he knew how those people by the lake had died, frozen in the postures of war. The cold was so intense that it knocked him backward and almost off the ledge. He recovered, crawled further away and raised his head, the spear poised. Already several of the warriors on the battlements were rigid and dead. Corum threw the spear Bryionak. He threw it at the blue eye.

For one moment it seemed that Bryionak had been frozen in the air. It hovered, suspended, and then appeared to make a conscious effort to continue, and the point, glowing bright orange now, as it had glowed against the ice phantoms, sliced into the eye.

Then Corum knew from which of the Fhoi Myore the honking had come. The hand dropped the wire and the eyelid closed even as the spear withdrew itself and returned to Corum. The travesty of a face twisted and the head turned this way and that, while the beast which pulled the chariot lurched round and began to retreat into the mist.

Corum felt a certain elation enter his mind. This Sidhi weapon had been especially made to fight the Fhoi Myore and it did its job well. Now one of the six was in retreat.

Corum called out to the people on the wall:

'Get back to the ground. Leave me here alone, for I have the spear Bryionak. Your weapons can do nothing against the Fhoi Myore. Let me stand here and fight them.'

Medhbh cried back: 'Let me stand with you, Corum, to die with you!'

But he shook his head and turned again to regard the advancing Cold Folk. Still it was hard to see them. A suggestion of a horned head. A hint of bristling hair. A glint which might have been the glint of an eye.

There came a roaring, then. Was that the voice of Kerenos, chieftain of the Fhoi Myore? No. The roaring came from behind the Fhoi Myore chariots.

An even larger, darker shape reared up behind them and Corum gasped as he recognized it. It was the Black Bull of Crinanass, grown huger but losing none of its mass. It lowered its horns and it plucked one of the Fhoi Myore from its chariot and it tossed the god up into the sky and caught the god on its horn and tossed the god again.

The Fhoi Myore were in panic. They wheeled their war-carts and began a sudden retreat. Corum saw Prince Gaynor, tiny and terrified, running with them. The mist moved faster than a tidal wave, back over the forest, out over the plain, and disappeared over the horizon leaving behind it a wasteland of corpses. The Black Bull of Crinanass, which had shrunk to its previous size, was now grazing contentedly on a patch of grass somehow left untrampled on the battlefield. But on its horns were dark smears and there were pieces of meat scattered about nearby; and some distance to the left of the Black Bull of Crinanass was a huge chariot, much bigger than the Bull, which had overturned, its wheel still spinning. It was a crude thing, of wood and wicker-work, poorly crafted.

The folk of Caer Mahlod were not jubilant, though they had been saved from destruction. They were stunned at what had happened. Very slowly they began to gather on the battlements to look at all the destruction.

Corum walked slowly down the steps, the spear Bryionak still held loosely in his silver hand. He walked through the tunnel and out of the gate of Caer Mahlod and he walked across the ruined earth to where the Bull was grazing. He did not know why he went to the Bull, and this time the creature did not move away from him but turned its huge head and stared into his eyes.

'You must slay me now,' said the Black Bull of Crinanass, 'and then my destiny will be complete.' It spoke in the pure tongue of the Vadhagh and the Sidhi. It spoke calmly, yet sadly.

'I cannot slay you,' said Corum. 'You have saved us all. You killed one of the Fhoi Myore so that now they number only six. Caer Mahlod still stands and many of her folk still live because of what you did.'

'It is what you did,' said the Bull. 'You found the spear Bryionak. You called me. I knew what must happen.'

'Why must I slay you?'

'It is my destiny. It is necessary.'

'Very well,' said Corum. 'I will do what you request.'

And he took the spear Bryionak and cast it into the heart of the Black Bull of Crinanass, and a great gout of blood burst from the Bull's side and the beast began to run, and this time the spear stayed where it was and did not return to Corum's hand.

Over the whole battlefield ran the Black Bull of Crinanass. Through the forest it ran and across the moors beyond. Along the cliffs by the sea it ran. And its blood washed the whole land, and where the blood touched the land it became green and flowers grew up and trees came into leaf. And slowly, above, the sky was clearing and the clouds fled in the wake of the Fhoi Myore and the sky became blue and the warm sun shone; and when the sun spread heat across all the world around Caer Mahlod the Bull ran towards the broken cliffs where Castle Erorn stood. And the Bull leapt the chasm which separated the cliff from the tower and it stood beside the tower for a moment, its knees buckling as the blood still trickled from its wound; it looked back at Corum, then staggered to the headland and flung itself over, into the sea. And the spear Bryionak still stayed in the side of the Black Bull of Crinanass and was never afterward seen again in mortal lands.

Epilogue

And that was the end of the Tale of the Bull and the Spear.

All signs of the struggle had disappeared from hill, forest and plain. Summer had come to Caer Mahlod at last and many believed that the blood of the Black Bull had made the land safe forever from the encroachment of the Cold Folk.

And Corum Jhaelen Irsei, of the Vadhagh folk, lived a life among the Tuha-na-Cremm Croich, and that, to them, was a further guarantee of their security. Even the old woman whom Corum had met on the frozen plain no longer muttered her gloomy warnings. All were happy. And they were happy that Corum lay with Medhbh, daughter of King Mannach, for it meant that he would stay with them. They harvested their crops and they sang in the fields and they feasted well, for the land was rich again where the Bull had run.

But sometimes Corum, lying beside his new love, would awake in the night and fancy that he heard the cool and melancholy strains of a harp and he would brood on that old woman's words and would wonder why he should fear the harp, a brother and, above all, beauty.

And at those times, of all the folk dwelling at Caer Mahlod, Corum was not happy.

The Oak and the Ram

FOR JARMILA

BOOK ONE

---

*In which Prince Corum finds himself
called to pursue the second of his
great quests . . .*

CHAPTER ONE
The Meeting of the Kings

And so Rhalina had died.

And Corum had found Medhbh, King Mannach's daughter, and in a short while (as Corum reckoned time) she too would die. If it was his weakness to fall in love with short-lived Mabden women, then he must reconcile himself to the knowledge that he would outlive many lovers, must experience many losses, many agonies. As it was, he did not think much about it, preferring to avoid the significance of such ideas whenever possible. Besides, the memories of Rhalina were growing dim and it was only with difficulty that he could remember the fine details of the life he had led in an earlier age than this, when he had ridden against the Sword Rulers.

Corum Jhaelen Irsei, who had been called the Prince in the Scarlet Robe (but, having since traded this robe to a wizard, was now known as Corum of the Silver Hand), stayed at Caer Mahlod for two months after the day when the Black Bull of Crinanass had run its fecund course and brought sudden spring to the land of the Tuha-na-Cremm Croich, the People of the Mound. It was two months since the misshaped Fhoi Myore had tried to slay the inhabitants of Caer Mahlod, to freeze and to poison this place so that it might, too, resemble Limbo whence the Fhoi Myore came and to which they were unable to return.

Now the Fhoi Myore appeared to have abandoned their ambitions of conquest. They were stranded upon this plane and had no love for its inhabitants, but they did not fight for the joy of fighting. The Fhoi Myore were only six. The Fhoi Myore had once been many. But they were dying of long-drawn-out diseases which would eventually rot them. In the meantime, however, they made themselves as comfortable as possible upon the Earth, turning the world into bleak and perpetual Samhain, a mid-winter world. And before they expired they would, casually, have destroyed the entire Mabden race as well.

But very few of the Mabden were in a mood to think about such a prospect. They had triumphed over the Fhoi Myore once and won their freedom. It seemed enough, for the summer was the richest and the hottest any remembered (some sweated and joked that they would welcome the return of the Cold Folk, they panted so much in the heat), as if the sun, giving no warmth to the rest of the Mabden lands, poured all its power into one small corner of the world.

The oaks were greener, the alders were stronger, the ash and the elms were the lushest they had ever been. In the fields there was wheat ripening where folk had never hoped to see another harvest.

There were poppies and cornflowers and marigolds, buttercups, woodbine, hollyhocks and daisies growing everywhere in profusion.

Only the cold, cold water pouring down in the rivers which flowed from the east reminded the folk of Tuha-na-Cremm Croich that their countrymen were all dead, or vassals of the Fhoi Myore, or both; that their High King – their Archdruid Amergin – was under a glamour, a prisoner in his own city at Caer Llud, a city now used as their capital by the Fhoi Myore. Only that reminded them, whenever they bent to drink. And many were made gloomy, brooding upon their incapacity to avenge their dead cousins, for the best they had done was defend their own land against the Cold Folk and even then they could not have accomplished the defence without the help of Sidhi magic and a demigod raised from his deep slumber beneath the Mound. That demigod was Corum.

The water flowed from the east and it fed the wide ditch they had dug around the conical mound on which was built the fortress city of Caer Mahlod, an old city, of grey and bulky granite; a city without much beauty but with considerable strength. Caer Mahlod had been abandoned at least once and re-occupied in times of war. It was the only city that remained to the Tuha-na-Cremm Croich. Once they had had several fairer cities, but these had been swept away by the ice which the Fhoi Myore brought.

But now many of those who had occupied the fortress town had returned to rebuild their ruined farms and tend the crops which had been revitalized by the Black Bull's lifeblood and only King Mannach and King Mannach's warriors and retainers and King Mannach's daughter and Corum remained at Caer Mahlod.

Sometimes Corum would stand on the battlements and look towards the sea and the ruins of his own home, which was now called Castle Owyn and thought a natural formation, and wonder upon the matter of the spear Bryionak and the Black Bull and the magic which had been worked. It seemed to him that he dreamed, for he could not explain the magic or how it had been brought about. He dreamed the dream of these people, who had called him from a dream. And for the most part he was content. He had Medhbh of the Long Arm (the nickname she had earned for her skill with spear and tathlum), with her thick red hair, her strong beauty, her intelligence and her laughter. He had dignity. He had the respect of his fellow warriors. They had become used to him now. They accepted his strange Vadhagh looks – 'elfin' looks, Medhbh called them – his artificial silver hand, his single yellow and purple eye and the patch over the other socket; the patch embroidered by Rhalina, Margravine of Moidel's Mount, who lay a thousand years at least in the past.

He had dignity. He had been true to this folk and he had been true to himself. He had pride.

And he had fine companionship. There was no question that his lot was improved since he had left Castle Erorn and answered the call of this folk. He wondered what had become of Jhary-a-Conel, Companion to Heroes. It had been Jhary, after all, who had advised him to do King

Mannach's bidding. But Jhary was the last mortal Corum knew who could still travel through the Fifteen Planes, apparently at will. Once all the Vadhagh could move between the planes, as could the Nhadragh, but with the defeat of the Sword Rulers the last vestiges of this power had been denied them.

And sometimes Corum would call a bard to him to sing one of the old songs of the Tuha-na-Cremm Croich, for he found such songs to his taste. One song was attributed to the first Amergin, ancestor to the High King, now a thrall of the Fhoi Myore, upon arriving in their new homeland:

I am the ocean wave;
I am the murmur of the surges;
I am seven battalions;
I am a strong bull;
I am an eagle on a rock;
I am a ray of the sun;
I am the most beautiful of herbs;
I am a courageous wild boar;
I am a salmon in the water;
I am a lake upon a plain;
I am a cunning artist;
I am a gigantic, sword-wielding champion;
I can shift my shape like a god.
In what direction shall we go?
Shall we hold our council in the valley or on the
  mountain-top?
Where shall we make our home?
What land is better than this island of the setting sun?
Where shall we walk to and fro in peace and safety?
Who can find you clear springs of water as can I?
Who can tell you the age of the moon but I?
Who can call the fish from the depths of the sea as
  can I?
Who can lure them near the shore as can I?
Who can change the shapes of the hills and the head-
  lands as can I?

I am a bard who is called upon by seafarers to prophesy.
Javelins shall be wielded to avenge our wrongs.
I prophesy victory.
I end my song by prophesying all other good things.

And then the bard would sing his own song as a kind of amplification of Amergin's:

I have been in many shapes before I attained congenial
*   form.*
I have been a narrow blade of a sword;
I have been a drop in the air;
I have been a shining star;
I have been a word in a book;
I have been a book in the beginning;
I have been a light in a lantern a year and a half;
I have been a bridge for passing over three score rivers;
I have journeyed as an eagle;
I have been a boat on the sea;
I have been a director in battle;
I have been a sword in the hand;
I have been a shield in a fight;
I have been the string of a harp;
I have been enchanted for a year in the foam of water;
There is nothing in which I have not been.

And in these old songs Corum would hear echoes of his own fate, which Jhary-a-Conel had explained to him – the fate to be eternally reborn, sometimes fully grown, as a warrior to fight in all the great battles of mortals, whether those mortals be Mabden, Vadhagh or some other race; to fight for the freedom of mortals oppressed by gods (for all that many believed the gods created *by* mortals). In those songs he heard an expression of the dreams he sometimes had – where he was the whole universe and the universe was him, where he was contained by the universe and simultaneously contained it and everything had an equal dignity, whether animate or inanimate, an equal value. Rock, tree, horse or man – all were equal. This was the mystical belief of many of King Mannach's folk. A visitor from Corum's world might have seen this as primitive worship of nature, but Corum knew that it was much more than that. Many a farmer there was in the land of the Tuha-na-Cremm Croich who would bow politely to a stone and murmur an apology before moving it from one place to another and he would treat his earth, his ox and his plough with as much courtesy as he would treat his father, his wife or his friend.

As a result, life among the Tuha-na-Cremm Croich had a formal, dignified rhythm which did not rob it of vitality or humour or, on occasions, anger. And this was why Corum found pride in fighting the Fhoi Myore, for the Fhoi Myore threatened more than life. The Fhoi Myore threatened the quiet dignity of this folk.

Tolerant of their own foibles, their own vanities, their own follies, the Tuha-na-Cremm Croich tolerated these qualities in others. It was ironical to Corum that his own race, the Vadhagh (called Sidhi by this folk now) had at the end been possessed of a similar outlook and had been robbed of it by the ancestors of this folk. He wondered if, in achieving such a noble way of life, a people became automatically vulnerable to destruction by those who had not achieved it. If so, it was an irony of cosmic proportions. And so Corum dismissed this line of reasoning, for he had become weary of cosmic proportions since his encounter with the Sword Rulers and his discovery of his own destiny.

Now King Fiachadh came a-visiting, risking much to cross the water from the west. His envoy arrived on a steaming horse which was wrenched to a skidding stop at the edge of the great water ditch surrounding the walls of Caer Mahlod. The envoy was clad in billowing pale green silk, silver breastplate and greaves, a silver battle-cap and a surcoat quartered in yellow, blue, white and purple. He panted as he called his business to the guards upon the gate-towers. Corum, running from the other side of the battlements, saw him and was astonished, for he was dressed in a style unlike anything he had seen before in this land.

'King Fiachadh's man!' called the envoy. 'Coming to announce our king's arrival on your shores.' He pointed to the west. 'Our ships have landed. King Fiachadh begs the hospitality of his brother, King Mannach!'

'Wait,' cried a guard. 'We shall tell King Mannach!'

'Then hurry, I beg of you, for we are anxious to seek the security of your walls. We have heard many tales of late concerning the dangers to be found abroad in your land.'

While Corum remained in the gate-tower, looking with polite curiosity at the envoy, King Mannach was summoned.

King Mannach was astonished for other reasons. 'Fiachadh? Why comes he to Caer Mahlod?' he murmured, calling out to the envoy: 'King Fiachadh knows that he is ever welcome in our town. But why journey you from the land of the Tuha-na-Manannan? Are you attacked?'

The envoy was still panting, at first managing only to shake his head.

'Nay, sire. My master wishes to confer with you and only recently we learned that Caer Mahlod had been freed of the Fhoi Myore frost. Thus we set sail speedily, without the usual formalities. For this King Fiachadh wishes you to forgive him.'

'There is nothing to forgive, unless it be the quality of our hospitality, tell King Fiachadh. We await him with pleasant anticipation.'

Another nod and the silk-clad knight forced his horse round to ride towards the cliffs, his loose jerkin and surcoat flapping, his silver cap and horse furniture flashing as he disappeared into the distance.

King Mannach laughed. 'Prince Corum, you will like my old friend Fiachadh. And at last we shall have news of how the folk of the Western Kingdoms fare. I had feared them conquered.'

*

'I had feared them conquered,' King Mannach said again as he spread his arms.

And the great gates of Caer Mahlod were opened and through the passage (which now led under the moat) came a great parade of knights, maidens and squires, bearing banner-decked lances, with samite cloaks, with buckles and brooches of finely worked red gold set with amethysts, turquoise and mother-of-pearl; with round shields engraved and enamelled in complicated, flowing designs, with silver-bound scabbards and gilded shoes. Tall, handsome women sat astride horses with ribbons plaited in their manes and tails. The men, too, were tall, and had long, thick moustaches of fiery red or warm yellow, their hair either flowing freely below their shoulders or bound in plaits or secured in bunches with little clasps of gold, brass or gem-set iron.

At the centre of this colourful party was a barrel-chested giant of a man with a bright red beard and piercing blue eyes and wind-browned cheeks, dressed in a long robe of red silk trimmed with the fur of the winter fox, and wearing no helmet, only an ancient iron circlet in which runes had been set in delicate, curling gold.

King Mannach's arms were still spread as he spoke joyfully:

'Welcome, old friend. Welcome, King Fiachadh of the Distant West, of the old, green land of our forefathers!'

And the great giant with the red beard opened his mouth and he bellowed with laughter, swinging one leg free over the saddle and sliding to the ground.

'I come in my usual style, you see, Mannach. In all my pomp, in all my bombastic majesty!'

'I see,' said King Mannach embracing the giant, 'and I am glad. Who would want a Fiachadh otherwise? You bring colour and enchantment to Caer Mahlod. See – my people smile with pleasure. See – their spirits rise. We shall feast tonight. We shall celebrate. You have brought joy to us, King Fiachadh!'

King Fiachadh laughed again, with pleasure at King Mannach's words, before turning to regard Corum who had stood back while the old friends greeted one another.

'And this is your Sidhi hero – your name hero – Cremm Croich!'

He stalked towards Corum and placed a huge hand upon Corum's shoulder, looking deeply into Corum's face and appearing to be satisfied. 'I thank you, Sidhi, for what you did to help my brother king. I bring magic with me and we shall talk together later of that. I bring a weighty matter, also . . .' he turned to King Mannach, 'and that we must all discuss.'

'Is that why you visit us, sire?' Medhbh stepped forward. She had been visiting a friend in a valley some way distant and had arrived just before King Fiachadh. She was still in riding costume, in leather and white linen, her unbound red hair flowing down her back.

'It is the main reason, lovely Medhbh,' said King Fiachadh bending to kiss the cheek she offered. 'You are grown as beautiful as I predicted! Ah, my sister lives again in you.'

'In all ways,' said King Mannach, and there appeared to be a significance in his words which Corum failed to identify.

Medhbh laughed. 'Your compliments are as huge as your vanity, Uncle!'

'But they are as sincere,' said Fiachadh. And he winked.

CHAPTER TWO

The Treasure Brought by King Fiachadh

King Fiachadh had brought a harpist with him and for an instant Corum felt a shiver run through him, the harpist's music was so unearthly. Corum thought he heard the harp which had sounded at Castle Owyn, but it was not that harp. This was sweeter. The bard's voice merged with the harp so that at times it was hard to tell which one heard. Corum sat with all the others in the great hall of Caer Mahlod, at a single vast table. Hounds ranged among the benches, nosing through reeds strewn upon the flagstones for scraps, for pools of sweet mead. Brands flared brightly, merrily, as if the laughter on all sides actually brightened the hall. Taking after their masters, King Fiachadh's knights and ladies sported with the men and women of Caer Mahlod and many songs were sung, many boasts shouted, many improbable tales told.

Corum sat between King Mannach and King Fiachadh and Medhbh sat next to her uncle, all at the head of the great dining board. King Fiachadh ate as lustily as he spoke, though Corum noticed that the king took little mead and was by no means as drunk as his retainers. Neither did King Mannach drink overmuch, and Corum and Medhbh followed his example. If King Fiachadh chose not to get drunk, there must be a particularly good reason, for evidently he liked to drink. He told several tall stories concerning his capacity while they ate.

The feasting went well, and slowly the hall emptied as, usually in couples, the guests and residents of Caer Mahlod bowed good night and left, and soon there were only a few snoring squires sprawled along the table, a big knight of the Tuha-na-Manannan spreadeagled under the table, a warrior and a maiden of the Tuha-na-Cremm Croich sprawled in each other's arms near the wall.

And King Fiachadh said in a deep, serious voice:

'You are the last I have visited, old friend.' He looked hard at King Mannach. 'I knew already what you would say. I fear I knew, too, what the others would say.'

'Say?' King Mannach frowned.

'To my proposal.'

'You have been visiting other kings?' said Corum. 'All the other kings whose folk are still free?'

King Fiachadh nodded his great, red head. 'All. I see that it is imperative we unite. Our only defence against the Fhoi Myore can be our unity. First I went to the land south of my own – to the folk called Tuha-na-Anu. Secondly I sailed north where dwell, among others, the Tuha-na-Tir-nam-Beo. A mountain people and fierce. Thirdly I sailed down the coast and guested with King Daffyn of the Tuha-na-Gwyddneu Garanhir. Fourthly I came to the Tuha-na-Cremm Croich. Three kings are cautious, thinking that to attract the attention of the Fhoi Myore will mean instant destruction to their lands. What does the fourth king say?'

'What does King Fiachadh ask?' said Medhbh reasonably.

'That all those who remain – four great peoples as far as I know – unite. We have some treasures which the power of the Sidhi could put to use in our favour. We have great warriors. We have your example of defeating them. We should carry the attack to Craig Dôn or Caer Llud, wherever the six remaining Fhoi Myore dwell. A large army. The remains of the free Mabden. What say you, King?'

'I say that I would agree,' said Mannach. 'Who would not?'

'Three kings would not. Each king thinks himself safer by staying in his own land and saying nothing, doing nothing. And all three kings are afraid. They say that with Amergin in the hands of the Fhoi Myore there is no point in fighting. The elected High King is not dead, so a new one cannot be made. The Fhoi Myore knew this when they spared Amergin's life . . .'

'It is not like your folk to let superstition bind them,' said Corum softly. 'Why do you not change this law and make a new High King?'

'It is not superstition,' said King Mannach without offence. 'For one thing, all the kings must meet to elect the new High King and I gather some are afraid to leave their own domain lest those lands be attacked in their absence or lest they are attacked while in other lands. An election of a High King takes many months. All the people must be consulted. All must hear the candidates, speak with them if they wish. Can we break such a law? If we do break our ancient laws, are our customs worth fighting for?'

Medhbh said:

'Make Corum your War Leader. Unify the kingdoms under him.'

'That suggestion has been made,' said King Fiachadh. 'I made it. None would hear of it. Most of us have no reason to trust gods. Gods have betrayed us in the past. We prefer to have no part of them.'

'I am not a god,' said Corum, reasonably.

'You are modest,' said King Fiachadh, 'but you are a god. A demigod at very least.' He stroked his red beard. 'That is what I think. And I have met you. Imagine, then, what those kings who do not know you think. They have heard the tales by now and those tales must have been greatly magnified by the time they reached them. For instance, I thought to meet a being at least twelve feet high!' King Fiachadh smiled, for he was taller than Corum. 'No, the only thing which would unite our folk would be the release of Amergin and the restoration of his full senses.'

'What has become of Amergin?' Corum asked. He had never heard the details of the High King's fate, for the Tuha-na-Cremm Croich were reluctant to discuss them.

'He is under a glamour,' said King Fiachadh soberly.

'An enchantment? What is its nature?'

'We are not sure,' said King Mannach. He continued reluctantly: 'Amergin is said to think of himself now as an animal. Some say he believes he is a goat, others a sheep, others a pig . . .'

'You see how clever are those who serve the Fhoi Myore?' Medhbh said. 'They keep our Archdruid alive but destroy his dignity.'

'And a gloom settles over all those who remain free,' King Fiachadh put in. 'That has much to do with why our fellow kings will not fight, Mannach. They have no soul for it, with Amergin crawling on all fours and eating grass.'

'Do not continue,' said King Mannach raising his hands. His old, strong face showed much grief. 'Our own High King symbolizes all our pride . . .'

'Do not confuse the symbol with the reality, however,' said Corum. 'Much pride remains amongst the Mabden race.'

'Aye,' said Medhbh. 'It is true.'

'Nonetheless,' said King Fiachadh, 'our people will only unite under an Amergin free from enchantment. Amergin was so wise. Such a great man was Amergin.' And a tear came to his blue eye. He turned his head away from them.

'Then Amergin must be rescued,' said Corum flatly. 'Should I find your king for you and bring him to the West?' He did not speak impetuously. From the beginning he had considered this. 'Disguised, I might reach Caer Llud.'

And when Fiachadh looked back he was not crying.

He was grinning.

'And I have the disguise,' he said.

Corum laughed aloud. He had been considering a decision, plainly, which King Fiachadh had also been considering – perhaps for much longer.

'You are a Sidhi . . .' began the king of the Tuha-na-Manannan.

'Related to them,' said Corum, 'as I discovered upon my last quest. We have looks in common and, I suppose, certain powers. I fail to understand, though, why I should possess such powers . . .'

'Because all believe,' said Medhbh simply, and she leaned towards him and touched his arm. The touch was like a kiss. He smiled tenderly at her. 'Very well,' he said. 'Because all believe. However, you may call me "Sidhi" if it suits you, King Fiachadh.'

'Then, Sir Sidhi, know this. In the land of the Distant West, the land of my folk, the Tuha-na-Manannan, came a year since a visitor. His name was Onragh . . .'

'Onragh of Caer Llud!' gasped King Mannach. 'In whose keeping . . .'

'. . . Were the Treasures of Llud, the Sidhi gifts? Aye, and Onragh lost them all from his chariot as he fled the Fhoi Myore and their vassals. Because the Hounds of Kerenos followed, he could not go back. So he lost them – all save one. And that Treasure he brought across the water to the Distant West, to the land of gentle mists and rain. And Onragh of Caer Llud was dying from his wounds which were of great variety. Half of one hand had been gnawed by the Hounds. An ear had been severed by a Ghoolegh flencher. Several knives had found his offal. Dying, he presented into my safekeeping the only Treasure he had saved, though it had not saved him. He could not use it. Only a Sidhi can use it, though I do not understand why, save that it was originally a Sidhi gift, like most of Caer Llud's Treasures, and must have worked for us once. And Onragh, doomed to die believing that he had failed our race, brought news of Amergin the High King. At that time Amergin was still in the great tower which stands by the river close to the centre of Caer Llud. This tower has always been the home of the High King. But Amergin was already under the glamour which makes him believe himself a beast. And he was guarded by many Fhoi Myore vassals – some of whom came with the Fhoi Myore from their own realm and others, the half-dead like the Ghoolegh, drawn from slain or captured Mabden. But guarded right well, my friends, if Onragh is to be believed. And not all the guards have human shape, I heard. But that is where, doubtless, Amergin is.'

'I will need an excellent disguise,' mused Corum, who

privately felt he was doomed to fail in his quest, but who also felt that he must attempt it if only to show his respect for these people.

'I hope I can suggest one,' said King Fiachadh and his massive bulk began to rise as he stood up. 'Is my chest where I asked it to be put, brother?'

King Mannach also rose, smoothing back his white hair. Corum remembered that not long since his hair had also had red in it. But that was before the Fhoi Myore had come. And King Mannach's beard was almost white now, too. Still he was a handsome man, standing almost as tall as broad-shouldered Fiachadh, the gold collar of his kingship around his firm throat. King Mannach pointed to a corner behind their seats.

'There,' he said. 'There is the chest.'

And King Fiachadh went to the corner and picked up the heavy chest by its golden handles and he carried the chest to the table and, with a grunt, put it down. Then from a pouch at his waist he took some keys and unlocked five strong locks. Then he paused, his piercing blue eyes staring at Corum. And he said something mysterious. He said:

'You are not a traitor, Corum, now.'

'I am not,' said Corum. 'Not now.'

'I trust a reformed traitor more than I trust myself,' said King Fiachadh, grinning cheerfully as he opened the lid.

But he opened the chest in such a way that Corum could not see the contents.

King Fiachadh reached into the chest and carefully began to draw something out.

'There,' he said. 'The last of the Treasures of Caer Llud.'

And Corum wondered if the king of the Tuha-na-Manannan were joking, still, for King Fiachadh was displaying in both hands a rather tattered robe; a robe such as the poorest of peasants might be too fastidious to wear. A robe which was patched, torn, faded so that it was impossible to tell the original colour.

Holding it almost gingerly and yet tenderly, as if in awe of the old robe, King Fiachadh offered it to Corum.

'This is your disguise,' said King Fiachadh.

CHAPTER THREE

Corum Accepts a Gift

'Did some hero wear it once?' Corum asked. It was the only explanation for the reverence with which King Fiachadh handled the tattered robe.

'Aye, a hero has worn it, according to our legends, during the first fights with the Fhoi Myore.' King Fiachadh seemed puzzled by Corum's question. 'It is often called just The Mantle, but sometimes it is called Arianrod's Cloak – so that strictly speaking it is a heroine's mantle, for Arianrod was a female Sidhi, of great fame and much loved by the Mabden.

'And so you treasure it,' said Corum. 'And well you might . . .'

Medhbh was laughing, for she knew what he thought.

'You come close to condescending to us, Sir Silverhand,' she said. 'Do you think King Fiachadh a fool?'

'Far from it, but . . .'

'If you knew our legends you would understand the power of that much-worn mantle. Arianrod used it for many great feats before she, herself, was slain by some Fhoi Myore during the last great battle between the Sidhi and the Cold Folk. Some say she slew a whole army of Fhoi Myore single-handed while wearing that cloak.'

'It makes the wearer invulnerable?'

'Not exactly,' said King Fiachadh, still proffering the mantle to Corum. 'Will you accept it, Prince Corum?'

'Gladly I will accept a gift from your hand, King Fiachadh,' said Corum, remembering his manners, and he reached out and took the cloak gently, in his fleshly hand and his hand of gleaming silver.

And both hands vanished at the wrists so that it seemed he was again crippled, though this time worse. Yet he could feel his fleshly hand and feel the texture of the cloth with his fingers, for all that the mantle had gone.

'It does work, then,' said King Fiachadh in tones of great satisfaction. 'I am glad you accepted it with hesitation, Sir Sidhi.'

Corum began to understand. He drew his fleshly hand away from under the cloak and there was his hand again!

'A mantle of invisibility?'

'Aye,' said Medhbh in awe. 'The same mantle used by Gyfech to enter the bedchamber of Ben while her father slept across the door. That mantle was much prized, even amongst the Sidhi.'

Corum said: 'I believe I know how it must work. It comes from another plane. Just as Hy-Breasail is part of another world, so is this mantle. It shifts the wearer into another plane, just as the Vadhagh could once move from plane to plane and remain aware of activities on different planes . . .'

They knew not of what he spoke, but they were too delighted to question him.

He laughed. 'Brought from the Sidhi plane, it has no true existence here. Yet why will it not work for Mabden?'

'It will not always work for Sidhi,' said King Fiachadh. 'There are some – Mabden or others – possessed of a sixth sense which makes them aware of you even when you are invisible to all others. Very few possess this sixth sense so that you may wear the mantle without detection most of the time. However, someone whose sixth sense is well-developed will see you just as I see you now.'

'And this is the disguise I must use to go to the Tower of the High King?' Corum said, handling the cloak with care and equally as much reverence as had King Fiachadh, marvelling as its folds hid first one portion and then another of his anatomy. 'Yes, it is a good disguise.' He smiled. 'There is none better.' He handed the mantle back to the king. 'Best keep it safely in its chest until it is needed.'

And when the chest was locked with all five keys, Corum

sank back in his chair, his expression thoughtful. 'Now,' he said, 'there is much to be planned.'

So it was late before Corum and Medhbh lay together in their wide, low bed, looking out through the windows at the summer moon.

'It was prophesied,' said Medhbh sleepily, 'that Cremm Croich should go upon three quests, face three great dangers, make three strong friendships . . .'

'Prophesied where?'

'In the old legends.'

'You have not mentioned this before.'

'There seemed no point. Legends are vague. You are not what the legends led us to expect, after all.' She smiled quietly.

He returned her smile. 'Well, then, I begin the second quest tomorrow.'

'And you will be gone long from my side,' said Medhbh.

'That is my fate, I fear. I came for duty, not for love, sweet Medhbh. The love must be enjoyed while it does not interfere with duty.'

'You could be killed, could you not? For all you are an elfin lord?'

'Aye, killed by sword, or poison. I could even fall from my horse and break my neck!'

'Do not mock my fears, Corum.'

'I am sorry.' He rose on one elbow and looked into her lovely eyes. He bent and kissed her lips. 'I am sorry, Medhbh.'

He rode a red horse, such as he had ridden when he first came to Cremmsmound. Its coat shone in the early morning sunshine. From beyond the walls of Caer Mahlod came the sound of birdsong.

He wore all his ceremonial fighting gear, the ancient gear of the Vadhagh. He wore a shirt of blue samite and his breeks were doeskin. He wore a peaked, conical silver helm with his runic name set into it (the runes were indecipherable to the Mabden) and he wore his byrnie, a layer of silver upon a layer of brass. He wore all save his scarlet robe, his Name-robe, for that he had traded to the wizard Calatin at the place he knew as Moidel's Mount. Upon the horse was a mantle of yellow velvet, and harness and saddle were of crimson leather with designs picked out in white.

For weapons Corum took a lance, an axe, a sword and a dirk. The lance was tall, its shaft strengthened with gleaming brass, its head of polished iron. The axe was double-headed, plain and long-hafted, also bound with bands of brass. The sword hung in a scabbard matching the horse's harness and its hilt was dressed in leather, bound with fine gold and silver wire, with a heavy round pommel of bronze. The dirk had been made by the same craftsman and matched the sword.

'Who could mistake you for anything but a demigod?' said King Fiachadh approvingly.

Prince Corum made a small smile and clutched his reins in his silver hand. He reached with his other hand to adjust the plain war-board which hung behind his saddle over one of the panniers containing as well as his provisions a tightly rolled fur cape which he would need as he advanced into Fhoi Myore lands. The other cape, the Sidhi cloak, Arianrod's Cloak, he had rolled and wrapped about his waist. Tucked into this were the gauntlets he would wear later, to protect one hand from the cold and to diguise the other so that he would not be easily recognized by any enemy.

Medhbh tossed back her long red hair and came forward to kiss his fleshly hand, looking up at him with eyes that were both proud and troubled.

'Have care with your life, Corum,' she murmured. 'Preserve it if you can, for all of us will need you even when this quest is over.'

'I shall not throw my life away,' he promised. 'Life has become good for me, Medhbh. But neither do I fear death at this moment.'

He wiped the sweat from his forehead. All his gear made him hot beneath the sun which was already blazing down, but he knew he would not be hot for long. He adjusted the embroidered eye-patch over the blind socket. He touched her gently upon her brown arm. 'I shall come back to you,' he promised.

King Mannach folded his arms across his chest and cleared his throat. 'Bring Amergin to us, Prince Corum. Bring our High King with you.'

'Only if Amergin is with me will I come back to Caer Mahlod. And if I cannot bring him, then I will make every effort to send him to you, King Mannach.'

'This is a great quest, this quest,' said King Mannach. 'Farewell, Corum.'

'Farewell, Corum,' said Fiachadh the red-bearded, putting a large, strong hand upon the Vadhagh's knee. 'Good luck in this.'

'Farewell, Corum,' said Medhbh, and her voice was now as steady as her gaze.

Then Corum kicked at the flanks of his red horse and he went from them.

It was with a calm mind that Corum rode from Caer Mahlod, across the gentle hills, into the deep, cool forest, going east to Caer Llud, listening to the birds, the rush of the little shining streams over old rocks, the whisper of the oaks and the elms.

Not once did Corum look back, not once did he feel a pang of regret, not once did he grieve or know fear or reluctance concerning his quest, for he knew that he fulfilled his destiny and that he represented a great ideal and he was, at that moment, content.

Such contentment was rare, thought Corum, for one destined to take part in the eternal struggle. Perhaps because he did not fight against his destiny this time, because he accepted his duty, he was rewarded with this peculiar peace of mind. He began to wonder if he would find peace only by accepting his fate. It would be a strange paradox – tranquillity attained in strife.

By the evening the sky had begun to grow grey, and heavy clouds could be seen in the horizon towards the east.

CHAPTER FOUR

A World Full of Death

Shivering, Corum pulled the heavy fur cloak around his shoulders and drew the hood over his helmeted head. Then he drove his fleshly hand deep into the fur-lined gauntlet he held ready, then he covered his silver hand with the other gauntlet. He stamped out the remains of his fire and looked this way and that across the landscape, his breath billowing white in the air. The sky was a hard, flat blue and it was sunless, for it was not yet true dawn. The land was almost featureless and the ground was dead, black, with a coating of pale frost. Here and there a stark, leafless tree stood out. In the distance was a line of snow-topped hills, as black as the ground. Corum sniffed the wind.

It was a dead wind.

The only scent on the wind was the scent of the killing frost. This part of the land was so desolate that it was evident the Cold Folk had spent some time here. Perhaps this was where they had camped before moving against Caer Mahlod in their war with that city.

Now Corum heard the sound he had thought he had heard before. This sound had caused him to spring up from his fire and disperse the smoke. The sound of hoofbeats. He looked to the south-east. There was a place where the ground rose and obscured his view. It was from beyond the rise that the hoofbeats were coming.

And now Corum heard another sound.

The faint baying of hounds.

The only hounds he might expect to hear in these parts were the devil hounds of Kerenos.

He ran to his red horse, who was showing signs of

nervousness, and mounted himself in his saddle, shaking his lance free from its scabbard and laying it across his pommel. He leaned forward and patted his horse's neck to calm the beast. He turned the horse towards the rise, ready to meet the danger.

A single rider appeared first, just as the sun began to rise behind him. The sun's rays caught the rider's armour and it flashed deep red. There was a naked sword in the rider's hand and the sword also reflected the rays of the sun so that for a second Corum could barely see. Then the armour turned to a fierce, burning blue, and Corum guessed the identity of the horseman.

The baying of those frightful hounds became louder, but still they had not appeared.

Corum urged his horse towards the rise.

Suddenly there was silence.

The voices of the hounds were stilled; the rider sat unmoving on his horse, but his armour changed colour again, from blue to greenish yellow.

Corum listened to the sound of his own breathing, the steady beating of his own horse's hooves upon hard, rimed earth. He began to ascend the rise, approaching the rider, his lance ready.

And then the rider spoke from within the featureless helm enclosing his head.

'Ha! I guessed so. It is you, Corum.'

'Good morning, Gaynor. Will you joust?'

Prince Gaynor the Damned threw back his head and laughed a bleak, hollow laugh and his armour changed from yellow to blazing black and he swept his sword into its scabbard.

'You know me, Corum. I am become wary. I do not have it in mind to make another journey into Limbo just yet. Here, at least, I have matters to occupy my time. There – well, there is nothing at all there.'

'In Limbo?'

'Aye. In Limbo.'

'Join a noble cause, then. Fight for my cause. Thus you could win redemption.'

'Redemption? Oh, Corum, you are simple-minded indeed. Who would redeem me?'

'No-one.'

'Then why do you speak of redemption?'

'You can redeem yourself. That is what I meant. I do not mean that you should placate the Lords of Law – if they still exist anywhere – or that you should bow to any authority save your own pride. I mean that there is within you, Prince Gaynor the Damned, something which could save you from the hopelessness now consuming you. You know those whom you serve to be degenerate, destructive, lacking in greatness of spirit. Yet wilfully you follow them, fulfil their ends for them, perpetrate great crimes and create monstrous miseries, spread evil, carry death – you know what you do and you know, too, that for you such crimes bring further agony of spirit.'

The armour changed from black to angry crimson. Prince Gaynor's faceless helm turned to stare directly into the rising sun. His horse stirred and he tightened his grip upon his reins.

'Join my cause, Prince Gaynor. I know that you respect it.'

'Law has rejected me,' said Prince Gaynor the Damned in a hard, weary voice. 'All that I once followed, all that I once respected, all that I once admired and sought to emulate – all have rejected Gaynor. It is too late, you see, Prince Corum.'

'It is not too late,' said Corum urgently, 'and you forget, Gaynor, that I alone have looked upon that face you hide behind your helm. I have seen all your guises, all your dreams, all your secret desires, Gaynor.'

'Aye,' said Prince Gaynor the Damned quietly, 'and that is why you must perish, Corum. That is why I cannot bear to know that you are alive.'

'Then fight,' said Corum with a sigh. 'Fight now.'

'I would not dare do that, not now that you have beaten me in combat once. I would not have you look upon all my faces again, Corum. No, you must die by other means than in single combat. The Hounds . . .'

Then Corum, guessing what was in Gaynor's mind, sent his horse into a sudden gallop, lance aimed directly at Gaynor's featureless helm, and rushed upon his ancient enemy.

But Gaynor laughed and wheeled his steed, thundering down the hill so that the white frost rose in glistening shards on all sides of him and the ground seemed to crack as he crossed it.

And Gaynor rode straight down the hill to where half a score of pale hounds squatted, their red tongues lolling, their yellow eyes glaring, their yellow fangs dripping yellow saliva, their long, feathery tails curled along their shaggy backs. And all their bodies were a glowing, leprous white, save for the tips of their ears which were the colour of fresh-drawn blood. Some, the largest, were the size of small ponies.

And now they were getting to their feet as Gaynor rode towards them. And now they were panting and grinning as Gaynor yelled to them.

Corum spurred his horse to greater efforts, hoping to plunge through the dogs and reach Gaynor before he escaped. He struck the pack with an impact which bowled several of the hounds over and his lance skewered one directly through the skull. And both these things combined to slow Corum down as he tried to tug the lance from the dog he had slain. His horse reared, screaming, and lashed at the dogs with its iron-shod hooves.

Corum abandoned his grip upon his lance and swung his double-bladed war-axe from his back, whirling it as he struck, first to his left and then to his right, cleaving the head from one dog and cracking the spine of another. But the dogs kept up their chill baying and this mixed with the horrible howling of the hound whose spine had been snapped, and yellow fangs clashed on Corum's byrnie and ripped at his great fur cloak and tried to drag the whistling war-axe from his hands. And Corum kicked his right foot free from his stirrup and drove his heel into the snout of one hound while with his axe he smashed down a dog which had got a grip upon his horse's harness. But the horse was tiring fast and Corum realized that it could hold out against the hounds only a few moments more before it collapsed beneath him with its throat torn, and there were still some six dogs to contend with.

Five. Corum sliced the rear legs from a dog which sought to spring at him and misjudged its distance. The thing flopped to the ground near the one which still died from a broken spine. The dog with the broken spine dragged itself to where its comrade writhed and sank its fangs into the red, exposed flanks, tearing hungrily at the flesh, taking a final meal before it expired.

Then Corum heard a yell and got an impression of something black moving to the right of him. Gaynor's men, no doubt, coming in to finish him. He tried a back-swipe with the axe, but missed.

The Hounds of Kerenos were regrouping, readying themselves for a more organized attack upon him. Corum knew he could not fight both the hounds and the new-comers, whoever they were. He looked for a gap in the ranks of the dogs through which he might gallop. But his horse stood panting now, its legs trembling, and he knew he could get nothing more from the beast. He transferred his axe to his silver hand and drew his sword. Then he began to jog towards the hounds, preferring to die attacking them rather than fleeing from them.

And again something black swept past him. A fast-moving pony with a rider crouched low upon its back, a curved sword in each hand, slicing into the white backs so that they yelped in surprise and scattered, whereupon Corum selected one and rode after it, bearing down on it. It turned, going for his horse's throat, but Corum stabbed and took the creature in the chest. Its long-clawed paws scrabbled at the body of the skittering horse for a moment before it fell to the ground.

And now only three hounds lived. Three hounds running after the black speck of a rider who could still be seen in the distance, his armour changing colour even as he rode.

Then Corum dismounted from his horse and drew a

deep breath and then regretted it for the stink of the hounds was worse in death than in life. He looked around him at the ruin of white fur and red vitals, at the gore which soaked the ground, and then he turned to look at the ally who had appeared to save his life.

His ally was still mounted. His ally grinned and sheathed first one curved sword and then another. He adjusted a broad-brimmed hat upon his long hair. He took a bag which hung from his saddle pommel and he opened it. From the bag crept a small black and white cat which was unusual in that it had a pair of wings neatly folded along its back.

Corum's ally grinned even more widely as he noted Corum's astonishment.

'This situation is not new to me, at least,' said Jhary-a-Conel, the self-styled Companion to Heroes. 'I am often in time to save some champion's life. It is my fate, just as it is his fate to struggle forever in the great wars of history. I sought you at Caer Mahlod, having some intimation that I would be useful but you had already gone. I followed as swiftly as I could, sensing that your life was in peril.'

Jhary-a-Conel swept off his wide-brimmed hat and bowed in his saddle. 'Greetings, Prince Corum.'

Corum was still panting from his fight. He could not speak. But he managed to grin back at his old friend.

'Do you quest with me, Jhary?' he said at last. 'Do you come with me to Caer Llud?'

'If the fates so will it. Aye. How fare you, Corum, in this world?'

'Better than I thought. And better still now that you are here, Jhary.'

'You know I might not be enabled to stay here?'

'I understood as much from our last conversation. And you? Have you had adventures on other planes since we last met?'

'One or two. One or two. I came to be involved in the strangest adventures concerning the nature of time. You'll recall the Runestaff, which came to our aid during the episode concerning the tower of Voilodion Ghagnasdiak?

Well, my adventures touched on the world most influenced by that peculiar stick. A manifestation of that eternal hero, of whom you, yourself, are a manifestation, he called himself Hawkmoon. If you think your tragedy is great, you would think it nothing when you heard of the tragedy of Hawkmoon . . .'

And Jhary told Corum the story of his adventures with Hawkmoon, who had gained a friend, lost a bride and two children, found himself inhabiting another's body, and spent what Corum considered a rather confusing time in a world which was not his own.

As Jhary talked, the two old friends rode from the scene of the slaughter, following in the tracks of Prince Gaynor the Damned who appeared to be riding hastily for Caer Llud.

And Caer Llud was still many, many days distant.

CHAPTER FIVE

The Lands Where the
Fhoi Myore Rule

'Aye,' said Jhary-a-Conel as he slapped gloved hands together over a fire which seemed reluctant to burn. 'The Fhoi Myore are fitting cousins to the Lords of Entropy, for they seem to seek the same ends. For all I know the Fhoi Myore are what those lords have become. There are so many fluctuations, these days. Caused partially, I should say, by Baron Kalan's foolish manipulation of time, partially as a result of the Million Spheres beginning to slide out of conjunction – though that will take a little while before it is fully accomplished. In the meantime we live in times which are uncertain in more ways than one. The fate of sentient life itself sometimes seems to me to be at stake. Yet do I fear? No, I think not. I place no special value upon sentience. I'd as cheerfully become a tree!'

'Who's to say they are not sentient?' Corum smiled as he set a pan upon the fire and began to lay strips of meat in the slowly boiling water.

'Well, then, a block of marble.'

'Again, we do not know . . .' Corum began, but Jhary cut him short with a snort of impatience.

'I'll not play such children's games!'

'You misunderstand me. You have touched on a subject I have been considering only lately, you see. I, too, am beginning to realize that there is no special value to being, as it were, able to think. Indeed, one can see many disadvantages. The whole condition of mortals is created by their ability to analyze the universe and their inability to understand it.'

'Some do not care,' said Jhary. 'I, for one, am content to

drift – to let whatever happens happen without bothering to ask why it happens.'

'Indeed, I agree that that is an admirable feeling. But we are not all endowed with such feelings by nature. Some must cultivate those feelings. Others may never cultivate them and they lead unhappy lives as a result. Yet does it matter if our lives are happy or unhappy? Should we place more value on joy than on sorrow? Is it not possible to see both as possessing the same value?'

'All I know,' said Jhary practically, 'is that most of us consider it better to be happy . . .'

'Yet we all achieve that happiness in a variety of ways. Some by cultivating carelessness, some by caring. Some by service to themselves and some by service to others. Currently I find pleasure in serving others. The whole question of morality . . .'

'Is as nothing when one's stomach rumbles,' said Jhary, peering into the pan. 'Is that meat done, do you think, Corum?'

Corum laughed. 'I think I am becoming a bore,' he said.

'It's nothing.' Jhary fished pieces of meat from the pan and dropped them into his bowl. He set one piece aside to cool for the cat which purred as it sat on his shoulder and rubbed its head against Jhary's. 'You have found a religion, that is all. What else can you expect in a Mabden dream?'

They rode beside a frozen river, along a track now completely hidden by snow, climbing higher and higher into the hills. They rode past a house whose stone walls had been cracked open as if by the blow of a gigantic hammer and it was only when they were close did they see the white skulls peering from the windows and the white hands gesturing in attitudes of terror. The bones shimmered in the pale sunshine.

'Frozen,' said Jhary. 'And cold it was which doubtless cracked the stones.'

'Balahr's work,' said Corum. 'He of the single, deadly eye. I know him. I have fought him.'

And they went past the house and over the hill and they found a town where the frozen corpses lay strewn about and these still had flesh on them and had plainly died before the cold had frozen them. And each male had been horribly desecrated.

'The work of Goim,' said Corum. 'The only female of the Fhoi Myore still surviving. She has a taste for certain morsels of mortal flesh.'

'We are at the borders of the lands where the Fhoi Myore hold full sway,' said Jhary-a-Conel, pointing ahead to where grey cloud boiled. 'Shall we suffer so? Shall Balahr or Goim find us?'

'It is possible,' Corum told him.

Jhary grinned. 'You are most sober, old friend. Well, console yourself that if they do these things to us we shall remain in a position of moral superiority.'

Corum grinned back.

'It does console me,' he said.

And they led their horses out of the town and down a steep snow-filled track, passing a cart full of the frozen bodies of children doubtless sent to flee the place before the Fhoi Myore descended.

And they entered a valley where the bodies of a whole army of warriors had been eaten by dogs and here they found fresh tracks – the tracks of a single rider and three large hounds.

'Gaynor also goes this way,' said Corum, 'a mere few hours ahead of us. Why does he dally now?'

'Perhaps he watches us. Perhaps he tries to guess the purpose of our quest,' Jhary suggested. 'With such information he can return to his masters and be welcomed.'

'If the Fhoi Myore welcome anyone. They do not recruit help, as such. There are some – the resurrected dead among them – who have no choice but to follow them and do their work for them, for they are welcome nowhere else.'

'How do the Fhoi Myore resurrect the dead?'

'There is one of the six called Rhannon, I believe. Rhannon breathes cold breath into the mouths of the dead and brings them to life. He kisses the living and introduces them to death. That is the legend. But few know much of the Fhoi Myore. Even the Fhoi Myore hardly know what they do or why they are upon this plane. Once they were driven away by the Sidhi who came from another plane themselves to help the people of Lwym-an-Esh. But with the decline of the Sidhi, the Fhoi Myore strength grew unchecked until they were able to return to the land and begin their conquerings. Their diseases must kill them soon. Few, I understand, will live for more than another thousand years. Then, when the Fhoi Myore die, the whole of this world shall be dead.'

'It would seem,' said Jhary-a-Conel, 'that we could do with a few Sidhi allies.'

'The only one I know is called Goffanon and he is weary of fighting. He accepts that the world is doomed and that nothing he can do will avert that doom.'

'He could be right,' said Jhary feelingly, looking about him.

And then Corum lifted his head, peering this way and that, his face troubled.

Jhary was surprised. 'What is it?'

'Do you not hear it?' Corum looked up into the hills from which they had come.

He could hear it quite plainly now – melancholy, wild, somehow mocking. The strains of a harp.

'Who would play music here?' Jhary murmured. 'Save a dirge?' He listened again. 'And it sounds as if it could be a dirge.'

'Aye,' said Corum grimly. 'A dirge for me. I have heard the harp more than once since I came to this realm, Jhary. And I have been told to fear a harp.'

'It is beautiful, however,' said Jhary.

'I have been told to fear beauty, also,' said Corum. He still could not find the source of the music. He realized that he was trembling and he controlled himself, urging his horse onward. 'I have been told that I shall be slain,' he continued, 'by a brother.'

And Jhary, asking questions, could get Corum to speak

no further on this subject. They rode for some miles in silence until they came out of the valley and looked upon a wide plain.

'The Plain of Craig Dôn,' said Corum. 'It is all it can be. This is thought a holy place by the Mabden. We are more than halfway to Caer Llud now, I think.'

'And well into the Lands of the Fhoi Myore,' added Jhary-a-Conel.

Even as they watched a blizzard swept suddenly over the great plain from east to west and was gone again, leaving fresh snow sparkling as a woman might lay a fresh sheet upon a bed.

'We'll leave good tracks in that,' said Jhary.

Corum was marvelling at the strange sight as the fast-moving blizzard moved away into the distance. Overhead the sun was fully obscured by clouds. The clouds were agitated. They swirled restlessly all the time, changing shape swiftly.

'I am reminded somewhat of the Realm of Chaos,' Jhary told him. 'And I have been told that such frozen landscapes as these are the ultimate landscapes of worlds where the Lords of Entropy are triumphant. This is what their wasteful variety achieves. But I speak of other worlds and other heroes – indeed, of other dreams. Shall we risk the dangers of detection upon that plain, or shall we circle the plain and hope that we are not seen?'

'We cross the Plain of Craig Dôn,' said Corum firmly. 'And if we are stopped and have time to speak, we shall say that we have come to offer our services to the Fhoi Myore, knowing that the Mabden cause is hopeless.'

'There seem few here of any intelligence, as I understand by intelligence,' said Jhary. 'Will they give us that time to converse, do you think?'

'We must hope that there are more like Gaynor.'

'An odd thing to hope!' exclaimed Jhary. He smiled at his cat, but it merely purred without apparently understanding its master's joke.

The wind howled then and Jhary bowed to it, pretending to assume that it was showing its appreciation.

Corum clutched his fur robe to him. Though it had been ripped in several places by the Hounds of Kerenos, it was still serviceable.

'Come,' he said. 'Let us cross the Plain of Craig Dôn.'

The snow was in constant movement beneath their horses' feet, eddying like an agitated river over rocks. The wind blew it this way and that. The wind made the snow-drifts heave and fall and reform. The wind drove into their bones so that sometimes they felt they would rather have cold steel in them than that wind. The wind sighed like a huntsman satisfied by his kill. The wind moaned like a satiated lover. The wind growled like a hungry beast. The wind shouted like a conqueror and it hissed like a striking snake. It blew fresh snow from the sky. Their shoulders would be heaped with this snow until it was blown clear again and a new deposit laid in its place. The wind blew roads through the snow for them and then sealed them up again. The wind blew from the east and from the north and from the west and the south. Sometimes it seemed that the wind blew from all directions at once, seeking to crush them as they pressed on across the Plain of Craig Dôn. The wind built castles and it tore them down. The wind whispered promises and roared threats. The wind toyed with them.

Then, through the swirl and the confusion, Corum saw dark shapes ahead. At first he thought them warriors and drew his sword, dismounting, for his horse would be of no help to him in this depth of snow. He sank to his knees in the stuff. Jhary remained on horseback, however.

'Fear not,' he said to Corum. 'They are not men. They are stones. They are the stones of Craig Dôn.'

And Corum realized that he had misjudged the distance, that the objects were still some good distance ahead.

'This is the holy place of the Mabden,' said Jhary.

'This is where they elect their High Kings and hold their important ceremonies,' said Corum.

'It is where they once did these things,' Jhary corrected him.

The wind appeared to drop as they approached the great stones. Even the wind seemed to show reverence for this great, old place. There were seven circles in all, each circle containing another until the centre was reached and the inner circle contained a large stone altar. Looking out from the centre and down the hill, Corum fancied the stone circles represented ripples upon a pool, planes of reality, representations of a geometry not wholly connected with earthly geometry.

'It is a holy place,' he murmured. 'It is.'

'Certainly it touches upon something I cannot explain,' Jhary agreed. 'Does it not remind you in some ways of Tanelorn?'

'Tanelorn? Perhaps. Is this their Tanelorn?'

'Geographically speaking, I think it might be. Tanelorn is not always a city. Sometimes it is a thing. Sometimes it is merely an idea. And this – this is the representation of an idea.'

'So primitive in its materials and the working of those materials,' said Corum. 'Yet so subtle in its conception. What minds created Craig Dôn, I wonder?'

'Mabden minds. Those you serve. This, too, is why they cannot bring themselves to unite against the Fhoi Myore. This was the centre of their world. It reminded them of their faith and their dignity. Now that they can no longer come upon their two great yearly visits to Craig Dôn their souls starve and, starving, rob them of their strength of will.'

'We must find a means of giving Craig Dôn back to them, then,' said Corum firmly.

'But first give them their High King, he who possesses all the wisdom of those who spend whole weeks fasting and meditating at Craig Dôn's altar.' Jhary leaned against one of the great stone pillars. 'Or so they say,' he added, as if embarrassed by having been caught uttering an approving word for the place. 'Not that it is my affair,' he went on. 'I mean, if . . .'

'Look who comes,' said Corum. 'And he appears to come alone.'

It was Gaynor. He had appeared at the outer circle of stones and seemed so small at that distance that he could only be identified by his armour which, as usual, constantly changed colour. He was not on horseback. He came walking through what was almost a tunnel made up of seven great arches and as he came in earshot he said:

'Some would have it that this temple, this Craig Dôn, is a representation of the Million Spheres, of the various planes of existence. But I do not think the local people sophisticated enough to understand such matters, do you?'

'Sophistication is not always measured by an ability to forge good steel or build large cities, Prince Gaynor,' said Corum.

'Indeed no. I am sure that you are right. I have known worlds where the complexity of the natives' thought was equalled only by the squalor of their living conditions.' The faceless helm turned to look up at the boiling sky. 'More snow coming, I'd say. What do you think?'

'Have you been here long, Prince Gaynor?' said Corum, his hand upon the hilt of his sword.

'On the contrary, you seem to have preceded me. I have just arrived.'

'But you knew we should be here?'

'I guessed this was your destination.'

Corum tried to hide his interest. Gaynor was wrong. This was not his destination. But did Gaynor know a secret concerning Craig Dôn? A secret which might be to the advantage of the Mabden.

'This place seems free of wind,' he said. 'At least, it is freer than the plain itself. And no signs of the Fhoi Myore in Craig Dôn itself.'

'Of course not. That is why you sought its sanctuary. You hope to understand why the Fhoi Myore fear it. You think you can find a means of defeating them here.' Gaynor laughed. 'I knew that was your quest.'

Corum restrained a secret smile. Without realizing it Gaynor had betrayed his masters.

'You are clever, Prince Gaynor.'

Gaynor had come to a stop under an arch in the third circle. He moved no closer.

In the distance Corum heard the baying of the Hounds of Kerenos. He smiled openly now.

'Your dogs fear this place, too?'

'Aye – they are Fhoi Myore dogs, come with them from Limbo. Their instincts warn them against Craig Dôn. Only Sidhi and mortals – even mortals such as I – can come here. And I fear the place, too, though I've little reason for my fears. The vortex cannot swallow Gaynor the Damned.'

Corum restrained his impulse to ask Prince Gaynor further questions. He must not let his old enemy know that he had not, until recently, any hint of Craig Dôn's properties.

'Yet you, too, are from Limbo,' Corum reminded Gaynor. 'I cannot understand why the – the vortex does not claim you.'

'Limbo is not my natural home. I was banished there – banished by you, Corum. Only those who came originally from Limbo need fear Craig Dôn. But what you think to gain from coming here, I know not. As naïve as ever, Corum, you doubtless hoped that the Fhoi Myore knew nothing of Craig Dôn and would follow you here. Well, my friend, I must tell you that my masters, while apparently stupid in some matters, have a proper regard for this place. They would not come an inch within the outer circle. Your journey has been for nothing.' Gaynor laughed his bleak laugh. 'Only once were your Sidhi ancestors successful in luring their foes to this place. Only once did the Fhoi Myore warriors find themselves engulfed and drawn back to Limbo. And that was many centuries ago. Beastlike, the remaining Fhoi Myore keep a safe distance from Craig Dôn, barely realizing why they do so.'

'They would not rather return to their own realm?'

'They do not understand that that is where they would go. And it is scarcely in the interest of those, like me, who *do* know, to try to communicate this knowledge to them. I have no wish to be abandoned here without their protecting power!'

'So,' said Corum as if to himself, 'my journey has been fruitless.'

'Aye. Moreover I think it unlikely you'll return to Caer Mahlod alive. When I go back to Caer Llud I shall tell them I have seen their Sidhi foe. Then all the hounds will come. All the hounds, Corum. I suggest you remain here, where you are safe.' Gaynor laughed again. 'Stay in this sanctuary. There is nowhere else in this land that you can escape the Fhoi Myore and the Hounds of Kerenos.'

'But,' replied Corum, pretending to miss Gaynor's meaning, 'we have food only for a while. We should starve here, Gaynor.'

'Possibly,' said Gaynor with evident relish. 'On the other hand I could come from time to time with food – when it pleased me. You could live for years, Corum. You could experience something of what I felt while I enjoyed my banishment in Limbo.'

'So that is what you hope for. That is why you did not harry us on our way here!' Jhary-a-Conel began to descend the hill, drawing one of his curved blades.

'No!' Corum cried out to his friend. 'You cannot harm him, Jhary, but he can slay you!'

'It will be pleasant,' Gaynor said, retreating slowly as Jhary came to a reluctant stop. 'It will be pleasant to see you squabbling for the scraps I bring. It will be pleasant to see your friendship die as hunger grows. Perhaps I'll bring you a hound's corpse – one that you slew, Jhary-a-Conel, eh? Would that be tasty? Or perhaps you will begin to find human flesh wholesome. Which one of you will first begin to desire to slay and eat the other?'

'This is an ignoble vengeance that you take, Gaynor,' said Corum.

'It was an ignoble fate you sent me to, Corum. Besides, I do not claim nobility of spirit. That is your province, is it not?'

Gaynor turned and his step was almost light as he walked away from them.

'I will leave the dogs,' he said. 'I am sure you'll appreciate their company.'

Corum watched Gaynor until he had reached the outer circle and climbed onto his horse. The wind made a low sound in the distance, a melancholy murmuring, as if it wished to enter the seven stone rings but could not.

'So,' said Corum musingly, 'we have gained something from the encounter. Craig Dôn is more than a holy place. It is a place of great power – an opening between the Fifteen Realms, perhaps – or even more. We were right to be reminded of Tanelorn, Jhary-a-Conel. But how is the gateway formed? What ritual opens it? Perhaps the High King will know.'

'Aye,' said Jhary, 'we have, as you say, gained something, Corum. But we have lost something, too. How are we to reach the High King now? Listen.'

And Corum listened, and he heard the ferocious baying of the frightful Hounds of Kerenos as they ranged about the outer stone circle. If they rode from the sanctuary of Craig Dôn, the dogs would instantly be upon them.

Corum frowned and he shivered as he drew his fur cloak about him. He squatted by the altar while Jhary-a-Conel paced back and forth and the horses snorted nervously as they pricked their ears and heard the hounds. It seemed to become colder as the evening settled upon the place of the seven stone circles. Craig Dôn's properties might protect them from the Fhoi Myore, but they could not protect them from the marrow-chilling cold, neither were there materials here from which they could build a fire.

Night came down. The noise of the wind increased, but it could not drown the persistent and terrible howling of the Hounds of Kerenos.

BOOK TWO

---

*In which Prince Corum makes use
of one Treasure only to discover
his lack of two others . . .*

CHAPTER ONE

A Sad City in the Mist

They stood between two of the great stone pillars of Craig Dôn and faced the prowling devil dogs of the Fhoi Myore. The Hounds of Kerenos were both fierce and wary; they snapped, they snarled, but they gave the stone circle wide clearance. Others of the dogs sat some distance off, barely visible against the wind-swirled snow which ruffled their shaggy coats. From somewhere Gaynor had added five more hounds.

Corum narrowed his eyes and fixed them on the nearest dog, then he drew back the arm which held the long and heavy lance, shifted his feet a little to get the best balance, and hurled the weapon with all the force of his fear, his anger and his desperation.

The lance flew true, driving deep into the canine body, knocking the hound from its feet.

'Now!' called Corum; and Jhary-a-Conel, who held the end of the rope, began to tug. Corum pulled too.

The line had been securely attached to the lance and the lance was buried deep in the dog's body so that this, too, was dragged back into the sanctuary of the stone circle. The hound still lived and when it realized what was happening to it it began to make feeble efforts to get free. It whined, it tried to snap at the shaft of the lance, but then it had been pulled under the arch and it became suddenly supine as if it accepted its doom. It died.

Corum and Jhary-a-Conel were jubilant. Putting his booted foot on the carcass Corum jerked his lance free and immediately ran back to the arch, selecting a fresh target, hurling his weapon out with the line flicking behind it, striking a second hound in the throat and instantly dragging the lance back. This time the lance came free from the corpse and bounced back through the snow to them. Now there were six beasts left. But they had become more wary. Not for the first time, Corum wished that he had brought his bone bow and his arrows upon this quest.

A hound came forward and sniffed at the corpse of its fellow. It nuzzled the throat from where the fresh blood poured. It began to lap the blood with its long, red tongue.

And a third hound paid dearly for its meal as the lance sprang out again from between the tall columns and plunged into its left flank. The hound yelled, whirled, tried to get free, fell writhing into the blood-flecked snow, rose again and wrenched itself away, leaving a large part of its flank in the head of the spear. It ran in circles for a while as its life-blood gushed from it and then, about a hundred yards from the corpse it had only recently been feeding from, it flopped down.

Feeling that they were at a safe distance from the deadly lance, its brother hounds moved in and began to feast of its still living flesh.

'It is our one great advantage,' said Corum as he and Jhary-a-Conel mounted their horses, 'that the Hounds of Kerenos possess no moral sense concerning the eating of their fellows! It is their weakness, I think.'

Then, while the hounds slavered around their feast, Corum and Jhary-a-Conel rode back through the seven circles, past the carved stone altar at the centre of the first circle, out again through the circles until they were on the far side from the hounds.

The hounds had not yet guessed Corum's plan. There were a few minutes in hand.

Digging their heels deep into the flanks of their horses, they galloped as fast as they could away from Craig Dôn, heading not for Caer Mahlod (as Gaynor would think they did) but for their original destination of Caer Llud. With any luck the wind would obscure their tracks and spread their scent in all directions and they would have time to reach Caer Llud and find Amergin the Archdruid before Gaynor or the Fhoi Myore had any hint of their plan.

Gaynor had spoken the truth when he had told them that they could never reach Caer Mahlod with all the Hounds of Kerenos hunting for them, but when Gaynor found them gone it was almost certain that for a while he would waste time riding in the wrong direction while his dogs cast for their scent. But Gaynor's jaundiced view of mortal character had worked this time to his disadvantage. He had reckoned without the quick thinking of Corum and Jhary-a-Conel, without their determination or their willingness to risk their lives for a cause. He had spent too long in the company of the weak, the greedy and the decadent. Doubtless he preferred such company, since he shone in it.

As he rode, Corum considered what he had learned from Gaynor the Damned. Did Craig Dôn still possess the properties Gaynor had described or had they only worked for the Sidhi? Was Craig Dôn now only a shell, avoided by the Fhoi Myore out of superstition rather than knowing respect for its powers? He hoped that there would come a time when he could discover the truth for himself. If Craig Dôn was still truly a place of power there might be a way found to make use of it again.

But now he must forget Craig Dôn as the pillars grew to black shadows in the distance and then were obscured entirely by the swirling snow. Now he must think ahead, of Caer Llud and Amergin under a glamour in his tower by the river, guarded both by men and things which were not men.

They were cold and they were hungry. The coats of their horses were rimed and their own cloaks sparkled with frost. Their faces were numbed by the cold wind and their bodies ached whenever they moved.

But they had found Caer Llud. They drew rein upon a hill and saw a wide, frozen river. On both banks of the river and connected by well-constructed wooden bridges was the City of the High King, pale granite coated with snow, some of the buildings rising several storeys. For this world it was a large city, perhaps the largest, and must once have contained a population of twenty or thirty thousand.

But now the city had the appearance of having been abandoned, for all that shapes could be seen moving through the mist which hung in its streets.

The mist was everywhere. Thinner in some places, it clung to Caer Llud like a threadbare shroud. Corum recognized the mist. It was Fhoi Myore mist. It was the mist which followed the Cold Folk wherever they travelled in their huge, poorly made wicker war-carts. Corum feared that mist, as he feared the primitive, amoral power of the surviving Lords of Limbo. Even as they watched, he saw a movement where the mist was thickest, close to the river bank. He saw a suggestion of a dark, horned head, of a gigantic torso which faintly resembled the body of a toad, of the outlines of a huge, creaking cart drawn by something as oddly formed as the rider. Then it had gone.

From Corum's frost-cracked lips came a single word:
'Kerenos.'

'He who is master to the Hounds?' Jhary sniffed.

'And master of much more,' Corum added.

Jhary blew his nose upon a large linen rag he took from under his jerkin. 'I fear this weather affects my health badly,' he said. 'I would not mind coming to blows with some of those who created such weather!'

Corum shook his head. 'We are not strong enough, you and I. We must wait. We must be as careful to avoid conflict with the Fhoi Myore as Gaynor is in avoiding direct conflict with me.' He peered through the mist and the eddying snow. 'Caer Llud is not guarded. Plainly they fear no attack from the Mabden. Why should they? That is to our advantage.'

He looked at Jhary's face which was blue with cold. 'I think we'd both pass for living corpses if we entered Caer Llud now. If stopped, we shall announce that we are Fhoi Myore men. While it is impossible to reason either with the

Fhoi Myore or their slaves, because of their primitive mentalities, it also means that they are slow to recognize a deception. Come.' Corum urged his horse down the hill towards that sad city, that once great city of Caer Llud.

Leaving the relatively clean air for the mist of Caer Llud was like going from midsummer into midwinter. If Corum and Jhary-a-Conel had considered themselves cold, it was now as nothing to the totality of coldness in which they now found themselves. The mist seemed virtually sentient, eating into their flesh, their bones and their vitals so that they were hard-put not to cry out and reveal their ordinary humanity. For Gaynor the Damned, for the Ghoolegh, the living dead, for the Brothers of the Pines like Hew Argech whom Corum had once fought, such cold doubtless meant little. But for mortals of the conventional mould it meant a great deal. Corum, gasping, shuddering, wondered if they could hope to live through it. With set faces they rode on, avoiding the worst of the mist as best they could, seeking the great tower by the river where they hoped Amergin was still imprisoned.

They said nothing as they rode, fearing to reveal their identities, for it was impossible to know who or what lurked on either side of them in the mist. The movement of their horses became sluggish, plodding, as the dreadful mist affected them. At last Corum bent over and spoke close to Jhary's head, finding speech painful as he said:

'There is a house just to the left of us which seems empty. See. The door is open. Ride directly through.'

And he turned his own horse into the doorway and entered a narrow passage already occupied by an old woman and a girl child who were huddled together, frozen and dead. He dismounted and led his horse into a room off the passage.

The room appeared untouched by looters. A glaze of frost covered food on the table which had been set for some ten people. A few spears stood in a corner and there were shields and swords against the wall. The men of the house had gone to fight the Fhoi Myore and had not returned for the meal. The old woman and the girl had died beneath the influence of Balahr's frightful eye. Doubtless they would find the corpses of others – old or young – who had not joined the hopeless battle against the Fhoi Myore when they had first come to Caer Llud. Corum desperately wished to light a fire, to warm his aching bones, to drive the mist from his body, but he knew that this would be risking too much. The living dead did not need fires to warm them and neither did the People of the Pines.

As Jhary-a-Conel led his own horse into the room, drawing a shuddering winged black and white cat from within his jerkin, Corum whispered: 'There will be clothing upstairs, perhaps blankets. I will see.' The small black and white cat was already climbing back inside Jhary's jacket, mewling a complaint.

Corum cautiously climbed a wooden staircase and found himself on a narrow landing. As he had guessed there were others here – two very old men and three babies. The old men had died trying to give their body-heat to the children.

Corum entered a room and found a large cupboard full of blankets stiff with cold. But they were not frozen through. He dragged out as many as he could carry and took them back down the stairs. Jhary seized them gratefully and began to drape them around his shoulders.

Corum was unwrapping something from his waist. It was the nondescript mantle, the gift of King Fiachadh, the Sidhi cloak.

Their plan was already made. Jhary-a-Conel would wait here with the horses while Corum sought Amergin. Corum unfolded the mantle, wondering again as it hid his hands from his own sight. This was the first Jhary had seen of the cloak and he gasped as, huddling in a mound of blankets, he saw what it did.

Then Corum paused.

From the street outside there came sounds. Cautiously he went to the shuttered windows and peered through a crack. Through the clinging mist he saw shapes moving – many shapes. Some were on foot and some were mounted, but all were of the same greenish hue. And Corum recognized them – the strange Brothers to the Pines who had once been men but now had sap instead of blood in their veins and they drew their vitality not from meat and drink but from the earth itself. These were the Fhoi Myore's fiercest fighters, their most intelligent slaves. And the horses they rode were also of the same, strange green colour, kept alive by the same elements which kept the People of the Pines alive. And yet even these were doomed, thought Corum as he watched, when the Fhoi Myore poisoned all the earth so that even the hardy trees could no longer live. But by that time the Fhoi Myore would no longer need their green warriors.

These were the creatures of whom Corum was most wary, with the exception of Gaynor himself, for they still retained much of their former intellect. He motioned Jhary to complete silence and barely breathed as he watched the throng pass by.

It was a large army and it had prepared itself for an expedition. It was leaving Caer Llud, it seemed. Was it to make a further attack on Caer Mahlod, or did they march elsewhere?

And then, behind this army, swam a thicker mist and from out of the mist came strange grumblings and gruntings, peculiar noises which might have been speech. The mist thinned a fraction and Corum saw the outline of lumbering, malformed beasts and a wicker chariot. He had to peer upward to see the faint outline of the one who rode in the chariot. He saw reddish fur, saw an eight-fingered hand, all gnarled and covered in warts, clutching what appeared to be a monstrous hammer, but the shoulders and the head were completely obscured. Then the creaking battle-cart had gone past the window and silence came again to the street.

Corum wrapped the Sidhi cloak about his body. It seemed to have been made for a much larger man, for its folds completely engulfed him.

And then it seemed, to his astonishment, that he saw two rooms, as if his eyes were slightly out of focus. Yet the rooms were subtly different. One was the room of death in which Jhary sat huddled in his blankets and one was light, airy, full of sunshine.

And Corum understood, then, the properties of the Sidhi cloak. It had been long since he had been able to shift his body from one plane into another. Effectively this was what the mantle had done for him. Like Hy-Breasail, it was not completely of this plane; it moved him sideways, as it were, through the dimensions separating one plane from another.

'What has happened?' said Jhary-a-Conel peering in Corum's direction.

'Why? Have I vanished?'

Jhary shook his head. 'No,' he said, 'but you have become a little shadowy, as if the mist thickens around you.'

Corum frowned. 'So the cloak does not work, after all. I should have tested it before I left Caer Mahlod.'

Jhary-a-Conel looked thoughtful. 'Perhaps it will deceive Mabden eyes, Corum. You forget that I am used to travelling between the realms. But those who cannot see, who have no knowledge such as we possess, perhaps they will not see you.'

Corum made a bitter smile. 'Well,' he said, 'we must hope so, Jhary!'

He turned towards the door.

'Go warily, Corum,' said Jhary-a-Conel. 'Gaynor – the Fhoi Myore themselves – many are not of this world at all. Some may see you clearly. Others may gain just an impression of your outline. But there is much danger in what you plan.'

And Corum said nothing in reply but left the room and entered the street and began to move towards the tower by the river with a steady, dogged stride, as a man might go bravely to his inevitable death.

CHAPTER TWO

A High King Brought Low

He stood directly in Corum's path as Corum went through the open gateway and began to ascend the gently rising steps which led to the entrance of the tall granite tower. He was big, barrel-chested, clad in leather, and in each white hand he held a cutlass. His red eyes glared. His bloodless lips curved in something which could have been a smile or a snarl.

Corum had met his kind before. This was one of the Fhoi Myore's living dead vassals, called the Ghoolegh. Often they rode as huntsmen with the Hounds of Kerenos, for they were drawn from the ranks of those who had been foresters before the Fhoi Myore came.

This must be the test, thought Corum. He stood less than a foot from the red-eyed Ghoolegh and assumed a martial position, one hand on his sword.

But the Ghoolegh did not respond. He continued to stare through Corum and plainly could not see him.

In some relief, his faith in the Sidhi cloak restored, Corum passed around the Ghoolegh guard and continued until he reached the entrance to the tower itself.

Here stood two more Ghoolegh and they were as unaware of Corum's presence as their fellow. He was almost cheerful as he walked through and began to mount the curving stairway leading up into the heart of the tower. The tower was wide and roughly square in shape. The steps were old and worn and the walls on both sides were either painted or carved with pictures of exceptionally beautiful workmanship. As with most Mabden art, they depicted famous deeds, great heroes, love stories and the doings of gods and demigods, yet they had a purity of conception, a beauty, which showed none of the darker aspects of superstition and religiosity. The metaphorical content of the old stories was completely understood by these Mabden and appreciated for what it was.

Here and there were the remains of tapestries which had been torn from the walls. Frost-coated, mist-rotted as they were, it was possible to see that they had been of immeasurable value, worked in gold and silver thread as well as rich scarlets, yellows and blues. Corum mourned at the destruction the Fhoi Myore and their minions had wrought.

He reached the first storey of the tower and found himself on a wide stone-flagged landing, almost a room in itself, with benches lined along the walls and decorative shields set above them. And from one of the rooms off this landing he heard voices.

Confident now in the powers of his cloak he approached the half-open door and to his surprise felt warmth issuing from it. He was grateful for the warmth, but puzzled, too. Becoming more cautious, he peered round the door and was shocked.

Two figures sat beside a big fire which had been built in the stone hearth. Both were swathed in layers of thick, white fur. Both wore fur gauntlets. Both had no business being in Caer Llud at all. On the other side of the room food was being set out by a girl who had the same white flesh and red eyes of the Ghoolegh guards and was doubtless, like them, one of the living dead. It meant that the two by the fire were not in Caer Llud illicitly. They were obviously guests, with servants put at their disposal.

One of these guests of the Fhoi Myore was a tall, slender Mabden with jewelled rings on his gloved hands and a jewelled, golden collar at his throat. His long hair and his long beard were both grey, framing a handsome, old face. And worn by a thong passed over his head so that it rested upon his chest was a horn. It was a long horn and there were bands of silver and gold around it. Corum knew that every one of those bands represented a different forest beast. The Mabden was the one he had met near Moidel's Mount and with whom he had traded a cloak – a cloak in exchange for the horn which the Mabden had, apparently, recovered. It was the wizard Calatin, who planned secret plans which had nothing to do with loyalty either to his Mabden countrymen or their Fhoi Myore enemies – or so Corum had thought.

But still more shocking to Corum was the sight of the wizard's companion – the one who had sworn he would never involve himself in the affairs of the world. And this man must truly be a renegade, for it was the one who was self-called a dwarf yet was eight feet tall and at least four feet broad at the shoulder – who had the fine, sensitive features which marked him as a cousin to the Vadhagh, for all that much of those features were covered in black hair. There was a glimpse of an iron breastplate beneath his many furs, there were polished iron greaves with gold inlays on his legs and he wore an iron polished helmet of similar workmanship. Beside him stood his huge double-bladed war-axe, not unlike Corum's axe, but much larger. This was Goffanon, the Sidhi smith of Hy-Breasail, who had given Corum the spear Bryionak and the bag of spittle which Calatin had wanted. How could Goffanon possibly have allied himself with the Fhoi Myore, let alone the wizard Calatin? Goffanon had sworn that he would never again involve himself in the wars between mortals and the Gods of Limbo! Had he deceived Corum? Had he been in league with the Fhoi Myore and the wizard Calatin all along? Yet, if so, why had he given Corum the spear Bryionak which had led to the defeat of the Fhoi Myore at Caer Mahlod?

Now, as if he sensed Corum's presence, Goffanon slowly began to turn his head towards the door and Corum withdrew hastily, not sure if the Sidhi would be able to see him.

There was something strange about Goffanon's face, something dull and tragic, but Corum had not had enough time to study the expression closely enough to be able to analyse it.

With heavy heart, horrified by Goffanon's treachery (though not over-surprised by Calatin's decision to league himself with the Fhoi Myore), Corum tiptoed back to the landing, hearing Calatin say:

'We shall go with them tomorrow when they march.'

And he heard Goffanon reply in a deep, distant voice:

'Now begins in earnest the conquest of the West.'

So the Fhoi Myore did prepare for battle and almost certainly they marched against Caer Mahlod again. And this time they had a Sidhi as an ally and there were no Sidhi weapons to thwart their ambitions.

Corum moved with greater urgency up the next stairway and had gone halfway when he turned a bend and saw a lump squatting so that it filled the whole stair and afforded him no room through which he could pass undetected.

The lump did not see him, but it lifted its snout and sniffed. Its three eyes, of disparate size, had a puzzled look. Its pink, bristle-covered flesh quivered as it pushed itself into a sitting position on its five arms. Three of the arms were human, seeming to have belonged to a woman, a youth and an old man. One of the arms was simian, that of a gorilla, and one of the arms seemed to have been the property of some kind of large reptile. The legs which the lump now revealed were short and ended in a human foot, a cloven hoof and a doglike paw respectively. The lump was naked, apparently sexless, and it was unarmed. It stank of excrement and of sweat and of corrupting food. It wheezed as it altered its position.

As silently as possible, Corum drew his sword as the three lids closed over the three mismatched eyes as the lump, seeing nothing, resettled itself to sleep again.

As the eyes closed Corum struck.

He struck through the oval mouth, through the roof of the mouth, into the brain. He knew that he could strike only once effectively before the lump made a noise which would bring other guards.

The eyes opened and instantly one closed again in a kind of obscene wink.

The others stared at the blade of the sword in astonishment, for it seemed to protrude from the thin air. The simian hand came up to touch the blade but it never completed the gesture. The hand fell limply back. The remaining eyes closed and Corum was sheathing his sword and clambering over the fat, yielding flesh as fast as he could, praying that none should find the lump's corpse before he had discovered the whereabouts of the Archdruid Amergin.

There were two Ghoolegh guards, their cutlasses at attention across their chests, at the top of this particular stair, but it was plain that they had heard nothing.

Hurriedly Corum slipped past them and mounted the next flight and there, on the landing above him, he saw two huge hounds, the largest of all the Hounds of Kerenos he had ever seen.

And these hounds were sniffing the air. They could not see him, but they had caught his scent. Both were voicing soft, deep growls.

Acting as rapidly as he had acted when he had seen the lump, Corum ran through the gap between the dogs and had the satisfaction of seeing them snap at the air and almost close their fangs on each other's throats.

And here was a great archway filled by a door of beaten bronze on which had been raised motifs of beautiful complexity. King Fiachadh had described it. This was the door to Amergin's apartments. And hanging on a brass hook beside the door, behind the head of one gigantic Ghoolegh guard, was a single iron key. And this was the key to the beautiful bronze door.

Behind Corum the Hounds of Kerenos, ordered not to leave their position, were whining and sniffing at the flagstones near where they sat. The Ghoolegh guard's dull features became curious. He lurched forward.

'What is it, dogs? Do strangers come?'

Corum stepped behind the Ghoolegh and silently drew the key from its hook, inserting it into the lock, turning it, opening the door and closing it behind him. With the distraction of the dogs to occupy his slow brain, the

Ghoolegh might not notice the absence of the iron key.

Corum found himself in an apartment full of rich, dark hangings. He sniffed and was surprised to recognize the smell of new-cut grass. The apartment was warm, too, heated by a fire even larger than the one at which Calatin and Goffanon sat two floors below.

But where was Amergin?

Stealthily Corum crept from one dark room to another, his hand on his sword, expecting some new trap.

And then, at last, he saw something. At first he took it for an animal, for it was upon all fours and eating from a golden tray piled high with the strands of some vegetable.

The head turned but the eyes did not see Corum, still draped in his Sidhi mantle. Large, soft eyes stared at nothing and the jaws moved slowly as they chewed the vegetation. The body was clothed in sheepskin garments with the wool still on them. The wool was dirty and full of filthy scraps of thistle, briar and burrs as if torn from the body of a wild mountain sheep. Jacket, shirt and leggings were all of the same coarse stuff and there was even a hood of sheepskin drawn around the head, exposing only the face. The man looked ridiculous and pathetic and Corum knew that this was Amergin, High King of the Mabden, Archdruid of Craig Dôn, and that he was truly under a glamour.

It had been a handsome face, possibly an intelligent face, but now it was neither. The eyes stared unblinking into nothing, the jaws continued to chew at the grass.

Corum murmured: 'Amergin?'

And Amergin ceased his chewing. He opened his mouth and he uttered a single, frightened bleat.

He began to crawl towards the shadows where doubtless he thought he would find security.

Sadly, Corum drew his sword.

CHAPTER THREE

A Traitor Sleeps,
a Friend Awakes

Without hesitation Corum reversed his grip upon his sword and brought the round pommel down hard on the back of Amergin's neck, then he picked up the body, surprised by its lightness. The man was slowly starving to death on the diet of grass he had been fed. Corum had been told that there would be little chance of releasing Amergin from his enchantment until they were far away from Caer Llud. He would have to carry the Archdruid to safety.

Somehow he managed to drape his mantle over Amergin's body as well as his own, checking in a mirror that both he and Amergin were invisible. Looking once around the room he turned and walked back to the bronze door, his sword still in his hand, though also covered by his mantle.

Cautiously he turned the key and opened the door. The Ghoolegh was standing up, close to the hounds. Both the devil dogs remained nervous, suspicious, but were still seated, their heads coming almost to the Ghoolegh's shoulder. The red, stupid eyes of the guard peered first down the stair and then about the landing and Corum was sure that he had seen the door closing, but then he looked again down the stairs and Corum was able to replace the key on its hook.

But he moved hastily. The key clinked against the stone of the wall. The dogs pricked up their ears. They snarled. Standing at the top of the stairs the Ghoolegh began to turn. Corum rushed forward and kicked the Ghoolegh off-balance. The undead creature yelled and fell, tumbling head over heels down the granite steps. The dogs glared and one snapped at Corum, but the Vadhagh prince lunged forward with his sword and cut through the hound's jugular as cleanly as he had slain the lump.

Then he felt a blow on his back and staggered, taking two involuntary bounds down the stairs and only barely managing to keep his balance, burdened as he was by the unconscious High King, staggering round as the remaining hound leapt from the top of the stair, its red jaws extended, its glistening yellow fangs dripping saliva, its fur bristling, its forelegs extended, and Corum only had time to bring up his sword before those gigantic paws had struck his chest and he was driven back against the wall, glimpsing from the corner of his single eye two Ghoolegh guards running to discover the cause of the commotion.

But his sword point had found the hound's heart and the beast had been dead even as it struck Corum. He dragged himself from under it, keeping a firm hold on Amergin, tugging his sword from the hound's corpse and then rearranging the Sidhi mantle about his body.

The Ghoolegh had seen something and they hesitated. They looked at the corpse of the hound, they looked at each other, uncertain what to do. Corum drew back, permitting himself a relieved grin as the Ghoolegh brandished their cutlasses and began to ascend the steps, plainly believing that whoever had slain the hound was still above.

Down the next flight Corum ran, clambering over the undetected corpse of the lump, down the rest of the steps until, panting, he reached the landing.

But Calatin and Goffanon had heard the sounds of strife and they were coming out of their room. Calatin was first. He was shouting.

'What is it? Who attacks?' He stared straight through Corum.

Corum made to move forward.

Then Goffanon said in a thick, slurred voice which had more curiosity in it than anger:

'Corum! What do you in Caer Llud?'

Corum made to put a finger to his lips, hoping that

Goffanon still had some loyalties to his Vadhagh cousin. Certainly Goffanon's great axe was still held loosely in his hand. He did not seem prepared to do battle.

'Corum?' Calatin whirled from where he stood on the first step. 'Where?'

'There,' said Goffanon pointing.

Calatin understood swiftly. 'Invisible! He must be slain. Slay him! Slay him, Goffanon!'

'Very well.' Goffanon began to get a grip on the haft of his axe.

'Goffanon! Traitor!' yelled Corum, and put up his own sword, revealing his position to Calatin who took a dagger from his belt and began to move towards him.

Goffanon was moving slowly, as if drugged. Corum decided to deal with Calatin first. He whirled his sword round in a poorly considered stroke which yet found Calatin's head and downed him, but the wizard was only knocked senseless by the flat of the sword. Corum gave Goffanon all his concentration, wishing desperately that he was not hampered by the burden of Amergin across his shoulder.

'Corum?' Goffanon frowned. 'Must I kill you?'

'It's no wish of mine, traitor.'

Goffanon began to lower his axe. 'But what does Calatin wish?'

'He wishes nothing.' Corum believed that he understood a little now of Goffanon's position. Amergin was not the only occupant of the tower under a glamour. 'He wishes you to protect me. That is what he wants. He wishes that you come with me.'

'Very well,' said Goffanon simply. And he fell in beside Corum.

'Hurry.' Corum stooped to wrench something from Calatin's body. From above came the puzzled voices of the Ghoolegh, and the Ghoolegh whom Corum had pushed down the steps was beginning to slither forward, though almost every bone must have been broken. They were hard to slay, those who were already dead. 'Those beyond the tower must soon realize that something is afoot here.'

They began to descend the last stairway.

There was a noise below and round the bend came the remaining Ghoolegh while at the same time Corum heard their comrades rushing down the steps, having decided that their enemies must somehow have escaped them.

Two above and three below. The Ghoolegh hesitated seeing only Goffanon. Doubtless they had been told that Goffanon was not an enemy and this confused them further. As quickly as he could, Corum crept past those who had blocked the path below and, as they began to climb towards Goffanon he did the only thing he could do against the living dead, he cut at the tendons of their legs so that they flopped down, using their arms to continue to crawl towards Goffanon, their cutlasses still in their hands. Goffanon turned with his axe and chopped at the legs of the two remaining Ghoolegh, severing those limbs. No blood spouted as the guards collapsed.

Then they were through the door, running into the cold, poisoned mist, down the steps from the tower, through the gateway, into the freezing streets, Goffanon loping beside Corum, keeping pace with him, his brows still drawn together as if in tremendous concentration.

Into the house they went and Jhary-a-Conel was already mounted, swathed still in coarse blankets so that only his face peeped through, holding Corum's horse ready for him. Jhary was astonished to see the Sidhi smith.

'Are you Amergin?'

But Corum was tearing the mantle of invisibility from him, revealing the starved figure in old sheepskins who lay over his shoulder.

'This is Amergin,' he explained curtly. 'The other's a cousin of mine I thought a traitor.' Corum heaved the prone Archdruid over his saddle, speaking to Goffanon. 'Do you come with us, Sidhi? Or do you remain to serve the Fhoi Myore?'

'Serve the Fhoi Myore? A Sidhi would not do that! Goffanon serves nobody!' The speech was still thick, the eyes still dull.

Having no time to waste either upon analysing the cause of Goffanon's strange actions or conversing with the great smith to learn more, Corum said roughly:

'Then come with us from Caer Llud.'

'Aye,' said Goffanon musingly. 'I would prefer to leave Caer Llud.'

They rode through the chilling mist, avoiding the massing of warriors on the far side of the city. Perhaps it was this which had allowed them to enter the city and leave it without detection – the Fhoi Myore thought only of their wars upon the West and gathered all their forces, all their attention, together for this single venture.

Whatever the reason, they were soon able to leave the outskirts of Caer Llud and were riding up a snow-covered hill, with the Dwarf Goffanon running easily beside their horses, his axe upon his shoulder, his beard and hair streaming behind him, his huge breath billowing in the air.

'Gaynor will soon understand what has happened and be most angry,' Corum told Jhary-a-Conel. 'He will realize that he has made a fool of himself. We can expect pursuit soon and he will be most vicious if he finds us.'

Jhary peered out from under his many blankets, refusing to relinquish a morsel of warmth.

'We must make speed for Craig Dôn,' he said. 'There we will have time to consider what to do next.' He managed to grin. 'At least we now have something the Fhoi Myore wish to keep – we have Amergin.'

'Aye. They'll be reluctant to destroy us if it means destroying Amergin too. But we cannot rely on that.' Corum adjusted the body more securely across his saddle.

'From what I know of the Fhoi Myore, they'll not think oversubtly upon the matter,' agreed Jhary.

'Always our good luck and our bad luck both, the mentality of the Fhoi Myore!' Corum grinned back at his old friend. 'For all that there is much danger ahead of us, Jhary-a-Conel, I cannot but feel right well-satisfied with today's accomplishments. Not long since I knew I went to my death, my quest unfilled. Now should I die, at least I shall know that I was partially successful!'

'It will not give me much satisfaction, however,' said Jhary-a-Conel feelingly. And he looked over his shoulder to Caer Llud in the distance as if he already heard the baying of the Hounds of Kerenos.

They left the mist behind and the air became relatively warmer. Jhary began to strip the blankets from him and drop them behind in the snow as they galloped on. The horses needed no urging this time. They were as glad to be free of Caer Llud and its unnatural mist as were their riders.

It was four days before they heard the noise of the Hounds. And Craig Dôn was still some distance off.

CHAPTER FOUR

Of Enchantments and Omens

'Of the few things I fear,' said Goffanon, 'I fear those dogs most.'

Since they had left Caer Llud far behind them, his speech had become increasingly coherent, his mind sharper, though he had said little about his association with the wizard Calatin. 'There must be still thirty miles of hard country before Craig Dôn is reached.'

They had come to stop upon a hill, searching through the dancing snow for signs of the dogs which pursued them.

Corum was thoughtful. He looked at Amergin who had woken the night after they had fled Caer Llud and had since been bound to stop his straying. Occasionally the High King would utter a bleat, but it was impossible to divine what he wanted from them, unless it was to indicate his hunger, for he had eaten little since they had fled the city. He spent most of his time in sleep and even when he was awake he was passive, resigned.

Corum said to Goffanon:

'Why were in you Caer Llud? I remember you telling me you intended to spend the rest of your days in Hy-Breasail? Did Calatin come to the Enchanted Isle and offer you a bargain which attracted you?'

Goffanon snorted. 'Calatin? Come to Hy-Breasail? Of course not. And what bargain could he offer me that was better than that which you offered? No, I fear that you were the instrument of my alliance with the Mabden wizard.'

'I? How?'

'Remember how I scoffed at Calatin's superstitions? Remember how thoughtlessly I spat into that little bag you gave me? Well, Calatin had a good reason for wanting that spittle. He has more power than I guessed – and a power I barely understand. It was the dryness which first came upon me, you see. No matter how much I drank I still felt thirsty – terrible, painful thirst. My mouth was forever dry, Corum. I was dying of thirst, though I near drained the rivers and streams of my island, gulping down the water as fast as I could, yet never satisfying that thirst. I was horrified – and I was dying. Then came a vision – a vision sent by that man of power, Corum, by that Mabden. And the vision spoke to me and told me that Hy-Breasail was rejecting me as it rejected the Mabden, that I should die if I remained there – die of this frightful thirst.'

The dwarf shrugged his huge shoulders. 'Well, I debated this, but I was already mad with thirst. At last I set sail for the mainland, where Calatin greeted me. He gave me something to drink. That drink did satisfy my thirst. But it also robbed me of my senses and put me completely in the wizard's power. I became his slave. He can still reach out for me. He could still trap me again and make me do his bidding. While he has that charm he made from my spittle – the charm which brings on the thirst – he can also control my thoughts to a large extent – he can somehow occupy my mind and cause my body to perform certain actions. And while he occupies my mind, I am not responsible for what I do.'

'So by delivering that blow to Calatin's head, I was able to break his influence over you?'

'Yes. And by the time he recovered we were doubtless beyond the range of his magic-working.' Goffanon sighed. 'I had never thought a Mabden could command such mysterious gifts.'

'And that is how the horn came back in Calatin's keeping?'

'Aye. I gained nothing from my bargain with you, Corum.'

Corum smiled as he drew something from beneath his cloak.

'Nothing,' he said. 'But I gained something from that most recent encounter.'

'My horn!'

'Well,' said Corum, 'I remember how mercenary you were, friend Goffanon, in the matter of bargains. Strictly speaking, I would say this horn is mine.'

Goffanon nodded his great head philosophically. 'That is fair,' he said. 'Very well, the horn is yours, Corum. I lost it, after all, through my own stupidity.'

'But through my unconscious connivance,' said Corum. 'Let me borrow the horn a while, Goffanon. When the time seems ripe, I will return it to you.'

'It is a better bargain than I made with you, Corum. I feel shamed.'

'Well, Goffanon, what do you plan to do? Return to Hy-Breasail?'

Goffanon shook his head. 'What should I gain by that? It seems my best interests lie with your cause, Corum, for if you defeat Calatin and the Fhoi Myore, then I am freed from Calatin's service forever. If I return to my island, Calatin can always find me again.'

'Then you are fully with us?'

'Aye.'

Jhary-a-Conel shifted nervously in his saddle. 'Listen,' he said, 'they come much closer now. I think they have our scent. I think we are in considerable danger, my friends.'

But Corum was laughing. 'I think not, Jhary-a-Conel. Not now.'

'Why so? Listen to their ghastly baying!' His lips curled in distaste. 'The wolves seek the sheep, eh?'

And, as if in confirmation, Amergin bleated softly.

Then Corum laughed. 'Let them come closer,' he said. 'The closer the better.'

He knew that it was wrong to leave Jhary in such suspense but he was enjoying the sensation – so often had Jhary made mysteries himself.

They rode on.

And all the while the Hounds of Kerenos came closer. They were in sight of Craig Dôn by the time the hounds appeared behind them, but they knew that the devil dogs could move faster than could they. There was no chance at all of reaching the seven stone circles before the hounds caught them.

Corum peered backwards at their pursuers, looking for signs of a suit of armour which constantly shifted its colours but there was none. White faces, red eyes – the Ghoolegh huntsmen controlled the pack. They were most expert at doing so, having been slaves of the Fhoi Myore for generations, bred beyond the sea in eastern lands before the Fhoi Myore began their re-conquest of the west. Gaynor, no doubt against his will, had been needed by the Fhoi Myore to lead the marching warriors who went against Caer Mahlod (if that was where they went) and so had been kept from the pursuit. This was just as well, thought Corum, unslinging the horn and putting its ornamental mouthpiece to his lips. He took a deep breath.

'Ride for Craig Dôn,' he told the others. 'Goffanon, take Amergin.'

The smith drew the limp body of the Archdruid from Corum's saddle and swung it easily over his massive shoulder.

'But you will die . . .' Jhary began.

'I will not,' said Corum. 'Not if I am careful in what I do now. Go. Goffanon will tell you the properties of this horn.'

'Horns!' Jhary exclaimed. 'I am sick of them. Horns for bringing the apocalypse, horns for calling demons – now horns for handling dogs! The gods grow unimaginative!' And with that peculiar observation he kicked his heels into the flanks of his horse and rode rapidly towards the tall stones of Craig Dôn, Goffanon loping behind him.

And Corum blew the horn once and though the Hounds of Kerenos pricked up their red, tufted ears, they still came running towards their quarry – running in a great pack made up of at least two score dogs. The Ghoolegh, mounted on pale horses, were, however, unsure. Corum could see that they hung back, where normally they would have chased behind the dogs.

Now the Hounds of Kerenos yelled in glee as they had Corum's scent and, veering slightly, sped towards him through the snow.

And Corum blew the horn a second time and the yellow eyes of the hounds, so close, so glaring, took on a somewhat puzzled expression.

Now other horns shouted as the Ghoolegh called their dogs off in panic, for they knew what would happen to them if the horn sounded a third time.

The Hounds of Kerenos were so near to Corum now that he could smell their stinking, steaming breath.

And suddenly they stopped in their tracks, whined and began reluctantly to trot back across the wind-blown snow to where the Ghoolegh waited.

And when the Hounds of Kerenos were in retreat, Corum blew the horn a third time.

He saw the Ghoolegh clutch their heads. He saw the Ghoolegh fall from their saddles. And he knew that they were dead, for the third blast of that horn always killed them – it was the punishing blast with which Kerenos slew those who failed to obey him.

The Hounds of Kerenos, whose last instructions had been to return, continued to lope back to where the dead Ghoolegh lay. And Corum whistled to himself as he tucked the horn into his belt and made for the Craig Dôn at an almost leisurely gait.

'Perhaps it is sacrilege, but it is a convenient place to put him while we debate the problem.' Jhary looked down at Amergin who lay upon the great altar stone within the inner circle of columns.

It was dark. A fire burned fitfully.

'I cannot understand why he eats only the few pieces of fruit or vegetables we brought. It is as if his innards have become sheep's innards, too. If this continues, Corum, we shall deliver a dead High King to Caer Mahlod!'

'You spoke earlier of being able to reach through to his

inner mind,' Corum said. 'Is that possible? If so, we can learn what to do to help him, perhaps.'

'Aye, with the aid of my little cat I might be able to do that, but it will take much time and considerable energy. I would eat before I begin.'

'By all means.'

And then Jhary-a-Conel ate, and he fed his cat almost as much food as he consumed himself, while Corum and Goffanon ate only sparingly and poor Amergin ate nothing at all, for their supplies of dried fruit and vegetables were almost gone.

The moon peered for a moment through the clouds and it struck the altar with its rays and the costume of sheepskin gleamed. Then the moon went away again and the only light came from the flickering fire which flung red shadows among the old stones.

Jhary-a-Conel whispered to his cat. He stroked his cat and the cat purred. Slowly, the cat in his arms, he began to approach the altar where starved, wasted Amergin lay, breathing shallow breaths as he slept.

Jhary-a-Conel put the little winged cat's head against the head of Amergin and then he drew his own head down so that it touched the other side of the cat's head. Silence fell.

There came a bleating, loud and urgent, and it was impossible for the watchers to judge whether it came from Amergin's mouth, from the cat's, or from Jhary's.

The bleating died away.

It became darker as, untended, the fire died. Corum could see the dirty white form of Amergin upon the altar, the faint outline of the cat as it pressed its tiny skull to the High King's, the tense features of Jhary-a-Conel.

Jhary's voice:

'Amergin . . . Amergin . . . noble druid . . . pride of your folk . . . Amergin . . . Amergin . . . come back to us . . .'

Another bleat, this time wavering and unsure.

'Amergin . . .'

Corum remembered the calling which had summoned him from his own world, the world of the Vadhagh, to this world. Jhary's incantation was not unlike that of King Mannach. And possibly this had something to do with Amergin's enchantment: he lived a different life entirely, the life of a sheep, perhaps in a world which was not quite this one. And if that were the case his 'real' self might be reached. Corum could not begin to understand what the people of this world called magic, but he knew something of the multiverse with its variety of planes which sometimes intersected and he believed that their power probably derived from some half-conscious knowledge of these realms.

'Amergin, High King . . . Amergin, Archdruid . . .'

The bleating became fainter and at the same time seemed to assume the qualities of human speech.

'Amergin . . .'

There was a catlike mewl, a distant voice which could have come from any one of the three upon the altar.

'*Amergin of the family of Amergin . . . the knowledge-seekers . . .*'

'Amergin.' This was Jhary's voice, strained and strange. 'Amergin. Do you understand your fate?'

'*An enchantment . . . I am no longer a man . . . Why should this displease me . . .?*'

'Because your own folk need your guidance, your strength, your presence amongst them!'

'*I am all things . . . we are all of us all things . . . it is immaterial, the form we take . . . the spirit . . .*'

'Sometimes it is important, Amergin. As now, when the fate of the whole Mabden folk rests upon your assuming your former role. What will bring you back to your folk, Amergin? What power will restore you to them?'

'*Only the power of the Oak and the Ram. Only the Oak Woman can call me home. If it matters to you that I return, then find the Golden Oak and the Silvern Ram, find one who understands their properties . . . Only – the Oak Woman – can – call me – home . . .*'

And then there came the agitated bleating of a sheep and Jhary fell back from the altar and the cat spread its wings and flew away to perch high on top of one of the great stone arches, crouching there as if in fear.

And the wind's melancholy voice came from the distance and the clouds seemed to grow darker in the sky and the bleating of a sheep filled the stone circle and then died away.

Goffanon was the first to speak, tugging at the hairs of his black beard, his voice a growl:

'The Oak and the Ram. Two of what the Mabden term their –"Treasures" – Sidhi gifts, both. It seems to me that I recall something of them. One of the Mabden who came to my island spoke of them before he died.' Goffanon shrugged. 'Yet most Mabden who came to my island spoke of such things. It was their interest in talismans and spells which brought them to Hy-Breasail.'

'What did he say?' Corum asked.

'Well, he told the tale of the lost Treasures – how the old warrior Onragh fled with them from Caer Llud and how they were scattered. These two were lost close to the borders of the land of the Tuha-na-Gwyddneu Garanhir, which is north of the land of the Tuha-na-Cremm Croich, across a sea – though there is a way by land, also. One of that folk found the Golden Oak and the Silvern Ram – large talismans both, of fine Sidhi workmanship – and took them back to his folk where they were held in great reverence and where, for all I know, they still are.'

'So we must seek the Oak and the Ram before we can restore Amergin to his senses,' said Jhary-a-Conel. He looked pale and exhausted. 'Yet I fear he will die before we can achieve that. He needs nourishment and the only nourishment which will keep him properly alive is that grass which the Fhoi Myore vassals fed him. It is a grass containing certain magical agents which, while they kept him firmly under his enchantment, also supplied his body's primary needs. Unless he is restored to his human identity shortly, he will die, my friends.'

Jhary-a-Conel spoke flatly and neither Corum nor Goffanon needed to convince themselves of the truth of his words. It was evident, for one thing, that Amergin was beginning to waste away, particularly since their supplies of fruit and vegetables were all but gone.

'Yet we must go to the land of the Tuha-na-Gwyddneu Garanhir if we are to find those things which will save him,' said Corum. 'And he will surely die before we reach that land. It seems that we are defeated.'

He looked down at the pathetic sleeping figure of he who had once been the symbol of Mabden pride. 'We sought to save the High King. Instead, we have slain him.'

CHAPTER FIVE

Dreams and Decisions

Corum dreamed of a field of sheep; a pleasant scene, save when all the sheep looked up at once and had the faces of men and women he had known.

He dreamed that he ran for the safety of his old home, Castle Erorn by the sea, but when he neared it he found that a great chasm had fallen between him and the entrance to the castle. He dreamed that he blew upon a horn and that this horn called all the gods to the Earth and the Earth became the field of their final battle. And he was consumed by an enormous sense of guilt, recalling many deeds which Corum awake could never recall: tragic deeds; the murder of friends and lovers, the betrayal of races, the destruction of the weak and of the innocent. And while a small voice reminded him that he had also destroyed the strong and the evil in his long career through a thousand incarnations, he was not consoled, for now he recalled Amergin and soon he would have Amergin's death upon his conscience. Once again his idealism had led to the destruction of another soul and he could not reconcile his tortured spirit.

And now gleeful music began to sound; mocking music, sweet music – the music of a harp.

And Corum turned from the chasm and he saw three figures standing there. One of the figures he recognized with pleasure. It was Medhbh, lovely Medhbh, in a smock of blue samite, with her red hair braided and bracelets of red gold upon her arms and ankles, a sword in one hand and a sling in the other. He smiled at her, but she did not return his smile. The figure next to her he also recognized now and he recognized that figure with horror. It was a youth whose flesh shone with the colour of pale gold. A youth who smiled without kindness and played upon the mocking harp.

Corum dreamed that he made to draw his sword, moving to attack the youth with the flesh of gold, but then the third figure advanced, raising a hand. This figure was the most shadowy of the three and Corum realized that he feared it more than he feared the youth with the harp, though he could not see the face at all. He saw that the raised hand was of silver and that the cloak the figure wore was of scarlet and then he turned his back again in horror, not daring to look upon the face because he was afraid he would see his own face there.

And Corum leapt into the chasm while the music of the harp grew louder and louder, more and more triumphant, and he fell through a night which had no ending.

And then there was a blinding whiteness which swallowed him and he realized that he had opened his eyes upon the dawn.

Slowly the great stones of Craig Dôn came into focus, dark and grim against the snow which surrounded them. He felt something gripping him and he tried to struggle free, fearing that Gaynor had found him, but then he heard Goffanon's deep voice saying:

'It is over, Corum. You are awake.'

Corum gasped. 'Such dreadful dreams, Goffanon . . .'

'What else did you expect if you sleep at the centre of Craig Dôn?' growled the Sidhi dwarf. 'Particularly after witnessing Jhary-a-Conel's work of last night.'

'It was similar to a dream I had when I first came to Hy-Breasail,' Corum said, rubbing at his frozen face and taking deep breaths of cold air as if he hoped thus to dispel the memory of the dreams.

'Because Hy-Breasail has similar properties to Craig Dôn, there is every reason why your dreams should be the same,' said Goffanon. He rose, his great bulk looming over Corum. 'Though some have pleasant dreams at Craig Dôn, and others have magnificent, inspiring dreams, I'm told.

'I have need of such dreams at present,' said Corum.

Goffanon shifted his war-axe from his right hand to his left and offered the free hand to Corum who took it and let the Sidhi smith help him to his feet. Amergin still slept upon the altar, covered by a cloak, and Jhary slept near the ashes of the fire, his cat curled up close to his face.

'We must go to the land of the Tuha-na-Gwyddneu Garanhir,' said Goffanon. 'I have been considering the problem.'

Corum smiled with his frozen lips. 'You league yourself fully with our cause, then?'

Goffanon shrugged with poor grace.

'It seems so. I've little choice. To reach that land we must go part of the way by sea. It will be the quickest way of making the journey.'

'But we are much burdened,' said Corum, 'and will make slow progress with Amergin.'

'Then one of us must take Amergin to the relative safety of Caer Mahlod,' said Goffanon, 'while the others make the longer journey to Caer Garanhir. Returning by sea, assuming that we have succeeded in finding the Golden Oak and the Silvern Ram, we should be able to get to Caer Mahlod with relative ease. It is the only way we have, if Amergin is to have even the faintest hope of living.'

'Then it is the way we must take,' said Corum simply.

Jhary-a-Conel had begun to stir. A hand reached out and found a wide-brimmed hat, cramming it on his head. He sat up, blinking. The cat made a small, complaining noise and curled itself sleepily upon his lap while Jhary stretched and rubbed at his eyes.

'How is Amergin?' he said. 'I dreamed of him. He led a great gathering here, at Craig Dôn, and all the Mabden spoke with a single voice. It was a fine dream.'

'Amergin still sleeps,' said Corum. And he told Jhary what he and Goffanon had discussed.

Jhary nodded his agreement. 'But which of us is to take Amergin to Caer Mahlod?' He got to his feet, cradling the black and white cat in his arm. 'I think it should be me.'

'Why so?'

'It is a simple task, for one thing, to travel from this point to another and deliver our sheepish friend. Secondly, I play no important part in the destinies involved. The folk of Gwyddneu Garanhir are more likely to show respect for two Sidhi heroes than for one.'

'Very well,' Corum agreed, 'you shall ride with Amergin for Caer Mahlod and there tell them all that has taken place and all we intend to do. Warn them, too, that the Fhoi Myore come again. With Amergin within the walls of Caer Mahlod, they could be saved from Balahr's frigid gaze and time might be bought as a result. Happily the Fhoi Myore do not travel with particular swiftness and there is a chance we can return before they reach Caer Mahlod . . .'

'If they do, indeed, head for Caer Mahlod,' said Goffanon. 'We know only that they plan to march west. It could even be that Craig Dôn itself is their destination, that they have some idea of destroying the place.'

'Why do they fear it so?' Corum said. 'Have they, any longer, the need?'

Goffanon rubbed at his beard. 'Possibly,' he said. 'Craig Dôn was built by Sidhi and Mabden both, at the time of our first great war with the Fhoi Myore. It was built according to certain metaphysical principles and it had several functions, both practical and symbolical. One of the practical functions was for it to act as a kind of trap which would swallow all the Fhoi Myore when they were lured here. It has the power – or, rather, it *had* the power – to restore those who do not belong in this realm to the realms where they do belong. However, it does not work for the Sidhi or I should have departed this world long since. It was our fate to accomplish its construction without being able to use it for our own ends. As it happened, we were not successful in luring all the Fhoi Myore here and ever since then those who survived have given the place wide clearance. There are rituals involved, too . . .'

Goffanon's expression became distant, as if he recalled the old days when he and all his brothers fought the might of the Fhoi Myore in their epic struggle. He looked out at the widening circles of stone columns.

'Aye,' he mused, 'this was a great place of power once, was Craig Dôn.'

Corum handed two things to Jhary-a-Conel. The first was the long, curved horn and the second was the Sidhi mantle.

'Take these,' he said, 'since you ride alone. The horn will protect you from the Hounds of Kerenos and the Ghoolegh huntsmen. The cloak will disguise you from the People of the Pines and others who pursue you. You will need both these things if you are to reach Caer Mahlod safely.'

'But what of you and Goffanon? Will you not need protection?'

Corum shook his head. 'We shall risk what we must risk. There are two of us and we are not burdened by Amergin.'

Jhary nodded. 'I accept the gifts, then.'

Soon they had mounted their horses and were riding through the stone arches, Goffanon running ahead with his war-axe upon his fur-clad shoulder, his helm of polished iron glinting in the cold light from the sky.

'Now you ride south-west and we ride north-west,' said Corum. 'Our ways will part soon, Jhary-a-Conel.'

'Let us pray they'll meet again.'

'Let us hope so.'

They spurred their horses and rode together for a while, enjoying one another's company but speaking little.

And a little later Corum watched from his motionless horse as Jhary rode rapidly for Caer Mahlod, his cloak billowing behind him, the semi-conscious figure of the enchanted High King tied across his horse's neck.

Far across the snow-shrouded plain rode Jhary-a-Conel, growing smaller and smaller and finally becoming obscured by a gust of wind-borne snow, blotted from Corum's sight but not from his thoughts.

Jhary and Jhary's fate was often in Corum's mind as he

rode for the coast, the tireless Goffanon loping always beside him.

And sometimes, too, Corum would recall the dream he had dreamed at Craig Dôn, and then he would ride still harder, as if he hoped to leave such memories behind him.

CHAPTER SIX

A Flight Across the Waves

Corum wiped his forehead free from the sweat which clung to it and gratefully dropped his byrnie and his helm into the bottom of the small boat.

The sun was high in a cloudless sky and while the day was actually only as warm as a day in early spring it seemed to be almost tropically hot both to Corum and Goffanon who, in their ride to the coast, had become used to the aching cold of those lands conquered by the Fhoi Myore. Corum was clad now only in his shirt and his leggings, his sword and dirk strapped about his waist and the rest of his war-gear tied across the back of his horse. He was reluctant to leave the horse behind him, but there were no easy means of transporting it across the ocean which gleamed ahead. The boat they had found was barely large enough to take Goffanon's great bulk, let alone Corum's.

Corum stood on the quay of the abandoned fishing village and wondered if Fhoi Myore minions had come here or if the inhabitants had been among those who had fled to Caer Mahlod during the first invasion of the Cold Folk. Whatever the circumstances of their flight, they had left much behind them, including several small boats. The larger boats, Corum guessed, had been taken either to the land of the Tuha-na-Gwyddneu Garanhir or even further to the land of the Tuha-na-Manannan, King Fiachadh's land. There were none of the usual signs of wanton Fhoi Myore slaying. It was his belief that the folk of the village had been hasty in their decision to leave. The white houses, the gardens in which flowers and vegetables grew, all looked as if they were still occupied and tended. The flight must have been comparatively recent.

Goffanon, complaining about the heat but refusing to remove his breastplate or war-cap, keeping, also, a firm grip on his double-headed axe, clambered from the short flight of stone steps and into the boat as Corum steadied it for him. Then Corum got cautiously into the bow and settled himself, laying his lance and his axe along the bottom of the boat and unshipping the oars (for Goffanon had insisted that he understood nothing of the art of rowing). Corum would dearly have given everything for a sail, but had been able to find nothing which would serve. He pushed off from the quay and manoeuvred the boat until his back was to the distant shoreline over the water, their destination. He began to row with long, strong strokes which at first wearied him but then, as he became used to the rhythm, involved seemingly less and less effort as Goffanon's weight increased their momentum through the clear, still waters of the sea.

The smell of the brine was good after the snow-laden air he had breathed so long and there was a sense of peace upon the sea which he had not known for a long while, even when he had sailed Calatin's boat for Hy-Breasail to meet (though he had not known it then) the huge self-styled dwarf who now sat in the stern and dangled a huge, heavily muscled hand in the water for all the world like a maiden being taken for a pleasure trip by her swain. Corum grinned, his liking for the Sidhi smith growing all the time.

'Perhaps at Caer Mahlod they will find herbs which will sustain Amergin,' said Goffanon, staring idly over the water as the coastline disappeared behind him. 'There, at least, they can grow such things. They grow in precious few parts of the old Mabden lands now.'

Corum, deciding to take a moment's rest from rowing, drew in the oars and took a deep breath.

'Aye,' he said, 'it's what I hope. Yet if the grass Amergin ate at Caer Llud was specially treated it might be hard to find something matching it exactly. However,' he grinned, 'this sunshine makes me feel considerably more confident.' And he began to row again.

It was some time later that Goffanon spoke again. He drew his black brows together and peered over Corum's shoulder, looking beyond Corum in the direction in which they rowed. 'Sea-fog ahead, by the look of it. Strange to find it so isolated and in such weather . . .'

Corum, reluctant to interrupt the rhythm of his rowing, did not look back but continued his steady strokes.

'Thick, too,' said Goffanon some moments later. 'It would probably be best to avoid it.'

And now Corum did pause in his rowing and turn to look. Goffanon was right. The sea-fog was spreading across a huge area, almost completely obscuring the sight of the land ahead. And now that Corum ceased his exertions he felt that it had become subtly colder, for all that the sun continued to shine.

'Bad luck for us,' he said, 'but it will take too long to row around it. We'll risk rowing through and hope that it does not cover too wide an area.' And Corum rowed on.

But soon the cold had actually become uncomfortable and he rolled down his sleeves. Still this was not enough and he paused to draw his heavy byrnie over his body and place his helmet upon his head and this seemed to impair his rowing and it was as if he dipped his oars in clinging mud. Tendrils of mist began to move around the boat and Goffanon frowned again, and Goffanon shivered.

'Can it be?' he growled, shifting so that the boat rocked wildly and they were almost pitched into the sea. 'Can it be?'

'You think it Fhoi Myore mist?' Corum murmured.

'I think it resembles Fhoi Myore mist most closely.'

'I think so, too.'

Now the mist was all around them and they could see only a few yards in all directions. Corum stopped rowing altogether and the boat drifted slower and slower until suddenly it stopped altogether. Corum looked over the side.

The sea had frozen. It had frozen almost instantly, for the waves had become ridges and on some of those ridges were delicate patterns which could only have been foam.

Corum's spirits sank and it was with resignation and despair that he stood up in the boat and bent to pick up his lance and his axe.

Goffanon, too, rose and tentatively put a fur-booted foot upon the ice, testing it. He lumbered from the boat and stood upon the sea, tying the thongs of his fur cloak together so that he was completely covered. His breath began to steam. Corum followed suit, wrapping his own cloak around him, staring this way and that. He heard a noise in the far distance. A grunt. A shout. And perhaps he heard the creaking of a great wicker battle-cart and the heavy footfalls of some malformed beast upon the ice. Was it thus that the Fhoi Myore built their roads across the sea, needing no ships? Was this ice their version of a bridge? Or did they know that Goffanon and Corum came this way and sought to thwart their progress?

They would know soon, thought Corum as he crouched beside the boat and watched. The Fhoi Myore and their minions were moving from east to west, in the same direction as Corum and Goffanon but at a slightly different angle. In the dim distance Corum saw dark shapes riding and marching and sniffed the familiar scent of pines, saw the bulky shapes of Fhoi Myore chariot-riders, and once he glimpsed the flickering armour of one who could only be Gaynor. And now he began to realize that the Fhoi Myore marched not against Caer Mahlod at all but most likely against Caer Garanhir, their own destination. And if the Fhoi Myore reached Caer Garanhir before them, the chances of finding the Oak and the Ram were very poor.

'Garanhir,' muttered Goffanon, 'they go to Garanhir.'

'Aye,' said Corum despairingly, 'and we have no choice now but to follow behind them, then hope to overtake them when they reach the land. We must warn Garanhir if we can. We must warn King Daffyn, Goffanon!'

Goffanon shrugged his massive shoulders and tugged at

his shaggy black beard and rubbed his nose. Then he spread his left hand and raised his double-headed war-axe in his right hand and he smiled. 'Indeed, we must,' he said.

They were thankful that the Hounds of Kerenos did not run with the Fhoi Myore army. These, doubtless, still scoured the countryside about Craig Dôn, looking for the three friends and Amergin. They would have had no chance at all of avoiding detection if those dogs had been present. Moving warily, Corum and Goffanon skulked in the wake of the Fhoi Myore, peering ahead in the hope that they would soon sight the land. The going was difficult, for the waves had formed small hills and dangerous ruts in the frozen sea. They were exhausted by the time they witnessed the landing of the Fhoi Myore and the People of the Pines on shores which had, an hour since, been green and lush and which were suddenly ice-covered and dead.

And the sea began to melt as the Fhoi Myore passed and Corum and Goffanon found themselves wading through water which was still freezing and which rose to Corum's chin and Goffanon's chest.

And, as he stumbled up the frosty beach, his throat choked with a mixture of sea and mist, Corum felt himself seized, weapons and all, about the waist and he was moving headlong up a hillside, borne by Goffanon who was wasting no time, running easily with Corum under one arm, his beard and hair flying in the wind, his greaves and his armour rattling on his massive body, apparently in no way slowed by his burden.

Corum's ribs ached but he managed to remark: 'You are a most useful dwarf, Goffanon. I am amazed at the energy possessed by one of such small stature as yourself.'

'I suppose I compensate for my shortness by cultivating stamina,' said Goffanon seriously.

Two hours later and they were well ahead of the Fhoi Myore force. They sat in a dip in the ground, enjoying the smell of grass and wild flowers, knowing miserably that it would not be long before these became rigid with cold and died. Perhaps that was why Corum relished the smell of the vegetation while it was still there.

Goffanon let out a great sigh as, tenderly, without picking the plant, he looked at a wild poppy.

'The Mabden lands are amongst the prettiest in this whole realm,' he said. 'And now these perish, as all the other lands have perished. Conquered by the Fhoi Myore.'

'What of the other lands in this realm?' Corum asked. 'What know you of them?'

'Long-since turned to poisoned ice by the diseased remnants of the Fhoi Myore race,' Goffanon said. 'These lands were safe partly because the Fhoi Myore remembered Craig Dôn and avoided the place, partly because this is where the surviving Sidhi made their homes. It took them a considerable length of time before they came back from the eastern seas and beyond.' He stood up. 'Would you sit upon my shoulders now? It will be more comfortable for you, I think.'

And Corum accepted the offer with courtesy and climbed upon the dwarf's shoulders. Then they were off again, for there was no time to be wasted.

'This proves the need for Mabden unity,' said Corum from his perch. 'If there were proper communications between the surviving Mabden, then all could gather to attack the Fhoi Myore force from several sides.'

'But what of Balahr and the rest? What have the Mabden in their armouries which can defend against Balahr's frightful gaze?'

'They have their Treasures. Already I have seen how one of them, the spear Bryionak which you gave me, can do much harm to the Fhoi Myore.'

'There was only one spear Bryionak,' said Goffanon in an almost melancholy tone, 'and now that has vanished – doubtless returning to my own home realm.'

They entered a narrow gorge between white limestone cliffs topped by green turf.

'As I recall,' said Goffanon, 'the city of Caer Garanhir lies but a short way on the other side of the pass.'

But as the pass wound up through the rocks and grew narrower at its farther end, they saw a group of figures awaited them there.

At first Corum thought that these were war-knights of the Tuha-na-Gwyddneu Garanhir, alerted of their coming and there to greet them. But then he noticed the greenish cast of riders and horses and he knew that these were not friends. And then the green ranks broke and another rider emerged – a rider whose armour shifted colour constantly and whose face was completely hidden by a blank, smooth helm.

And Goffanon stopped and took Corum from his shoulders and put him upon the pale clay of the ground and looked back as he heard a sound. Corum looked also.

Riding green horses down the steep slopes of the gorge came another group of green riders and the whole air was thick with their piny scent. The riders reached the bottom of the pass and paused.

Gaynor's voice echoed through the narrow walls of the gorge and his voice was gay, triumphant:

'You could have prolonged your life so easily, Prince Corum, if you had chosen to remain as my guest at Craig Dôn. Where is the little lamb Amergin, whom you stole?'

'Amergin was dying, the last I saw of him,' said Corum truthfully, unslinging his axe from his back.

Goffanon murmured: 'It is time for the hewing of pines, I think, Corum,' and he moved so that he stood facing those at their rear while Corum confronted those at their front. Goffanon hefted his own huge axe, turning its polished iron so that it flashed in the bright summer sunshine. 'At least we shall die in the summer warmth,' Goffanon said, 'and not have our bones eaten by the Cold Folk's mist.'

'You should have been warned,' said Prince Gaynor the Damned. 'He eats a diet of rare grasses only. And now the High King of the Mabden is perished, a mere carcass of mutton. No matter.'

In the distance, behind him, Corum heard a great roaring noise and he knew that this must be the Fhoi Myore on the march, moving much faster than he had thought possible.

Goffanon cocked his head on one side and listened almost curiously.

Then, from both sides, the green-faced horsemen began to bear down on them so that the sides of the gorge shook and Gaynor's bleak laughter grew wilder and wilder.

Corum whirled his war-axe and made a great wound in the neck of the first horse, seeing greenish, viscous liquid ooze from the gash. It halted the horse's momentum, but it did not kill it. Its green eyes rolled and its green teeth snapped and its green rider brought a dull iron sword down at Corum's head. Corum had fought Hew Argech, one of the People of the Pines, and he knew how to counter such blows. He chopped deliberately at the wrist as it swept down and wrist and sword flew earthward like a bough lopped from a tree. He chopped next at the horse's legs so that it crashed on to the dusty clay and lay there unsuccessfully trying to regain an upright position. This helped to confuse the next rider who came at Corum and was unable to strike a clean blow without snaring his horse's legs in those of the wounded animal. The scent of pines was now almost overpowering as the sap oozed from the wounds Corum wrought. It was a scent he had once loved but which now sickened him. It was sweet and it was odious.

Goffanon had brought at least three of the Pine Folk down and was chopping at their bodies, slicing off limbs so that they could not move, though they still lived, their green eyes glaring, their green lips snarling. These had once been the flower of Mabden warriors, probably from Caer Llud itself, but their human blood had been drawn from their veins and pine sap poured into them instead, and now they served the Fhoi Myore for they were ashamed of what they had become and at the same time most proud of their distinction.

As he fought, Corum tried to glance about him to see if there was any means of escaping from the gorge, but Gaynor had chosen the best place to attack – where the sides were steepest and the passage narrowest. This meant that Corum and Goffanon could defend themselves longer but could never hope to get away. Eventually they would be overwhelmed by the People of the Pines, vanquished by these living trees, these brothers of the oak's oldest enemy. Like a rustling, marching forest, they rushed again at the one-eyed Vadhagh with the silver hand, at the eight-foot Sidhi with the bristling black beard.

And Gaynor, at a safe distance, laughed on. He was indulging in his favourite sport – the destruction of heroes, the conquest of honour, the extermination of virtue and idealism. And he indulged himself thus because he had never quite succeeded in driving these qualities from his own self. Thus Gaynor sought to still any voice which dared remind him of the hope he dared not hope, the ambition he feared to entertain – the possibility of his own salvation.

Corum's arms grew weary and he staggered now as he chopped at green arms, slashed at green heads, cracked the skulls of green horses and grew dizzy with the scent of the pine sap which was now sticky underfoot.

'Farewell, Goffanon,' he shouted to his comrade. 'It heartened me much when you joined our cause, but I fear your decision has led you to your death.'

And Corum was astonished when he heard Goffanon's laughter blending with that of Prince Gaynor the Damned.

CHAPTER SEVEN

A Long-lost Brother

Then Corum realized that only Goffanon laughed.

Gaynor laughed no longer.

Corum tried to peer through the mass of green warriors to the far end of the pass where he had last seen Gaynor, but there was no sign of the flickering, fiery armour. It seemed that Prince Gaynor the Damned had deserted the scene of his triumph.

And now the Warriors of the Pines were falling back, looking fearfully into the sky. And Corum risked glancing up and he saw a rider there. The rider was seated upon a shining black horse all dressed in red and gilded leather, the buckles of its harness of sea-ivory and the edges all stitched with large and perfect pearls.

And overwhelming the stink of the pines came the fresh, warm smell of the sea. And Corum knew that the smell came from the smiling rider who sat the horse with one hand upon his hip and the other upon his bridle.

And then, casually, the rider stepped his horse over the gorge and turned so that he could look down into the pass from the other side. It gave Corum some idea of the size of horse and rider.

The rider had a light, golden beard and his face was that of a youth of some eighteen summers. His golden hair was braided and hung down his chest. He wore a breastplate which was fashioned from some kind of bronze and decorated with motifs of the sun and of ships, as well as whales and fish and sea-serpents. Upon the rider's great, fair-skinned arms were bands of gold whose patterns matched those on the breastplate. He wore a blue cloak with a great circular pin at the left shoulder. His eyes were a clear, piercing green-grey. At his hip was a heavy sword which was probably longer than Corum's full height. On his left arm was a shield of the same glowing bronze as his breastplate.

And Goffanon was crying delightedly up to the gigantic rider on the gigantic horse, even as he continued to fight the People of the Pines.

'I heard you coming, brother!' cried Goffanon. 'I heard you and knew who it was!'

And the giant's laughter rumbled down the gorge. 'Greetings, little Goffanon. You fight well. You always fought well.'

'Do you come to aid us?'

'It seems so. My rest was disturbed by the Fhoi Myore vermin laying ice across my ocean. For years I have been at peace in my underwater retreat, thinking to have no more irritation from the Cold Folk. But they came, with their ice and their mist and their silly soldiers, and so I must attempt to teach them a lesson.'

Almost carelessly he drew his great sword from its scabbard and with the flat reached down into the gorge to sweep away the Brothers of the Pines so that they began to retreat in panic in both directions.

'I will meet you at the far end of this pass,' said the giant, shaking the reins of his horse and making it move away from the brink. 'I fear I would stick if I tried to join you there.'

The ground shook as the gigantic rider disappeared and a little while later they trudged up to the end of the gorge to meet him and Goffanon in spite of his weariness ran forward with his arms wide open, the axe falling from his grip, shouting joyfully:

'Ilbrec! Ilbrec! Son of my old friend! I did not know you lived!'

Ilbrec, twice Goffanon's height, swung himself from his saddle, laughing.

'Aha, little smith, if I had known that you survived I should long since have sought you out!'

Corum was astonished to see the Sidhi Goffanon seized in Ilbrec's great arms and embraced. Then Ilbrec turned his attention upon Corum and said: 'Smaller and smaller, eh! Who is this who so resembles our ancient Vadhagh cousins?'

'Vadhagh he is, brother Ilbrec. A champion of the Mabden since the Sidhi left.'

Corum felt ridiculously tiny as he bowed to the great, laughing youth. 'Greetings to you, cousin,' he said.

'And how fared your father, the great Manannan?' Goffanon asked. 'I heard that he had been slain in the Island of the West and lies now beneath his own Hill.'

'Aye – with a Mabden folk named for him. He has honour in this realm.'

'And deservedly, Ilbrec.'

'Are there more of our folk surviving?' Ilbrec asked. 'I had thought myself the last.'

'None to my knowledge,' Goffanon told him.

'And how many Fhoi Myore are there?'

'Six. There were seven, but the Black Bull of Crinanass took one before it departed this realm – or died – I know not which. The Black Bull was the last of the great Sidhi herd.'

'Six.' Ilbrec sat himself down upon the turf, his golden brow darkening. 'What are their names, these six?'

'One is Kerenos,' said Corum. 'Another is Balahr, another is Rhannon and another is Goim. The other two I do not know.'

'Neither have I seen them,' said Goffanon. 'They hide, as usual, in their mist.'

Ilbrec nodded. 'Kerenos with his dogs, Balahr with his eye, Rhannon with his breath and Goim – Goim with her teeth. An unsavoury quartet, eh? And hard to fight, those four alone. They were four of the most powerful. Doubtless it is why they linger on. I should have thought them all rotted and forgotten by now. They have vitality, these Fhoi Myore.'

'The vitality of Chaos and Old Night,' agreed Goffanon, fingering the blade of his axe. 'Ah, if only all our comrades were with us. What a reaving then, eh? And if those comrades wielded the Weapons of Light, how we should drive back the coldness and the darkness . . .'

'But we are two,' said Ilbrec sadly. 'And the greatest of the Sidhi are no more.'

'Yet the Mabden are courageous,' said Corum. 'They have a certain power. And if their High King can be restored to them . . .'

'True,' said Goffanon, and he began to tell his old friend of all that had passed in recent months, since the coming of the Fhoi Myore to the islands of the Mabden. Only when he spoke of Calatin and the wizard's charm did he become reticent, but managed to speak of the matter nonetheless.

'So the Golden Oak and the Silvern Ram still exist,' mused Ilbrec. 'My father spoke of them. And Fand the Beautiful, she prophesied that one day they would give power to the Mabden. My mother Fand was a great seeress, for all she had weaknesses in other directions.' Ilbrec grinned and spoke no more of Fand. Instead, he rose up and went to where his black horse cropped the grass. 'Now, I suppose, we must make speed for Caer Garanhir and see what defences they can build and how best we can help them when the Fhoi Myore attack. Do you think all six ride against that city?'

'It is possible,' said Corum. 'Yet usually the Fhoi Myore do not move in the front of their vassals but bring up the rear. They are cunning, in some ways, those Fhoi Myore.'

'They were ever that. Would you ride with me, Vadhagh?'

Corum smiled. 'If your horse agrees that he will not mistake me for a flea upon his back, I'll ride with you, Ilbrec.'

And, laughing, Ilbrec swung Corum up and sat him down so that he could place a leg either side of his great pearl-studded pommel. Still unused to the hugeness of the Sidhi (and understanding at last how Goffanon could regard himself as a dwarf), Corum felt weak in the presence of Ilbrec who now seated himself with a creak of leather breeks and saddle behind him, calling out:

'Onward, Splendid Mane. Onward, beautiful horse, to where the Mabden gather.'

And as soon as he had become used to the huge movements of the cantering horse, Corum began to enjoy the sensation of riding the beast, listening to the conversation of the two Sidhi as Goffanon continued his steady pace beside the horse.

'It seems to me,' said Ilbrec thoughtfully, 'that my father bequeathed a chest to me containing some armour and a spear or two. Perhaps they would be useful in this struggle of ours, though they have lain unused for many scores of years now. If I could find that chest I would know.'

'Yellow Shaft and Red Javelin?' Goffanon asked eagerly. 'The sword your father named Retaliator?'

'Most of his arms were lost in the last battle, as you know,' said Ilbrec. 'And others were of a sort which drew their strength from our original realm and thus could not be used properly or could only be used once. Nonetheless, there could be something of use in that chest. It is in one of the sea-caverns I have not visited since that battle. For all I know it has gone, or rotted, or,' he smiled, 'been devoured by some sea monster.'

'Well, we shall know soon enough,' said Goffanon. 'And if Retaliator should be there . . .'

'We'd be best advised to consider our own abilities,' said Ilbrec laughing again. 'Rather than put our faith in weapons which might not even exist in this realm any longer. Even with them, the strength of the Fhoi Myor is greater than ours.'

'But added to the Mabden strength,' said Corum, 'it could be great indeed.'

'I have always liked the Mabden,' Ilbrec told him, 'though I am not sure I share your faith in its powers. Still, times change and so do races. I will give you my judgement of the Mabden when I have seen them do battle against the Fhoi Myore.'

'That opportunity should come quite soon,' said Corum, pointing ahead.

He had seen the towers of Caer Garanhir. And they were tall, those towers, rivalling the buildings of Caer Llud in size and outshining them in beauty. Towers of shining limestone and dark-veined obsidian from which banners flew. Towers surrounded by the battlements of a massive wall which spoke of invincible strength.

Yet Corum knew that the impression of strength was deceptive, that Balahr's horrid eye could crack that granite and destroy all who sheltered behind it. Even with the giant Ilbrec as an ally they would be hard-put to resist the forces of the Fhoi Myore.

CHAPTER EIGHT

The Great Fight at
Caer Garanhir

Corum had smiled when he saw the expressions of those who had come to the battlements when Ilbrec had shouted, but now his face was dark as he stood in King Daffyn's magnificent hall, all hung with jewelled flags, and tried to speak to a man who was barely able to stand and yet continued to sip from a mead-cup as he tried to listen to Corum's words.

Half of King Daffyn's war-knights were sprawled insensible beside benches covered with stained samite. The other half leaned on anything which would give them support, some with drawn swords calling out silly boasts, while some sat with mouths hanging open, staring at Ilbrec who had managed to squeeze himself into the hall and crouched behind Corum and Goffanon.

They were not prepared for war, the Tuha-na-Gwyddneu Garanhir. They were prepared for nothing but drunken slumber now, for they had been celebrating a marriage – the marriage of the king's son, Prince Guwinn, to the daughter of a great knight of Caer Garanhir.

Those still awake were impressed well enough by the appearance of what they saw as three Sidhi of varying size, but some were still certain that they suffered the effects of feasting and drinking too much.

'The Fhoi Myore march in strength against you, King Daffyn,' said Corum again. 'Many hundreds of warriors, and most hard to slay they are!'

King Daffyn's face was red with drink. He was a fat, intelligent-looking man, but his eyes held little intelligence at that moment.

'I fear you overpraised the Mabden, Prince Corum,' said Ilbrec tolerantly. 'We must do what we can without them.'

'Wait!' King Daffyn came unsteadily down the steps from his throne, mead-horn still in his hand. 'Are we to be slain in our cups?'

'It seems so, King Daffyn,' said Corum.

'Drunk? Slain without dignity by those who slew – who slew our brothers of the East?'

'Just so!' said Goffanon, turning away impatiently. 'And you deserve little better.'

King Daffyn fingered the great medallion of rank which he wore about his neck. 'I shall have failed my people,' he said.

'Listen again,' said Corum. And he re-told his tale, slowly, while King Daffyn made a considerable effort to understand, even throwing away the mead-horn and refusing more mead when a blustering knight offered it to him.

'How many hours are they from Caer Garanhir?' asked the king when Corum had finished.

'Perhaps three. We travelled rapidly. Perhaps four or five. Perhaps they will not attack at all until the morning.'

'But three hours – we have three hours for certain.'

'I think so.'

King Daffyn staggered about his hall, shaking sleeping knights, shouting at those who were still in some stage of wakefulness. And Corum despaired.

Ilbrec voiced that despair. 'This will not do at all,' he said. He began to squeeze himself back through the doors. 'Not at all.'

Corum barely heard him as he continued to remonstrate with King Daffyn who was fighting with his own disinclination to hear bad news on such a day as this.

Goffanon turned and left the hall shouting: 'Do not abandon them, Ilbrec. You see them at their worst . . .'

But there came a shaking of the earth, a thundering of hooves, and Corum now ran from the hall in time to see the huge black horse, Splendid Mane, leap the battlements of Caer Garanhir's walls.

'So,' said Corum, 'he has gone. Plainly he feels he would best save his strength for a better cause. I cannot say that I blame him.'

'He is headstrong,' said Goffanon. 'Like his father. But his father would not have left friends behind.'

'You wish to go, too?'

'No. I'll stay. I've told you my decision. We are lucky to be here and not fallen to the Pine Folk. We should be grateful that Ilbrec saved our lives once.'

'Aye.' Wearily, Corum turned back into the hall to find King Daffyn shaking two of the prone warriors.

'Wake up!' said King Daffyn. 'Wake up. The Fhoi Myore come!'

They stood blinking upon the battlements, their eyes red, their hands shaking, and they made much use of the water-skins which the young lads brought round. Some were still in their formal wedding finery and others had donned armour. Now they sighed and groaned and held their heads as they looked out from the walls of Caer Garanhir and waited for the enemy.

'Yonder!' said a boy to Corum, lowering his water-skin and pointing. 'I see a cloud!'

Corum looked and he saw it. A cloud of boiling mist on the far horizon.

'Aye,' he said. 'That is the Fhoi Myore. But many come ahead of them, look. Look lower. See the riders.'

It seemed for a moment that a green tidal wave washed towards Caer Garanhir.

'What is that, Prince Corum?' said the boy.

'It is the People of the Pines,' said Corum, 'and they are exceptionally hard to slay.'

'The mist moved towards us, but now it has paused,' said the boy.

'Aye,' Corum replied, 'that is how the Fhoi Myore always fight, sending their vassals to weaken us first.'

He looked along the battlements. One of King Daffyn's war-knights was leaning out and groaning as he vomited. Corum turned away in grim despair. Other warriors were coming up the stone stairways now, nocking arrows to long bows. These, it appeared, had not celebrated the marriage of Prince Guwinn with quite the same abandon as the knights. They wore shining shirts of bronze mail and there were bronze war-caps upon their dark red heads. Some wore leathern breeks, and others had mail leggings. As well as the quivers on their backs they had javelins and there were swords or axes at their belts. Corum's spirits lifted a little as he saw these soldiers, but they dropped again when he heard, from the far distance, the cold, booming, wordless voices of the Fhoi Myore. No matter how bravely or how well they fought this day, the Fhoi Myore remained and the Fhoi Myore had the means of destroying all within Caer Garanhir's splendid walls.

Now the sound of hooves drowned the voices of the Fhoi Myore. Pale green horses and pale green riders, all of the same shade, with pale green clothing and pale green swords in pale green hands. The riders spread out as they approached the walls, circling to find the weakest parts of the defences before they closed in.

And the sweet, nauseating smell of the pines drifted closer on the wind and that same wind brought a chill which made all who stood upon the battlements shiver.

'Archers!' King Daffyn cried, raising his long sword high. 'Let fly!'

And a wave of whirring arrows met the wave of green riders and had no more effect upon them than if the archers had shot their shafts into so many trees. Faces, bodies, limbs were struck, horses were struck, and the People of the Pines did not waver.

A young knight in a long samite robe, over which had hastily been thrown a mail surcoat, ran up the steps, buckling a sword about his waist. He was a handsome youth, his brown hair unbound, his dark eyes dazed and puzzled. His feet were bare, Corum noticed.

'Father!' the youth cried, approaching King Daffyn. 'I am here!' And this must be Prince Guwinn, less drunk than his fellows. And Corum thought to himself that

Prince Guwinn had most to lose this day, for he must have come straight from his marriage bed.

Now Corum saw fire flickering in the distance and knew that Gaynor came to war. At the head of his Ghoolegh infantry, Gaynor the Damned lifted up his faceless helm as if he sought Corum amongst the defenders, his yellow plume dancing and his naked sword glowing sometimes silver, sometimes scarlet, sometimes gold and sometimes blue, the eight-arrowed Sign of Chaos pulsing on his breastplate, his strange armour glowing with as many different colours as his sword. Gaynor's tall horse pranced before the white-faced Ghoolegh infantry. Corum saw red, bestial eyes gleaming in a thousand faces. And yet still there seemed to be more fire, fire burning on the fringes of the Fhoi Myore mist. Was this some new form of enemy Corum had not yet encountered?

The People of the Pines were driving closer and from their mouths came laughter – rustling laughter like the sound of wind through leaves. Corum had heard such laughter before and he feared it.

He saw the reaction in the faces of the knights and warriors who waited on the battlements. They all felt terror strike them as they realized fully that they faced the supernatural. Then each man controlled his terror as best he could and prepared to stand against the Brothers to the Trees.

Another wave of arrows flew out, and another, and every single arrow found its target and now virtually every pine warrior rode forward with a red-fletched arrow protruding from his heart.

And the rustling laughter increased.

The warriors rode slowly and relentlessly forward. Some bristled with arrows. A few had javelins sticking completely through them. But their blank faces grinned blank grins and their cold eyes remained fixed upon the defenders. Reaching the foot of the walls, they dismounted.

More arrows flew and some of the People of the Pines began to take on the appearance of strange, sharp-spined animals, so many arrows quivered in their bodies.

And then they began to climb the walls.

They climbed as if they needed no hand- or foot-holds at all. They climbed as ivy climbed. Green tendrils moving up the walls towards the defenders.

One or two of the knights gasped and fell back, unable to accept this sight. Corum hardly blamed them. Nearby Goffanon growled in distaste.

And the first of the pale green warriors, eyes still fixed, grins still rigid, reached the battlements and began to attempt to climb over.

Corum's war-axe flashed in the sunlight and its blade smashed the head completely from the first warrior he saw. That warrior he pushed backward and it fell, but immediately another appeared and Corum's axe again struck off the head. Green sap spouted from the neck and clung to the blade of the axe, spattered across the stones of the battlements as he drew back his arms to strike again at the next head. He knew that he must tire of this soon or that parts of the defences would weaken and he would be attacked from both sides, but he did what he could while the People of the Pines swarmed up the walls, apparently in inexhaustible numbers.

There came a momentary pause when Corum was able to look beyond the Pine Warriors and see Gaynor ordering his Ghoolegh forward. They carried great logs in leathern harness which swung between them and they were plainly intent on battering down the gates of the city. Knowing that the Mabden were not, these days, used to fighting sieges, Corum could think of no way to resist the battering rams. The Mabden had fought hand to hand for centuries, each man picking another from the ranks of his enemies. Many tribes had not even fought to kill, feeling it ignoble to slay a man when he had been defeated. And while this was a Mabden strength it was, in any fight with Fhoi Myore forces, a great weakness.

Corum yelled to King Daffyn to prepare his people for the appearance of the Ghoolegh in their streets, but King

Daffyn was kneeling, his face gleaming with tears, and a Pine Warrior was running along the battlements towards Corum.

Corum saw that King Daffyn knelt beside the body of one whom the Pine Warrior had just slain. The body was dressed in white samite and a mail coat. Prince Guwinn would not be returning to his marriage bed.

Corum swung the axe low and chopped the Pine Warrior at the waist so that the torso toppled from the legs as a tree might topple. For moments the warrior continued to live, the legs moving forward, the arms waving from where the torso lay upon the flagstones. Then it died and turned brown almost immediately.

Corum ran up to King Daffyn crying savagely:

'Do not weep for your son – avenge him! Fight on, King Daffyn, or you and your folk are surely lost.'

'Fight on? Why? What I lived for has died. And we shall all die soon, Prince Corum. Why not now? I care not how I perish.'

'For love,' said Corum, 'and for beauty. For those things must you fight. For courage and pride!' But even as he spoke such words they rang hollow as he looked upon the corpse of the youth and he saw the tears spring again into the eyes of the youth's father. He turned away.

From below came the crashing and creaking noises as the battering rams repeatedly struck the gates. On the battlements Pine Warriors were now almost as thick as the defenders.

Goffanon could be seen, his huge bulk rising above a mass of the People of the Pines, his double-bladed axe swinging with the regularity of a pendulum as it chopped and chopped at the tree folk. There seemed to be a song on Goffanon's lips, almost a dirge, as he fought, and Corum caught some of the words.

I have been in the place where was slain Gwendoleu,
The son of Ceidaw, the pillar of songs,
When ravens screamed over blood.

I have been in the place where Bran was killed,
The son of Iweridd, of far extending fame,
When the ravens of the battlefield screamed.

I have been where Llacheu was slain,
The son of Urtu, extolled in songs,
When the ravens screamed over blood.

I have been where Meurig was killed,
The son of Carreian, of honourable fame,
When the ravens screamed over flesh.

I have been where Gwallawg was killed,
The son of Goholeth, the accomplished,
The resister of Lloegyr, the son of Lleynawg.

I have been where the soldiers of the Mabden were slain,
From the east to the north:
I am the escort of the grave.

I have been where the soldiers of the Mabden were slain,
From the east to the south:
I am alive, they in death!

And Corum realized that this was Goffanon's death-song, that the Sidhi smith prepared himself for his own inevitable slaying.

I have been to the graves of the Sidhi,
From the east to the west:
Now the ravens scream for me!

CHAPTER NINE

The Defence of the King's Hall

Corum realized that the position upon the battlements was all but lost and he smashed through the Pine Warriors to stand beside Goffanon, crying:

'To the hall, Goffanon! Fall back to the hall!'

Goffanon's song ended and he looked at Corum with calm eyes.

'Very well,' he said.

Together they went slowly back to the steps, fighting all the way, the People of the Pines crowding in on all sides, fixed grins, fixed eyes, sword-arms rising and falling. And the rustling, terrifying laughter hissing forever from their lips.

The knights and warriors who survived followed Corum's example and barely made the street as the timbers of the gates burst and the brass-shod battering ram smashed through. Two knights escorted King Daffyn who was still weeping and at length they reached the king's hall and drew the great brass doors close, barring them.

The signs of festivity were still everywhere about the hall. There were even a few too drunk to be roused who would probably die without realizing what had happened. Brands guttered, jewelled flags drooped. Corum went to peer through the narrow windows and saw that Gaynor was there, riding triumphantly at the head of his half-dead army, the eight-arrowed Sign of Chaos glowing as radiantly as ever upon his chest. For a while at least, Corum hoped, the people of the city would be reasonably safe while Gaynor concentrated his attack upon the hall. Corum saw the Ghoolegh behind Gaynor. They still carried their battering rams. And still the Fhoi Myore had not moved forward. Corum wondered if they would advance at all, knowing that Gaynor, the Ghoolegh and the People of the Pines would accomplish the defeat of Caer Garanhir without their help.

Yet even if, by hard fighting, the Fhoi Myore vassals could be vanquished, Corum knew that the Fhoi Myore could not be.

Pale green faces began to appear at the windows and stained glass smashed as the People of the Pines attempted to gain entrance to the hall. Again the knights and warriors of the Tuha-na-Gwyddneu Garanhir ran to defend themselves against the inhuman invaders.

Swords of notched and shining iron met the pale green swords of the Pine Warriors and the fight continued while outside the steady pounding of the battering rams began to sound on the bronze doors of the hall.

And while the fight raged, King Daffyn sat upon his throne, his head upon his hands, and wept for the death of Prince Guwinn, taking no interest in how the battle progressed.

Corum ran to where at least ten of the Pine Warriors bore down on two of King Daffyn's war-knights. His axe was blunted now and his fleshly hand was sore and bleeding. If it had not been for his silver hand, he might long since have been forced to drop the weapon. As it was, his arms were weary as he lifted the double-bladed axe to chop at the neck of a Pine Warrior who was about to slide his sword into the unprotected side of a tall knight already engaged with two more of the Pine Folk.

Several of the Pine Warriors came at Corum then, swords slashing, laughter rustling from their pale green lips, and Corum took first one step backward and then another as they pressed him towards the far wall of the hall. Elsewhere Goffanon was engaged with three of the warriors and unable to help Corum. The Vadhagh prince swung the axe back and forth, up and down, and swords ripped his byrnie and found his flesh and began to draw blood from a dozen shallow wounds.

Then Corum felt the stones of the wall behind him and knew he could retreat no further. Above him a brand flickered, casting his shadow over the bodies of the Pine Folk as, grinning, they moved to finish him.

A sword bit into the haft of his axe. Desperately he wrenched the weapon free and struck at the one who held the sword, a warrior who had been handsome but whose face was now pierced by three red-fletched arrows. He struck the axe deep into the skull, splitting it. Green gore spouted, the warrior fell but he took the head and part of the haft of Corum's axe with him. Corum turned and leapt for the ledge above his head, getting his balance and drawing his sword, steadying himself with his silver hand by clinging to the bracket in which the brand flared. The Pine Warriors began to move up the wall towards him. He kicked one back, chopped at another with his sword, but they were clutching at his feet now, still grinning, still laughing, cold eyes still staring. Desperately he released his grip upon the bracket and seized the brand, plunging it into the face of the nearest warrior.

And the warrior screamed.

For the first time a Pine Warrior yelled in pain. And his face began to burn, the sap sizzling from the wounds he had already received but which had not appeared to harm him.

The other warriors fell away in panic, avoiding their blazing comrade as he ran about the hall screaming and burning until at last he fell over the remains of another of his kind. The brown body caught, too, and began to burn.

And then Corum cursed himself for not understanding that the only weapon likely to be feared by tree-folk was fire. He called to the others:

'Get brands! Fire will destroy them! Take the torches from the walls!'

And he saw that the bronze doors of the hall were bulging now and could not last much longer before the onslaught of the Ghoolegh battering rams.

Now all who could still move were springing to the torches and tearing them down, turning them upon their enemies, and soon the hall was full of cloudy smoke – smoke which choked Corum and the others – sweet, pine-scented smoke.

The People of the Pines began to retreat, trying to reach the windows, but the war-knights of the Tuha-na-Gwyddneu Garanhir stopped them, thrusting the brands into their bodies and making them shriek and fall upon the bloody flagstones as they burned.

And then there fell a silence in the hall – a silence broken only by the steady beating of the rams upon the door. And there were no more People of the Pines, only grey ash and smoke and a sweet, nauseating stink.

Here and there the jewelled flags had caught and were beginning to smoulder. Elsewhere wooden beams were burning, but the defenders ignored them as they massed near the front of the hall and waited for the Ghoolegh to come.

And this time each surviving warrior, including Corum and the battered Sidhi smith, Goffanon, had a brand in his hand.

The bronze door bulged. The hinges and the bars creaked.

Light began to show through as the doors were beaten out of shape.

Again the rams struck. Again the doors creaked.

Through the gap Corum thought he saw Gaynor directing the work of the Ghoolegh.

Another blow and one of the bars snapped and flew across the hall to land at the feet of the king who still wept in his throne at the far end.

Another blow and the second bar snapped and a hinge clattered to the flagstones, the door tilting and beginning to swing inward.

Another blow.

And the bronze doors fell and the Ghoolegh paused in surprise as a wedge of men came running towards them from the smoky gloom of the hall at Caer Garanhir, brands in their left hands, swords or axes in their right hands, moving to attack.

Gaynor's black horse reared and the Damned Prince almost dropped his glowing sword in astonishment as he saw the battle-weary, smoke-blackened, tattered force, led by the Vadhagh Corum and the Sidhi Goffanon, rushing at him. 'What? What? Some still live?'

Corum ran straight for Gaynor, but still Gaynor refused to do combat with him, turning the rearing horse and seeking to cut a path through his own Ghoolegh half-dead so that he might escape.

'Come back, Gaynor! Fight me! Oh, fight me, Gaynor!' cried Corum.

But Gaynor laughed his bleak laugh as he retreated. 'I shall not return to Limbo – not while the prospect of death awaits me in this realm.'

'You forget that the Fhoi Myore are already dying. What if you outlive them? What if they perish and the world is renewed?'

'That cannot happen, Corum. Their poisons spread and are permanent! You fight for nothing, you see!'

Then Gaynor had gone and the Ghoolegh with their cutlasses and their knives were lumbering forward, nervous of the brand-fire, for fire had no place in the Fhoi Myore lands. Though the Ghoolegh did not burn as the People of the Pines had burned, they feared the flames heartily and were loath to move forward, particularly now that Gaynor had retreated and could be seen in the distance turning his horse to watch the fray from safety.

The Ghoolegh outnumbered the survivors of Garanhir by more than ten to one, yet the war-knights and the warriors were forcing them backward, yelling their battle-cries, shouting their battle-songs, hacking and stabbing at the half-dead warriors, shoving the brands deep into their faces so that they grumbled and whined and put up their hands to ward away the flames.

And Goffanon was no longer singing his own death-song. He was laughing and shouting out to Corum: 'They retreat! They retreat! See how they retreat, Corum!'

But Corum felt no gaiety, for he knew that the Fhoi Myore had not yet attacked.

Then he heard Gaynor's voice calling:

'Balahr! Kerenos! Goim!' Gaynor called. 'It is time! It is time!'

Gaynor the Damned rode back to the gates of Caer Garanhir.

'Rhannon! Arek! Sreng! It is time! It is time!'

And Gaynor went shouting through the ruined gates of Caer Garanhir, his Ghoolegh creeping behind him, thinking that he retreated.

Corum and Goffanon and the few knights and warriors of the Tuha-na-Gwyddneu Garanhir roared their triumph as they saw their enemies flee.

'For all that it shall be our only victory this day,' said Corum to Goffanon, 'I savour it greatly, my Sidhi friend.'

And then they waited for the Fhoi Myore to come.

But the Fhoi Myore did not come, though it began to grow dark. In the distance the Fhoi Myore mist remained and a few Ghoolegh milled here and there, mixing with the People of the Pines, but the Fhoi Myore, unused to defeat, were perhaps debating what to do next. Perhaps they recalled the spear Bryionak and the Black Bull of Crinanass which had defeated them once, slaying their comrade, and seeing their vassals driven back, became fearful that another Bull came against them. Just as they avoided Craig Dôn it was possible that they now avoided Caer Mahlod because they associated it with defeat and were considering avoiding Caer Garanhir for the same reason.

Whatever made the Fhoi Myore remain upon the horizon Corum did not care. He was glad for the reprieve and the time for the dead to be counted, the wounded tended, the old and the children to be taken to places of greater security, the warriors and knights (many of whom were women) to be properly equipped and for the gates to be shored up as well as possible.

'They are cautious, the Fhoi Myore,' said Goffanon reminiscently. 'They are like cowardly carrion dogs. It is what has allowed them to survive so long, I think.'

'And Gaynor follows their example. As far as I know he has no great reason to fear me, but it worked to our advantage this day. Yet the Fhoi Myore will come soon, I think,' said Corum.

'I think so,' agreed the Sidhi. He stood on the battlements beside Corum and sharpened the blades of his axe with the whetstone he carried, his great, black brows drawn together. 'Yet do you see something which flickers close to the mist? And do you see a darker mist blending with that of the Fhoi Myore?'

'I saw it earlier,' Corum said, 'and cannot explain it. I think it is some other Fhoi Myore tool which they shall send against us before long.'

'Ah,' said Goffanon pointing. 'Here comes Ilbrec. Doubtless he saw that our battle went well and comes to join us again.' Goffanon's tone was bitter.

They watched the gigantic, golden youth riding the proud black stallion towards them. Ilbrec was smiling and he carried a sword in his hand. The sword was not that which he still bore at his belt, but another. And it made the sword he bore at his belt seem crude and poor by comparison, for it blazed as brightly as the sun and its hilt was all worked in fine gold and there were jewels in it and a pommel which glowed like a ruby and yet was the size of Corum's head. Ilbrec tossed his braids and waved the sword high.

'You were right to remind me of the Weapons of Light, Goffanon! I found the chest and I found the sword. Here it is! Here is Retaliator, my father's sword with which he fought the Fhoi Myore. Here is Retaliator!'

And Goffanon said sullenly, as Ilbrec came closer to the walls, his huge head level with theirs as they stood upon the battlements: 'But you came with it too late, Ilbrec. We have finished our fight now.'

'Too late? Did I not use the sword to draw a circle around the Fhoi Myore ranks so that even now they are confused, unable to move towards the city, unable to direct their troops?'

'So it was your work!' Corum began to laugh. 'You

saved us, after all, Ilbrec, when you seemed to have deserted us.'

Ilbrec was puzzled. 'Desert you? Leave what will be the last struggle between Sidhi and Fhoi Myore ever to take place? I would not do that, little Vadhagh!'

And Goffanon was laughing now.

'I know you would not, Ilbrec. Welcome back to us! And welcome, too, to the great sword Retaliator!'

'It still has all its powers,' said Ilbrec, turning the blade to make it blaze yet more brightly. 'It is still the mightiest weapon ever drawn against the Fhoi Myore. And they know it! Ah, they know it, Goffanon! I drew this burning circle around their poison mist, containing the mist and containing them at the same time, for they cannot move unless their mist moves with them. And there they stay.'

'For ever?' Corum said hopefully.

Ilbrec shook his head and smiled. 'No. Not for ever, but for a while. And before we leave I will draw a defence about Caer Garanhir so that the Fhoi Myore and their warriors will fear to attack.'

'We must go to King Daffyn and interrupt his grieving, I fear,' said Corum. 'Time grows short if we are to save Amergin's life. We need the Golden Oak and the Silvern Ram.'

King Daffyn raised his red eyes and looked upon Corum and Goffanon who stood in the hall before him. A slender girl of little more than sixteen summers sat upon the arm of the king's chair and stroked the king's head.

'Your city is safe now, King Daffyn, and will be so for some time. But now we ask a boon of you!'

'Go,' said King Daffyn. 'I suppose that I shall be grateful to you later, but I am not grateful now. Please leave me. Sidhi warriors bring the Fhoi Myore upon us.'

'The Fhoi Myore marched before we came here,' said Corum. 'It was our warning that saved you.'

'It did not save my son,' said King Daffyn.

'It did not save my husband,' said the maiden who sat beside the king.

'But other sons were saved – and other husbands – and more will be saved, King Daffyn, with your help. We seek two of the Mabden Treasures – the Oak of Gold and the Ram of Silver. Do you have them?'

'They are no longer mine,' said King Daffyn. 'And I would not part with them if they were.'

'These are the only things which will revive your Archdruid Amergin from the enchantment put upon him by the Fhoi Myore,' said Corum.

'Amergin? He is a prisoner in Caer Llud. Or dead, by now.'

'No. Amergin lives – just. We saved him.'

'Did you?' King Daffyn looked at the two with a different expression in his eyes. 'Amergin lives and is free?' The despair seemed to fall away as Fhoi Myore snow had melted when touched by the Black Bull's blood. 'Free? To guide us?'

'Aye – if we can get to Caer Mahlod in time. For that is where he is. At Caer Mahlod, but dying. The Oak and the Ram alone will save him. Yet if they are not yours, whom must we ask to give them to us?'

'They were our wedding gifts,' said the sweet-faced girl. 'They were the king's gifts to his son and me this morning, when Guwinn lived. You may have the Oak of Gold and the Ram of Silver.'

And she left the hall and returned shortly bearing a casket. And she opened the casket and revealed a model of a spreading oak tree all worked in gold and so fine as to seem completely real. And beside it rested the silver image of a ram, each curl of wool seeming to be set in relief by the craftsman who made it. A ram with great, sweeping horns. A rampant ram whose silver eyes stared with a strange wisdom from the silver head.

And the maiden bowed her fair head and she closed the lid of the casket and she handed it to Corum who accepted it with gratitude, thanking her, thanking King Daffyn.

'And now we go back to Caer Mahlod,' said Corum.

'Tell Amergin, if he revives, that we shall follow him in any decision he cares to make,' said King Daffyn.

'I will tell him,' said Corum.

Then the Vadhagh Prince and the Sidhi dwarf left that hall of mourning and went out through the gates of Caer Garanhir and joined their comrade Ilbrec, son of Manannan, the greatest of the Sidhi heroes.

And the fire still flickered around the distant mist and now a peculiar fire had begun to sprout some distance from the walls of Caer Garanhir.

'The Sidhi fire protects this place,' said Ilbrec. 'It will not last but it will dissuade the Fhoi Myore from attacking, I think. Now, we ride!' He stuffed the sword Retaliator into his belt and bent to pick up Corum who clung to his casket as he was lifted into the air and sat upon Ilbrec's saddle near the pommel.

'We shall need a boat when we reach the sea,' said Corum as they began to move.

'Oh, I think not,' said Ilbrec.

BOOK THREE

---

*In which Prince Corum is witness
to the power of the Oak and the
Ram and the Mabden people
find new hope*

CHAPTER ONE

The Road Across the Water

They had reached the beach before Corum became aware that Goffanon was lagging behind. He craned his head back and saw that the Sidhi dwarf was some distance off, almost stumbling now and shaking his shaggy head from side to side.

'What ails Goffanon?' Corum asked.

Ilbrec had not noticed. Now he, too, looked back. 'Perhaps he tires. He has fought long today and he has run many miles.' Ilbrec looked west, to where the sun was sinking. 'Should we rest before crossing the sea?'

The gigantic horse Splendid Mane tossed his head as if to say that he did not wish to rest, but Ilbrec laughed and patted his neck.

'Splendid Mane hates to rest and loves only to be galloping the world. He has slept for so long in the caverns beneath the sea that he is impatient to be on the move! But we must let Goffanon catch up with us and then ask him what he feels.'

Corum heard Goffanon's panting breath behind him and turned again, smiling, to ask the Sidhi smith what he wished to do.

But Goffanon's eyes were glaring and Goffanon's lips were curled back in a foam-flecked snarl and the great double-bladed war-axe was aimed directly at Ilbrec's skull.

'Ilbrec!' Corum flung himself towards the ground and landed with a crash, managing to keep the chest containing the Oak and the Ram tucked firmly under his left arm. He drew his sword as he sprang upright, while Ilbrec turned, calling in puzzlement:

'Goffanon! Old friend? What's this?'

'He is enchanted!' Corum yelled. 'A Mabden wizard has put him under a glamour. Calatin must be nearby!'

Ilbrech reached out to grasp the haft of the dwarf's war-axe, but Goffanon was strong. He pulled the giant from his saddle and the two immortals began to struggle upon the ground, close to the sea-washed beach, while Corum and Splendid Mane looked on, the horse severely puzzled by his master's behaviour.

Corum cried: 'Goffanon! Goffanon! You fight a brother!'

Another voice floated down from above and looking up Corum saw a tall man standing on the edge of the cliff, a tendril or two of white, clinging mist above his shoulders.

The world grew grey as the sun sank.

The figure on the cliff-edge was the wizard Calatin, in a long pleated surcoat of soft leather stained a rich, deep blue. Upon his slender, gloved fingers were jewelled rings and at his throat a collar of jewelled gold, while his samite robe was embroidered with mystical designs. He stroked his grey beard and he smiled his secret smile.

'He is my ally now, Corum of the Silver Hand,' said the wizard Calatin.

'And thus the ally of the Fhoi Myore!' Corum looked for a pathway up the cliff which would take him to the wizard and all the while Goffanon and Ilbrec tumbled over and over on the sand, grunting and snorting in their exertions.

'For the moment, at least,' said Calatin. 'But one does not have to be loyal to either Mabden or Fhoi Myore – or Sidhi – there are other loyalties, loyalties to oneself among them, are there not? And, who knows, but you could be an ally of mine soon!'

'Never that!' Corum began to run up a steep cliff path towards the wizard, his sword in his fleshly hand. 'Never that, Calatin!'

Out of breath, Corum reached the top of the cliff and approached the wizard, who smiled and began to retreat slowly.

It was then that Corum saw the mist behind the wizard and he recognized the mist for what it was.

'Fhoi Myore! One of them is free!'

'He was never trapped by Ilbrec's sword. We followed behind the main force. This is Sreng. Sreng of the Seven Swords.'

And the mist began to move towards Corum as darkness covered the world and from below on the beach he still heard the pantings and the gruntings of the two fighting Sidhi.

And through the mist he saw a huge wicker battle-cart, large enough to take one as large as Ilbrec himself. The cart was drawn by two massive creatures which seemed most to resemble lizards, though they were not lizards. And from the cart now stepped a vast being with a white body all covered in red, pulsing warts, and the body was naked save for a belt. The belt was festooned with swords, making a sort of kilt. Corum looked up and he saw a face which was human in some respects and resembled the face of one he had known, long ago. The eyes were fierce and tragic. They were the eyes of the Earl of Krae, of Glandyth who had first struck off Corum's hand and put out his eye and so begun the long history of the fight against the Sword Rulers. But the eyes did not know Corum, though there was a flicker of recognition as they saw the silver hand fixed to his left wrist.

And from the torn folds of the mouth there sounded a booming noise.

'Lord Sreng,' said the wizard Calatin. 'This is he who helped in the destruction at Caer Mahlod. This is he who engineered this day's defeat. This is Corum.'

And Corum put down the casket in which reposed the Oak of Gold and the Ram of Silver and he spread his legs so that he stood firmly over the casket, and he reached to his belt and he took his dirk in his silver hand, and he prepared to defend himself against Sreng of the Seven Swords.

Sreng moved slowly, as if in pain, drawing two of his great swords from his belt.

'Slay Corum, Lord Sreng, and give me his body. Slay Corum and the Fhoi Myore will no longer be plagued by the resistance of the Mabden.'

Again the strained, booming noise came from the ragged mouth. The red warts pulsed on the vast expanse of pale flesh. Corum noted that one of the giant's legs was shorter than the other so that his gait was rolling as he moved. He saw that Sreng had only three teeth in his mouth and that the little finger of his right hand was covered in a yellow mould speckled with white and black. Then Corum saw that other parts of the giant's body, particularly about the thighs covered by the swords, also had patches of this mould growing upon them. And from Sreng of the Seven Swords there escaped a foulness of stench reminding Corum of long-dead fish and the excrement of cats.

From the dark below came the grunts of the fighting Sidhi. Calatin was barely visible, chuckling from the night. Only Sreng, framed against the mist he must carry always with him, was clearly seen.

Corum felt that he did not wish to die at the hands of this decrepit god, this Sreng. Sreng himself was already dying, as were the other Fhoi Myore, of diseases which might take a hundred years to kill him.

'Sreng,' said Corum, 'would you return to Limbo, return to your realm where you would not perish? I could help you go back to your world, the plane where your disease will not flourish. Leave this realm to enjoy its natural state. Take back your coldness and your death.'

'He deceives you, Lord Sreng,' said the wizard Calatin from the darkness. 'Believe me. He deceives you.'

And then a word, a booming word escaped the torn lips. And that word echoed the word Corum had spoken, as if it were the only word in human speech which the lips could form.

The word was: 'Death.'

'Your own realm awaits you – there is a way through.'

A diseased arm began to raise a crude sword of roughly cast iron. Corum knew that he could not block any blow from that sword. It whistled down at his head and then struck the ground near his feet with horrible force. He realized that Sreng had not deliberately missed him but that the Fhoi Myore was hard-put to control his limbs. Knowing this Corum stooped, picked up the casket containing the Oak and the Ram, and ran inside Sreng's guard, driving his sword deep into the giant's shin.

The Fhoi Myore's voice boomed in pain. Corum ran under his legs and hacked at him behind his knee where grew more of the disgusting mildew. Sreng began to turn, but then the leg buckled and he fell, searching for Corum while Calatin yelled:

'There, Lord Sreng! There! Behind you!'

Now Corum shuddered as the chilling mist began to eat at his bones. All his instincts made him wish to run clear of the mist and into the night, but he held his ground as a gigantic hand came hunting for him. He hacked at the sinews of the hand and then another huge sword whistled over his head forcing him to duck, almost striking him.

And Sreng fell backward upon Corum, his neck pressing the Vadhagh prince to the ground, his hand still searching for the mortal who fought him with such temerity.

Corum sweated to pull himself free, not knowing if any of his bones were broken, while the diseased fingers brushed his shoulder, sought to pluck him up, missed and began to search again. The stench of the Fhoi Myore's rotting flesh almost robbed Corum of his consciousness; the texture of that flesh made him shudder; the chilling mist robbed him of the last of his strength, but at least, he assured himself, he would have died valiantly against one of the great enemies of those whose cause he championed.

Was the voice he now heard Calatin's?

'Sreng! I know you, Sreng!'

No, the voice was Ilbrec's. So Ilbrec had won the fight and doubtless Goffanon now lay dead upon the beach. Corum had the impression of a huge hand coming down upon him, but then it seized Sreng by what was left of the

Fhoi Myore's hair and pulled the head up so that Corum was able to scramble free. Then, as Corum staggered back, still keeping his hold upon the casket containing the Oak and the Ram, he saw golden Ilbrec draw the great sword Retaliator, the sword of his father, from his belt and place the point against Sreng's breast and drive that point deep into the Fhoi Myore's corrupting heart so that Sreng let forth a yell.

Sreng's last yell frightened Corum more than any of the previous events had done. For Sreng's last yell had been a shout of pleasure, a wavering, delighted sound as Sreng found the death he had longed for.

Ilbrec stepped back from the Fhoi Myore body.

'Corum? Are you safe?'

'Safe enough, thanks to you, Ilbrec. I am bruised, that is all.'

'Thank yourself. What you did against Sreng was valiant. You have brains and great courage, Vadhagh. You saved yourself, for I should not have come in time otherwise.'

'Calatin,' said Corum. 'Where is he?'

'Fled. There is nothing we can do at present, for it becomes urgent to leave this place.'

'Why did Calatin want my body from Sreng?'

'Is that what he asked?' Ilbrec drew Corum up in the crook of his huge arm while he sheathed the sword Retaliator. 'I have no idea. I know nothing of Mabden needs.'

Ilbrec returned to the beach where the black horse Splendid Mane cropped at the grass of the cliff, its pearl harness sparkling in the light of the moon which had now risen in the sky.

Corum saw a dark shape lying upon the beach.

'Goffanon?' he said. 'You were forced to slay him?'

'He showed every intention of slaying me,' said Ilbrec. 'I remembered what he told me of Calatin's enchantment. I suppose Calatin followed us and came close enough to Goffanon to re-exert his sorcerous influence. Poor Goffanon.'

'Should we bury him here?' said Corum. He was full of misery, only now realizing the strength of his affection for the Sidhi smith. 'I would not like the Fhoi Myore to find him. Neither would I care for Calatin to – to make use of the body.'

'I agree that that would not be good,' said Ilbrec. 'But I think it unwise to bury him, you know.' He placed Corum again upon the saddle of Splendid Mane and he crossed to where Goffanon's body lay, heaving it up with some difficulty by placing Goffanon's limp arm around his neck and carrying the dwarf upon his back. 'He is a very heavy dwarf,' Ilbrec said.

Corum was distressed by Ilbrec's lightness of tone. But perhaps the giant simply hid his melancholy well.

'Then what shall we do?'

'Take him with us, I think, to Caer Mahlod.' Ilbrec put his foot in his stirrup and prepared to mount. He grunted and cursed as he got into the saddle after several attempts. 'Ach! The dwarf has bruised me all over. Damn him!' Then he smiled in his golden beard as he looked down and saw the expression upon Corum's face. 'Do not grieve, yet, for Goffanon the smith. Sidhi dwarfs are very hard to slay. This one, for instance, has merely had his silly senses knocked from him for a while.'

Ilbrec leaned back in his saddle, letting Splendid Mane take some of the weight of the dwarf. He held Goffanon's war-axe in the same hand which held the reins, resting it behind Corum across his saddle. 'Well, Splendid Mane, you carry three with you. I hope that you have lost none of your old skills.'

Corum's face broke into a smile. 'So he lives! Yet still we shall have to move swiftly to escape Calatin's power. And our boat was abandoned out there. How shall we cross the water?'

'Splendid Mane knows certain paths,' said Ilbrec. 'Paths not quite of this dimension, if you understand me. Now, horse of my father, gallop. And gallop straight. Find the pathways through the sea.'

Splendid Mane snorted, lifted himself on his hind-legs

for a moment, and plunged towards the sea.

Ilbrec laughed in delight, then, at Corum's considerable astonishment as Splendid Mane's hooves touched the sea but did not sink.

Soon they were galloping out over the ocean, over the surface, beneath a huge moon which made the water shine, galloping for Caer Mahlod, galloping along the road across the water.

'You understand much concerning the Fifteen Realms, Vadhagh,' said Ilbrec as they rode, 'so you will understand that it is Splendid Mane's great talent to find certain veins, as it were, which do not belong exactly in this realm, just as my sea-caverns do not belong. These veins can be found most particularly upon the surface of the sea and sometimes in the air itself. A Mabden would marvel and call such abilities sorcery, but we know otherwise. They make, however, a good spectacle when one wishes to impress the poor Mabden.'

And Ilbrec laughed again as Splendid Mane galloped on. 'We shall be in Caer Mahlod before morning!'

CHAPTER TWO

The Place of Power

The folk of the Tuha-na-Cremm Croich looked with awe upon the three as they approached the conical mound on which Caer Mahlod was built.

Goffanon was awake now and striding beside Splendid Mane. He grumbled of the bruises Ilbrec had inflicted, but his tone was good-humoured for he knew that Ilbrec had in reality saved both his life and his pride.

'So this is Caer Mahlod,' said the golden-haired son of Manannan as he brought Splendid Mane to a halt beside the water-ditch which now protected the citadel. 'It has changed little.'

'You have been here before?' asked Corum curiously.

'Indeed. In the old days there was a place near here where the Sidhi would gather. I remember being brought here by my father shortly before he went off to fight in the battle which took his life.'

Ilbrec dismounted and gently lifted Corum from the saddle to place him upon the ground. Corum was weary, for they had ridden all night over those strange, other-realm pathways across the sea; but he still kept the casket, the gift of King Daffyn and his daughter-in-law, tightly under his arm. His mail coat was torn and his helmet was much-dented. The sword at his side was notched and blunted; he bore the signs of many small wounds, and when he walked it was painfully and slowly. But there was pride, too, in his bearing as he called for the drawbridge to be lowered:

'It is Corum come back to Caer Mahlod,' he cried, 'bringing two friends, allies of the Mabden.' He lifted the casket in his two hands, the one of flesh and the other of silver. 'And, see, here are the Oak of Gold and the Ram of Silver which will give you back your High King.'

The bridge was lowered and on the other side waited Medhbh of the Long Arm and Jhary-a-Conel with his cat upon his shoulder and his hat upon his head. Medhbh ran forward to embrace Corum, kissing his bruised face, taking off his helmet and stroking his hair.

'My love,' she said. 'My elfin love, come home.' And she was weeping.

Jhary-a-Conel said soberly: 'Amergin is close to death. A few more hours and he will bleat his last, I fear.'

Grave-faced Mannach appeared. With dignity he welcomed the two Sidhi.

'We are much honoured. Corum brings fine, good friends to Caer Mahlod.'

Looking about the morning streets at the people who were beginning to gather, Corum saw none of King Fiachadh's people.

'Has King Fiachadh gone?'

'He had to leave, for there were rumours that the Fhoi Myore marched over an ice-bridge to attack his land.'

'The Fhoi Myore marched,' said Corum, 'and they made an ice-bridge over the sea right enough, but it was not King Fiachadh's folk they attacked. They went to Caer Garanhir and there we fought them, Goffanon, Ilbrec and I.' And he told King Mannach of all that had befallen him since he and Goffanon had parted from Jhary-a-Conel.

'But now,' he ended, 'I would eat, for I am famished, and doubtless my friends are hungry, too. And I would rest for an hour or two, since we have ridden through the whole night to be here.'

'You slew a Fhoi Myore!' said Medhbh. 'So they can be slain by others than the Black Bull?'

'I helped slay one – a very minor one, a very ill one,' smiled Corum. 'But if it had not been for Ilbrec here, I should now be crushed beneath the monster.'

'I owe you much, great Ilbrec,' said Medhbh, bowing her head to the Sidhi. Her thick, red hair fell down over her face and she brushed it back as she tilted back her head to look up into the smiling eyes of the giant Sidhi. 'I should be mourning now if it were not for you.'

'He's brave, this little Vadhagh.' The golden-bearded youth laughed, seating himself casually upon the flat roof of a nearby house.

'He is brave,' agreed Medhbh.

'But come,' King Mannach said urgently, taking Corum's arm, 'you must see Amergin and tell me what you think of his condition.' King Mannach looked up at Ilbrec. 'I fear you could not enter our low doors, Lord Sidhi.'

'I'll wait here cheerfully until I'm needed,' said Ilbrec. 'But you go, Goffanon, if that is fitting.'

Goffanon said: 'I should like to see what has happened to the Archdruid, we took so much trouble saving him.' He left his axe standing near Ilbrec's right foot and followed after King Mannach, Medhbh, Jhary-a-Conel and Corum as they entered the king's hall and crossed it, waiting while King Mannach opened a door and led them inside.

The room was lit brightly with brands. No attempt had been made to remove Amergin's sheepskin clothing, but it had been cleaned. The High King lay beside a number of plates on which various kinds of grasses had been laid.

'We sought desperately to discover which would sustain him best, but none of them have done more than prolong his life by a few hours,' King Mannach said. He opened the casket Corum had handed him. He frowned as he inspected the two beautifully made images. 'How are these to be used?'

Corum shook his head. 'I know not.'

'He did not tell us,' Jhary-a-Conel said.

'Then has your quest been fruitless?' Medhbh asked.

'I think not,' said Goffanon, stepping forward. 'I know something of the properties of the Oak and the Ram. There was a legend amongst our folk that they had been fashioned for a particular purpose, when the Mabden race would be in great danger and few Sidhi to help them in their struggles. I recall that there was a Sidhi called Oak Woman who gave a pledge to the Mabden, but the nature of that pledge I do not know. We must take the Oak and the Ram to a place of power, perhaps to Craig Dôn . . .'

'It would be too far to journey,' Corum said reasonably. 'Look – life flees Amergin even as we speak.'

'It is true,' said Medhbh. The High King's breath was shallow and his flesh as pale as his woollen garments. His face looked old and lined whereas previously, perhaps because he was untroubled in his guise of a sheep, it had seemed young.

'Cremmsmound,' said Jhary-a-Conel. 'That is a place of power.'

'Aye,' said King Mannach with a faint smile. 'It is. At Cremmsmound we summoned you, Prince Corum, to come to our aid.'

'Then perhaps there we can release the magic of the Oak and the Ram,' Goffanon said, frowning and tugging at his matted black beard. 'Could you ask Amergin, Jhary-a-Conel, if Cremmsmound is a good place?'

But Jhary shook his head. 'My cat reports that the Archdruid is too weak. To speak with him now would be to shock what remains of his life from him.'

'This is an irony I do not like,' said King Mannach. 'To be defeated now, after so many deeds of courage have been performed.'

And, as if in agreement with the king, there came from the figure on the floor a faint, melancholy bleat.

His body trembling with sudden emotion, King Mannach turned away. He groaned. 'Our High King! Our High King!'

Goffanon laid a huge, gnarled hand upon Mannach's shoulder. 'Let us take him, anyway, to Cremmsmound, to that place of power. Who knows what will happen? Tonight the moon shall be at its fullest and will shine upon the mistletoe and the oaks. It is an excellent night for the working of incantations and charms, I am told, for the fullness of the moon indicates when the Fifteen Planes intersect most closely.'

'Is that why folk regard the full moon as having particular properties?' Medhbh had been told something of the realms beyond the Earth by Corum. 'It is not simply superstition?'

'The moon itself has no power,' said Goffanon. 'It is merely, in this case, a measuring instrument. It tells us roughly how the different planes of the Earth move in relation to each other.'

'Strange,' said King Mannach, 'how we are inclined to reject such knowledge simply because it becomes corrupted by primitive minds. A year ago I should not have believed in the legends of the Sidhi, in the legends of Cremm Croich, in the folktales of our people or in any of our old superstitions. And in a way I would have been right, for there are those who have an interest in using legends and superstitions for their own ends. They cherish such notions not for their own sake but for the use to which they can be put. Poor, wretched people who cannot love life seek for something beyond life, something they prefer to regard as better than life. And, as a result, they corrupt the knowledge they discover and, in turn, associate their own weaknesses with this knowledge – at least, in the minds of others like myself.

'But the knowledge you have brought us, Corum – that extends our appreciation of life. You speak of a variety of worlds where mankind flourishes. You offer us information which brings light to our understanding, where the corrupt and the lost speak only of mysteries and dark superiorities and seek to elevate themselves in their own eyes and the eyes of their fellows.'

'I follow you,' said Corum, for he had some experience himself of what King Mannach meant. 'Yet even when the minds are primitive and the knowledge corrupt, this can spawn a huge and ugly power of its own. And can the power of Light exist without the presence of the power of Dark? Can generosity survive without greed or knowledge survive without ignorance?'

'That is ever the puzzle of the Mabden dream,' said Jhary-a-Conel, almost to himself, 'and that, doubtless, is why I am encouraged to remain in that dream wherever, in all the Fifteen Realms and beyond, it manifests itself.' Then he spoke more briskly: 'But this particular dream will fade very soon unless we find a means of reviving Amergin. Come, let us bear him swiftly to this place of power, this Cremmsmound.'

And it was only as they prepared to leave for the mound in the oak grove that Corum realized he had a profound reluctance to accompany them.

He realized that he feared Cremmsmound, for all that it was the place he had first seen when King Mannach and his folk called him from their past, from Castle Erorn and his brooding and his memories of Rhalina.

Corum mocked himself, realizing that he was both tired and hungry and that when he had rested a little and eaten a little and spent a little time in the company of his lovely Medhbh he would no longer experience such silly feelings.

Yet they remained with him until the evening when King Mannach, Medhbh of the Long Arm, Jhary-a-Conel, Goffanon the dwarf, Ilbrec of the Sidhi riding on Splendid Mane, Corum and all King Mannach's folk from the fortress city of Caer Mahlod, took the near-dead body of the High King Amergin forth and bore it towards the forest where, in a glade, rose the mound under which, according to legend, Corum – or a previous incarnation of Corum – had been buried.

A little faint sunlight lingered among the great trees of the forest, creating dark and mysterious shadows which seemed to Corum to contain more than rhododendrons and brambles, more than squirrels or foxes or birds.

Twice he shook his head, cursing his own weariness for putting stupid notions into his mind.

And then at last the party reached Cremmsmound in the oak glade.

They reached the place of power.

CHAPTER THREE

The Golden Oak and the Silvern Ram

For a moment, as he entered the oak grove, Corum felt a cold enter his body which was even more profound than that which he had experienced at Caer Llud and he felt that this was the coldness of death.

He began to remember the prophecy of Ieveen the Seeress whom he had met on the way to Hy-Breasail. She had told him to fear a harp – well, he did fear a harp. She had told him to fear a brother, too. Did his 'brother' rest under the grassmound in the oak grove, under the artificial hill surrounded by oaks of all ages, the holy place of the folk of Caer Mahlod? Was there another Corum – the real hero Cremm, perhaps – who would rise from the earth to slay him for his presumption?

Was it Cremm he had seen in his dream while he slept at Craig Dôn?

The mount was a silhouette against the sinking sun and the moon was already rising. A hundred faces turned upwards to look at the moon, but these were not the faces of superstitious men and women. Each face reflected a curiosity and a sense of impending wonderment. It was quiet in the oak grove as they stood in a circle about the mound.

Then Ilbrec lifted the puny body of the High King in his great arms and Ilbrec walked up the mound and placed the High King at the very top. And then Ilbrec, too, turned his face up to look at the moon.

Ilbrec walked slowly back down the mound to stand beside his old friend Goffanon.

Next came King Mannach to the mound, walking

slowly up and holding the open casket in his arms. From within the casket gleamed gold and silver. King Mannach placed the golden oak at Amergin's head, where it faced the fading sun, and the oak shone brightly, seeming to absorb all the remaining rays. And King Mannach placed the image of the silver ram at Amergin's feet so that the rays of the moon would fall upon it, and already the silver ram burned white and cold.

Corum thought that, save for their size, those two images could be a living tree and a living ram, so fine was their workmanship. The gathering pressed closer around the mound as King Mannach descended, all eyes upon the prone body of the High King and the oak and the ram. Only Corum hung back. The cold had gone from his body, yet he still shivered, still fought the fear which sought to fill his mind.

Then came Goffanon the smith, his double-bladed axe, which he had forged himself centuries before, upon his broad shoulder, the gold of the oak and the silver of the ram reflected in his helm, greaves and breastplate of polished iron. And Goffanon walked halfway up the mound and paused, lowering his axe so that the blade rested upon the turf and his hands rested upon the shaft.

Corum smelled the rich and subtle scents of the trees, the brambles, the rhododendrons and the grass of the forest. Those scents were warm and good and should have lulled the sense of fear in Corum, but they did not. Still he did not join the throng, but remained at the edge of the gathering wishing that Medhbh had not pressed forward with the rest, wishing that she stood beside him to comfort him. But none knew what Corum felt. All eyes were upon the figure of the High King, upon the image of the oak at his head and the image of the ram at his feet. And Corum became conscious of a silence descending upon the forest; there was neither the sound of animals nor the rustle of leaves. There was a stillness as if nature itself waited to learn what events would now come to pass.

And Goffanon lifted his huge and bearded head towards the moon and he began to sing in the clear, deep voice which had earlier sounded his own death-song, when he thought that the Brothers to the Pines would slay him. And though the words were spoken in the Sidhi tongue, which was related to the tongues of the Vadhagh and the Mabden, Corum heard many of them and understood them.

Ancient were the Sidhi
    Ere before the Calling
They died abroad
    In noble circumstance.

Binding vows they made,
    Stronger than blood,
Greater than love,
    To aid the Mabden race.

In clouds they came
    To the islands of the West,
Their weapons and their music
    In their arms.

Gloriously they fought,
    And nobly died
In battle and in grief,
    Honouring their vows.

Ancient were the Sidhi,
    Proud in word and deed;
Ravens followed them
    In alien realms.

Ancient were the Sidhi!
    E'en in death
They swore the fulfilment
    Of all oaths.

Chariots and treasures,
   Mounds and caverns,
Are their monuments,
   And their names.

Of these heroes few remain
   To guard against the Pines.
The oaks are dying.
   Unearthly winter slays them.

Ancient were the Sidhi,
   Brothers to the Oak,
Friends of the Sun,
   Enemies of the Ice.

The ravens grew fat
   On Sidhi flesh.
Who is there now
   To aid the Oak?

Once Oak Woman stood amongst us,
   Sharing her strength;
Her knowledge brought us courage
   And the Fhoi Myore fell.

The Fhoi Myore fell.
   Sunlight swept the West,
And Oak Woman slept.
   Her work was done.

Ancient were the Sidhi!
   Few there were who lived.
Prophetic voices spoke,
   But the Sidhi would not hear.

Oak woman stirred,
   Pledges she made.
If cold returned,
   She would wake.

Mystic talismans
    She fashioned,
Against the Winter's might;
    To save her Oaks.

Sleeping, Oak woman smiled,
    Safe against the snow,
Her oath ensured,
    Her word made strong.

In nine fights the Fhoi Myore fell;
    In nine fights died the Sidhi;
Few heroes left the final field.
    Manannan died and all his throng.

Dying, great Manannan knew peace,
    In vain he had not fought,
For he recalled Oak Woman's vow
    To aid tomorrow's race.

Oak Woman slept in sanctuary.
    A word would wake her.
The tenth great fight grew near.
    The word was sought.

The word was lost.
    Three heroes sought it.
Goffanon sang a song.
    The word was found.

None moved as Goffanon's song ended. The Sidhi smith lowered his head and rested his chin upon his chest, waiting.

From the prone figure who lay upon the crown of the mound there came a small, weak sound, at first little more than the familiar, tragic bleating.

Goffanon raised his head, listening carefully. The note of the bleating changed for a brief instant and then faded.

Goffanon turned to face those who waited.

He spoke in a low, tired voice. He said:

'The word is "Dagdagh".'

And as he heard the word Corum gasped, for an awful shock ran through his whole body and made him stagger, made his heart pound and his head swim, though the word meant nothing to his conscious mind. He saw Jhary-a-Conel turn, white-faced, and stare at him.

And then the harp began to play.

Corum had heard the harp before. It was the harp which had sounded from Castle Erorn when he had first come to Caer Mahlod. It was the harp he had heard in dreams. Now only the tune was different. This tune was rousing and triumphant; a tune of bounding confidence, a laughing tune.

He heard Ilbrec whisper in astonishment: 'The Dagdagh harp! I thought it stilled forever.'

Corum felt that he drowned. He drew great gulps of air into his lungs as he sought to control his terror. He looked fearfully behind him amongst the dark trees, but he saw nothing save the shadows.

And when he looked back at the mound he was half-blinded, for the Golden Oak was growing, its golden branches spreading over the heads of those who watched and emitting a marvellous radiance. And Corum's fear was forgotten in his wonderment. Still the Golden Oak grew until it seemed to cover the whole mound and Amergin's body could just be discerned beneath it.

And all who watched were transfixed as from the oak there stepped a maiden as tall as Ilbrec himself; a woman whose hair was the green of oak-leaves and whose garment was the deep brown of an oak's trunk and whose skin was as pale as the flesh of the oak which lies beneath the bark. And she was Oak Woman, smiling and speaking:

'I recall my pledge. I recall the prophecy. I know you, Goffanon, but I do not know these others.'

'They are Mabden, save for Corum and Ilbrec. They are a good folk, Oak Woman, and they revere the oaks. See, oaks grow all around, for this is their Place of Power, their Holy Place.' Goffanon spoke almost hesitantly, seeming as impressed by this vision as were the Mabden. 'Ilbrec is your friend's son, Manannan's son. Of the Sidhi only he and I remain. And Corum is our kinsman, of the Vadhagh race. The Fhoi Myore have returned and we fight them, but we are weak. Amergin, High King of the Mabden, lies at your feet, enchanted. His soul has become the soul of a sheep and we cannot find the soul he lost.'

'I will find his soul,' said Oak Woman, smiling slightly, 'if that is your need.'

'It is, Oak Woman.'

The Oak Woman looked down upon Amergin. She bent and listened to his heart, then listened near his lips.

'His body dies,' she said.

There was a groan from all who watched save Corum and Corum was listening for the sound of the terrible harp, but it sounded no longer.

Then Oak Woman took the Silvern Ram from Amergin's feet.

'This was the prophecy,' she said, 'that the Ram must be given a soul. Now the soul of Amergin begins to leave his body and provides a soul for the Ram. Amergin must die.'

'No!' a score of lips shouted the word.

'But you must wait,' said Oak Woman chidingly with a smile. She placed the Ram at Amergin's head, crying:

> *'Soul speeding to the Mother Sea;*
> *Lamb bleating at the rising moon;*
> *Pause soul, silence lamb!*
> *Here is your home!'*

Now the bleating began afresh, but this time it was a lusty bleating, the bleating of a new-born lamb. And the voice came from the Silvern Ram as the moonlight fell upon its silver fleece and even as they watched they saw it grow and the bleating grew deeper and turned to a deep, lowing sound and the Silvern Ram turned its head and its eyes had the same intelligence which Corum had witnessed in the eyes of the Black Bull of Crinanass and he knew then that this animal, like the Bull, was one of a flock which the Sidhi had brought with them when they came to this realm. The Ram saw the Oak Woman and it ran to her and nuzzled her hand.

Then Oak Woman smiled again, turning her head towards the sky, calling:

> *'Soul dwelling in the Mother Sea,*
> *Leave your tranquil haven.*
> *Your earthly destiny is yet unfinished.*
> *Here is your home!'*

And the body of the High King stirred as if in sleep. And the hands crept to the face and the eyes opened and upon those blank features there was now written an expression of peace and wisdom and where age had lined the flesh there was now youth and where the limbs had been feeble there was now strength. And a cool, well-timbred voice said with faint astonishment:

'I am Amergin.'

Then the Archdruid rose up, tearing off the sheepskin hood and releasing his fair hair so that it fell upon his shoulders. And he ripped the sheepskin clothing from his body to reveal a form that was naked and beautiful and clad only in bracelets of hammered red gold.

And now Corum knew why the folk had mourned for their High King, for Amergin radiated both humility and dignity, wisdom and humanity.

'Yes,' he said, touching his breast and speaking wonderingly, 'I am Amergin.'

Now a hundred swords flashed in the moonlight as the Mabden saluted their Archdruid.

'Hail, Amergin! Hail, Amergin of the family of Amergin!'

And many men were there who wept for joy and embraced each other, and even the Sidhi, Goffanon and Ilbrec, raised their weapons in salute to Amergin.

The Oak Woman lifted her hand and she pointed a white finger through the throng to where Corum stood, still full of fear and unable to join the others in their joy.

'You are Corum,' said Oak Woman. 'You saved the High King and you found the Oak and the Ram. You are the Mabden champion now.'

'So I am told,' said Corum in a small, tortured voice.

'You shall be great in the memories of this folk,' said Oak Woman, 'yet you shall know little lasting happiness here.'

'I understand that also,' said Corum, and he sighed.

'Your destiny is a noble one,' continued Oak Woman, 'and I thank you for your dedication to that destiny. You have saved the High King and enabled me to keep my word.'

'You have slept all this time in the Golden Oak?' said Corum. 'You have waited for this day?'

'I have slept and I have waited.'

'But what power kept you upon this plane?' he asked, for this question had been puzzling him ever since Oak Woman had appeared. 'What great power was it, Oak Woman?'

'The power of my pledge,' she said.

'Naught else?'

'Why should aught else be necessary?'

And then the Oak Woman stepped back into the trunk of the Golden Oak and was followed by the Silvern Ram and the light from the oak began to fade and then the outlines of the oak itself began to fade and then the Golden Oak, the Silvern Ram and Oak Woman were gone and were never afterward seen again in mortal lands.

CHAPTER FOUR

The Dagdagh Harp

Now the folk of Caer Mahlod carried their High King Amergin joyfully back to their fortress city and many danced as they moved through the moonlit forest and there were broad grins upon the faces of Goffanon and Ilbrec, who was mounted on his black horse Splendid Mane.

And only Corum's brow was clouded, for he had heard words from Oak Woman which were less than cheering, and he lagged behind and was late in entering the king's hall.

Their own good spirits clouding their vision, none of the others saw that Corum did not smile, and they slapped him upon his shoulders and they toasted him and they honoured him as much as they honoured their own High King.

And the feasting began, and the drinking, and the singing to the sound of the Mabden harps.

So Corum, seated beside Medhbh on one side and King Mannach on the other, drank a considerable amount of sweet mead and tried to drive the memory of the harp from his mind.

He saw King Mannach lean across to where Goffanon was seated next to Ilbrec (who was manfully showing no discomfort as he sat cramped and cross-legged beside the bench) and ask: 'How knew you the incantation which raised the Oak Woman, Sir Goffanon?'

'I knew no special incantation,' said Goffanon, lifting a cauldron of mead from his lips and setting it upon the table. 'I trusted to my hidden memories and the memories of my people. I hardly heard the words of the song myself. They came almost unbidden from my lips. I relied upon this to reach both the Oak Woman and Amergin's spirit where it drifted. It was Amergin himself who gave me the word which in turn produced that music which, in its turn, began the transformation.'

'Dagdagh,' said Medhbh, unaware that Corum shuddered at the sound. 'An old word. A name, perhaps?'

'A title, also. A word of many meanings.'

'A Sidhi name?'

'I think not – though it is associated with the Sidhi. The Dagdagh led the Sidhi into battle on more than one occasion. I am young, you see, as the Sidhi measure age, and I took part in only two of the nine historic fights against the Fhoi Myore and by that time the name of Dagdagh was no longer spoken. I know not why, save that there was a hint that Dagdagh had betrayed our cause.'

'Betrayed it? Not this night, surely?'

'No,' said Goffanon, his brow darkening a trifle. 'Not this night.' And he raised the cauldron to his lips and took a thoughtful swig.

Jhary-a-Conel left his seat and came to stand behind Corum. 'Why so pensive, old friend?'

Corum was grateful that Jhary had noticed his mood and at the same time did not wish to spoil Jhary's celebration. He smiled as best he could and shook his head: 'Weariness, I suppose. I've slept little of late.'

'That harp,' continued Medhbh and Corum wished that she would stop. 'I recall hearing a similar harp.' She turned to Corum. 'At Castle Owyn when we rode there once.'

'Aye,' he murmured. 'At Castle Owyn.'

'A mysterious harp,' said King Mannach, 'but I for one am grateful to it and would hear its music again if it brings us such gifts as the restoration of our High King,' and he raised his mead-horn to toast Amergin who sat smiling and calm, but drinking little, at the head of the table.

'Now we shall mass,' said King Mannach, 'all the folk of the Mabden who remain. We shall build a great army and we shall ride against the Fhoi Myore. And this time we shall leave none alive!'

'Brave words,' said Ilbrec, 'but we need more than

courage. We need weapons such as my sword Retaliator. We need cunning – aye, and caution where it suits our cause.'

'You speak wisely, Sir Sidhi,' said Amergin. 'You echo my own thoughts.' His old and yet youthful face was full of good humour as if he were not troubled one bit by the great problem of the Fhoi Myore. He wore a robe, now, of loose yellow samite bordered with designs of blue and red and his hair was braided and lay upon his back.

'With Amergin to counsel us and Corum to lead us into war,' said King Mannach, 'I believe that I am not foolish to show some optimism.' He smiled at Corum. 'We grow stronger. Not long since our lives seemed lost and our race destroyed, but now . . .'

'Now,' said Corum finishing a whole horn of mead and wiping his lips upon the back of his silver hand, 'now we celebrate great victories.' Unable to control himself he rose from the bench, stepped over it, and strode from the hall.

He walked into the night, through the streets of Caer Mahlod – streets which were filled with merrymakers, with music and with laughter – and he went through the gate and over the turf towards where the distant sea boomed.

And at last he stood alone upon the brink of the chasm which separated him from the ruins of his old home, Castle Erorn, which this folk called Castle Owyn and thought a formation of natural rock.

In the moonlight the ruins glowed and Corum wished that he could fly across the gulf and enter Castle Erorn and find a gateway back to his own world. There he had been lonely, but that was not the loneliness he felt now. Now he had a sense of complete desolation.

And then he saw a face staring back at him from out of the broken windows of the castle. It was a handsome face, a face with a skin of gold; a mocking face.

Corum called hoarsely:

'Dagdagh! Is it Dagdagh?'

And he heard laughter which became the music of a harp.

Corum drew his sword. Below him the sea foamed and leapt on the rocks at the foot of the cliff. He prepared to leap the gulf, to seek the youth with the skin of gold, to demand why the youth plagued him so. He poised himself, caring not if he fell and died.

And then he felt a soft, strong hand upon his shoulder. He tried to shake it free, still crying:

'Dagdagh! Let me be!'

Medhbh's voice said close to his ear, 'Dagdagh is our friend, Corum. Dagdagh saved our High King.'

Corum turned towards her and saw her troubled eyes staring into his single eye.

'Put away your sword,' she said. 'There is no-one there.'

'Did you not hear the music of his harp?'

'I heard the wind making music in the crannies of Castle Owyn. That is what I heard.'

'You did not see his face, his mocking face?'

'I saw a cloud move across the moon,' she said. 'Come back now, Corum, to our celebrations.'

And he sheathed his sword and he sighed and he let her lead him back to Caer Mahlod.

Epilogue

And that was the end of the Tale of the Oak and the Ram.

Messengers went across the sea, taking the news to all: The High King was restored to his folk. They sailed to the west to tell King Fiachadh of the Tuha-na-Manannan (named for Ilbrec's own family, Corum now knew) and they sailed to the north where the Tuha-na-Tir-nam-Beo were told the news. And they told the Tuha-na-Anu and they told King Daffyn of the Tuha-na-Gwyddneu Garanhir. And wherever they found Mabden tribes they told them that the High King dwelled at Caer Mahlod, that Amergin debated the question of war against the Fhoi Myore and that the representatives of all the tribes of the Mabden race were called there to plan the last great fight which would decide who ruled the Islands of the West.

In the smithies there was a clanging and roaring as swords were fashioned, and axes made and spears honed under the direction of that greatest of all smiths, Goffanon.

And there was excitement and optimism in the homes of the Mabden as they wondered what Corum of the Silver Hand and Amergin the Archdruid would decide and where the battle would take place and when it would begin.

And others listened to Ilbrec who would sit in the fields and tell them the tales he had heard from his father, whom many thought to be the greatest of the Sidhi heroes, tales of the Nine Fights against the Fhoi Myore and the deeds which were done. And they were heartened by these tales (some of which they knew) and glad to understand that the heroism which had been thought to be the fanciful invention of bards had actually taken place.

And only when they saw Corum, pale and pensive, his head bent as if he listened for a voice he could not quite hear, did they consider the tragedy of those tales, of the great hearts which had been stilled in the service of their race.

And at those times did the folk of Caer Mahlod become thoughtful and at those times they understood the enormity of the sacrifice made for their cause by the Vadhagh Prince called Corum of the Silver Hand.

The Sword
and the Stallion

FOR JUDITH

BOOK ONE

In which armies are gathered and plans debated regarding an assault upon the Fhoi Myore and Caer Llud. Sidhi advice is requested and gladly given; yet, as is often the case, the advice creates further perplexity . . .

CHAPTER ONE

Considering the Need for Great Deeds

So they came to Caer Mahlod; all of them. Tall warriors garbed in their finest gear, riding strong horses, bearing good weapons. They had a look of practical magnificence. They made the country around Caer Mahlod blaze with the bright colours of their samite pavilions and their embroidered battle flags, the gold of their bracelets, the silver of their cloak clasps, the burnished iron of their helmets, the mother-of-pearl inlaid upon their carved beakers or set into their travelling chests. These were the greatest of the Mabden and they were also the last, the People of the West, the Stepsons of the Sun, whose cousins of the East had long since perished in fruitless battle with the Fhoi Myore.

And in the centre of the encampments stood a tent much larger than the rest. Of sea-blue silk, it was otherwise unadorned and no battle banner stood near its entrance, for the size of the tent alone was enough to announce that it contained Ilbrec, the son of Manannan-mac-Lyr, who had been the greatest of the Sidhi heroes in the old fights against the Fhoi Myore. Tethered near this tent stood a huge black horse, large enough to seat the giant; a horse of evident intelligence and energy: a Sidhi horse. Though welcome in Caer Mahlod itself, Ilbrec could find no hall high enough to contain him and had thus pitched his tent with those of the gathering warriors.

Beyond the fields of pavilions there were green forests of pleasant trees, there were gentle hills dotted with clumps of wild flowers and shrubs whose colours sparkled like jewels in the warming rays of the sun; and to the west of all this glowed a blue, white-crested ocean over which black and grey gulls drifted. Though they could not be seen from the walls of Caer Mahlod, there were many ships on all the nearby beaches. The ships had come from Gwyddneu Garanhir and they had come from Tir-nam-Beo. They were ships of several different designs and divergent purposes, some being warships and others being trading ships, some used for fishing the sea and some for travelling broad rivers. Every available ship had been utilized to bring the Mabden tribes to this massing.

Corum stood upon Caer Mahlod's battlements, the dwarf Goffanon at his side. Goffanon was a dwarf only by Sidhi standards, being considerably taller than Corum. Today he did not wear his polished iron helm; his huge unkempt mane of black hair flowed down his shoulders, meeting his heavy black beard so that it was impossible to tell which was which. He wore a simple smock of blue cloth, embroidered at collar and cuffs in red thread and gathered at the waist by his great leather belt. There were leggings and high-laced sandals on his legs and feet. In one huge, scarred hand was a mead horn from which he would sip occasionally; the other hand rested on the haft of his inevitable double-bladed war-axe, one of the last of the Weapons of Light, the Sidhi weapons especially forged in another realm to fight the Fhoi Myore. The Sidhi dwarf looked with satisfaction upon the tents of the Mabden.

'They still come,' he said. 'Good warriors.'

'But somewhat inexperienced in the kind of warfare we contemplate,' Corum said.

He watched as a column of northern Mabden crossed the ground beyond the main gate and the moat. These were tall and tough, in scarlet plaids which made them sweat, in winged or horned helmets or simple battle-caps; red-bearded men for the most part, soldiers of the Tir-nam-Beo, armed with big broadswords and round iron shields, disdaining all other weapons save the knives sheathed in the belts which criss-crossed their chests. Their dark features were painted or tattooed in order to emphasize their already fierce appearance. Of all the surviving Mabden, these men of the high northern mountains were the only ones who still lived, for the most part, by war, cut off by their own chosen terrain from what they regarded as the softer aspects of Mabden civilization. They reminded Corum somewhat of the old Mabden, the Mabden of the Earl of Krae who had hunted him once across these same downs and cliffs, and for a moment Corum wondered again at his willingness to serve the descendants of that cruel, animal-like folk. Then he recalled Rhalina and he knew why he did what he did.

Corum turned away to contemplate the roofs of the fortress-city of Caer Mahlod, leaning his back against the battlements, relaxing in the warmth of the sunshine. It had been over a month since he had stood at night upon the brink of the chasm separating Castle Owyn from the mainland and shouted his challenge to the Dagdagh harpist whom he was convinced inhabited the ruin. Medhbh had worked hard to console him and make him forget his nightmares and she had been largely successful; he now saw his experiences in terms of his exhaustion and his dangers. All he had needed was rest and with that rest had come a certain degree of tranquillity.

Jhary-a-Conel appeared on the steps leading to the battlements. He had on his familiar slouch hat, and his little winged black and white cat sat comfortably on his left shoulder. He greeted his friends with his usual cheerful grin.

'I've just come up from the bay. More ships have arrived – from Anu. The last, I heard. They have none left to send.'

'More warriors?' asked Corum.

'A few, but mainly they bring fur garments – all that the people of Anu can muster.'

'Good.' Goffanon nodded his great head. 'At least we'll be reasonably well-equipped when we venture into the Frostlands of the Fhoi Myore.'

Removing his hat, Jhary wiped sweat from his brow. 'It's hard to imagine that the world is so cold such a comparatively short distance from here.' He put his hat back on his head and reached inside his jerkin, taking out a piece of herbal wood and broodingly picking his teeth with it as he joined them. He stared out over the encampment. 'So this is the whole Mabden strength. A few thousands.'

'Against five,' said Goffanon, almost defiantly.

'Five gods,' said Jhary, giving him a hard stare. 'In keeping our spirits high we must not let ourselves forget the power of our enemies. And then there is Gaynor – and the Ghoolegh – and the Pine Warriors – and the Hounds of Kerenos – and,' Jhary paused, adding softly, almost regretfully, 'and Calatin.'

The dwarf smiled. 'Aye,' he said, 'but we have learned how to deal with almost all these dangers. They are no longer quite the threat they were. The People of the Pines fear fire. And Gaynor fears Corum. And as for the Ghoolegh, well, we still have the Sidhi horn. That gives us power, too, over the Hounds. As for Calatin . . .'

'He is mortal,' said Corum. 'He can be slain. I intend to make it my particular business to slay him. He has power only over you, Goffanon. And, who knows? That power could well be on the wane.'

'But the Fhoi Myore themselves fear nothing,' said Jhary-a-Conel. 'That we must remember.'

'They fear one thing in this plane,' Goffanon told the Companion to Heroes. 'They fear Craig Dôn. It is what we must ever remember.'

'It is what they ever remember, also. They will not go to Craig Dôn.'

Goffanon the smith drew his black brows together. 'Perhaps they will,' he said.

'It is not Craig Dôn, but Caer Llud we must consider,' Corum told his friends. 'For it is that place we shall attack. Once Caer Llud is taken, our morale will rise considerably. Such a deed will give our men increased strength and enable them to finish the Fhoi Myore once and for all.'

'Truly great deeds are needed,' Goffanon agreed, 'and also cunning thoughts.'

'And allies,' said Jhary feelingly, 'more allies like yourself, good Goffanon, and golden Ilbrec. More Sidhi friends.'

'I fear that there are no more Sidhi save we two,' murmured Goffanon.

'It is unlike you to express such gloom, friend Jhary!' Corum clapped his silver hand upon the shoulder of his companion. 'What causes this mood? We are stronger than we have ever been before!'

Jhary shrugged. 'Perhaps I do not understand the Mabden ways. There seems too much joy in all these newcomers, as if they do not understand their danger. It is as if they come to a friendly tourney with the Fhoi Myore, not a war to the death involving the fate of their whole world!'

'Should they grieve, then?' Goffanon said in astonishment.

'No . . .'

'Should they consider themselves in death or in defeat?'

'Of course not . . .'

'Should they entertain one another with dirges rather than with merry songs? Should their faces be downturned and their eyes full of tears?'

Jhary began to smile. 'You are right, I suppose, you monstrous dwarf. It is simply that I have seen so much. I have attended many battles. Yet never before have I seen men prepare for death with such apparent lack of concern.'

'That is the Mabden way, I think,' Corum told him. He glanced at Goffanon, who was grinning broadly. 'Learned from the Sidhi.'

'And who is to say that they prepare for their own deaths and not the deaths of the Fhoi Myore?' added Goffanon.

Jhary bowed. 'I accept what you say. It heartens me. It is merely that it is strange, and the strangeness is doubtless what I find discomforting.'

Corum was, himself, disconcerted to find his normally insouciant friend in such a mood. He tried to smile.

'Come now, Jhary, this brooding demeanour suits you ill. Normally it is Corum who mopes and Jhary who grins . . .'

Jhary sighed.

'Aye,' he said, almost bitterly, 'it would not do, I suppose, to forget our rôles at this particular time.'

And he moved away from them, pacing along the battlements until he reached a spot where he paused, staring into the middle distance, plainly desiring no further conversation with his comrades.

Goffanon glanced at the sun.

'Nearly noon. I am promised to advise the blacksmiths of the Tuha-na-Anu on the special problems involved in the casting and weighting of a kind of hammer we have devised together. I hope to talk with you further this evening, Corum, when we all meet to debate our plans.'

Corum raised his silver hand in a salute as the dwarf went down the steps and strode through a narrow street in the direction of the main gate.

For a moment Corum had the impulse to join Jhary, but it was most obvious that Jhary required no company at this time. After a while Corum, too, descended the steps, going in search of Medhbh, for suddenly he felt a great need to seek the consolation of the woman he loved.

It occurred to him as he made his way towards the king's hall that perhaps he was becoming too dependent upon the girl. Sometimes he felt that he needed her as another man might need drink or a drug. While she seemed to respond eagerly to this need, it could be that it was not fair to her to make the demands he did. As he walked to find her, he saw clearly that there were the seeds of considerable tragedy in the relationship which had developed between them. He shrugged. The seeds need not be nurtured. They could be destroyed. Even if his main destiny was pre-determined there were certain aspects of his personal life which he could control.

'Surely that must be so,' he muttered to himself. A woman passing him on the street glanced at him, believing herself to be addressed. She was carrying a sheaf of staves which would be used for spears.

'My lord?'

'I observed that our preparations go well,' Corum told her, embarrassed.

'Aye, my lord. We all work for the defeat of the Fhoi Myore.' She lifted her load in her arms. 'Thank you, my lord . . .'

'Aye.' Corum nodded, hesitating. 'Aye, good. Well, good morning to you.'

'Good morning, my lord.' She seemed amused.

Corum strode on, his head down, his lips firmly shut until he reached the hall of King Mannach, Medhbh's father.

But Medhbh was not there. A servant said to Corum: 'She is at her weapons, Prince Corum, with some of the other women.'

Prince Corum walked through a tunnel and into a high, wide chamber decorated with old battle flags and antique arms and armour, where a score of women practised with bow, with spear, with sword and with sling.

Medhbh herself was there, whirling her sling at a target at the far end of the chamber. She was famous for her skill with the sling and the tathlum, that awful missile made from the brains of a fallen enemy and thought to be of considerable supernatural effectiveness. As Corum entered Medhbh let fly at the target and the tathlum struck it dead centre, causing the thin bronze to ring and the target, which hung by a rope from the ceiling, to spin round and round, flashing in the light from the brands which helped light the chamber.

'Greetings,' called Corum his voice echoing. 'Medhbh of the Long Arm!'

She turned, glad that he had witnessed her skill. 'Greetings, Prince Corum.' She dropped the sling and ran to him, embracing him, looking deep into his face. She frowned. 'Are you melancholy, my love? What thoughts disturb you? Is there fresh news of the Fhoi Myore?'

'No.' He held her to him, conscious that others of the women glanced at them. He said quietly: 'I merely felt the need to see you.'

She smiled tenderly back at him. 'I am honoured, Sidhi prince.'

This particular choice of words, emphasizing the differences of blood and background between them, had the effect of disturbing him still more. He looked hard into her eyes and the look was not a kind one. She, recognizing this stare, looked surprised, taking a step back from him, her arms falling to her sides. He knew that he had failed in the purpose of his visit, for she, in turn, was disturbed. He had driven her from him. Yet had not she first created the alienation by her remark? For all that her smile had been tender, the phrase itself had somehow cut him. He turned away, saying distantly:

'Now that need is satisfied,' he said, 'I go to visit Ilbrec.'

He wanted her to tell him to stay, but he knew she could not, no more than he could bear to remain. He left the hall without a further word.

And he cursed Jhary-a-Conel for introducing his gloomy thoughts into the day. He expected better of Jhary.

Yet, in fairness, he knew that too much was expected of Jhary and that Jhary had begun to resent it – if only momentarily – and he understood that he, Corum, was placing too much reliance on the strength of others and not enough upon himself. What right had he to demand such strength if he indulged his weaknesses?

'Eternal Champion I might be,' he murmured, as he reached his own chambers, which he now shared with Medhbh, 'but eternal pitier of myself, also, it sometimes seems.'

And he lay down upon his bed and he considered his own character and at length he smiled and the mood began to leave him.

'It's obvious,' he said. 'Inaction suits me poorly and encourages the baser aspects of my character. My destiny is that of a warrior. Perhaps I should consider deeds and leave the question of thoughts to those better able to think.' He laughed, becoming tolerant of his own weaknesses and resolving to indulge them no further.

Then he left his bed and went to find Ilbrec.

CHAPTER TWO

A Red Sword is Lifted

Corum crossed the field, stepping over guy-ropes and around the billowing walls of the tents, on his way to Ilbrec's pavilion. He arrived, at last, outside the pavilion whose sea-blue silk rippled like little waves, and he called:

'Ilbrec! Son of Manannan, are you within?'

He was answered by a regular scraping noise which he was hard-put, at first, to recognize, then he smiled, raising his voice:

'Ilbrec – I hear you preparing for battle. May I enter?'

The scraping noise ceased and the young giant's cheerful, booming voice replied:

'Enter, Corum. You are welcome.'

Corum pushed aside the tent-flap. The only light within was the sunlight itself, piercing the silk, and giving the impression of a blue and watery cavern, not unlike part of Ilbrec's own domain beneath the waves. Ilbrec sat upon a great chest, his huge sword Retaliator across his knees. In his other hand was a whetstone with which he had been honing the sword. Ilbrec's golden hair hung in loose braids to his chest and today his beard was also plaited. He wore a simple green smock and sandals laced to his knees. In one corner of his tent lay his armour, his breastplate of bronze with its reliefs showing a great, stylized sun whose circle was filled with pictures of ships and of fish; his shield, which bore only the symbol of the sun; and his helmet, which had a similar motif. His lightly tanned arms had several heavy bracelets, both above and below the elbows, and these were of gold and these, too, matched the design of the breastplate. Ilbrec, son of the greatest of the Sidhi heroes, was a full sixteen feet high and perfectly proportioned.

Ilbrec grinned at Corum and began, again, to hone his sword.

'You look gloomy, friend.'

Corum crossed the floor of the tent and stood beside Ilbrec's helmet running his fleshly hand over the beautifully worked bronze. 'Perhaps a premonition of my doom,' he said.

'But you are immortal, are you not, Prince Corum?'

Corum turned at this new voice which was even younger in timbre than Ilbrec's.

A youth of no more than fourteen summers had entered the tent. Corum recognized him as King Fiachadh's youngest son, called Young Fean by all. Young Fean resembled his father in looks, but his body was lithe where King Fiachadh's was burly and his features were delicate where his father's were heavy. His hair was as red as Fiachadh's and he had something of the same humour almost constantly in his eyes. He smiled at Corum; and Corum, as he always did, thought there was no creature in the world more charming than this young warrrior who had already proved himself one of the cleverest and most proficient knights in all the company gathered here.

Corum laughed. 'Possibly, Young Fean, aye. But somehow that thought does not console me.'

Young Fean was sober for a moment, pushing back his light cloak of orange samite and removing his plain, steel helmet. He was sweating and had evidently just come from weapons practice.

'I can understand that, Prince Corum.' He made a slight bow in the direction of Ilbrec who was plainly glad to see him. 'Greetings to you, Lord Sidhi.'

'Greetings, Young Fean. Is there some service I can do you?' Ilbrec continued to hone Retaliator with long, sweeping movements.

'None, I thank you. I merely came to talk.' Young Fean hesitated, then replaced his helmet on his head. 'But I see that I intrude.'

'Not at all,' said Corum. 'How, in your opinion, do our men show?'

'They are all good fighters. Therre is not one who is poor. But they are few, I think,' said Young Fean.

'I agree with both your judgements,' said Ilbrec. 'I was considering the problem as I sat here.'

'I have also discussed it,' said Corum.

There was a long pause.

'But there is nowhere we can recruit more soldiers,' said Young Fean, looking at Corum as if he hoped Corum would deny this statement.

'Nowhere at all,' said Corum.

He noticed that Ilbrec said nothing and that the Sidhi giant was frowning.

'There is one place I heard of,' said Ilbrec. 'Long ago, when I was younger than Young Fean. A place where allies of the Sidhi might be found. But I heard, too, that it is a dangerous place, even for the Sidhi, and that the allies are fickle. I will consult with Goffanon later and ask him if he recalls more.'

'Allies?' Young Fean laughed. 'Supernatural allies? We have need of any allies, no matter how fickle.'

'I will talk with Goffanon,' said Ilbrec, and he returned to the honing of his sword.

Young Fean made to leave. 'I will say nothing, then,' he told them. 'And I look forward to seeing you at the feast tonight.'

When Young Fean had left, Corum looked enquiringly at Ilbrec, but Ilbrec pretended an intense interest in honing his sword and would not meet Corum's eye.

Corum rubbed at his face. 'I recall a time when I would have smiled at the very idea of magical forces at work in the world,' he said.

Ilbrec nodded abstractedly as if he did not really hear what Corum said.

'But now I have come to rely on such things.' Corum's expression was ironic. 'And must, perforce, believe in them. I have lost my faith in logic and the power of reason.'

Ilbrec looked up. 'Perhaps your logic was too narrow and your reason limited, friend Corum?' he said quietly.

'Maybe.' Corum sighed and moved to follow Young Fean through the tent-flap. Then, suddenly, he stopped short, putting his head on one side and listening hard. 'Did you hear that sound?'

Ilbrec listened. 'There are many sounds in the camp.'

'I thought I heard the sound of a harp playing.'

Ilbrec shook his head. 'Pipes – in the distance – but no harp.' Then he frowned, listening again. 'Possibly, very faint, the strains of a harp. No.' He laughed. 'You are making me hear it, Corum.'

But Corum knew he had heard the Dagdagh harp for a few moments and he was, again, troubled. He said nothing more of it to Ilbrec, but went out of the tent and across the field hearing a distant voice crying his name:

'Corum! Corum!'

He turned. Behind him a group of kilted warriors was resting, sharing a bottle and conversing amongst themselves. Beyond these warriors Corum saw Medhbh running over the grass. It was Medhbh he had heard.

She ran round the group of warriors and stopped a foot or so from him, hesitantly stretching out her arm and touching his shoulder. 'I sought you out in our chambers,' she said softly, 'but you had gone. We must not quarrel, Corum.'

At once Corum's spirits lifted and he laughed and embraced her, careless of the warriors who had turned their attention upon the couple.

'We shall not quarrel again,' he said. 'Blame me, Medhbh.'

'Blame no-one. Blame nothing. Unless it be Fate.'

She kissed him. Her lips were warm. They were soft. He forgot his fears.

'What a great power women have,' he said. 'I have recently been speaking with Ilbrec of magic, but the greatest magic of all is in the kiss of a woman.'

She pretended astonishment. 'You become sentimental, Sir Sidhi.'

And again, momentarily, he sensed that she withdrew from him.

Then she laughed and kissed him once more. 'Almost as sentimental as Medhbh!'

Hand in hand they wandered through the camp, waving to those they recognized or those who recognized them.

At the edge of the camp several smithies had been set up. Furnaces roared as bellows forced their flames higher and higher. Hammers clanged on anvils. Huge, sweating men in aprons plunged iron into the fires and brought it out white and glowing and making the air shimmer. And in the centre of all this activity was Goffanon, also in a great leathern apron, with a massive hammer in one hand, a pair of tongs in the other, deep in conversation with a black-bearded Mabden whom Corum recognized as the master-smith Hisak, whose nickname was Sun-thief, for it was said he stole the stuff of the sun itself and made bright weapons with it. In the nearby furnace a narrow piece of metal was immersed even now. Goffanon and Hisak watched this with considerable concentration as they talked and plainly it was this piece of metal they discussed.

Corum and Medhbh did not greet the two, but stood to one side and watched and listened.

'Six more heartbeats,' they heard Hisak say, 'and it will be ready.'

Goffanon smiled. 'Six and one quarter heartbeats, believe me, Hisak.'

'I believe you, Sidhi. I have learned to respect your wisdom and your skills.'

Already Goffanon was extending his tongs into the fire. With a strange gentleness he gripped the metal and then swiftly withdrew it, his eye travelling up and down its length. 'It is right,' he said.

Hisak, too, inspected the white-hot metal, nodding. 'It is right.'

Goffanon's smile was almost ecstatic and he half-turned, seeing Corum. 'Aha, Prince Corum. You come at the perfect moment. See!' He lifted the strip of metal high.

Now it glowed red hot, the colour of fresh blood. 'See, Corum! What do you see?'

'I see a sword blade.'

'You see the finest sword blade made in Mabden lands. It has taken us a week to achieve this. Between us, Hisak and I have made it. It is a symbol of the old alliance between Mabden and Sidhi. Is it not fine?'

'It is very fine.'

Goffanon swept the red sword back and forth through the air and the metal hummed. 'It has yet to be fully tempered, but it is almost ready. It has yet to be given a name, but that will be left to you.'

'To me?'

'Of course!' Goffanon laughed in delight. 'Of course! It is your sword, Corum. It is the sword you will use when you lead the Mabden into battle.'

'Mine?' Corum was taken aback.

'Our gift to you. Tonight, after the feast, we will return here and the sword will be ready for you. It will be a good friend to you, this sword, but only after you have named it will it be able to give you all its strength.'

'I am honoured, Goffanon,' said Corum. 'I had not guessed . . .'

The great dwarf tossed the blade into a trough of water and steam hissed. 'Half of Sidhi manufacture, half of Mabden. The right sword for you, Corum.'

'Indeed,' Corum agreed. He was deeply moved by Goffanon's revelation. 'Indeed, you are right, Goffanon.' He turned to look shyly at the grinning Hisak. 'I thank you, Hisak. I thank you both.'

And then Goffanan said quietly and somewhat mysteriously: 'It is not for nothing that Hisak is nicknamed the Sunthief. But still there is a song to be sung and a sign to be placed.'

Respecting the rituals, but privately believing that they had no real significance, Corum nodded his head, convinced that an important honour had been done to him, but unable to define the exact nature of that honour.

'I thank you again,' he said sincerely. 'There are no

words, for language is a poor thing which does no justice to the emotions I should like to express.'

'Let there be no further words on this matter until the time comes for the sword-naming,' said Hisak, speaking for the first time, his voice gruff and understanding.

'I had come to consult you upon another matter,' said Corum. 'Ilbrec spoke of possible allies earlier. I wondered if this meant anything to you.'

Goffanon shrugged. 'I have already said that I can think of none.'

'Then we will let the subject pass until Ilbrec has had time to speak to you himself,' said Medhbh, touching Corum's sleeve. 'We will see you tonight at the feast, my friends. Now we go to rest.'

And she led a thoughtful Corum back towards the walls of Caer Mahlod.

CHAPTER THREE

At the Feast

Now the great hall of Caer Mahlod was filled. A stranger entering would not have guessed that the folk here prepared themselves for a final desperate war against an almost invincible foe; indeed the gathering seemed to have the spirit of a celebration. Four long oaken tables formed a hollow square in the centre of which sat, not altogether comfortably, the golden-haired giant, Ilbrec, with his own beaker, plate and spoon set out before him. At the tables, facing inwards, sat all the nobles of the Mabden, with the High King – slender, ascetic Amergin – in the place of greatest prominence, wearing his robe of silver thread and his crown of oak and holly leaves; Corum, with his embroidered eye-patch and his silver hand, was seated directly opposite the High King. On both sides of Amergin sat kings, and beside the kings sat queens and princes, and beside the princes sat princesses and great knights with their ladies. Corum had Medhbh on his right and Goffanon on his left and beside Medhbh sat Jhary-a-Conel, and beside Goffanon sat Hisak Sunthief the Smith who had helped forge the unnamed blade. Rich silks and furs, garments of doeskin and plaid, ornaments of red gold and white silver, of polished iron and burnished bronze, of emerald and ruby and sapphire, brought blazing colour to a hall lit by brightly burning brands of reeds soaked in oil. The air was full of smoke and the smell of food as whole beasts were roasted in the kitchens and brought quartered to the tables. Musicians, with harps and pipes and drums, sat in one corner playing sweet melodies which managed to blend with the voices of the company; the voices were cheerful and the conversation and the laughter were easy. The food was consumed lustily by all save Corum who was in reasonable spirits but for some reason lacked an appetite. Exchanging a few words occasionally with Goffanon or Jhary-a-Conel, sipping from a golden drinking horn, he glanced around him at the gathering, recognizing all the great heroes and heroines of the Mabden folk who were there. Apart from the five kings – King Mannach, King Fiachadh, King Daffyn, King Khonun of the Tuha-na-Anu and King Ghachbes of the Tuha-na-Tir-nam-Beo – there were many who had known glory and were already celebrated in the ballads of their people. Amongst these were Fionha and Cahleen, two daughters of the great dead knight Milgan the White; blonde-haired, creamy-skinned, almost twins, dressed in costumes of identical cut and colour save that one was predominantly red trimmed with blue and the other blue trimmed with red, warrior maidens both, with honey-coloured eyes and their hair all wild and unbound to below their shoulders, flirting with a pair of knights apiece. And nearby was the one called the Branch Hero, Phadrac-at-the-Crag-at-Lyth, almost as huge and as broad-shouldered as Goffanon, with green, glaring eyes and a red laughing mouth, whose weapon was a whole tree with which he would sweep his enemies from their horses and stun them. The Branch Hero laughed rarely, for he mourned his friend Ayan the Hairy-handed whom he had killed during a mock fight when drunk. And on the next table was Young Fean, eating and drinking and flirting as heartily as any man, the darling of the nobles' daughters who giggled at every word he said and stroked his red hair and fed him tidbits of meat and fruit. Near him sat all of the Five Knights of Eralskee, brothers who, until recent times, had refused to have aught to do with the folk of the Tuha-na-Anu, for they had harboured a blood grudge against their uncle, King Khonun, whom they believed to be their father's murderer. For years they had remained in their mountains, venturing out to raid King Khonun's lands or to try to raise an army against him. Now they were sworn to forget their grudge until the matter of the Fhoi Myore was done. They were all similar in appearance, save that the youngest had black hair and an expression not quite as grim as that of his brothers, all sporting the high-peaked conical helmets bearing the Owl Crest of Eralskee, all big men and very hard men who smiled as if the action were new to them. Then there was Morkyan of the Two Smiles, a scar on his face turning the lip on the left side upwards and the lip on the right side downwards, but this was not why he was called Morkyan of the Two Smiles. It was said that only Morkyan's enemies saw those two smiles – the first smile meant that he intended to kill them and the second smile meant that they were dying. Morkyan was splendid in dark blue leather and a matching leathern cap, his black beard trimmed to a point and his moustaches curling upwards. He wore his hair short and hidden entirely by the tight-fitting cap. Leaning across two friends and speaking to Morkyan was Kernyn the Ragged who looked like a beggar and had impoverished himself through his strange habit of giving generous amounts of money to the kin of men he had slain. A demon in battle, Kernyn was always remorseful after he had killed an enemy and would make a point of finding the man's widow or family and bestowing a gift upon them. Kernyn's brown hair was matted and his beard was untidy. He wore a patched leather jerkin and a helmet of plain iron and his long, mournful face was presently lit up as he regaled Morkyan with some reminiscence of a battle in which they had fought on different sides. Grynion Ox-rider was there, too, his arm around the ample waist of Sheonan the Axe-maiden, another woman of outstanding martial abilities. Grynion had earned his nickname for riding a wild ox into the thick of a fight when he had lost his horse and weapons and was wounded almost mortally. Helping himself from a huge side of beef, which he attacked with a large, sharp knife, was Ossan the Bridlemaker, renowned for his leather-working skill. His jerkin and his cap were made of embossed, finely-tooled hide, covered in a variety of flowing designs. He was a man nearing old age but his movements were those of a youth.

He grinned as he forced meat into his mouth, the grease running into his ginger beard, and turned to listen to the knight who told a joke to those within hearing of him. And there were many more: Fene the Legless, Uther of the Melancholy Dale, Pwyll Spinebreaker, Shamane the Tall and Shamane the Short, The Red Fox Meyahn, Old Dylann, Ronan the Pale and Clar from Beyond the West among them. Corum had met them all as they had come to Caer Mahlod and he knew that many of them would die when they battled, at last, with the Fhoi Myore.

Now Amergin's clear, strong voice rang out, calling to Corum:

'Well, Corum of the Silver Hand, are you satisfied with the company you lead to war?'

Corum answered gracefully, 'My only doubt is that there are many here better able to lead such great warriors than I. It is my honour that I am elected to this task.'

'Well spoken!' King Fiachadh lifted his mead-horn. 'I toast Corum, the slayer of Sreng of the Seven Swords, the saviour of our High King. I toast Corum, who brought back the Mabden pride!'

And Corum blushed as they cheered and drank his health and when they had finished he stood up and raised his own horn and he spoke these words:

'I toast that pride! I toast the Mabden folk!'

The company roared its approval and all drank.

Then Amergin said:

'We are fortunate in having Sidhi allies who have chosen to aid us in our struggle against the Fhoi Myore. We are fortunate in that many of our great Treasures were restored to us and used to defeat the Fhoi Myore when they sought to destroy us. I toast the Sidhi and the gifts of the Sidhi.'

Again the whole company, save an embarrassed Ilbrec and a bemused Goffanon, drank and cheered.

Ilbrec was the next to speak. He said:

'If the Mabden were not courageous; if they were not a fine-spirited folk, the Sidhi would not help them. We fight for that which is noble in all living beings.'

Goffanan grunted his agreement with this sentiment. 'By and large,' he said, 'the Mabden are not a selfish folk. They are not mean. They respect one another. They are not greedy. They are not, in the main, self-righteous. Aye, I've a liking for this people. I am glad that finally I chose to fight in their cause. It will be good to die in such a cause.'

Amergin smiled. 'I hope you do not expect death, Sir Goffanon. You speak of it as if it were an inevitable consequence of this venture.'

And Goffanon lowered his eyes, shrugging.

King Mannach put in quickly: 'We shall defeat the Fhoi Myore. We must. But I'll admit we could make use of any further advantages that Fate cares to send us.' He looked meaningly at Corum who nodded.

'Magic is the best weapon against magic,' he agreed, 'if that is what you meant, King Mannach.'

'It is what I meant,' said Medhbh's father.

'Magic!' Goffanon laughed. 'There's little of that left now, save the kind the Fhoi Myore and their friends can summon.'

'Yet I heard of something . . .' Corum hardly realized he was speaking. He paused, reconsidering his impulse.

'Heard what?' said Amergin, leaning forward.

Corum looked at Ilbrec. 'You spoke of a magical place, Ilbrec. Earlier today. You said you might know of somewhere where magical allies might be found.'

Ilbrec glanced at Goffanon, who frowned. 'I said I might know of such a place. It was a dim memory . . .'

'It is too dangerous,' said Goffanon. 'As I told you before, Ilbrec, I wonder at your suggesting it. We are best engaged in using to fullest advantage the resources we have now.'

'Very well,' said Ilbrec. 'You were ever cautious, Goffanon.'

'In this case rightly,' grunted the Sidhi dwarf.

But now there was a silence in the hall as everyone listened to the exchange between the two Sidhi.

Ilbrec looked about him, addressing all. 'I made a

mistake,' he said. 'Magic and such stuff has a habit of recoiling on those who use it.'

'True,' said Amergin. 'We will respect your reserve, Sir Ilbrec.'

'It is well,' said Ilbrec, but it was plain he did not really share Goffanon's caution. Caution was not part of the Sidhi youth's character, just as it had not been part of the great Manannan's nature.

'Your folk fought the Fhoi Myore in nine great fights,' said King Fiachadh, wiping his mouth clean of the sticky mead which clung to it. 'You know them best, therefore. And therefore we respect any advice you give us.'

'And do you give us advice, Sir Sidhi?' Amergin asked.

Goffanon looked up from where he had been staring broodingly into his drinking beaker. His eyes were hard and sharp; they burned with a fire none had previously seen there. 'Only that you should fear heroes,' he said.

And no-one asked him what he meant, for all were profoundly disturbed and perplexed by his remark.

At length King Mannach spoke:

'It is agreed that we march directly for Caer Llud and make our first attack there. There are disadvantages to this plan – we go into the coldest of the Fhoi Myore territories – yet we have the chance of surprising them.'

'Then we retreat again,' said Corum. 'Making the best speed we can for Craig Dôn where we shall have left extra weapons, riding beasts and food. From Craig Dôn we can make forays against the Fhoi Myore knowing that they will be unwilling to follow us through the seven circles. Our only danger will be if the Fhoi Myore are strong enough to hold Craig Dôn in siege until our food is gone.'

'And that is why we must strike hard and strike swiftly at Caer Llud, taking as many of them as we can and conserving our own strength,' said Morkyan of the Two Smiles, fingering his pointed beard. 'There must be no display of courage – no glory-deeds at Caer Llud.'

His words were not particularly well received by many in the company.

'War-making is an art,' said Kernyn the Ragged, his long

face seeming to grow still longer, 'though a terrible and immoral art. And most of us gathered here are artists, priding ourselves upon our skills – aye, and our style, too. If we cannot express ourselves in our individual ways, then is there any point to fighting at all?'

'Mabden fights are one thing,' said Corum quietly, 'but a war of Mabden against Fhoi Myore is another. There is more to lose than pride in the battles we contemplate tonight.'

'I understand you,' said Kernyn the Ragged, 'but I am not sure I entirely agree with you, Sir Sidhi.'

'We could give up too much in order to save our lives,' said Sheonan the Axe-maiden, disengaging herself from Grynion's embrace.

'You spoke of what you admired in the Mabden.' The Branch Hero, Phadrac, addressed Goffanon. 'Yet there is a danger that we should sacrifice all the virtues of our folk merely in order to continue to exist.'

'You must sacrifice nothing of that,' Goffanon told him. 'We merely counsel prudence during the assault on Caer Llud. One of the reasons that the Mabden lost so badly to the Fhoi Myore was because the Mabden warriors fight as individuals whereas the Fhoi Myore organize their forces as a single unit. At Caer Llud, if nowhere else, we must emulate these methods, using cavalry for fast-striking, using chariots as moving platforms from which to cast missiles. It would be pointless to stand and fight against Rhannon's horrible breath, would it not?'

'The Sidhi speak wisely,' agreed Amergin, 'and I beg all my folk to listen to them. That is why we are gathered here tonight, after all. I saw Caer Llud fall. I saw fine, brave war-knights fall before they could strike a single blow against their enemies. In the old times, in the times of the Nine Fights, Sidhi fought Fhoi Myore, one to one; but we are not Sidhi. We are Mabden. We must, in this instance, fight as a single folk.'

The Branch Hero leaned his great body backwards on the bench, nodding. 'If Amergin decrees this, then I will fight as the Sidhi suggest. It is enough,' he said.

And the others murmured their assent.

Now Ilbrec reached into his jerkin and drew out a rolled sheet of vellum.

'Here,' he said, 'is a map of Caer Llud.'

He unrolled the sheet and turned, displaying it.

'We attack simultaneously from four sides. Each force will be led by its king. This wall is considered the weakest and so two kings and their people will attack it. Ideally, we could move in to crush the Fhoi Myore and their slaves at the centre of the city, but in actuality we shall probably not be successful in this and having struck as hard as we can will be forced to retreat, saving as many of our lives as possible for the second fight, at Craig Dôn . . .' And Ilbrec went on to explain the details of the plan.

Although one of those mainly responsible for the plan, Corum privately considered it over-optimistic, yet there was no better plan and so it would have to stand. He poured himself more mead from the pitcher at his elbow, passing the pitcher to Goffanon. Corum still wished that Goffanon had allowed Ilbrec to speak of the mysterious magical allies he considered too dangerous to enlist.

As he accepted the pitcher, Goffanon said quietly: 'We must leave here soon for midnight approaches. The sword will be ready.'

'There is little more to discuss,' Corum agreed. 'Let me know when you wish to go and I will make our excuses.'

Now Ilbrec was answering the close questioning of some of the number who wished to hear how such-and-such a wall would be breached and how long ordinary mortals might be expected to survive in the Fhoi Myore mist and what kind of clothing would offer the best protection and so on. Seeing that he had no more to add to the discussion Corum stood up, courteously taking his leave of the High King and the rest of the gathering and, with Medhbh, Goffanon and Hisak Sunthief beside him, strolling from the crowded hall into narrow streets and a cool night.

The sky was almost as light as day and the heavy buildings of the fortress-city were outlined blackly against it. A few pale, blue-tinted clouds flowed over the moon and flowed on to the horizon in the direction of the sea. They walked to the gate and crossed the bridge which spanned the moat, making their way round the edge of the camp and going towards the trees beyond. Somewhere a great owl hooted and there was a crack of wings, the squeal of a young rabbit. Insects chittered in the tall grass as they waded through it and entered the forest.

While the trees were still thin, Corum looked up into the clear sky noting that once again, as it had been the last time he had entered this wood, the moon was full.

'Now,' said Goffanon, 'we go to the place of power where the sword awaits us.'

And Corum found that he paused, reluctant to visit that mound where he had first entered this strange Mabden dream.

There came a sound from behind. Corum turned nervously, seeing, to his relief, that Jhary-a-Conel came to join them, his winged cat on his shoulder.

Jhary grinned. 'The hall was becoming too stuffy for Whiskers here.' He stroked the cat's head. 'I thought I might join you.'

Goffanon seemed a trifle suspicious, but he nodded. 'You are a welcome witness to what will transpire tonight, Jhary-a-Conel.'

Jhary gave a bow. 'I thank you.'

Corum said: 'Is there no other place we can go, Goffanon? Must it be Cremmsmound?'

'Cremmsmound is the nearest place of power,' said Goffanon simply. 'It would be too far to travel elsewhere.'

Corum still did not move. He listened carefully to the sounds of the forest. 'Do you hear the strains of a harp?' he asked.

'We are not close enough to the hall to hear the musicians,' said Hisak Sunthief.

'You hear no harp in the wood?'

'I hear nothing,' said Goffanon.

'Then I do not hear it,' said Corum. 'I thought for a moment it was the Dagdagh harp. The harp we heard when we summoned Oak Woman.'

'An animal cry,' said Medhbh.

'I fear that harp.' Corum's voice was almost a whisper.

'There would be no need,' Medhbh told him. 'For the Dagdagh harp is wise. It is our friend.'

Corum reached out and took her warm hand. 'It is your friend, Medhbh of the Long Arm, but it is not mine. The old seeress told me to fear a harp, and that is the harp of which she spoke.'

'Forget that prophecy. The old woman was plainly deranged. It was not a true prophecy.' Medhbh stepped closer to him, her grip tightening. 'You, of all of us, should not give in to superstition now, Corum.'

Corum made a great effort and pushed the fear into the back of his mind. Then, momentarily, he met Jhary's eye. Jhary was troubled. He turned away, adjusting his wide-brimmed hat on his head.

'Now we must go quickly,' growled Goffanon. 'The time is near.'

And, fighting off that morbid sense of doom, Corum followed the Sidhi dwarf deeper into the forest.

CHAPTER FOUR

The Sword Song of the Sidhi

It was as Corum had seen it before, Cremmsmound, with the white rays of the moon striking it, with the leaves of the oak trees shining like dark silver, all still.

Corum studied the mound and wondered what lay beneath it. Did the mound really hide the bones of one who had been called Corum of the Silver Hand? And could those bones indeed be his own? The thought barely disturbed him at that moment. He watched Goffanon and Hisak Sunthief digging in the soft earth at the base of the mound, eventually drawing out a finished sword, a heavy, finely-tempered sword whose hilt was of plaited ribbons of iron. The sword seemed to attract the light of the moon and reflect it with increased brightness.

Careful not to touch the handle, holding the sword below the hilt, Goffanon inspected it, showing it to Hisak who nodded his approval.

'It will take much to dull the edge of this,' said Goffanon. 'Save for Ilbrec's sword Retaliator, there is no blade like it now in all the world.'

'Is it steel?' Jhary-a-Conel stepped closer, peering at the sword. 'It does not shine like steel.'

'It is an alloy,' said Hisak proudly. 'Partly steel, partly Sidhi metal.'

'I thought there was no Sidhi metal left upon this plane,' Medhbh said. 'I thought it all gone, save for that in Ilbrec's and Goffanon's weapons.'

'It is what remains of an old Sidhi sword,' said Goffanon. 'Hisak had it. When we met he told me that he had kept it for many years, knowing no way in which to temper it. He got it from some miners who found it while they were digging for iron ore. It had been buried deep. I recognized it as one of a hundred swords I forged for the Sidhi before the Nine Fights. Only part of the blade remained. We shall never know the circumstances of how it came to be buried. Together Hisak and I conceived a way in which to blend the Sidhi metal with your Mabden metal and produce a sword containing the best properties of both.'

Hisak Sunthief frowned. 'And certain other properties, I understand.'

'Possibly,' said Goffanon. 'We shall learn more in time.'

'It is a fine sword,' said Jhary, reaching towards it, 'may I try it?'

But Goffanon withdrew it swiftly, almost nervously, shaking his head.

'Only Corum,' he said. 'Only Corum.'

'Then . . .' Corum made to take the sword. Goffanon raised his hand.

'Not yet,' said the dwarf. 'I have still to sing the song.'

'Song?' Medhbh was curious.

'My sword song. A song was always sung at such a time as this.' Goffanon lifted the sword towards the moon and it took on the aspect, for a moment, of a living thing; then it was a solid black cross framed against the great disc of the moon. 'Each sword I make is different. Each must have a different song. Thus its identity is established. But I shall not name the blade. That task is Corum's. He must name the sword with the only name right for it. And when it is named, then the sword will fulfil its ultimate destiny.'

'And what is that?' asked Corum.

Goffanon smiled. 'I do not know. Only the sword will know.'

'I thought you above such superstition, Sir Sidhi!' Jhary-a-Conel stroked his cat's neck.

'It is not superstition. It is something to do with an ability, at such times as these, to see into other planes, into other periods of time. What will happen will happen.

Nothing we do here will change that, but we will have some *sense* of what is to come and that knowledge could be of use to us. I must sing my song, that is all I know.' Goffanon looked defensive. Then he relaxed, turning his face to the moon. 'You must listen and be silent while I sing.'

'And what will you sing?' asked Medhbh.

'As yet,' murmured Goffanon, 'I do not know. My heart will tell me.'

And, instinctively, they all fell back into the shadows of the oaks while Goffanon climbed slowly to the crest of Cremmsmound, the sword held by the blade in his two hands and lifted towards the moon. On the top of the mound he paused.

The night was full of heavy scents, of rustlings and the voices of small animals. The darkness in the surrounding grove was almost impenetrable. The oak trees were still. Then the sounds of the forest seemed to die away and Corum heard only the breathing of his companions.

For a long moment Goffanon neither moved nor spoke. His huge chest rose and fell rapidly and his eyes had closed. Then he moved slowly, lifting the sword to eight separate points before returning to his original position.

Then he began to sing. He sang in the beautiful, liquid speech of the Sidhi which was so like the Vadhagh tongue and which Corum could easily understand. This is what Goffanon sang:

Lo! I made the great swords
Of a hundred Sidhi knights.
Nine and ninety broke in battle.
Only one came home.

Some did rot in earth; some in ice;
Some in trees; some under seas;
Some melted in fire or were eaten.
Only one came home.

One blade, all broken, all torn,
  Of the Sidhi metal
Not enough for a sword,
  So iron was added.

Sidhi strength and Mabden strength
  Combine in Goffanon's blade.
His gift for Corum.
  Weakness, too, this war-knife holds.

Now Goffanon shifted his grip slightly upon the sword, raising it a little higher. He swayed, as one in a trance, before continuing:

Forged in fire, tempered in frost,
  Power from the sun, wisdom from the moon,
Fine and fallible,
  This brand is fated.

Ah! They will hate it,
  Those ghosts of the yet-to-come!
Even now the sword thirsts for them.
  Their blood grows chill.

It seemed almost that Goffanon balanced the blade by its tip and that it stood upright under its own volition.

(And Corum recalled a dream and he recoiled. When had he handled such a sword before?)

Soon will come the naming,
  Then the foe shall shudder!
Here is a handsome needle,
  To stitch the Fhoi Myore shroud!

Glaive! Goffanon made thee!
  Now you go to Corum!
Worms and carrion eaters
  Will call you 'Friend'.

> *Harsh shall be the slaughter,*
> *Ere the winter's vanquished*
> *Good, red reaping*
> *For a Sidhi scythe!*

> *Then must come the naming;*
> *Then must come the tally.*
> *Sidhi and Vadhagh both shall*
> *Pay the score.*

Now a frightful shuddering possessed Goffanon's bulky body and he came close to losing his grip on the sword.

Corum wondered why the others did not seem to hear Goffanon when he groaned. He looked at their faces. They stood entranced, uncomprehending, overawed.

Goffanon hesitated, rallied himself, and went on:

> *Unnamed blade, I call thee Corum's sword!*
> *Hisak and Goffanon claim thee not!*
> *Black winds cry through Limbo!*
> *Blind rivers await my soul!*

These last words Goffanon screamed. He appeared terrified by what he saw through his closed eyes, but his sword song still issued from his bearded lips.

(Had Corum ever seen this sword? No. But there had been another like it. This sword would prove useful against the Fhoi Myore, he knew. But was the sword really a friend? Why did he consider it an enemy?)

> *This was a fated forging;*
> *But now that it is done*
> *The blade, like its destiny,*
> *Cannot be broken.*

Corum could see only the sword. He found that he was moving towards it, climbing the mound. It was as if Goffanon had disappeared and the blade hung in the air, burning sometimes white like the moon, sometimes red like the sun.

Corum reached out for the handle with his silver fingers, but the sword seemed to retreat. Only when Corum stretched his left hand, his hand of flesh, towards it did it allow him to approach.

Corum still heard Goffanon's song. The song had begun as a proud chant; now it was a melancholy dirge. And was the dirge accompanied, in the far distance, by the strains of a harp?

> Here is a fitting sword,
>   Half mortal, half immortal,
> For the Vadhagh hero.
>   Here is Corum's sword.
>
> There is no comfort in the blade I made,
>   It was forged for more than war;
> It will kill more than flesh;
>   It will grant both more and less than death.
>
> Fly, blade! Rush to Corum's grip!
>   Forget Goffanon made thee!
> Doom only the Mabden's foes!
>   Learn loyalty, shun treachery!

Suddenly the sword was in Corum's left hand and it was as if he had known such a sword all his life. It fitted his grasp perfectly; its balance was superb. He turned it this way and that in the light of the moon, wondering at its sharpness and its handling.

'It is my sword,' he said. He felt that he was united with something he had lost long since and then forgotten about. 'It is my sword.'

> Serve well the knight who knoweth thee!

Abruptly, Goffanon's song ended. The great dwarf's eyes opened; his expression was a mixture of tormented guilt, sympathy for Corum, and triumph.

Then Goffanon turned to peer at the moon.

Corum followed his gaze and was transfixed by the great silver disc which apparently filled the whole sky. Corum felt as though he were being drawn into the moon. He saw faces there, scenes of fighting armies, wastelands, ruined cities and fields. He saw himself, though the face was not his. He saw a sword not unlike the one he now held, but the other sword was black, whereas his was white. He saw Jhary-a-Conel. He saw Medhbh. He saw Rhalina and he saw other women, and he loved them all, but of Medhbh alone he felt fear. Then the Dagdagh harp appeared and changed into the form of a youth whose body shone with a strange golden colour and who, in some way, was also the harp. Then he saw a great, pale horse and he knew that that horse was his but he was wary of where the horse would take him. Then Corum saw a plain all white with snow and across this plain came a single rider whose robe was scarlet and whose arms and armour were those of the Vadhagh and who had one hand of flesh and one of metal and whose right eye was covered by an elaborately embroidered patch and whose features were the features of a Vadhagh, of Corum. And Corum knew that this rider was not himself and he gasped in terror and tried not to look as the rider came closer and closer, an expression of mocking hatred upon his face and in his single eye the unequivocal determination to kill Corum and take his place.

'No!' cried Corum.

Clouds moved across the moon and the light dimmed and Corum stood upon Cremmsmound in the oak grove, the place of power, with a sword in his hand that was unlike any sword forged before this day; and Corum looked down the mound and saw that Goffanon now stood with Hisak Sunthief and Jhary-a-Conel and Medhbh the red-haired, Medhbh of the Long Arm, and all four stared at Corum as if they wished to help him and could not.

Corum did not know why he replied to their expressions in the way he did when he raised the sword high over his head and said to them in a quiet, firm voice:

'I am Corum. This is my sword. I am alone.'

Then the four walked up the mound and they took him back to Caer Mahlod where many still feasted, unaware of what had taken place in the oak grove when the moon had been at its fullest.

CHAPTER FIVE

A Company of Horsemen

Corum slept long into the following morning, but it was not a dreamless sleep. Voices spoke to him of untrustworthy heroes and noble traitors; he had visions of swords, both the one he had been given during the ceremony in the oak grove and others, in particular one other, a black blade which seemed, like the Dagdagh harp, to have a complex personality, as if inhabited by the spirit of a particularly powerful demon. And between hearing these voices and seeing these visions he heard the words repeated over and over again:

'You are the Champion. You are the Champion.'

And sometimes a chorus of voices would tell him:

'You must follow the Champion's Way.'

And what, he would wonder, if that way were not the way of the Mabden whom he had sworn to help?

And the chorus would repeat:

'You must follow the Champion's Way.'

And Corum awoke, eventually, saying aloud:

'I have no liking for this dream.'

He spoke of the dream into which he had awakened.

Medhbh, dressed, fresh-faced and determined, had been standing beside the bed. 'What dream is that, my love?'

He shrugged and tried to smile. 'Nothing. Last night's events disturbed me, I suppose.' He looked into her eyes and he felt a little fear creep into his mind. He reached out and took hold of her soft hands, her strong, cool hands. 'Do you really love me, Medhbh?'

She was disconcerted. 'I do,' she said.

He looked beyond her to the carved chest on the lid of which rested the sword Goffanon had given him. 'How shall I name the sword?'

She smiled. 'You will know. Is that not what Goffanon told you? You will know what to call it when the time comes and then the sword will be informed with all its powers.'

He sat up, the covers falling away from his broad, naked chest.

She went to the far side of the chamber and signalled to someone in the next room. 'Prince Corum's bath. Is it ready?'

'It is ready, my lady.'

'Come, Corum,' said Medhbh. 'Refresh yourself. Wash away your unpleasant dreams. In two days we shall be ready to march. There is little left for you to do until then. Let us spend those two days as enjoyably as we can. Let us ride, this morning, beyond the woods and over the moors.'

He drew a deep breath. 'Aye,' he said lightly. 'I am a fool to brood. If my destiny is set, then it is set.'

Amergin met them as they mounted their horses an hour later. Amergin was tall, slender and youthful but had the dignity of a man much older than he looked. He wore the blue and gold robes of the Archdruid and there was a simple coronet of iron and raw gems set upon his head of long, fair hair.

'Greetings,' said the High King. 'Did your business go well last night, Prince Corum?'

'I think so,' said Corum. 'Goffanon seemed satisfied.'

'But you do not carry the sword he gave you.'

'It is not a sword, I think, to be worn casually.' Corum had his old, good sword at his side. 'I shall carry Goffanon's gift into battle, however.'

Amergin nodded. He looked down at the cobbles of the courtyard, apparently in deep thought. 'Goffanon told you no more of those allies Ilbrec mentioned?'

'I took it that Goffanon did not regard them, whoever they are, as allies, necessarily,' said Medhbh.

'Just so,' said Amergin. 'However, it would seem to me it would be worth risking much if it meant that our chances of defeating the Fhoi Myore were improved.'

Corum was surprised by what he guessed to be the import of Amergin's words. 'You do not think we shall be successful?'

'The attack on Caer Llud will cost us dear,' said Amergin quietly. 'I meditated on your plan last night. I believe I had a vision.'

'Of defeat?'

'It was not a vision of victory. You know Caer Llud, Corum, as do I. You know how utterly cold it is now that the Fhoi Myore inhabit it. Cold of that order affects men often in ways they do not fully comprehend.'

'That is true.' Corum nodded.

'That is all that I thought,' said Amergin. 'A simple thought. I cannot be more specific.'

'You do not need to be, High King. But I fear there is no better means of making war against our enemies. If there were . . .'

'We should all know it.' Amergin shrugged and patted the neck of Corum's horse. 'But if you have the opportunity to reason with Goffanon again, beg him at very least to tell us the nature of these allies.'

'I promise you that I shall, Archdruid, but I do not anticipate any success.'

'No,' said Amergin, his hand falling away from the horse. 'Neither do I.'

Corum and Medhbh rode out from Caer Mahlod, leaving behind them a thoughtful Archdruid, and soon they were galloping through the oak woods and up into the high moorlands where curlews rose and sank above their heads and the smell of the bracken and the heather was sweet in their nostrils and it seemed that no power in the universe could change the simple beauties of the landscape. The sun was warm in a soft blue sky. It was a kindly day. And soon their spirits had risen higher than ever before, and they dismounted from their horses and wandered through the knee-high bracken and then sank down into it so that all they could see was the sky and the cool, restful green of the ferns on all sides; and they held each other and they made gentle love, then lay close together in silence, breathing the good air and listening to the quiet sounds of the moorlands.

They were allowed an hour of this peace before Corum detected a faint pulsing from the ground beneath him and put his ear to the source, knowing what it must mean.

'Horses,' he said, 'coming nearer.'

'Fhoi Myore riders?' She sat up, reaching for her sling and her pouch which she carried everywhere.

'Perhaps. Gaynor or the People of the Pines, or both. Yet we have outriders everywhere at present to warn us of an attack from the east and we know that all the Fhoi Myore gather in the east at present.'

Cautiously he began to raise his head. The horsemen were coming from the north-west, more or less from the direction of the coast. His view was blocked by the rise of a hill, but now, very faintly, he thought he could hear the jingle of harness. Looking behind him, Corum could see that their horses would be clearly visible to anyone approaching over that hill. He drew his sword and began to creep towards the horses. Medhbh followed him.

Hastily, they clambered into their saddles, riding towards the hill, but at an angle to the approaching horsemen, so that, with luck, they would not immediately be seen if they crested the hill.

An outcrop of white limestone offered them some cover and they drew rein behind this, waiting until the riders came in sight.

Almost immediately the first three appeared. The ponies they rode were small and shaggy and dwarfed by the size of the broad-shouldered men on their backs. These men all had the same blazing pale red hair and sharp blue eyes. The hair of their beards was plaited into a dozen narrow braids and the hair of their heads hung in four or five very thick braids into which were bound strands of beads, glinting. They had long oval shields strapped to their left arms and these shields appeared to be of hide and wicker reinforced with rims and bands of brass hammered into bold, flowing designs. The shields appeared to have sheaths attached to their inner surfaces and into these were stuck two iron-headed spears shod with brass. On their hips the men sported short, wide-bladed swords in leather, iron-studded sheaths. Some wore their helmets and others carried them over their saddle pommels and the helmets were all roughly of the same design – conical caps of leather ribbed by iron or brass and decorated with the long, curving horns of the mountain ox. In some cases the original horn had been completely obscured by the polished pebbles, bits of iron or brass or even gold, set into it. Thick plaid cloaks predominantly of red, blue or green were flung over their shoulders. They had kilts either of plaid or of leather and their legs were naked; only a few wore any kind of footgear and of these most wore a simple sandal strapped at the ankle.

They were, without doubt, warriors, but Corum had seen none quite like these, though to a degree they resembled the folk of Tir-nam-Beo and the ponies reminded him of those ridden by his old enemies of the forests near Moidel's Mount. Eventually all the riders came into sight – about a score of them – and as they rode closer it was evident they had lately experienced hardship. Some had broken limbs, others had wounds bound up and two of the men were strapped tightly to their saddles so that they would not fall from their ponies.

'I do not think they mean harm to Caer Mahlod,' said Medhbh. 'These are Mabden. But what Mabden? I thought all warriors had been summoned by now.'

'They have travelled far and hard by the look of them,' murmured Corum. 'And over the sea, too. Look, their cloaks bear the stains of sea-water. Perhaps they have left a boat near here. Come, let us hail them.' He urged his horse from its cover behind the limestone crag, calling out to the newcomers:

'I bid you good afternoon, strangers. Where are you bound?'

The burly warrior in the vanguard reined in his pony

suddenly, his red brows coming together in a suspicious scowl, his heavy, gnarled hand reaching towards the handle of his sword, and when he spoke his tone was deep and coarse.

'I bid you a good afternoon, also,' he said, 'if you mean us no harm. As for where we are bound – well, that is our business.'

'It is also the business of those whose land this is,' Corum answered reasonably.

'That could be,' the warrior answered. 'But if it be not Mabden land, then you have conquered it and if you have conquered it, then you are our enemy and we must slay you. We can see that you are not Mabden.'

'True. But I serve the Mabden cause. And this lady, she is Mabden.'

'She resembles a Mabden, certainly,' said the warrior, dropping none of his caution. 'But we have seen too many illusions on our journey here to be deceived by what is apparently so.'

'I am Medhbh,' said Medhbh fiercely, offended. 'I am Medhbh of the Long Arm, famous in my own right as a warrior. And I am the daughter of King Mannach, who rules this land from Caer Mahlod.'

The warrior became a trifle less suspicious, but he kept his hand upon the hilt of his sword and the others spread out as if they prepared to attack Medhbh and Corum.

'And I am Corum,' said Corum, 'once called the Prince in the Scarlet Robe, but I traded that robe to a wizard and now I am called Corum of the Silver Hand.' He held up his metal hand which, up to that point, he had concealed. 'Have you not heard of me? I fight for the Mabden against the Fhoi Myore.'

'That is he!' one of the younger warriors behind the leader shouted and pointed at Corum. 'The scarlet robe – he does not wear it now – but the features are the same – the eye-patch is the same. That is he!'

'You have followed us, then, Sir Demon,' said the leading warrior. He sighed, turned in his saddle and looked back at his men. 'These are all that are left, but perhaps we can defeat you and your she-demon consort.'

'He is no demon and neither am I!' cried Medhbh angrily. 'Why do you accuse us of this? Where have you seen us before?'

'We have not seen you before,' said the leader. He steadied his nervous pony with a movement of the reins. His harness clattered and his metal stirrup struck the rim of his long shield. 'We have seen only this one.' He nodded at Corum. 'In those foul and sorcerous islands back there.'

He jerked his head in the direction of the sea.

'The island where we beached eight good longships and ten rafts of provisions and livestock, going ashore for fresh water and meat. You will recall,' he continued, staring with hatred at Corum, 'that when we left it was with but a single ship, no women or children, no livestock save our ponies, and few provisions.'

Corum said: 'I assure you that you have not seen me until this moment. I am Corum. I fight the Fhoi Myore. These last weeks I have spent at Caer Mahlod. I have not left at any time. This is the first journey I have taken beyond the immediate confines of the city in a month!'

'You are the one who came against us on the island,' said the youth who had first accused Corum. 'In your red cloak, with your helm of mock-silver, with your face all pale like that of a dead thing, with your eye-patch and your laughter . . .'

'A Shefanhow,' said the leader. 'We know you.'

'It has been literally a lifetime since I heard that word used,' said Corum sombrely. 'You are close to angering me, stranger. I speak the truth. You must have come to blows with an enemy who resembled me in some way.'

'Aye!' the youth laughed bitterly. 'To the extent of being your twin! We feared you would follow us. But we are ready to defend ourselves against you. Where do your men hide?' He looked about him, his braids swinging with the movement of his head.

'I have no men,' said Corum impatiently.

The leader laughed harshly. 'Then you are foolish.'

'I will not fight you,' Corum told him. 'Why are you here?'

'To join those who gather at Caer Mahlod.'

'It is as I thought.' All Corum's earlier forebodings had returned and he fought to hold them off. 'If we give you our weapons and take you to Caer Mahlod, will you believe that we mean you no harm? At Caer Mahlod you will learn that we speak the truth, that we have never seen you before and that we are not your enemies.'

The loud-voiced youth called: 'It could be a trick, to lure us into a trap.'

'Ride with your swords at our throats if you like,' said Corum carelessly. 'If you are attacked, you may kill us.'

The leader frowned. 'You have none of the manner of that other we met on the island,' he said. 'And if you lead us to Caer Mahlod at least we shall have reached our destination and thus gained something from this meeting.

'Artek!' shouted the youth. 'Be wary!'

The leader turned. 'Silence, Kawanh. We can always slay the Shefanhow later!'

'I would ask you, in courtesy,' said Corum evenly, 'not to employ that term when you refer to me. It is not one I like and it does not make me sympathetic to you.'

Artek made to answer, a hard smile half-forming on his lips. Then he looked into Corum's single eye and thought better of his reply. He grunted and ordered two of his men forward. 'Take their weapons. Hold your swords at them as we ride. Very well – Corum – lead us to Caer Mahlod.'

Corum derived some pleasure from the looks of shock on the strangers' faces as they rode to the outskirts of the camp and saw the expressions of concern and anger in the eyes of every Mabden who became aware that Corum and Medhbh were prisoners. Now it was Corum's turn to smile and his smile was broad as the crowd around the twenty riders became thicker and thicker until they were no longer able to advance and came to a halt in the middle of the camp, still some distance from the hill on which Caer Mahlod was built. A war-chief of the Tir-nam-Beo glared at Artek, whose sword pressed upon Corum's chest.

'What mean you by this, man? Why do you hold hostage our princess? Why threaten the life of our friend, Prince Corum?'

Artek's embarrassment was so complete that he blushed a deeper red than his hair and beard. 'So you spoke the truth . . .' he muttered. But he did not lower his sword. 'Unless this is some monstrous illusion and all these are your demon followers.'

Corum shrugged. 'If they are demons, Sir Artek, then you are doomed, anyway, are you not?'

Miserably Artek sheathed his sword. 'You are right. I must believe you. Yet your resemblance to the one who attacked us on that hateful and haunted isle is so close – you would not blame me, Prince Corum, if you saw him.'

Corum answered so that only Artek could hear. 'I think that I have seen him in a dream. Later, Sir Artek, you and I must talk about this, for I believe the evil which was worked against you will soon be directed against me – and the results will be even more tragic.'

Artek darted him a puzzled glance but, respecting the tone of Corum's words, said nothing further.

'You must rest and you must eat,' said Corum. He had taken a liking to the barbarian in spite of the poor circumstances of their meeting. 'Then you must tell us all your tale in the great hall of Caer Mahlod.'

Artek bowed. 'You are generous, Prince Corum, and you are courteous. Now I see why the Mabden respect you.'

CHAPTER SIX

Concerning the Voyage of the People of Fyean

'We are an island folk,' said Artek, 'living mainly off the sea. We fish –' he paused – 'well, in the past, until recently, we – well, we were sea-raiders, in short. It is a hard life on our islands. Little grows there. Sometimes we raided nearby coasts, at other times we attacked ships and took what we needed to survive . . .'

'I know you now.' King Fiachadh laughed heartily. 'You are pirates, are you not! You are Artek of Clonghar. Why, the folk of our sea-ports pass water at the very mention of your name!'

Artek made a feeble gesture and again he blushed. 'I am that same Artek,' he admitted.

'Fear not, Artek of Clonghar,' smiled King Mannach, leaning across the table and patting the pirate upon the hand, 'all old scores are forgotten in Caer Mahlod. Here we have only one enemy – the Fhoi Myore. Tell us how you came here.'

'One of the ships we raided was from Gwyddneu Garanhir – on its way to Tir-nam-Beo, we discovered, with a message for the king of that land. From that ship we learned of the great massing against the Fhoi Myore. While we have never encountered this folk – living in the remote north-west as we do – we felt that if all the Mabden were joining together against the Cold Folk then we should help also – that their fight was our fight in this case.' He grinned, recovering some of his buoyancy. 'Besides – without your ships, how should *we* live? So it was in our interest to ensure that you survived. We readied all our own boats – more than a score – and built strong, watertight rafts to tow behind them, taking all our folk from Fyean – our whole island's name – since we did not wish to leave our women and children unprotected.'

Artek stopped, lowering his eyes. 'Ah, how I wish we had left them. Then, at least, they might have died in their own homes and not on the shifting shores of that terrible island.'

Ilbrec, who had squeezed himself into the hall to hear Artek's story, said quietly: 'Where is this island?'

'A little to the north and west of Clonghar. The storm drove us in that direction. During the same storm we lost most of our water and much of our meat. Do you know the place, Sir Sidhi?'

'Has it a single high hill, very even in its proportions, at its centre?'

Artek inclined his head. 'It has.'

'And does one huge pine tree grow on the peak of that hill at the exact centre?'

'There is the biggest pine I have ever seen there,' agreed Artek.

'When you have landed does everything seem to shimmer and threaten to change its appearance, save for that hill which remains sharp and solid in outline?'

'You have been there!' said Artek.

'No,' said Ilbrec. 'I have only heard of the place.' And he darted a very hard stare at Goffanon who affected to be without interest in this island and looked studiously bored. But Corum knew the dwarf well enough to see that Goffanon was deliberately ignoring the import of Ilbrec's glance.

'We sea-warriors have passed the island before, of course, but since it is often surrounded by mist and there are hidden rocks at various points off its coast, we have never actually landed there. We have never had the necessity to do so.'

'Though some have been thought ship-wrecked there in the past and never found,' added the eager youth Kawanh. 'There are superstitions about the place – that it is inhabited by Shefanhow and such . . .' His voice trailed off.

'Is it sometimes called Ynys Scaith, this place?' asked Ilbrec, still thoughtful.

'I have heard it called that, aye,' Artek agreed. 'It is an old, old name for the place.'

'So you have been to Shadow Island.' Ilbrec shook his fair head, half-amused. 'Fate draws at more threads than we guessed, eh, Goffanon?'

But Goffanon pretended that he had not heard Ilbrec, though later Corum saw him offer his fellow Sidhi a secret, warning glare.

'Aye, and that is where we saw Prince Corum here – or his double . . .' blurted Kawanh, then stopped. 'I apologize, Prince Corum,' he said. 'I had not meant . . .'

Corum smiled. 'Perhaps it was my shadow you saw. After all, the place is called Ynys Scaith – the Isle of Shadows. An evil shadow, however.' The smile faded on his face.

'I have heard of Ynys Scaith.' Until this moment Amergin had said nothing beyond a formal greeting to Artek and his men. 'A place of dark sorcery where evil druids would go to work their magic. A place shunned even by the Sidhi . . .'

Now it was Amergin's turn to look meaningfully at both Ilbrec and Goffanon, and Corum guessed that the wise Archdruid had also noticed the exchange of glances between the two Sidhi. 'Ynys Scaith, so I was taught as a novice, existed even before the coming of the Sidhi. It shares certain properties with the Sidhi isle of Hy-Breasail, but is in other ways unlike that place. Where Hy-Breasail was supposed to be a land of fair enchantments, Ynys Scaith was said to be an island of black madness . . .'

'Aye,' growled Goffanon. 'It is, to say the least, inhospitable to Sidhi and Mabden alike.'

'You have been there, Goffanon?' Amergin asked gently.

But Goffanon had become wary again. 'Once,' he said.

'Black madness and red despair,' put in Artek. 'When we landed there we found ourselves unable to return to our ships. Disgusting forests grew up in our path. Mists engulfed us. Demons attacked us. All kinds of misshapen beasts lurked in wait for us. They destroyed all our children. They slew all our women and most of our menfolk. We are the only ones, of the whole race of Fyean, who survived – and that by luck, stumbling accidentally upon one of our ships and sailing directly for your shores.' Artek shuddered. 'Even if I knew my wife was still alive and trapped upon Ynys Scaith I would not return.' Artek clenched his two hands together. 'I could not.'

'She is dead,' said Kawanh gently. He was comforting his leader. 'I saw it happen.'

'How could we be sure that what we saw was in any way reality!' Artek's eyes filled with agony.

'No,' said Kawanh. 'She is dead, Artek.'

'Aye,' Artek's hands parted. His shoulders slumped. 'She is dead.'

'Now you know why I would have no part of your idea,' murmured Goffanon to Ilbrec.

Corum looked away from the still shaking Artek of Clonghar. He looked at the two Sidhi. 'Is that where you thought we should find allies, Ilbrec?'

Ilbrec motioned with his hand, dismissing his own idea. 'It was.'

'Nothing but evil comes from Ynys Scaith,' Goffanon said. 'Only evil, no matter how disguised.'

'I had not realized . . .' Amergin reached out and touched Artek upon the shoulder. 'Artek, I will give you a potion that will make you sleep and will ensure that you will not dream. In the morning you will be a man again.'

The sun was setting over the camp. Ilbrec and Corum walked towards the Sidhi's blue tent. From a score of cooking fires came the mingled smells of a variety of meals. Nearby a boy sang of heroes and great deeds in a high, melancholy voice. They entered the tent.

'Poor Artek,' said Corum. 'What allies had you hoped to find on Ynys Scaith?'

Ilbrec shrugged. 'Oh, I thought that the inhabitants – certain of them, at least, might be bribed to side with us. I suppose that my judgement was poor, as Goffanon said.'

'Artek and his followers thought they saw me there,'

Corum told him. 'They thought I was one of those who slew their companions.'

'That puzzles me,' said Ilbrec. 'I have heard of nothing like that before. Perhaps you do have a twin . . . Did you ever have a brother?'

'A brother?' Corum was reminded of the old woman's prophecy. 'No. But I was warned to fear one. I thought the warning might apply to Gaynor who, spiritually in some ways, is a brother. Or whoever it is lying under the hill in the oak grove. But now I think that brother awaits me in Ynys Scaith.'

'Awaits you?' Ilbrec was alarmed. 'You do not mean to visit the Isle of Shadows?'

'It occurred to me that those powerful enough to destroy the best part of the people of Fyean, fearsome enough to terrify one as brave as Artek, would be good allies to have,' said Corum. 'Besides, I would face this "brother" and discover who he is and why I should fear him.'

'It is unlikely that you would survive the dangers of Ynys Scaith,' mused Ilbrec, seating himself in his giant chair and drumming his fingers upon his table.

'I am in a mood to take most risks with my own destiny,' said Corum softly, 'so long as it is not to the disadvantage of these Mabden we serve.'

'I, too.' Ilbrec's sea-blue eyes met Corum's eye. 'But the Mabden march to Caer Llud the day after tomorrow and you must lead them in their war.'

'That is what stops me from sailing immediately to Ynys Scaith,' said Corum. 'That is all.'

'You fear not for your own life – your sanity – perhaps your soul?'

'I am called Champion Eternal. What is death or madness to me, who shall live many more lives than this? How can my soul be trapped if it is needed elsewhere? If anyone has the chance of visiting Ynys Scaith and returning, then surely it is Corum of the Silver Hand?'

'Your logic has flaws,' said Ilbrec. He looked broodingly into the middle-distance. 'But you are right in one point – you are the best fitted to seek Ynys Scaith.'

'And there I could attempt to employ its inhabitants in our service.'

'They would be of great use to us,' admitted Ilbrec.

Cold air came into the tent as the flap parted. Goffanon stood there, his axe upon his shoulder. 'Good evening, my friends,' he said.

They greeted him. He sat himself down on Ilbrec's war-chest, placing his axe carefully beside him. He looked from Corum to Ilbrec and back again. He read something in both their faces that disturbed him.

'Well,' he said, 'I hope you heard enough just now to dissuade you from the foolhardy scheme Ilbrec was considering earlier.'

'You planned to go there?' Corum asked.

Ilbrec spread his hands. 'I had thought . . .'

'I have been there,' interrupted Goffanon. 'That was my bad luck. My good luck was that I managed to escape. Evil druids used that island before the Mabden grew to power on this plane. It existed as a place before the rising of the Vadhagh and the Nhadragh, even – though it was not then on this plane.'

'Then how came it here?' asked Corum.

Ilbrec cleared his throat. 'An accident. For some reason there were those who grew powerful enough in its own plane to be able to destroy it. As Fate would have it, this was at the time when we Sidhi were coming through to help the Mabden against the Fhoi Myore. The inhabitants of Ynys Scaith were able to break through to this plane under cover of our own movements so, indirectly, the Sidhi are responsible for that place of horror existing here. Thus Ynys Scaith escaped the vengeance of the people of its own world, yet I heard that this world is inhospitable to them – they cannot leave their island without certain aids or they inevitably die. They seek a means of returning to their own plane or some other more hospitable to them. Thus far they have been unsuccessful. That is why I thought we might bargain with them to come to our aid – if we offered to help them.'

'They would betray us, no matter what bargain they made with us,' Goffanon said. 'It is as much in their nature to do so as it is in our nature to breathe air.'

'We should have to guard against such a happening,' said Ilbrec.

Goffanon gestured impatiently. 'We could not. Listen to me, Ilbrec! Once I had the notion to visit Ynys Scaith, during the quiet times following the defeat of the Fhoi Myore. I knew what the Mabden said of Hy-Breasail, my own home – that it was inhabited by demons. I thought, therefore, that probably Ynys Scaith was a similar place – that while Mabden perished there, Sidhi would survive. I was wrong. What Hy-Breasail is to the Mabden, so Ynys Scaith is to the Sidhi. It belongs neither to this plane nor to ours. Moreover, the inhabitants use the properties of their land deliberately to torture and to slay all visitors not of their own kind.'

'Yet you escaped,' put in Corum. 'And Artek and a few others survived.'

'By luck in both cases. Artek told you that they found their ship by purest chance. Similarly, I stumbled into the sea. Once clear of Ynys Scaith I could not be followed by the inhabitants. I swam for more than a day before I reached an island little more than a crag of rock jutting from the sea. There I remained until sighted by a ship. They were wary of me, but they took me aboard and eventually I made my way back to Hy-Breasail and never left thereafter.'

'You mentioned nothing of this when first we met,' said Corum.

'For good reason,' growled the Sidhi smith. 'I would have mentioned nothing now, save that Artek spoke out.'

'Yet you speak only of general terrors, not of specific dangers,' said Ilbrec reasonably.

'That,' said Goffanon, 'is because the specific dangers are indescribable.' He got up. 'We fight the Fhoi Myore without seeking such allies as the folk of Ynys Scaith. That way some of us might survive. The other way – we are all doomed. I speak the truth.'

'As you see it,' Corum could not resist saying.

At this, Goffanon's face hardened. He picked up his axe, flung it onto his shoulder and left the tent without another word.

CHAPTER SEVEN

In Which Old Friendships Appear Suddenly Discarded

Amergin came to Corum's chambers that night while Medhbh was elsewhere visiting her father. He entered without knocking, and Corum, who had been staring through the window at the fires of the camp, turned as he detected a footfall.

Amergin spread his thin hands. 'I apologize for my rudeness, Prince Corum, but I wished to speak with you privately. I gather that you have angered Goffanon in some way.'

Corum nodded. 'There was a dispute.'

'Concerning Ynys Scaith?'

'Aye.'

'You had considered visiting the place?'

'I am due to lead your army on the day after tomorrow. Clearly it would be impossible for me to do both.' Corum indicated a carved chair. 'Be seated, Archdruid.'

Corum sat down upon his bed as Amergin lowered himself into the chair.

'Yet you would go, if you had no responsibilities here?' The High King spoke slowly, without looking at Corum.

'I think so. Ilbrec is for the venture.'

'Your chances of survival would seem to be exceptionally slender.'

'Perhaps.' Corum rubbed at his eye-patch. 'But then if we cared considerably about our survival we would not be engaged in this war against the Fhoi Myore.'

'That is reasonable,' said Amergin.

Corum tried to interpret the import of what Amergin was saying.

'There are many reasons,' he said, 'why I should lead the Mabden. Morale must be kept as high as possible while we march through the cold lands.'

'True,' said Amergin. 'I have been debating all this in my mind, as no doubt have you. But you will remember that I asked you earlier to persuade Goffanon to reveal the nature of these potential allies?'

'You spoke of it this morning.'

'Exactly. Well, since then I have meditated on this whole matter further and my conclusions are the same – we shall fare badly at Caer Llud. We shall be defeated by the Fhoi Myore unless we have magical assistance. We require supernatural aid, Prince Corum, beyond anything I can summon, beyond anything the Sidhi have at their disposal. And it appears that the only place whence such help can be got is Ynys Scaith. I tell you all this knowing that you are discreet. Needless to say, our armies must set forth with every confidence of defeating the Fhoi Myore. Their morale would be harmed if you did not lead them, yet I think even with your leadership we should still be beaten. Thus, reluctantly, I conclude that our only hope lies in your being able to bargain with the folk of Ynys Scaith to come to our assistance.'

'And what if I fail?'

'Dying men will curse you for a traitor, but your name will not be dishonoured for long, for there will be no Mabden left to hate you.'

'Is there no other way? What of the lost Treasures of the Mabden, the Sidhi gifts?'

'Those that remain are in Fhoi Myore hands. The Healing Cauldron is at Caer Llud. So is the Collar of Power. There was one other, but we were never sure of its nature nor why it was amongst our Treasures. That is lost.'

'What was it?'

'An old saddle of cracked leather. We kept it faithfully, as we kept our other Treasures, but I think it came with them by mistake.'

'So you cannot recover this cauldron and collar until the Fhoi Myore are defeated.'

'Just so.'

'Do you know anything more of the folk of Ynys Scaith?'

'Only that they would, if they could, leave this plane of ours forever.'

'So I have learned. Yet we are not, surely, powerful enough to help them to do this.'

'If I had the Collar of Power,' said Amergin, 'I might, with other knowledge, be able to achieve their end for them.'

'Goffanon thinks that any bargain with the folk of the Shadow Isle will cost us dear – too dear.'

'If some of us survive, the cost will not be too much,' said Amergin, 'and I think some of us would live on.'

'Perhaps life is not at stake. What other damage could they do?'

'I do not know. If you think the risk too great . . .'

'I have my own reasons, as well as yours, for visiting Ynys Scaith,' Corum said.

'It would be best if you left without much ceremony,' Amergin told him. 'I would inform our men that you have embarked upon a quest and that you will, if possible, rejoin us before the attack on Caer Llud. In the meantime, if Goffanon will not go to Ynys Scaith, let us hope he will lead the Mabden in your stead, for he knows Caer Llud.'

'But he has a weakness, remember that,' said Corum. 'The wizard Calatin has power over him which can only be broken if Calatin loses the bag of spittle he holds. When you attack Caer Llud and if I have perished, seek Calatin out and slay him at once. I think of all those who side with the Fhoi Myore that Calatin is the most dangerous, for he is the most human.'

'I will remember what you say,' answered the Archdruid. 'But I do not think you will perish upon Ynys Scaith, Corum.'

'Perhaps not.' Corum frowned. 'Yet I sense that this world becomes increasingly inhospitable to me, as it does to the folk of the Isle of Shadows.'

'You could speak truly,' Amergin agreed. 'The specific

conjunction of the planes might, in your case, be un-
lucky.'

Corum smiled. 'That sounds like mysticism of doubtful
veracity, High King.'

'Truth often sounds so.' The Archdruid rose. 'When
would you set forth for Ynys Scaith?'

'Soon. I must consult Ilbrec.'

'Leave all other things to me,' said Amergin, 'and, I beg
you, do not discuss our plan too fully with anyone, even
Medhbh.'

'Very well.'

Corum watched Amergin leave, wondering if the
Archdruid were playing an even more complex game than
he had guessed and that Corum was a piece he was
preparing to sacrifice. He shrugged the thoughts away.
Amergin's logic was good, particularly if his vision had
been accurate and the Mabden army stood the chance of
being totally defeated at Caer Llud. And soon after
Amergin had gone, Corum followed him, making his way
out of the fortress-city, down the hill to Ilbrec's great tent.

Corum had returned to his chambers and was arming
himself when Medhbh came in. She had expected to find
him asleep and instead saw him dressed for war.

'What's this? Do we march tomorrow?'

Corum shook his head. 'I go to Ynys Scaith,' he told
her.

'You embark upon a private quest when you are due to
lead us against Caer Llud?' She laughed, wishing to
believe that he joked.

Corum remembered Amergin's wish that he should say
as little as possible about his reasons for the journey. 'It is
not a private quest,' he replied. 'Not wholly, at any rate.'

'No?' Her voice was shaking.

She paced the room several times before continuing.
'We should never have trusted one not of our own race.
Why should we expect you to feel loyalty to our cause?'

'You know that I feel that loyalty, Medhbh.' He
walked towards her, arms outstretched, but she shook his
hand away, turning to glare at him.

'You go to madness and death if you go to Ynys Scaith. You heard what Artek told us!' She tried to control her emotion. 'If you go to Caer Llud with us the worst that can happen to you is that your death will be a noble one.'

'I will rejoin you at Caer Llud if that is possible. The army will travel much slower than shall I. There is every chance of my rejoining it even before the assault on Caer Llud.'

'There is every chance of your never returning from Ynys Scaith,' she said grimly.

He shrugged.

This gesture angered her further. Some word came half-formed from her lips, then she walked to the door, opened it and shut it with a crash behind her.

Corum began to follow her, then thought better of it, knowing that further argument would lead to further misunderstanding. He hoped that Amergin might explain his predicament to Medhbh at some time, or at least convince her that his need to visit Ynys Scaith was not wholly the result of a private obsession.

But it was with a heavy heart indeed that he left the castle and returned to the camp where Ilbrec awaited him.

The golden giant was caparisoned for war, his great sword Retaliator sheathed at his hip, his huge horse Splendid Mane prepared for riding. He was smiling, plainly excited by the prospect of their adventure; but Corum could feel nothing but pain as he tried to return the Sidhi's smile.

'There is no time to waste,' said Ilbrec. 'As we agreed, we shall both ride Splendid Mane. He gallops faster than any mortal horse and will have us to Ynys Scaith and back in no time. I got the chart from Kawanh. There is naught else to keep us here.'

'No,' said Corum. 'Naught else.'

'You are irresponsible fools!'

Corum wheeled round to confront a Goffanon whose face was dark with rage. The Sidhi dwarf shook the fist which held his double-bladed war-axe and he snarled at them. 'If you come back from Ynys Scaith alive then you will not be sane. You will be good for nothing. We need you on this march. The Mabden are expecting the three of us to lead them. Our presence gives them confidence. Do not go to Ynys Scaith. Do not go!'

'Goffanon,' said Ilbrec reasonably, 'in most things I respect your wisdom. In this matter, however, we must follow our own instincts.'

'Your instincts are false if they lead you to destruction, to the betrayal of those you have sworn to serve! Do not go!'

'We go,' said Corum in a quiet voice. 'We must.'

'Then an evil demon drives you and you are no longer my friends,' said Goffanon. 'You are no longer my friends.'

'You should respect our motives, Goffanon . . .' began Corum, but he was cut off by the dwarf's cursing.

'Even if you return sane from Ynys Scaith – and I doubt that you will – you will bring your own doom with you. That is unquestionable. I have seen it. There has been a hint of it in my dreams of late.'

With a certain defiance, Corum said: 'The Vadhagh had a theory that dreams tell more about the man who dreams than about the world he dwells in. Could you have other motives for not wishing us to visit Ynys Scaith . . .?'

Goffanon glared at him contemptuously. 'I go with the Mabden to Caer Llud,' he said.

'Be careful of Calatin,' said Corum earnestly.

'I think that Calatin was a better friend than are you two.' Goffanon's back was bowed as he made to leave the camp.

'Well, must I decide?' The voice was light and ironic. It belonged to Jhary-a-Conel who had emerged from the shadows and stood with his hand on his hip, his other hand to his chin, staring at the three of them from under tightly drawn brows. 'Must I decide between travelling to Ynys Scaith or Caer Llud? Are my loyalties divided?'

'You go to Caer Llud,' said Corum. 'Your wisdom and knowledge are required here. They are greater than mine . . .'

'Whose would not be?' burst out Goffanon, still with his back to Corum.

'Go with Goffanon, Jhary,' said Corum softly to the Companion to Heroes. 'Help guard him against Calatin's sorcery.'

Jhary nodded. He touched Corum on the shoulder. 'Goodbye, treacherous friend,' he murmured. And the little smile on his lips was melancholy.

As they spoke, Ilbrec mounted Splendid Mane, his harness clattering. 'Corum?'

Corum spoke sharply. 'Goffanon, I am sure that I do what is most necessary to serve our cause best.'

'You will pay a price,' said Goffanon. 'You will pay, Corum. Heed my warning.'

Corum tapped a silver finger against the sword he now wore at his side. 'My danger is lessened, however, thanks to your gift. I have faith in this blade you made. Do you say it will not protect me at all?'

Shaking his huge head from side to side as if in pain Goffanon groaned. 'That depends upon the uses to which it is put. But, by the souls of all the Sidhi heroes, great and dead, I wish that I had not forged it.'

BOOK TWO

---

*On Ynys Scaith many terrors are
experienced, many deceptions
revealed, and several reversals
brought about . . .*

CHAPTER ONE

The Enchantments of Ynys Scaith

Splendid Mane had not forgotten the old roads between the planes and now the Sidhi horse galloped apparently upon the very waters of the sea as dawn found Ilbrec and Corum, both mounted on the same steed, out of sight of any land at all. The cool ocean rolled, blue veined with white, on all sides of them, turning to pink, to gold and back to blue again as the sun climbed the sky.

'Amergin said that Shadow Isle existed even before the coming of the Sidhi.' Corum sat behind Ilbrec, clinging to the giant's great belt. 'Yet you told me it only came to this plane when the Sidhi came.'

'There were always adepts in certain arts who could travel between the planes, as you well know,' explained Ilbrec, delighting in the feel of the spray upon his face, 'and doubtless there were Mabden druids who visited Ynys Scaith before it properly arrived here.'

'And who, originally, were the folk who dwell now upon Ynys Scaith? Were they Mabden?'

'Never. An older race, like the Vadhagh, who were gradually superseded by Mabden. Living in virtual exile upon their island they became inbred and cruel – and they had already been inbred and cruel before the island became their only home.'

'What was this race called?'

'That I do not know.' Ilbrec drew Kawanh's chart from inside his armour, inspecting the parchment closely and then leaning forward to murmur something in the ear of Splendid Mane.

Almost at once the horse began to alter its direction slightly, making for the north-west.

Grey clouds began to appear, bringing with them a light rain which was not particularly uncomfortable, and soon they had passed into the sunshine again. Corum found himself half-asleep as he clung to Ilbrec's belt, and he deliberately took the opportunity to rest his body and his mind as much as possible, knowing that he would need all his resources when they came to Ynys Scaith.

Now it was that the two heroes rode across the sea and came at length to Ynys Scaith: a small island, shaped like the peak of a mountain and shrouded by dark cloud where all about it the sky was blue and clear. They could hear the breakers booming on its bleak beaches, they could see the hill at the island's very centre and, soon, they saw the single tall pine standing upon the top of the hill, but of the rest of the island, though they rode still closer, they could make out little. With a soft word and a light movement of his hand, Ilbrec reined in Splendid Mane and the horse and its riders came to a halt while the sea swirled everywhere around them.

Corum adjusted his silvered, conical helm upon his head and leaned to tighten the straps of his greaves of gilded brass, at the same time shrugging his silver byrnie into a more comfortable fit upon his body. Over his shoulder went his quiver of arrows and his unstrung bow. Onto his left arm went his shield of white hide, and now he clenched a long-hafted war-axe in his silver hand, leaving his right hand free to clutch Ilbrec's belt or to draw his strange sword when the occasion demanded.

In front of him Ilbrec threw back his heavy cloak so that the sun glanced off his golden, braided hair, his bronze armour and shield, his bracelets of gold. He turned to look back at Corum and his green-grey eyes were identical in colour to the sea. And Ilbrec smiled. 'Are you ready, friend Corum?'

Corum could not imitate the devil-may-care smile of the Sidhi; his own smile was a little grimmer as he inclined his head slightly. 'Let us ride on to Ynys Scaith,' he said.

So Ilbrec shook Splendid Mane's reins and the huge horse began to gallop again, the spray rising high into the air as they went faster and faster towards the isle of enchantments.

Now Splendid Mane was almost upon the beach, yet it was still impossible to define any clear images in the general, shadowy appearance of the island. There was a suggestion of heavy, tangled forest, of half-ruined buildings, of beaches littered with a variety of jetsam, of swirling mist, of large-winged flapping birds, of burly beasts prowling through the wreckage and the trees; but every time the eye seemed about to focus on something it would shift again and become dim. Once Corum thought he saw a great face, larger than Ilbrec's, staring at him from over a rock, but then both face and rock seemed to become a tree, or a building, or a beast. There was something unclean and dolorous about Ynys Scaith; it had none of the beauty of Hy-Breasail. It was almost as if this particular magic isle were the reverse of the first Corum had visited. Soft, unpleasant sounds issued from the interior; sometimes it was as if voices whispered to him. A smell of corruption was carried to his nostrils by an unpleasant wind. Ynys Scaith's chief impression was one of decay – of a soul in decay – and in this it had something in common with the Fhoi Myore. Corum was filled with foreboding. Why should the folk of Ynys Scaith throw in their lot with the Mabden? They would seem likelier to wish to help the Cold Folk.

Again Ilbrec reined in Splendid Mane, a foot or two from the shore, and he flung up his left hand, calling out:

'Hail, Ynys Scaith! We are willing visitors to your land! Would you welcome us?'

It was an old greeting, a traditional Mabden greeting, but Corum felt it would mean little to whomever dwelled in this place.

'Hail, Ynys Scaith! We come in peace to discuss a bargain with you!' called the gigantic youth.

There was a suggestion of an echo, but no other reply.

Ilbrec shrugged. 'Then we must visit the island uninvited. Poor courtesy . . .'

'Which could well be returned by the inhabitants,' said Corum.

Ilbrec urged Splendid Mane forward and the horse's hooves at last touched the grey beach of Ynys Scaith, whereupon the forest ahead of them turned suddenly to blazing scarlet fronds, agitated and whimpering, rustling and chuckling. Looking back, Corum could no longer see the sea. Instead he saw a wall of liquid lead.

Deliberately, Ilbrec rode towards the fronds and, as he approached, they flattened themselves, like supplicants hailing a conqueror. Splendid Mane, disturbed and unwilling to continue, snorted and set his ears back, but Ilbrec clapped his heels against the beast's flanks and on they went. No sooner had they crossed a few feet of these fronds than they sprang up again and the two heroes were surrounded by the plants which reached feathery fingers out and touched their flesh and sighed.

And Corum felt that the fronds reached through his skin and stroked his bones and he was hard put not to lash out at the things with his sword. He could understand the terror of the Mabden when confronted with such monstrous foliage, but he had experienced much more in his time and knew how to control his panic. He attempted to speak casually to Ilbrec who also pretended to ignore the plants.

'Interesting flora, Ilbrec. I've seen nothing like it elsewhere upon this plane.'

'Indeed it is, friend Corum.' Ilbrec's voice shook only a little. 'It seems to have some kind of primitive intelligence.'

The whispering increased, the touch of the plants became more insistent, but the two rode steadfastly on through the forest, their eyes aching from the scarlet blaze.

'Could this be an illusion, even?' Corum suggested.

'Possibly, my friend. A clever one.'

The fronds thinned, giving way to pavements of green marble which lay beneath an inch or two of yellowish liquid smelling several times worse than a stagnant pond. All kinds of small insect life existed in the liquid, and occasionally clouds of flying things would rise out of it and hover round their heads as if inspecting them. To their right were several ruins: colonnades covered in festering ivy, partially collapsed galleries, walls of rotting granite and eroded quartz on which grew vines whose livid blooms emitted a sickly stench; while ahead of them they could see two-legged animals bending to drink the liquid, looking at them through glazed, white eyes before stooping to drink again. Something wriggled across Splendid Mane's path. Corum thought at first he had seen a pale snake, but then he wondered if the thing had not had the shape of a human being. He looked for it, but it had disappeared. An ordinary black rat swam steadily through the deeper reaches of the liquid; it ignored Ilbrec and Corum. Then it dived and disappeared through a narrow crack in the surface of the marble.

By the time they had reached the far side of this expanse the two-legged creatures had gone and Splendid Mane walked on a lawn of spongy grass which gave off disgusting sucking noises whenever the horse pulled its hooves free. So far nothing had menaced them directly and Corum began to think that the Mabden who had landed here had been victims of their own terrors instilled in them by such ghastly sights as these. Now his nose detected a stench not unlike that of cow dung, but rather stronger. It was a nauseating stench and he drew a scarf from under his byrnie and tied it around his mouth, though it made only the slightest difference. Ilbrec cleared his throat and spat upon the turf, guiding Splendid Mane towards a pathway of cracked lapis lazuli leading into a dark corridor of trees which were like and yet unlike ordinary rhododendrons. Large, dark, sticky leaves brushed their faces and soon the corridor had become pitch black, save for a few yellow lights which flickered in the recesses of the foliage on both sides of them. Once or twice it seemed to Corum that the lights revealed grinning faces whose features had been partially eaten away, but he guessed that his imagination, fed by the obscene visions of the recent past, was responsible for these sights.

'Let us hope this path leads us somewhere,' murmured Ilbrec. 'The stench gets worse, if anything. Could it be, I wonder, the distinctive odour of Ynys Scaith's inhabitants?'

'Let us hope not, Ilbrec. It will make communication with them that much more difficult. Do you know in what direction we head now?'

'I fear not,' replied the Sidhi youth. 'I am not sure if we go south, north, east or west. All I know is that the branches above us are getting damnably low and it would be wise if I, at least, dismounted. Will you take a grip on the saddle, Corum, while I get off?'

Corum did so, and felt Ilbrec get down from his saddle, heard the creak of harness and a jingle as Ilbrec took Splendid Mane's reins and began to plod on. Without the bulk of the giant to reassure him, Corum felt much more exposed to the dangers – imaginary or otherwise – of this reeking arbour. Did he hear laughter from the depths on either side? Did he hear bodies moving menacingly, keeping pace with him, ready to pounce? Was that a hand which reached out and pinched his leg?

More lights flickered, but this time they were directly ahead.

Something coughed in the forest.

Corum took a firmer grip on his sword. 'Do you feel we are watched, Ilbrec?'

'It is possible.' The young giant's voice was firm, but tense.

'Everything we have seen speaks of a great civilization which died a thousand years ago. Perhaps there are no longer any intelligent inhabitants on Ynys Scaith?'

'Perhaps . . .'

'Perhaps we have only animals to fear – and diseases. Could the air affect the brain and infest it with unpleasant thoughts, terrifying visions?'

'Who knows?'

And the voice which replied to Corum was not Ilbrec's voice.

'Ilbrec?' whispered Corum, afraid that his friend had suddenly vanished.

There was a pause.

'Ilbrec?'

'I heard it also,' said Ilbrec, and Corum felt him move back a pace and reach out a huge hand to touch Corum's arm and squeeze it gently. Then Ilbrec raised his voice: 'Where are you? Who was it that spoke to us?'

But there came no further reply and so they pressed on, coming at length to a place where thin sunlight broke through the branches and the tunnel divided into three separate paths. The shortest was the middle one for, though it was gloomy, the sky could be seen at its far end.

'This would seem the best,' Ilbrec said, remounting. 'What think you, Corum?'

Corum shrugged. 'It is tempting – almost a trap,' he said. 'As if the folk of Ynys Scaith wished to lure us somewhere.'

Ilbrec said: 'Let them lure us, if they will.'

'My feelings, too.'

Without further comment, Ilbrec urged Splendid Mane into the tunnel.

Slowly the lattice above them opened out until the cracked path widened and they rode down an avenue of stunted bushes, seeing ahead of them tall, broken columns around which climbed the stems of some long-dead lichen, brown and black and dark green. And it was only when they had passed between those columns, carved with demonic creatures and grinning, bestial heads, that they realized they were now upon a bridge built over an immensely wide and dreadfully deep chasm. Once there had been a wall on either side of the bridge, but in most places the wall had fallen away and they could see down to the floor of the chasm where a stretch of black water boiled and in which reptilian bodies of all descriptions threshed and snapped and yelled.

And over the bridge there now moaned a miserable wind, a cold, clinging wind which dragged at their cloaks and even seemed to threaten to toss them off the swaying stonework of the bridge and down into the chasm.

Ilbrec sniffed, tugging his cloak about him, looking over

the edge with an expression of distaste upon his features.

'They are large, those reptiles. I have seen none larger. Look at the teeth they have in their mouths! Look at those glaring eyes, those bony crests, those horns. Ach! I am glad they cannot reach us, Corum!'

Corum nodded his agreement.

'This is no world for a Sidhi,' Ilbrec murmured.

'Nor a Vadhagh,' said Corum.

By the time they had reached the middle of the bridge the wind had increased and Splendid Mane found it difficult to push even his great bulk against it. It was then that Corum looked up and saw what he thought at first were birds. There was about a score of them, flying in a rough formation, and as they came closer he saw that they were not birds at all but winged reptiles with long snouts filled with sharp, yellow fangs. He tapped Ilbrec upon his shoulder, pointing.

'Ilbrec,' he said. 'Dragons.'

They were dragons, indeed, albeit scarcely larger than the great eagles which inhabited the northern mountains of Bro-an-Mabden, and they were plainly bent on attacking the two who sat upon Splendid Mane's back.

Corum stuck his feet into the horse's girth strap so that the wind should not blow him from its back, and with some difficulty he managed to unsling his bow, string it, and take an arrow from his quiver. He fitted the arrow to the string, drew it back, sighted along the arrow, did his best to allow for the strength of the wind, and let fly at the nearest dragon. His arrow missed the beast's body, but pierced the wing. The dragon yelled, twisted in the air, snapping at the arrow with its teeth. It began to fall, righted itself clumsily, but then began to spin round and round, falling towards the dark water below where other reptiles hungrily awaited it. Two more arrows Corum let fly, but both went wide of their targets.

Then a dragon had swept in at Ilbrec's head and its teeth grazed against the rim of the giant's shield as he put it up to defend himself, at the same time swinging Retaliator up in an attempt to stab the dragon's belly. Splendid Mane reared, whinnying, hooves flailing, eyes rolling, and the bridge shuddered at this new movement. A fresh crack appeared in it and a piece at the edge broke off and tumbled into the gorge. Corum felt his stomach turn as he saw the masonry go hurtling down. He shot another arrow and this again missed its mark completely, but plunged into the throat of the next dragon. But now they were surrounded by the flap of leathery wings, the snap of sharp teeth, and claws almost like human hands reached out to tear at them. Corum had to drop the bow and draw his unnamed sword, Goffanon's gift. Half-blinded by the silvery light which issued from the metal, he slashed at random at the attacking reptiles and felt the beautifully honed blade slice into cold-blooded flesh. Now wounded dragons scuttled around Splendid Mane's legs and, from the corner of his eye, Corum saw at least three fall over the jagged edge of the bridge. And Corum saw Ilbrec's bright, golden sword all dripping with the dragons' blood and he heard the voice of the youth as it sang a Sidhi song (for it was ever the Sidhi way to sing when death confronted them):

> Foes from the east we ever faced;
> And fearless foes they were.
> In fifty fights the Sidhi fought,
> Ere they were clad in gore.
> Fierce were we in war.
> Fierce were we in war.

Corum felt something settle on his back and cold claws touched his flesh. With a shout he slashed backwards and his blade carved into scaly skin and brittle bone, and a dragon coughed and vomited blood over his silvered helm. Clearing the chill and sticky stuff from his eye, Corum was in time to stab upward at a dragon who dived down at Ilbrec's unprotected head, its claws outstretched.

And Ilbrec sang on:

Lest Sidhi bodies clay should claim,
Pray let that clay be known.
Let mortal heroes sing our fame,
In Sidhi soil rest Sidhi bones.
In foreign earth we lie alone.
In foreign earth we lie alone.

Corum guessed the meaning of Ilbrec's song, for he, too, disliked the idea of his life being stolen by these mindless creatures, of dying in this nameless place with none knowing how he died.

At least half the dragons had now been slain or so badly wounded that they were harmless, but the movement of the great Sidhi steed as he reared and trampled the corpses of the reptiles was causing more and more pieces of masonry to fall from the bridge and now a sizeable hole had appeared ahead of them. His attention divided between the potential disaster and the immediate one, Corum failed to see a dragon swoop in on him, its claws digging into his shoulders, its snout snapping at his face. With a strangled gasp he brought his shield rim up, jamming it into the dragon's soft belly and at the same time forcing his unnamed sword into the thing's throat. The reptile's corpse lost its grip and flopped onto the stone of the bridge and at that moment the bridge itself gave way and Ilbrec, Splendid Mane and Corum were hurtling downward to where the swimming things swarmed in the black waters of the chasm.

Corum heard Ilbrec yelling:

'Cling to my belt, Corum. At all costs do not lose your grip.'

And though Corum obeyed, he saw little point in the Sidhi's instructions. After all, they were soon to be dead. But first, of course, would come the pain. He hoped it would not last too long.

CHAPTER TWO

The Malibann Reveal Themselves

There was a moment when they were falling and then a moment when they were rising, but Corum, preparing himself for death, had not noticed when the change had come about. Somewhat circuitously, Splendid Mane appeared to be galloping in the sky, back towards the broken bridge. The dragons had gone, doubtless unwilling to follow their quarry down to the bottom of the chasm and contest ownership with their larger cousins.

And Ilbrec was laughing, guessing what Corum must feel.

'The old roads are everywhere,' he said, 'and thank my ancestors that Splendid Mane can still find them!'

The horse slowed to a leisurely trot, still apparently treading thin air, and then continued towards the far edge of the chasm.

Corum sighed with relief. For all that he had good reason to trust Splendid Mane's powers, it was hard for him to believe in the horse's ability to ride across the water, let alone the air. Once again the hooves touched ground which Corum could see was solid and the horse came to a halt. Another pathway led through low hills covered in a kind of fungus, multicoloured, unhealthy. Ilbrec and Corum dismounted to inspect their wounds. Corum had lost his bow and his quiver was empty – he threw it aside – but the dragons' claws had produced little more than flesh wounds in his arms and shoulders. Ilbrec was similarly unharmed. They grinned at each other and it was plain to both that neither had expected to live on that shuddering bridge.

Ilbrec took his water bottle from his saddle bag and offered it to Corum. It was the size of a small barrel and Corum had difficulty lifting it to his lips, but he was grateful for the drink.

'What puzzles me,' said Ilbrec, accepting the bottle back and raising it, 'is the size of Ynys Scaith. From the sea it looks a comparatively small island. Yet from here it appears to be a sizeable land, going on as far as the eye can see. And look –' he pointed into the distance where the hill and the single pine tree stood out sharply, though the scenery all around it was misty – 'the hill seems further away from us than ever. There is no question in my mind, Corum, that this place is under a glamour of considerable power.'

'Aye,' agreed the Vadhagh Prince, 'and I have the feeling that we have hardly begun to understand the extent of it as yet.'

With this, they remounted and followed the path on through the hills until they turned a corner and saw that the hills ended sharply, giving way to a plain seemingly made of hammered copper, shimmering as it reflected the light of the sun; and far away, in what Corum judged to be the centre of this plain, some figures stood. Whether the figures were of beasts or of men, Corum could not tell, but he loosened Goffanon's gift-sword in its sheath and he adjusted the shield more firmly upon his arm as Splendid Mane began to trot over the plain, his hooves ringing and clanging as they struck the metal.

Corum put his hand to his eyes to protect them against the glare of the copper, straining to make out more detail, but it was a long time before he was certain that the figures were indeed human and a longer time before he realized that they were Mabden – men, women and children – and that only a few of the group stood upright. Most lay upon the plain of hammered copper and were very still.

Ilbrec shook Splendid Mane's reins and the great horse slowed to a walk.

'Artek's people?' said Ilbrec.

'It would seem so,' said Corum. 'They have a similar look to them.'

Still a little wary, the two dismounted again and began to walk towards the group of figures who now stood in such sharp outline against the landscape of hammered copper.

As they came within earshot they began to hear voices – small moans, whimperings, groans and whispers – and they saw that all were naked and that most of those upon the ground were dead. All appeared to have been burned by fire. Those who stood had red, blistered skins and it was a wonder that they could remain upon their feet at all. Corum could feel the heat of the hammered copper through his thick-soled boots and he could imagine how fierce it must be on bare feet. These people could not have come willingly unclad to the centre of the plain; they had been driven here. They were dying, roasting to death. Some cruel intelligence had forced them here. Corum swallowed his anger, finding it almost impossible to understand the minds of creatures who could conceive of such cruelty. He noticed now that several of the men and women had their hands tied behind them and that they were trying, futilely, to protect those few children who still remained alive.

As they realized that Corum and Ilbrec had come, the Mabden peered at them in fear through purblind eyes. Blistered lips moved pleadingly.

'We are not your enemies,' said Corum. 'We are friends of Artek. Are you the People of Fyean?'

One man turned his ruined face towards Corum. His voice was like the sound of a distant wind. 'We are. All that remain.'

'Who did this to you?'

'The island. Ynys Scaith.'

'How did you come to the plain?'

'Have you not seen the centaurs – and the monstrous spiders?'

Corum shook his head. 'We came over the bridge. Over the chasm where the giant reptiles dwell.'

'There is no chasm . . .'

Corum paused, then said: 'There was for us.' Drawing a small knife from his belt he stepped forward to sever the man's bonds, but the wretch stumbled backward fearfully.

'We are friends,' Corum told him again. 'We have spoken with Artek who told us what had befallen you. It is largely because we met him that we came here.'

'Artek is safe?' A woman spoke. It was possible that she was young, that she had been beautiful. 'He is safe?' She stumbled towards Corum. Her hands, also, were secured behind her back. She fell and struggled to her knees, whimpering in pain. 'Artek?'

'He is safe – and about a score more of your folk.'

'Ah,' she breathed. 'Oh, I am glad . . .'

'His wife,' said the man to whom Corum had first spoken, but Corum had already guessed this. 'Did Artek send you here to rescue her?'

'To rescue you all,' said Corum. It was a lie he was happy to tell. These people were dying. It would not be long before the last perished.

'Then you are too late,' said Artek's wife.

Corum stooped to cut her bonds, and then the voice he had heard in the forest came again from nowhere:

'*Do not free her. She is ours now.*'

Corum looked about him but, save that the air seemed to shimmer all the more, he could see nothing.

'I shall free her, however,' he said. 'So that she might at least die with her hands unbound.'

'*Why do you seek to anger us?*'

'I seek to anger no-one. I am Corum Llaw Ereint.' He held up his silver hand. 'I am the Champion Eternal. I came in peace to Ynys Scaith. I mean no harm to its inhabitants – but I will not see further harm done to these people.'

'Corum . . .' began Ilbrec softly, his hand upon the hilt of Retaliator. 'I think we confront, at last, the folk of Ynys Scaith.'

Corum ignored him and cut the ropes away from the woman's burned flesh.

'Corum . . .'

Methodically Corum went amongst the folk of Fyean and he offered them his water bottle and those who were bound he freed. He looked nowhere else.

'Corum!'

Ilbrec's voice was more urgent and when Corum had finished his work and looked up he saw that Ilbrec and Splendid Mane were surrounded by tall, slim figures of a brownish yellow colour, whose skins were seamed and whose hair was sparse. They wore little more than belts supporting large swords. The flesh of their lips was drawn back from their teeth, their cheeks were sunken, as were their eyes, and they had the appearance of corpses long preserved. When they moved, small pieces of dried skin or flesh fell from their bodies. If they had expressions upon their faces, Corum could not tell what they were. He could only stand and look upon them in horror.

One wore a spiked crown set with sapphires and rubies. The precious stones seemed to contain more life than did his face and body. White eyes peered at Corum; yellow teeth clashed as the being spoke.

'We are the Malibann and this island is our home. We have a right to protect ourselves against invaders.' His accent was unusual but his words were easy to understand. 'We are ancient . . .'

Ilbrec nodded a sardonic agreement.

The Malibann leader was quick to notice Ilbrec's expression. He inclined his mummified head. 'We use these bodies rarely, he said by way of explanation. 'But be assured that we have little need of them. It is not in physical prowess that we pride ourselves, but in our wizardly power.'

'It is great,' agreed Ilbrec.

'We are ancient,' continued the leader, 'and we know much. We can control almost anything we wish to control. We can stop the sun from rising, should we wish it.'

'Then why exert petty spite upon these people?' Corum asked him. 'These are not the actions of demigods!'

'It is our whim to punish those who invaded our island.'

'They meant you no harm. They were forced upon your shores by unkind elements.'

Studying the horrible, decaying faces of the Malibann, Corum became slowly aware that in many ways they shared characteristics of features with the Vadhagh. He wondered if these were Vadhagh folk, exiled centuries before. Were they the original inhabitants of Ynys Scaith?

'How they came – how you came – is immaterial to us. You came – they came – you must be punished.'

'Are all who land here punished?' Ilbrec asked thoughtfully.

'Almost all,' said the leader of the Malibann. 'It depends upon their reasons for visiting us.'

'We came here to speak with you,' said Corum. 'We came to offer help in return for aid from you.'

'What can you offer the Malibann?'

'Escape,' said Corum, 'from this plane – back to a plane more hospitable to you.'

'That matter is already in hand.'

Corum was astonished. 'You have help?'

'The Malibann never seek help. We have employed someone to perform a service for us.'

'Someone of this world?'

'Yes. But now we grow weary of conversing with such primitive intellects as yourselves. First we shall dismiss this filth.'

The eyes of the Malibann glowed a fiery red. There came a shrill, despairing wailing from the people of Fyean and then they had all vanished. And with them vanished the plain of hammered copper.

Now Corum and Ilbrec and Splendid Mane stood in a hall whose roof had partially fallen in. Evening sunshine filtered through the gaps in roof and walls and revealed rotting tapestries, crumbling sculpture, faded murals.

'Where is this place?' Corum asked of the Malibann who stood in the shadows near the walls.

The leader laughed. 'You do not recognize it? Why, it is where all your adventures took place – or most of them.'

'What? Within the confines of this hall?' Ilbrec stared

around him in dismay. 'But how could such a thing have been accomplished?'

'We have great powers, the Malibann, and I, Sactric, have the greatest power of all, that is why I am Emperor of Malibann . . .'

'This isle? You style it an empire?' Ilbrec smiled faintly.

'This isle is the hub of an empire so magnificent it would make your most marvellous civilization seem like the encampment of a baboon tribe. When we return to our own plane – from which we were banished by a trick – we shall reclaim that empire and Sactric shall reign over it.'

'Who is it that aids you in this ambition?' Corum asked. 'One of the Fhoi Myore?'

'The Fhoi Myore? The Fhoi Myore are merely mad beasts. What help could they give us? No, we have a subtler ally. We await his return at this moment. Perhaps we shall let you live long enough to meet him.'

Ilbrec murmured to Corum, 'The sun is only just setting. Can we have been here such a short time?'

And Sactric laughed at him. 'Is two months a short time in your terms?'

'Two months? What mean you?' Corum made a movement towards Sactric.

'I mean only that the passage of time on Ynys Scaith and the passage of time in your world proceed at different speeds. Effectively, Corum Llaw Ereint, you have been here for at least two months.'

CHAPTER THREE

A Ship Comes Sailing to the Isle of Shadows

'Ah, Ilbrec,' said Corum to his friend, 'then how have the Mabden fared against the Fhoi Myore?'

Ilbrec could not reply to this. Instead he shook his head, saying: 'Goffanon spoke the truth. We were fools. We should not have come here.'

'At least we are all agreed in one thing,' came Sactric's dry voice from the shadows. The gems in his crown glinted as he moved. 'And having heard that admission I am inclined to spare your lives for a while. Moreover I shall grant you the freedom of this island you call Ynys Scaith.' Then, rather more casually than would seem necessary to him, he added, 'You know one named Goffanon?'

'We do,' said Ilbrec. 'He warned us against coming here.'

'Goffanon is sensible, it seeems.'

'Aye. It seems so,' said Corum. He was still angry, still bewildered, still considering attacking Sactric, though he guessed he would have little satisfaction even if he managed to put to the sword that already dead body. 'You are acquainted with him?'

'He visited us once. Now we must deal with your horse.' Sactric's eyes began to glow red again as he gestured towards Splendid Mane.

Ilbrec cried out and ran to his steed but already Splendid Mane's pupils became fixed and glazed and the horse was frozen to the spot.

'He is not harmed,' said Sactric. 'He is too valuable for that. When you are dead, we shall use him.'

'If he will let you,' muttered Ilbrec ferociously, into his beard.

Then the Malibann withdrew into the deeper shadows and were gone.

Listlessly the two heroes climbed through the ruins and out into what remained of the evening light. Now they saw the island for what it really was. Save for the hill (at whose foot they now stood) and the single pine, the rest of the island was a wasteland of jetsam, of carrion, of decaying stone, vegetation, metal and bones. Here were the remains of all the ships which had ever landed on the shores of Ynys Scaith, and here were the remains, too, of the cargoes and their crews. Rusting armour and weapons lay all about; yellow bones of men and of their beasts were much in evidence, some complete skeletons, some scattered, while occasionally Corum and Ilbrec came upon a pile consisting entirely of skulls or another pile consisting of rib-cages. Weather-rotted fabrics, silks, woollens, cotton garments, fluttered in the chill wind which also bore a faint, terrible stink of putrefaction; leather breastplates, jerkins, caps, horse furniture, boots and gauntlets, were cracked, disintegrating. Iron and bronze and brass weapons lay rusted together in heaps, jewels had lost their sheen and looked sickly, as if they, too, rotted; grey ash blew like an ever-moving tide across these scenes and nowhere was there any evidence of a living creature, not even a raven or a cur to feast upon those bodies still fresh enough to have flesh on their bones.

'In a way I prefer the Malibann illusions,' said Ilbrec, 'for all that they were terrifying and came close to killing us!'

'The reality is in a sense more terrifying,' murmured Corum, pulling his cloak about him as he stumbled over the waste of detritus, following Ilbrec. The night was closing in and Corum did not look forward to spending it surrounded by so much evidence of death.

Ilbrec's eye had been casting through the gloom as the giant had walked and now it fixed on something. Ilbrec paused, changed his direction a little, and plunged through rubble until he came to an overturned chariot which still had the bones of a horse between its shafts. He reached into the chariot and the skeleton of the driver fell with a clatter at the movement. Ignoring this Ilbrec straightened his back, holding something dusty and shapeless in his hand. He frowned.

'What have you found, Ilbrec?' Corum asked, reaching his companion's side.

'I am not sure, Vadhagh friend.'

Corum inspected Ilbrec's discovery. It was an old saddle, of cracked leather; its straps did not seem strong enough to hold it to the lightest of horses. The buckles were dull, rusty and half falling off, and altogether Corum considered it the most worthless of discoveries.

'An old saddle . . .'

'Just so.'

'Splendid Mane has a good saddle of his own. Besides, that would not fit him. It is made for a mortal horse.'

Ilbrec nodded. 'As you say, it would not fit him.' But he held onto the saddle as they made their way down to the beach and found a place relatively clear of debris, settling down to rest, since there was little else to do that night.

But before he went to sleep, Ilbrec sat cross-legged, turning the old saddle over and over in his great hands. And once Corum heard him murmur:

'Are we all that are left, we two? Are we the last?'

And then the morning dawned.

First the water was white and wide and then it turned slowly to scarlet, as if some great dying sea-beast beneath the surface were spreading its life-blood in its final throes, and it pulsed as the red sun rose, making the sky blossom with deep yellows and watery purples and a flat, rich orange.

And the magnificence of this sunrise further emphasized the contrast between the calm beauty of the ocean and the island which it surrounded, for the island had the appearance of a place where all civilizations had come to dump their unwanted waste, an elaborate version of a farmer's dung-heap. And this was Ynys Scaith with all its glamours gone, this was what Sactric had called the Empire of Malibann.

The two men rose slowly and stretched painfully, for their sleep had not been peaceful. Corum flexed first the fingers of his artificial silver hand, then he flexed the fingers of his fleshly hand which had become so numb it was almost impossible to tell apart from the unnatural one. He straightened his back and he groaned, grateful for the wind from the sea which blew away the stink of putrefaction and brought instead a cleansing brine. He rubbed at his eye-sockets; the one which lay under the patch itched and seemed a trifle inflamed. He pushed back the patch to let the air get at it, the white, milky scar revealed. Normally he spared himself and others the pain of exposing the wound. Ilbrec had unbraided his golden hair and combed it; now he was plaiting the hair again, weaving in threads of red gold and yellow silver: these braids, thick and strengthened by metal, were the only protection he had for his head, for it was his pride never to fight with a helmet upon his locks.

Then both men walked down to the edge of the sea and washed themselves as best they could in the salt water. The water was cold. Corum could not help wondering if soon it would be frozen. Had the Fhoi Myore already consolidated their victories? Was Bro-an-Mabden now nothing but a dead waste of ice from shore to shore?

'Look,' said Ilbrec. 'Can you see it, Corum?'

The Vadhagh Prince raised his head but could see nothing on the horizon.

'What did you think you saw, Ilbrec?'

'I can still see it – a sail, I am sure, coming from the direction of Bro-an-Mabden.'

'I trust it is not friends bent on our rescue,' Corum said miserably. 'I would not wish others to fall into this trap.'

'Perhaps the Mabden were victorious at Caer Llud,' said Ilbrec. 'Perhaps we see the first of a squadron of ships armed with Amergin's full magic.'

But Ilbrec's words were hollow and Corum could feel no

hope. 'If it is a ship you see,' he said, 'I fear it brings further doom to us and those we love.' And now he thought he, too, could see a dark sail on the horizon. A ship moving at considerable speed.

'And there –' Ilbrec pointed again – 'is that not a second sail?'

Sure enough, for a moment Corum thought he detected another sail, a smaller sail, as if a skiff followed in the wake of the galley, but he did not see it after the first few moments and guessed that it had been a trick of the light.

In trepidation they watched the ship approach. It had a high, curved prow, with a figurehead in the shape of an elongated lion, inlaid with silver, gold and mother-of-pearl. Its oars were shipped and it sailed by the power of the wind alone, its huge black and red sail taut at the mast, and soon there was no question in their minds that it did head for Ynys Scaith. Both Ilbrec and Corum began to shout and yell to the ship, trying to warn it to circumnavigate the island and go on to a more favourable landing place, but its movement was implacable. They saw it go past a promontory and disappear, plainly with the idea of anchoring in the bay. At once, and without ceremony, Ilbrec picked Corum up and placed the Vadhagh upon his shoulders, setting off at a loping pace towards the place where the ship had last been seen. They covered the ground swiftly, for all the debris in their path, and finally Ilbrec arrived, panting, at a natural harbour, in time to see a small boat putting out from the ship, whose sail was not furled.

There were three figures in the boat, but only one, swathed in bulky furs, was rowing. His companions sat in the prow and the stern respectively and they, too, were muffled in heavy capes.

Well before the three men had landed, Ilbrec and Corum had plunged into the sea and were waist-deep, yelling at the tops of their voices.

'Go back! Go back! This is a land of terror!' cried Ilbrec.

'This is Ynys Scaith, the isle of shadows. All mortals who land here are doomed!' Corum warned them.

But the bulky figure continued to row and his companions made no sign that they had heard the shouted words, so that Corum began to wonder if the Malibann had already enchanted the newcomers.

At last Corum and Ilbrec reached the boat itself as it came close to the shore. Corum clung to the side while Ilbrec towered over the boat, looking for all the world like the sea-god his father had been in the legends of the Mabden.

'It is dangerous,' boomed Ilbrec. 'Can you not hear me?'

'I fear they cannot,' said Corum. 'I fear they are under a glamour, just as we were.'

And then the figure in the prow pushed back his hood and smiled. 'Not at all, Corum Jhaelen Irsei. Or, at least, extremely unlikely. Do you not recognize us?'

Corum knew the face well. He recognized the old, handsome features framed by long, grey ringlets and the thick, grey beard; he recognized the hard, blue eyes, the thick, curved lips, the golden collar, inset with jewels, at the throat and the matching jewels on the long, slender fingers. He recognized the warm, mellow voice which was full of a profound wisdom gained at considerable expense of time and mental energy. He recognized the wizard Calatin whom he had first met in Laahr forest when he had sought the spear Bryionak, all that long time ago in what seemed to him now to be a happier period of his life.

And at the moment Corum recognized his old enemy Calatin, Ilbrec said in a voice which shook:

'Goffanon! Goffanon!'

For sure enough the bulky figure who had rowed the boat was none other than the Sidhi dwarf, Goffanon of Hy-Breasail. There was a glassy look in his eyes and his face was slack, but he spoke – he said:

'Goffanon serves Calatin again.'

'He has you in his power! Oh, I knew that I did not welcome that sail.'

Then Corum said urgently: 'Even you, Calatin, cannot survive on Ynys Scaith. The people here have enormous powers for the making of lethal illusions. Let us all return to your ship and sail away from here, there to settle our disputes in a pleasanter clime.'

Calatin looked around him. He looked at the third figure in the boat who had not revealed his face but kept it thoroughly hidden in his hood. 'I find nothing to say against this island,' he said.

'It is because you do not see it for what it is,' Corum insisted. 'Make a bargain, Calatin, to take us back to your ship . . .'

Calatin shook his head and smoothed his grey beard. 'I think not. I am tired of sailing. I have never been at my best while crossing water. We shall disembark.'

'I warn you, wizard,' grumbled Ilbrec, 'that the moment you set foot on this island, you are as doomed as all the other wretches who preceded you.'

'We shall see. Goffanon, drag the boat high onto the beach so that I shall not wet my garments when I leave the boat.'

Obediently Goffanon clambered from the boat and began to haul it through the water and thence onto the beach while Corum and Ilbrec watched helplessly.

Then Calatin stepped elegantly onto the beach and looked around him, stretching his arms so that the surcoat, covered all over in occult symbols, was revealed. He took a deep, appreciative breath of the tainted air, then snapped his fingers, whereupon the other figure, still completely muffled and unrecognizable, rose from the seat in the stern and joined Calatin and Goffanon.

For a moment they stood there, confronting one another with the boat separating them.

'I hope that you are fugitives,' said Ilbrec at last. 'From Mabden victory over the Fhoi Myore.'

And Calatin smiled and hid his lips with his bejewelled hand.

'Are your Fhoi Myore masters all dead, then . . .?' Corum said aggressively, but without much conviction.

'The Fhoi Myore are not my masters, Corum,' replied Calatin chidingly, softly. 'They are my sometime allies. We work to our mutual advantage.'

'You speak as if they are still alive.'

'Still alive, aye. They are alive, Corum.' Calatin voiced these words in the same controlled tone, his blue eyes full of humour and malice. 'And triumphant. And victorious. They hold Caer Llud and now pursue what remains of the Mabden army. Soon all the Mabden will be dead, I fear.'

'So we did not win at Caer Llud?'

'Did you expect that you could? Shall I tell you some of those who died there?'

Corum shook his head, turning away, but then he groaned, 'Very well, wizard, who died?'

'King Mannach died there, his own battle-standard driven through his body. You knew King Mannach, I believe.'

'I knew him. I honour him now.'

'And King Fiachadh? Another friend?'

'What of King Fiachadh?'

'He was a prisoner for a few hours, I understand, of my lady Goim.'

'Of Goim?' Corum shuddered. He recalled the stories he had heard of the female Fhoi Myore's horrible tastes. 'And his son, Young Fean?'

'He shared his father's fate, I believe.'

'What others?' whispered Corum.

'Oh, there were many. Many of the Mabden's heroes.'

Goffanon said in distant, unnatural tones:

'Ayan the Hairy-handed's friend, the Branch Hero, was torn to pieces by the Hounds of Kerenos, as were Fionha and Cahleen, the warrior-maidens . . .'

'And of the Five Knights of Eralskee only the youngest remains alive, if the cold has not taken him by now. He fled on a horse, pursued by Prince Gaynor and the People of the Pines,' continued Calatin with relish. 'And King Daffyn lost his legs and froze to death not a mile from Caer Llud – he had crawled that mile. We saw his body on our way here. And King Khonun of the Tuha-na-Anu we found hanging from a tree not ten yards from him, discovered by the Ghoolegh, we think. And do you know of one called

Kernyn the Ragged, a man of singular dress and unsanitary habits?'

'I know Kernyn the Ragged,' said Corum.

'With a group of those he led, Kernyn was found by my lord Balahr's eye and froze to death before he could strike a single blow.'

'Who else?'

'King Ghachbes was slain, and Grynion Ox-rider, and Clar from Beyond the West, and the Red Fox, Meyahn, and the two Shamanes, both the Tall and the Short, and Uther of the Melancholy Dale. Also were slain in great numbers warriors of all the Mabden tribes. And Pwyll Spinebreaker was wounded, probably mortally. The same is true of Old Dylann and Sheonan Axe-maiden and perhaps Morkyan of the Two Smiles . . .'

'Stop,' said Corum. 'Are none of the Mabden left alive?'

'By now I would think it unlikely, though we have travelled for some time. They had little food and were heading for Craig Dôn where they could be sure of temporary sanctuary, but they will starve there. They will die at their holy place. Perhaps it is all they want. They know their time upon the earth is over.'

'But you are a Mabden,' said Ilbrec. 'You speak of the race as if it were not your own.'

'I am Calatin,' said the wizard, as if addressing a child, 'and I have no race. Once I had a family, that was all. And the family has gone, too.'

'Sent to its deaths on your behalf, as I recall,' Corum said savagely.

'They were dutiful sons, if that is what you mean.' Calatin laughed lightly. 'But I have no natural heirs, it is true.'

'And having none of your own, you would see the whole race die?'

'Perhaps that is my motive for doing what I do,' agreed Calatin equably. 'Then again, an immortal has no need of heirs, has he?'

'You are immortal?'

'I hope so.'

'By what means did you achieve this?' Corum asked him.

'By the means you know. By choosing my allies properly and using my skills wisely.'

'And is that why you visit Ynys Scaith, in the hope of finding more allies, even more despicable than the Fhoi Myore?' said Ilbrec, putting his hand upon the hilt of his sword. 'Well, I should warn you that the Malibann have no need of the likes of you and that they will deal with you as they have dealt with us. We have had no luck in convincing them to come to our aid.'

'That does not surprise me.' Calatin's tone was still equable.

'They will destroy you when they destroy us,' said Corum with a certain grim satisfaction.

'I think not.'

'Why so?' Ilbrec glowered at the wizard who held his old friend Goffanon in thrall. 'Why so, Calatin?'

'Because this is by no means my first visit to Ynys Scaith.' He gestured towards the cowled figure on his right. 'You said I have no heirs, but it was on Ynys Scaith, with the help of the Malibann, that my son was born. I like to think of him as my son. And it was on Ynys Scaith that I learned many new powers.'

'Then it is you!' said Ilbrec. 'You are the ally of the Malibann – the one they mentioned.'

'I think I must be.'

Calatin's smirk was so self-satisfied that Corum drew his sword and ran towards him, but then the flat of Goffanon's axe slammed against his armoured chest and he was knocked down onto the filthy beach while Calatin shook his head in mock despair and said:

'Direct your anger at yourself, Prince Corum of the Silver Hand. You have received poor counsel and followed it. Perhaps if you had been at Caer Llud to lead the Mabden the battle would not have gone so ill . . .'

Corum began to rise, reaching for his sword, which lay a few feet from him, but again black-bearded Goffanon used his axe to push the sword away.

'Prince Corum,' said Calatin, 'you must know that the surviving Mabden blame you for their defeat. They call you turncoat. They believe that you joined sides with the Fhoi Myore and fought against them.'

'How could they believe that? Now I know you for a liar, Calatin. I was here all the time. What evidence have they?'

Calatin chuckled. 'They have good evidence, Prince Corum.'

'Then some glamour was put upon them. One of your illusions!'

'Oh you do me too much honour, Prince Corum.'

'Jhary-a-Conel – was he not there?'

'Little Jhary-a-Conel joined with me for a while, when he realized how the battle went, then he vanished – doubtless shamed at his decision, though I considered it sensible.'

Then Corum began to weep, feeling even more distressed by the knowledge that his enemy Calatin was witness to his grief.

And as Corum wept a voice came from somewhere. It was Sactric's dry, dead voice and it held a note of impatience.

'Calatin. Escort your company to the Great Palace. We are anxious to see what you have brought us and if you have kept your bargain.'

CHAPTER FOUR

On a Hill, Bargaining for the World's Fate

The Great Palace was no longer a palace but a place where a palace had once been. The huge pine tree which stood on the very top of Ynys Scaith's only hill had once grown at the centre of the palace, but now there were only traces of the original foundations.

The mortals and the Sidhi sat upon grass-covered blocks of masonry while Sactric's mummified figure stood at the spot where, he said, their great throne had once rested; this throne, he had told them, had been carved from a single gigantic ruby, but none believed him.

'You will see, Emperor Sactric,' began Calatin, 'that I have fulfilled the last part of our bargain. I have brought you Goffanon.'

Sactric inspected the expressionless face of the Sidhi dwarf. 'The creature resembles that one whom I desired to meet again,' he admitted. 'And he is completely in your power?'

'Completely.' Calatin brandished the little leather bag which Corum remembered from when he himself had bargained with the wizard. It was the bag into which Goffanon had spat. It was the bag which Corum had given to Calatin and whose contents Calatin had used to secure his power over the great dwarf. Corum looked at that bag and he was filled with hatred for Calatin even more intense than he had felt before, but his hatred for himself was even stronger. With a groan he buried his face in his hands. Ilbrec cleared his throat and muttered something, an attempt at comfort, but Corum could not hear the words.

'Then give me the bag which contains your power.'

The decaying hand reached towards Calatin, but Calatin replaced the little bag in his robe and smiled. 'The power must be transferred willingly, as you know, or it will cease to be. I must first be sure, Sactric, that you will complete that part of the bargain which is yours.'

Sactric said bleakly: 'We give our word rarely, we of Malibann. When we give it, we are bound to keep it. You requested our help first in destroying what remains of the Mabden race and then in imprisoning the Fhoi Myore in an illusion from which they will be unable to escape, leaving you free to use this world as you feel fit. You have agreed to bring us Goffanon and to help us leave this plane forever. Well, you have brought Goffanon and that is good. We must trust that you have the power to help us depart this world and find another, pleasanter place in which to live. Of course, if you do not succeed in that, we shall punish you. You know this, also.'

'I know it, Emperor.'

'Then give me the bag.'

Calatin showed considerable reluctance to comply as he once more drew out the leather bag, but at last he handed it to Sactric, who accepted it with a hiss of pleasure.

'Now, Goffanon, listen to your master Calatin!' Calatin began, while the dwarf's friends looked on in misery. 'You have a new master, now. It is this great man, this emperor, this Sactric.' Calatin stepped forward and took Goffanon's huge head in his jewelled fingers and turned it so that the eyes stared directly at Sactric. 'Sactric is your master now and you will obey him as you have obeyed me.'

Goffanon's words were slurred, the speech of an idiot, but they heard him say:

'Sactric is my master now. I will obey him as I have obeyed Calatin.'

'Good!' Calatin stepped back with a look of considerable self-importance on his handsome face. 'And now, Emperor Sactric, how do you intend to dispose of my two enemies here?' He indicated Corum and Ilbrec. 'Would you allow me to devise a means . . .?'

'I am not yet sure I wish to dispose of them,' said Sactric.

'Why slaughter good animals before they need to be eaten?'

Corum saw Ilbrec pale a little at Sactric's choice of phrase and he, himself, found the words distressing. Desperately, he tried to devise a method of capturing Sactric, at very least, but he knew that Sactric was able to enter and leave his mummified corpse at will and to invoke lethal illusions at a moment's whim. There was little either he or Ilbrec could do but pray that Calatin would not get his will.

Calatin shrugged. 'Well, they must die at some time. Corum, in particular . . .'

'I will not discuss the question until I have tested Goffanon.' Sactric returned his attention to the Sidhi smith. 'Goffanon. Do you remember me?'

'I remember you. You are Sactric. You are now my master,' rumbled the dwarf, and Corum groaned to see his old friend brought so low.

'And do you remember that you were once here before, on this island you call Ynys Scaith?'

'I was on Ynys Scaith before.' The dwarf closed his eyes and moaned to himself. 'I remember. The horror of it . . .'

'But you left again. Somehow you overcame all the illusions we sent you and you went away . . .'

'I escaped.'

'But you took something with you. You used it to protect yourself until you could leave. What became of that which you took?'

'I hid it,' said Goffanon. 'I did not wish to look at it.'

'Where did you hide it, dwarf?'

'I hid it.' Goffanon's face now had upon it an idiot grin. 'I hid it, Lord Sactric.'

'That thing was mine, as you know. And it must be returned to me. I must have it again, ere we leave this plane. I shall not leave without it. Where did you hide it, Goffanon?'

'Master, I do not remember!'

Sactric's voice now had anger in it and almost, Corum thought, desperation. 'You must remember!' Sactric wheeled, pointing a finger from which dusty flesh dropped even as he spoke. 'Calatin! Have you lied to me?'

Calatin was alarmed. His air of complacency had disappeared to be replaced with a look of anxiety. 'I swear to you, your majesty. He must know. Even if it is buried in his memory, the knowledge is there!'

Sactric now placed his clawlike hand upon Goffanon's broad shoulder, shaking the dwarf. 'Where is it, Goffanon? Where is that which you stole from us?'

'Buried . . .' said Goffanon vaguely. 'Buried, somewhere. I put it in safety. There was a charm to ensure that it could never be found again, save by me . . .'

'A charm? What kind of charm?'

'A charm . . .'

'Be more specific, slave!' Sactric's voice was high; it shook. 'What did you do with that which you stole from me?'

It had become plain to Corum that the Emperor of Malibann had no wish to reveal to the others what Goffanon had taken and it began to dawn on the Vadhagh Prince that if he listened carefully he might discover some weakness in the apparently invulnerable sorcerer.

Again Goffanon's answer was vague. 'I took it away, master. She . . .'

'Be silent!' Sactric wheeled to address Calatin again. The wizard looked ill. 'Calatin, upon your word that you would deliver Goffanon to me I helped you make the Karach, I helped you infuse life into it, as you desired, but now I find that you deceived me . . .'

'I swear to you, Lord Sactric, that I did not. I cannot explain the dwarf's inability to answer your questions. He should do all you tell him without hesitation . . .'

'Then you *have* deceived me – and deceived yourself, moreover. Something has died in this Sidhi's brain – your magic has proved unsubtle. Without his secret we cannot leave this plane – would have no desire to leave this plane. Therefore our bargain ends . . .'

'No!' shrieked Calatin, rising, seeing his own terrible death suddenly appearing in Sactric's cold, blazing eyes. 'I swear to you – Goffanon has the secret – let me speak to him . . .Goffanon, listen to Calatin. Tell Sactric what he wishes to know . . .'

And Goffanon's voice answered flatly:

'You are not my master now, Calatin.'

'Very well,' said Sactric. 'You must be punished, wizard . . .'

Then, in a panic, Calatin cried out: 'Karach! Karach! Destroy Sactric!'

The hooded figure rose swiftly, tearing off its outer robe and drawing a great sword from a scabbard at its belt, and Corum shouted in fear at what he saw.

The Karach had a Vadhagh face. It had a single eye and another covered by a patch. It had a hand which shone like silver and another made of flesh. It wore ornate armour almost exactly the same as Corum's own. It had a conical cap with a peak and engraved over the peak in Vadhagh lettering was a name – 'Corum Jhaelen Irsei' – which meant Corum, the Prince in the Scarlet Robe.

And the Scarlet Robe, Corum's Name-robe, flapped on the Karach's body as it strode towards Sactric.

And the Karach's face was alike in every major detail to Corum's.

And Corum knew now why Artek and his followers had accused him of attacking them on Ynys Scaith. And he knew why the Mabden had been deceived into thinking that he fought with the Fhoi Myore against them. And he knew, too, why Calatin had made that bargain with him, long ago, for his Name-robe. Calatin had been planning all this for some time.

And looking upon that face that was not his own face Corum shuddered and his veins became cold.

Now Sactric disdained to use his magic against the Karach, the doppelgänger (or perhaps his magic was useless against a creature which was already, itself, an illusion), and he cried to his new servant:

'Goffanon! Defend me!'

Obediently the massive dwarf leapt forward to block the Karach's path, his giant axe swinging.

And, fascinated and full of fear, Corum watched the fight, believing that he at last looked upon the 'brother' of the old woman's prophecy, the one whom he had to fear.

Calatin was screaming at Corum: 'There! There is the Karach, Corum! There is the one destined to kill you and to take your place. There is my son! There is my heir! There is the immortal Karach!'

But Corum ignored Calatin and watched the battle as the Karach, its face expressionless, its body apparently tireless, aimed blow after blow at Goffanon, who parried with his double-bladed war-axe, the war-axe of the Sidhi. Corum could see that Goffanon was tiring, that he had been exhausted before he ever reached the island, and that soon the dwarf would fall to the Karach's sword, and it was then that Corum drew his own sword and ran towards his double, while Sactric laughed:

'You hurry to defend me, too, Prince Corum?'

Corum darted a look of hatred at the corrupt form of the Malibann before he brought his sword, the cross-forged sword which Goffanon had made for him down upon the shoulder of the Karach and made the thing turn.

'Fight me, changeling!' Corum growled. 'It is what you were created to do, was it not?'

And he drove his sword at the Karach's heart, but the creature stepped aside and Corum could not stop his own momentum and the blade went past the Karach's body and then buried itself in flesh, but it was not the Karach's flesh.

It was Goffanon's flesh that the sword found and Goffanon groaned as the blade pierced his shoulder, while Corum gasped in horror at what, inadvertently, he had done. And Goffanon fell back and it must have been that the sword-blade had lodged itself in a bone for the movement of the dwarf's falling wrenched the sword from Corum's hand and left him without weapons so that the Karach, with a terrible fixed grin on its face, a glitter in its single, soulless eye, advanced to slay him.

Ilbrec now drew his own bright blade Retaliator and came striding to Corum's assistance, but before he could cross the space Calatin rushed past him and began to flee down the hill, having given up any notion of defeating Sactric and plainly hoping to reach his boat before the Malibann realized he had gone.

But Goffanon saw Calatin and he raised his hand to grasp the sword he had made and which now stuck in his shoulder (and still he was careful not to touch the handle) and he wrenched it from the wound and he turned it, poised it, then flung it with great force after the retreating wizard.

The moon-coloured sword whistled across the distance between Goffanon and Calatin and the point found the wizard between the shoulder blades.

Calatin continued to run for some moments, apparently unaware that the sword pierced his body. Then he faltered. Then he fell, croaking:

'Karach! Karach! Avenge me. Avenge me, my only heir! My son!'

The Karach turned, its expression softening, searching for the source of those words, its sword falling to its side. At last its eyes found Calatin (who was still not dead but was attempting to get to his knees and crawl on towards the shore and the boat in which, such a short time before, he had sailed in triumph) and Corum felt sure he detected genuine misery in the Karach's expression as it realized the plight of its dying master.

'Karach! Avenge me!'

And the Karach began stiffly to walk down the hill in the wake of its master until it reached the enfeebled Calatin, whose fine, occult robes were now all smeared with his own blood. From this distance it seemed to Corum that he, himself, paused beside the wizard and sheathed his sword. It was as if he watched a tableau from the past or the future in which he was the main actor; it was as if he dreamed, for he could not bring himself to move as he watched his double, the Karach, the changeling, stoop and look at Calatin's face in puzzlement, wondering why its master groaned and writhed in this way. It reached out to touch the sword which jutted from Calatin's shoulder blades but then it withdrew its hand as if the sword had been hot.

Again it seemed puzzled. Calatin was panting out more words to the Karach, words which the onlookers could not hear, and the Karach put its head on one side and listened carefully.

Calatin's dying hands found a rock. Painfully the wizard pulled his body onto the rock and the moon-coloured sword was pushed free, falling to the ground. Then the Karach sheathed its own sword and bent to lift its master, its creator, in its arms.

Sactric spoke now, from behind the three who stood on the hill watching this scene. He said:

'Goffanon, I am still your master. Go after the changeling and destroy it.'

But Goffanon spoke in a new voice, a voice full of its old, gruff assurance. And Goffanan said:

'It is not yet time to slay the Karach. Besides, it is not my destiny to slay it.'

'Goffanon! I command this!' shouted Sactric, holding up the little leathern bag which contained his power over the Sidhi smith.

But Goffanon merely smiled and began to inspect the wound which the sword he had forged himself had made in his shoulder. 'You have no right to command Goffanon,' he said.

There was a deep bitterness in Sactric's dry, dead voice when he spoke next:

'So I have been fully deceived by the mortal wizard. I shall not allow my judgement to be clouded so again.'

Now the changeling Corum was carrying its master to the beach, but it did not walk towards the boat; instead it began to walk directly into the sea so that soon its scarlet robe was lifted on the surface of the water and surrounded both the creature and the dying wizard like so much thick blood.

'The wizard did not deceive you willingly,' said Goffanon. 'You must know that truth, Sactric. I was no more in his power when I came here than I was in yours. I let him think he commanded me, for I wished to discover if my friends were still alive and if I could help them . . .'

'They'll not live for long,' swore Sactric, 'and neither will you, for I hate you most deeply, Goffanon.'

'I came of my free will, as I said,' the dwarf continued, ignoring Sactric's threats, 'for I would make the bargain with you that Calatin hoped to make . . .'

'Then you do know where you hid that which you stole?' Hope had returned to Sactric's tone.

'Of course I know. It is not something I could easily forget.'

'And you will tell me?'

'If you agree to my conditions.'

'If they are reasonable, I will agree.'

'You will gain everything you hoped to gain from Calatin, and you will gain it more honourably . . .' said Goffanon. There was a renewed dignity in the dwarf's bearing, for all his wound evidently caused him pain.

'Honour? That's a Mabden conception . . .' began Sactric.

Goffanon cut him off, turning to Corum: 'You have much to do now, Vadhagh, if you are to make amends for your stupidities. Go, fetch your sword.'

And Corum obeyed, his eyes still fixed on his double. The body of the wizard had sunk completely beneath the waves but the head and shoulders of the changeling could still be seen, and Corum saw that head turning to look at him. Corum felt a shock run through him as single eye met single eye. Then the changeling's face twisted and its mouth opened and it let out such a sudden, dreadful howling that Corum was stopped in his tracks just by the stone where his sword lay.

Then the Karach continued on until its head had disappeared under the surface of the sea. For a second or two Corum saw the scarlet surcoat, his Name-robe, drifting on the water before it was pulled down and the Karach was gone.

Corum bent and picked up his sword, Goffanan's gift, and he looked at its strange, silvery whiteness, and it was now smeared with his old enemy's blood, but he was glad, for the first time, that he held the sword, and now he knew that he had a name for it, though it was not a noble name, not the name he would have expected to have given it. But it was the right name. He knew it, just as Goffanon had said he would know it when the moment came.

He carried the sword back to the top of the hill where the single pine grew and he lifted the sword towards the sky and he said in a grim, quiet voice:

'I have a name for the sword, Goffanon.'

'I know that you have,' said the dwarf, his own tone echoing Corum's.

'I call the sword Traitor,' said Corum, 'for the first blood it drew was from he who forged it and the second blood it drew was from the one who thought he was that man's master. I call my sword Traitor.'

And the sword seemed to burn more brightly and Corum felt renewed energy flow through him. (Had there been another time, another sword like this? Why did the sensation seem familiar?) And he looked at Goffanon and saw that Goffanon was nodding, that Goffanon was satisfied.

'Traitor,' said Goffanon, and he laid a large hand against the wound in his shoulder.

Then Ilbrec said, apparently inconsequentially: 'Now that you have a named sword, you will need a good horse. They are the first requisites of a war-knight.'

'Aye, I suppose they are,' said Corum. He sheathed the sword.

Sactric gestured impatiently. 'What is the bargain you seek to make with the Malibann, Goffanon?'

Goffanon was still staring at Corum. 'An apt name,' he said, 'but you give it a dark power now, not a light one.'

'That must be,' said Corum.

Goffanon shrugged and gave his attention to Sactric, speaking practically. 'I have what you want and it shall be yours, but you, in turn, must agree to help us against the Fhoi Myore. If we are successful and if our great Archdruid Amergin is still alive, and if we can recover the last of the Mabden Treasures which still reside at Caer Llud, then we promise that we shall let you leave this plane and find another better suited to you.'

Sactric nodded his mummified head. 'If you can keep your bargain, we shall keep ours.'

'Then,' said Goffanon, 'we must work speedily to accomplish the first part of our task, for time runs out for the beleaguered remnants of the Mabden army.'

'Calatin spoke the truth?' said Corum.

'He spoke the truth.'

Ilbrec said: 'But Goffanon, we knew you to be wholly in the wizard's power while he held that bag of spittle. How could it be that you were at no time in his power on your journey here?'

Goffanon smiled. 'Because the bag did not contain my spittle . . .' He was about to explain further when Sactric interrupted.

'Do you expect me to accompany you back to the mainland?'

'Aye,' said Goffanon. 'That will be necessary.'

'You know it is hard for us to leave this island.'

'But it is necessary,' said Goffanon. 'At least one of you must come with us and it should be the one in whom all the power of the Malibann is invested – namely yourself.'

Sactric thought for a moment. 'Then I will need a body,' he said. 'This one will not do for such a journey.' He added: 'Best if you are not trying to deceive the Malibann, Goffanon, as you deceived them once before . . .' His tone had become haughty again.

'It is not, this time, in my interest,' said the dwarf. 'But know you this, Sactric, I have no relish for making bargains with you and, if it were only my decision, I would perish rather than give you back what I stole from you. However, the die has been cast so thoroughly that the only way to save the situation now is to continue with what my friends here started. But I think it will go ill for some of us, at least, when your full power is restored to you.'

Sactric shrugged his flaking, leathery shoulders. 'I would not deny that, Sidhi,' he said.

'The question remains,' said Ilbrec, 'how is Sactric to travel beyond Ynys Scaith if the world outside is inhospitable to him?'

'I need a body.' Sactric looked speculatively at the three and caused Corum, at least, to shudder.

'Few human bodies could contain that which is Sactric,' said Goffanon. 'It is a problem which, for a solution, might require an act of considerable self-sacrifice on the part of one of us . . .'

'Then let that one be me, gentlemen.'

The voice was a new one in the company, but it was familiar. Corum turned and saw to his great relief that it was Jhary-a-Conel, as cocky as ever, leaning against a rock with his wide-brimmed hat over one eye and the small, winged, black and white cat on his shoulder.

'Jhary!' Corum rushed forward to embrace his friend. 'How long have you been upon the island?'

'I have witnessed most of what has taken place today. Very satisfactory.' Jhary winked at Goffanon. 'You deceived Calatin perfectly . . .'

'I should not have had the opportunity if it had not been for you, Jhary-a-Conel,' said Goffanon. He turned to speak to the others. 'It was Jhary who, as soon as it was obvious that the day was going badly for the Mabden, pretended to be a turncoat and offered his services to Calatin who (appreciating his own deviousness and thinking all men like him in that respect) accepted. Thus, by sleight of hand, was Jhary able to substitute the bag containing the spittle for one like it which contained nothing but a little melted snow. Then, to find out what Calatin planned against the Mabden, I had only to pretend to be still in his power, while Jhary lost himself in the general confusion after the retreat from Caer Llud, following discreetly until we came to Ynys Scaith . . .'

'So I did see a smaller sail on the horizon earlier!' said Corum. 'It was your skiff, Jhary?'

'Doubtless,' said the self-styled Companion to Heroes. 'And now, as to the other matter, I know that cats have a certain resilience men lack, when it comes to containing the souls of other creatures. I remember a time once when my name was different and my circumstances were different, when a cat was used to great effect to contain (and in this case imprison) the soul of a very great sorcerer – but no more of that . . . My cat will carry you, Sactric, and I think you'll experience little discomfort . . .'

'A beast?' Sactric began to shake his mummified head. 'As Emperor of Malibann I could not . . .'

'Sactric,' said Goffanon sharply, 'you know very well that soon, unless you get free of this plane, you and yours will have perished completely. Would you risk that because of a small point of pride?'

Sactric said savagely: 'You speak too familiarly, dwarf. Why, if I were not bound by my word . . .'

'But you are,' said Goffanon. 'Now, sir, will you enter the cat so that we can leave, or do you not require back that which I took from you?'

'I want it more than life.'

'Then, Sactric, you must do as Jhary suggests.'

There seemed to be no reaction from Sactric, save that he stared at the black and white cat in some disdain for a moment; then there came yowling from the cat, its fur stood on end and it clawed at the air before subsiding. And suddenly Sactric's mummy fell heavily to the ground and lay there in a tangled heap.

The cat said:

'Let us go quickly. And remember, I have lost none of my powers merely because I inhabit this body.'

'We shall remember,' said Ilbrec, picking up the old saddle he had found and dusting it off.

The Sidhi youth, the wounded smith, Goffanon, Corum of the Silver Hand, and Jhary-a-Conel with that which was now Sactric balancing on his shoulder, began to make their way to the beach and the boat which waited for them.

BOOK THREE

---

*In which Mabden, Vadhagh, Sidhi
and Malibann and Fhoi Myore struggle
for possession of the Earth herself and
in which enemies become allies and
allies enemies. The Last Battle against
the Cold Folk, against the
Frost Eternal . . .*

CHAPTER ONE

That Which Goffanon
Stole from Sactric

The journey had been uneventful, with Ilbrec riding on Splendid Mane and guiding the ship on the shortest course to the mainland. And now they all stood upon a cliff at the foot of which a white, angry sea thundered, and Goffanon raised his double-bladed war-axe high above his head, using his one good arm, and then he drove the axe down into the turf which had, until a few minutes earlier, been marked by a small cairn of stones.

The extraordinarily intelligent eyes of the black and white cat watched Goffanon intensely and sometimes those eyes seemed to burn ruby red.

'Be careful you do not harm it,' said the cat in Sactric of Malibann's voice.

'I have still to remove the charm I laid,' said Goffanon.

Having cut away the turf to expose a patch of earth measuring some eighteen inches across, the Sidhi dwarf knelt over this and ran some of the earth through his fingers, muttering what seemed to be a series of simple, rhymed couplets. When this was done he grunted, took out his knife and began to dig carefully in the soft ground.

'Ugh!' Goffanon found what he sought and his face was screwed up in an expression of considerable disgust. 'Here it is, Sactric.'

And he withdrew from the ground, by its thin strands of hair, a human head, as mummified as Sactric's own had been, yet having an air not only of undeniable femininity but also, strangely, of beauty, though there was nothing evidently beautiful about the severed head.

'Terhali!' sighed the little black and white cat and now

there was plain adoration in its eyes. 'Has he harmed you, my love, my sweet sister?'

And now they all gasped as the head opened eyes which were pure, and clear, and icy green. And the rotting lips replied:

'I hear your voice, Sactric, my own, but I do not see your face. Perhaps I am still a little blind?'

'No, I have had to inhabit this cat for the nonce. But soon we shall be in new bodies, bodies which can accept us, on some other plane. There is a chance that we might escape from this plane at last, my love.'

They had brought a casket with them from Ynys Scaith and into this box of bronze and gold they now lowered the head. As the lid closed the eyes stared from the gloom.

'Farewell, for the moment, beloved Sactric!'

'Farewell, Terhali!'

'And that is what you stole from Sactric,' murmured Corum to Goffanon.

'Aye, the head of his sister. It is all that is left of her. But it is enough. She has power equal to her brother's. If she had still been on Ynys Scaith when you went there, I doubt you would have survived at all.'

'Goffanon is right,' said the black and white cat, staring hard at the box which the dwarf now tucked under his arm. 'That is why I would not leave this plane until she was restored to me. She is all that I love, Terhali.'

Jhary-a-Conel reached up and gave the cat's head a sympathetic pat. 'It is what they say, is it not, about even the worst of us having tenderness for something . . .' And he brushed away an imaginary tear.

'And now,' said Corum, 'we must make haste for Craig Dôn.'

'Which way?' asked Jhary-a-Conel, looking around him.

'That way,' said Ilbrec, pointing east, 'towards the winter.'

Corum had almost forgotten how fierce was the Fhoi Myore winter and he was grateful that they had come upon the abandoned village and found riding horses there, and thick furs to wear, for without both they would now be in a sorry plight. Even Ilbrec was muffled in the pelts of the snow-fox and the marten. Four nights had passed and each night seemed to herald a colder morning. Everywhere they had seen the familiar signs of the Fhoi Myore victories – ground cracked open as if from the blow of a gigantic hammer, frozen bodies twisted in the contours of agony, mutilated corpses of human folk as well as beasts, ruined towns, groups of warriors frozen on the spot by the power of Balahr's eye, children ripped into a dozen pieces by the teeth of the Hounds of Kerenos – the signs of that frightful, unnatural winter which was destroying the very grass of the fields and leaving desolation wherever the ice formed.

Through deep drifts of snow they forced their way, falling often, stumbling frequently, and occasionally losing track of their direction altogether – blundering on towards Craig Dôn which might already be the graveyard of the last of the Mabden.

And the white snow continued to fall from the grey and endless sky, and their blood felt like ice in their veins, and their skins cracked and their limbs grew stiff and painful so that even breathing hurt their chests and, leading their horses, they were often tempted to lie down in the soft snow and forget their ambitions and die as they knew their comrades must have died, already.

At night, when they would light a poor fire and sit close to it, they would scarcely be able to move their lips to speak and it seemed that their minds were as numbed by the cold as their bodies; often the only sound would be the murmur of the small black and white cat as it curled beside the bronze and gold casket and spoke to the head within, and they would hear the head reply, but they would feel no curiosity concerning the nature of the conversation between Sactric and Terhali.

Corum was not sure how many days and nights had passed (he was merely faintly surprised that he was still alive) when they came to the crest of a low hill and looked out across a wide plain over which fell a thin drift of snow;

and there in the distance they saw a wall of mist and they recognized the mist for what it was – the mist which went everywhere that the Fhoi Myore went and which some believed was created by their foul breath or which others thought was necessary to sustain the diseased lives of the Cold Folk. And they knew that they had come to the Place of the Seven Stone Circles, the holy place of the Mabden, their greatest Place of Power, Craig Dôn. As they rode closer they began to hear the horrid howling of the Hounds of Kerenos, the strange, melancholy booming tones of the Fhoi Myore, the rustlings and whisperings of the Fhoi Myore vassals, the People of the Pines who had once been men but were now brothers to the trees.

'This means,' said Jhary-a-Conel, riding close to Corum on a horse which pushed wearily through snow which sometimes came up to its neck, 'that some of our comrades still live. The Fhoi Myore would not remain so close to Craig Dôn unless there was something to keep them here.'

Corum nodded. He knew that the Fhoi Myore feared Craig Dôn and would normally avoid the place at all costs; Gaynor had revealed that when he thought he had trapped them there, months before.

Ilbrec rode ahead on Splendid Mane, driving a path through the snow which the others could follow. If it had not been for the Sidhi giant, their progress would have been much slower and, indeed, it was likely that they would never have reached Craig Dôn before the cold consumed them. Goffanon went next, on foot as always, his axe over his shoulder, the box containing Terhali's head under his arm. His wound had begun to heal, but the shoulder was still stiff.

'The Fhoi Myore circle is complete,' said Ilbrec. 'We shall not get through their ranks undetected, I fear.'

'Or unscathed.' Corum watched his own breath billow white upon the freezing air and he tugged the thick furs tighter to his shivering body.

'Could not Sactric conjure some illusion for us that would allow us to pass through the besiegers without being seen?' Jhary suggested.

Goffanon did not like this suggestion. 'It would be best to save the illusions for later,' he said, 'so that none will suspect the truth when the crucial moment comes . . .'

'I suppose that is wise,' agreed Jhary-a-Conel reluctantly. 'Then we must make a dash for it, I would say. At least they expect no-one to attack them from beyond Craig Dôn.'

'No-one in their right mind would,' said Corum with a faint smile.

'I do not think we are sane, at present,' Jhary replied. And he managed to wink.

'What do you think, Sactric?' Ilbrec asked the black and white cat.

Sactric frowned. 'I would rather that my sister and I conserved our strength until the last moment. What you ask of us is considerable, for it is much harder to use our power away from Ynys Scaith.'

Ilbrec accepted this. 'I will go first to clear the path. Keep close behind me.' He drew the great blade Retaliator and it shone strangely in the cold light; it was a thing of the sun and the sun had not been seen on this plain for some long while. Warmth glowed from it and seemed to melt the snowflakes as they fell. And Ilbrec laughed and his ruddy face was full of golden radiance and he cried to his horse: 'On, Splendid Mane! On to Craig Dôn! On to the Place of Power!'

Then he was galloping so that the snow flew in huge clouds on either side of him and his comrades followed close behind, yelling and waving their weapons, both to sustain their spirits and to keep themselves as warm as possible as Ilbrec vanished first into the unnaturally cold Fhoi Myore mist, leading the way to Craig Dôn.

Then Corum had also entered this mist, keeping his eyes fixed as closely as he could on his gigantic comrade, and now he had an impression of huge, dark, bulky shapes moving through the mist, of hounds barking warnings, of riders with green-tinged skins trying to detect the nature of those who had suddenly charged into their camp, and he heard a voice he recognized crying:

'Ilbrec! It is the giant! The Sidhi come to Craig Dôn! Rally, Ghoolegh! Rally!'

It was Prince Gaynor's voice – the voice of Gaynor the Damned, whose fate was so closely linked to Corum's.

Now the hunting horns of the Ghoolegh sounded as they called their fierce dogs to them and the mist was filled with a frightful yapping, yet still Corum could not see the pale beasts with their blood-red ears and their hot, yellow eyes, the beasts which his friend Goffanon feared above all other things.

A huge groaning answered Gaynor's warning, a voice full of pain, and Corum knew that this was the voice of Kerenos himself, wordless, anguished, bleak; the voice of one of the Lords of Limbo, as desolate as the plane from which these dying gods had originated. Corum hoped that Kerenos's brother, Balahr, was not close by, for Balahr had only to direct his gaze upon them to freeze them for eternity.

Suddenly Corum found his path blocked by four or five slack-faced creatures with skins almost as white as the surrounding snow; creatures armed with thick-bladed flenchers more suitable for hacking the carcasses of game than for fighting, but he knew that these were the favoured weapons of the Ghoolegh and it was Ghoolegh he faced now.

With his moon-coloured sword Corum sliced about him, astonished at the ease with which the metal slid through flesh and bone, and he realized that the sword had, indeed, attained its full power now that it had been named. And, though it was almost impossible to kill the Ghoolegh, he maimed his opponents so badly that they ceased to be any danger to him and he was able to pass easily through their ranks and catch up with Ilbrec who could still be seen ahead, Retaliator rising and falling like living flame and slaying pine-folk and the few Hounds who had so far answered the call of the Ghoolegh horns.

For a while, in the exhilaration of battle, Corum was barely aware of the Fhoi Myore mist he breathed, but slowly he realized that his throat and lungs felt as if ice formed solidly in them and his movements were becoming more sluggish, as were the movements of his horse. And desperately he shouted his battle-cry:

'I am Corum! I am Cremm Croich of the Mound! I am Llaw Ereint, the Silver Hand! Tremble, lackeys of the Fhoi Myore, for the Mabden heroes have returned to the Earth! Tremble, for we are the enemies of Winter!'

And the sword called Traitor flashed and brought cold death to a snapping dog, while elsewhere Goffanon sang a dirgelike song as he whirled his axe with one hand in a circle of deadly metal, and Jhary-a-Conel, the black and white cat clinging to his shoulder, a blade in each hand, struck about him, screaming something which seemed more like a scream of fear than a battle-song.

Now they were closing in from all sides and Corum heard the fearful creaking of the Fhoi Myore battle-carts and knew that Balahr and Goim and the others must be close by, and that once the Fhoi Myore found them they would be doomed, but now, too, he could see the shadowy outlines of the first great stone circle of Craig Dôn – huge, rough-cut pillars which were topped by stone slabs almost as long as those which supported them.

Seeing the great Place of Power so close gave Corum the extra strength to force his horse through the green- faced Pine Warriors who rode at him, to hack this way and that with Traitor and draw saplike blood which filled the air with the cloying stink of the pine-tree. He saw Goffanon beset by a pack of white Hounds, go down on one knee, his black head thrown back, his deep voice roaring his defiance, and he burst into the pack, slicing at a throat here, a belly there, giving Goffanon time to rise and stumble into the sanctuary of the first circle and stand panting with his broad back against a granite pillar. Then Corum himself had reached the circle and was safe; within seconds Ilbrec and Jhary had joined them and they all stood there, grinning at one another unable to believe that they still lived.

From beyond the stone circle they heard Prince Gaynor shouting:

'Now we have them all! They will starve as the others starve!'

But the booming, miserable voices of the Fhoi Myore seemed to contain a note of concern, and the howling of the Hounds of Kerenos had an uncertain quality to it, and the Ghoolegh and the Pine Warriors who clustered on the outskirts peered at the four comrades with wary respect and Corum called back to his old enemy, his brother in destiny:

'Now the Mabden will rally and drive you away forever, Gaynor!'

And Gaynor's voice was amused. 'Are you sure they will rally to you, Corum? After you turned against them? I think, my friend, that you will find them reluctant even to speak to you, for all that they are near-dead and you are their only hope . . .'

'I know of Calatin's trick and what he did to destroy the Mabden morale. I will explain this to Amergin.'

Gaynor made no further reply in words, but his laughter cut deeper into Corum's spirit than could the sharpest of retorts.

Slowly the four heroes made their way through the archways of the stone circles, passing wounded men and dead men, and mad men, and weeping men, and men who stared unseeingly into space, until at last they came to the central circle where a few tents had been erected and a few fires flickered and men in broken armour, in torn furs, crouched shivering beside their tattered battle banners and waited for death.

Amergin, slender, frail, very proud, stood beside the stone altar of Craig Dôn where once he had lain after Corum had rescued him from Caer Llud. Amergin had a gloved hand resting upon that altar now as he looked up and recognized the four. His face was grim, but he did not speak.

Then another figure emerged from behind the High King – a woman whose red hair fell to below her shoulders. There was a crown on her head and she was clad in heavy chain mail from throat to ankle, a heavy, bronze-buckled belt around her waist, a fur cloak on her back. And her eyes burned green and fierce as she looked with contempt upon Corum. And it was Medhbh.

Corum made a movement towards her, murmuring: 'Medhbh, I have brought . . .'

But her voice was colder than Fhoi Myore mist as she drew herself up, her hand upon the golden pommel of her sword, and said:

'Mannach is dead. It is Queen Medhbh now. I am Queen Medhbh and I lead the Tuha-na-Cremm Croich. Under our High King, Amergin, I lead all the Mabden, those who are not already slain as a result of your monstrous treachery.'

'I did not betray you,' said Corum simply. 'You were tricked by Calatin.'

'We saw you, Corum . . .' began Amergin gently.

'You saw a changeling – you saw a Karach created by Calatin for the very purpose of making you think me a traitor.'

'It is true, Amergin,' said Ilbrec. 'We all saw the Karach, on Ynys Scaith.'

Amergin raised his hand to his temple. It was plain that even that movement cost him dear. He sighed. 'Then we must have a trial,' he said, 'for that is the Mabden way.'

'A trial?' Medhbh smiled. 'At this time?' She turned her back on Corum. 'He has proven himself guilty. Now he tells incredible lies; he thinks we are so dazed by defeat that we will believe them.'

'We fight for our beliefs, Queen Medhbh,' said Amergin, 'just as much as we fight for our lives. We must continue to conduct our affairs according to those beliefs. If we do not then we have no justification for living. Let us question these people fairly and listen to their answers before we judge them innocent or guilty.'

Medhbh shrugged her beautiful shoulders. And Corum knew agony then. He knew that he loved Medhbh more than he had ever loved her before.

'We shall find Corum guilty,' she said. 'And it will be my pleasure to deliver the sentence.'

CHAPTER TWO

The Yellow Stallion

There was hardly a man or woman there who could stand unaided. Gaunt, frozen, half-starved faces looked upon Corum and, for all that they were familiar faces, he saw no sympathy in them; all judged him a turncoat and blamed him for the huge losses they had sustained at Caer Llud. Beyond the seventh circle of stones, the outer circle, the unnatural mist swirled, the bleak voices of the Fhoi Myore boomed and echoed and the Hounds of Kerenos maintained a constant howling.

And Corum's trial began.

'Perhaps I was mistaken in seeking allies on Ynys Scaith,' commenced Corum, 'and thus I am guilty of poor judgement. But of all else, I am innocent.'

Morkyan of the Two Smiles, who had only been slightly wounded at Caer Llud, drew his dark brows together and fingered his moustache. His scar was white against his swarthy skin.

'We saw you,' said Morkyan. 'We saw you riding side by side with Prince Gaynor, with the wizard Calatin, with that other traitor Goffanon – all riding together, leading the Pine Warriors, the Ghoolegh, the Hounds of Kerenos against us. I saw you cut down Grynion Ox-rider and one of the sisters, Cahleen, daughter of Milgan the White, and I heard that you were directly responsible for the death, also, of Phadrac-at-the-Crag-at-Lyth, that you lured him to his death when he thought you still fought for us . . .'

Hisak, nicknamed Sunthief, who had helped Goffanon forge Corum's sword, growled from where he sat with his back against the altar, his left leg in splints, 'I saw you kill many of our people, Corum. We all saw you.'

'And I say that it was not I whom you saw,' Corum insisted. 'We came to help. We have been on Ynys Scaith all this time – under a glamour which made us think a few hours had passed when really months had passed . . .'

Medhbh's laughter was harsh. 'A folk tale! We cannot believe such childish lies!'

Corum said to Hisak Sunthief: 'Hisak, do you remember the sword that the one supposed to be me carried? Was it this sword?'

And he drew forth his moon-coloured blade and strange, pale light pulsed from it.

'Was it this sword, Hisak?'

And Hisak shook his head. 'Of course it was not. I should have recognized that sword. Was I not present at the ceremony?'

'You were. And if I had a sword of such power, would I not have used it in battle?'

'Probably . . .' admitted Hisak.

'And look!' Corum held up his silver hand. 'What is that metal?'

'It is silver, of course.'

'Aye! Silver! And did the other – this Karach – did it have a hand of silver . . .?'

'I recall now,' said Amergin, frowning, 'that the hand did not seem to be exactly silver. More some kind of mock silver . . .'

'Because silver is deadly to the changeling!' said Ilbrec. 'All know that!'

'This is merely a complicated deception,' said Medhbh, but she was no longer so sure in her accusations.

'But where, then, is this changeling now?' said Morkyan of the Two Smiles. 'Why does one vanish and another appear? If we saw both together we could be more easily convinced.'

'The Karach's master is dead,' said Corum. 'Goffanon slew him. The Karach took Calatin into the sea. It was the last we saw of both. We have already fought this changeling, you see.'

Corum looked from weary face to weary face and he saw that the expressions were changing. Most were at least prepared to listen to him now.

'And why did you all return,' said Medhbh, pushing back her long red hair, 'when you knew that the position was hopeless here?'

'What could we gain by aiding you? Is that what you mean?' said Jhary-a-Conel.

Hisak pointed a finger at Jhary. 'I saw you riding with Calatin, also. Ilbrec is the only one here who was not evidently in league with our enemies.'

'We returned,' said Corum, 'because we had achieved the object of our quest to Ynys Scaith and brought you aid.'

'Aid?' Amergin looked hard at Corum. 'Of the kind we discussed?'

'Of exactly that kind.' Corum indicated the black and white cat and the bronze and gold casket. 'Here it is . . .'

'It does not take the form I expected,' said Amergin.

'And there is this . . .' Ilbrec was dragging something from one of his panniers. 'Doubtless brought in some ship wrecked upon the shores of Ynys Scaith. I recognized it at once.' And he displayed the cracked, ancient saddle he had found on the beach.

Amergin sighed with surprise and stretched his hands towards the saddle. 'I know it. It is the last of our Treasures to remain unlocated, save for the Collar and the Cauldron which still reside in Caer Llud.'

'Aye,' said Ilbrec, 'and doubtless you know the prophecy attached to this saddle?'

'I do not recall any definite prophecy,' Amergin said. 'I was always puzzled as to why such an evidently useless old saddle was included in our Treasures.'

'It is Laegaire's saddle,' said Ilbrec. 'Laegaire was my uncle. He died in the last of the Nine Fights. He was half-mortal, you'll recall . . .'

'And he rode the Yellow Stallion,' said Amergin, 'which could only be ridden by one who was pure in spirit and who fought in a just cause. So that is why this saddle has been preserved with our other Treasures.'

'That is why. But I do not mention all this merely in order to pass the time. I know how to call the Yellow Stallion. And thus I might have the means of proving to you that Corum does not lie. Let me call the Stallion, then let Corum try to ride the beast. If it accepts him, then you will know that he is pure in spirit and that he fights in a just cause – your cause.'

Amergin looked at his companions. 'This seems fair,' said the High King.

Only Medhbh was reluctant to accept Amergin's judgement. 'It could be a sorcerous trick,' she said.

'I will know if it is,' said Amergin. 'I am Amergin. Forget not that, Queen Medhbh.'

And she accepted her High King's rebuke and turned away.

'Let a space be cleared near the altar,' said Ilbrec, carrying the saddle carefully to the great stone slab and placing it thereon.

They stood away from the altar, on the fringes of the first circles of monoliths, and they watched as Ilbrec turned his golden head towards the cold sky and spread his huge arms so that what little light there was gleamed on his red gold bracelets and Corum was suddenly impressed anew by the power emanating from this noble, barbaric god, the son of Manannan.

And Ilbrec began to chant:

> In all nine great fights did Laegaire struggle.
>   Small though he was, his bravery was huge.
> No Sidhi fought better and none more cunningly
>   For the Mabden cause.

> Laegaire was his name, of undying honour,
>   Famous for his humility, he rode the Yellow Steed,
> And led the charge at Slieve Gullion,
>   Though few warriors then remained.

The day was won, but Goim's javelin had found him,
  And Laegaire lay in warm, wet crimson,
His head upon his saddle, dying a warrior's death.
  While his yellow horse wept.

Few were left to hear it when Laegaire named his heir,
  Calling to the oak and alder as witness,
Saying that he had owned nothing but life and his steed,
  His life he gave willingly to the Mabden.

To the Yellow Stallion Laegaire granted freedom,
  Making only one condition on him:
If again Old Night threatened, he must return
  And a pure champion serve in the Mabden cause.

So, dying, Laegaire told his witnesses to take his saddle,
  A reminder of his noble oath,
Saying that he who could sit in it would prove true,
  That the Yellow Stallion would know him.

In summer fields the Stallion grazes,
  Awaiting Laegaire's heir;
Now in Laegaire's name we call him;
  To charge again upon Old Night.

Now Ilbrec sank upon his knees before the altar on which the old, cracked saddle stood, and his last words were uttered in what was almost an exhausted sigh.

Save for the noises in the distance, the boomings and the howlings, there was silence. None moved. Ilbrec remained where he was, his head lowered. They waited.

Then there came a new sound from somewhere, but none could tell from which direction, whether from above them or below, but it was the unmistakable sound of a horse's hooves galloping closer. This way and that they looked, but nowhere could they see the horse, yet still it came closer until it seemed to be within the stone circle. They heard a snorting, a high, proud whinnying, the stamping of metal-shod hooves on frozen ground.

Then suddenly Ilbrec lifted his head and laughed.

And a yellow horse stood there on the other side of the altar, an ugly horse which yet had nobility in its bearing and a look of warm intelligence in its marigold-coloured eyes. Its breath poured from its flared nostrils and it tossed its mane and it looked expectantly at Ilbrec who got slowly from his knees and picked the saddle up in his two huge hands and placed it gently upon the back of the Yellow Stallion, and patted the beast's neck, and spoke to it lovingly, mentioning Laegaire's name frequently.

Ilbrec turned, gesturing towards Corum:

'Now, Corum, try to mount the horse. If he accepts you it will prove to all that you can be no betrayer of the Mabden.'

Hesitantly, Corum stepped forward. At first the Yellow Stallion snorted and backed away, flattening its ears against its head, studying Corum with those intelligent eyes.

Corum put a hand upon the pommel of the saddle and the Yellow Stallion turned its head to inspect him, sniffing him. Corum climbed carefully into the saddle and the Yellow Stallion lowered its long head to the ground and unconcernedly began to nose about in the snow for grass. It had accepted him.

So now the Mabden cheered him, calling him Cremm Croich, Llaw Ereint, and the Hero of the Silver Hand, their champion. And Medhbh, who was now Queen Medhbh, came forward with tears in her eyes, stretching out her soft hand to Corum but saying nothing. And Corum took her hand, bent his head and kissed her hand with his lips.

'And now we must consult,' said Goffanon, his voice brisk. 'What are we to do against the Fhoi Myore?' He stood beneath one of the arches, resting his hand upon the haft of his axe, and he stared beyond the stone circles of Craig Dôn, into a mist which appeared to be thickening.

Sactric, in the form of the black and white cat, spoke in a quiet, dry tone. 'Ideally, I would gather, it would suit you if the Fhoi Myore were where you are now and you were elsewhere . . .'

Amergin nodded. 'That is assuming that the Fhoi Myore have a real reason to avoid Craig Dôn. If it is merely a superstition, then we are lost.'

Sactric said: 'I do not think it merely superstition, Amergin. I, too, understand the power of Craig Dôn. I must consider how best I can help you, but I must have your assurance that you, in turn, will help me if I am successful on your behalf.'

'Once I have the Collar of Power again,' said the Archdruid, 'I can help you. Of that I am certain.'

'Very well, you have made the bargain.' Sactric seemed satisfied.

'Aye,' said Goffanon grimly from where he stood, 'we have made the bargain.'

Corum looked enquiringly at his friend, but the Sidhi dwarf would say no more.

Medhbh whispered in Corum's ear as he dismounted: 'I thought I would not be able to do this, but now I know that I was mistaken, there is a charm I have which will help you, of that I have been assured.'

'A charm?'

She said: 'Give me that hand of silver for a little while. I have the means to make it stronger than it is.'

He smiled. 'But, Medhbh, I need no extra strength . . .'

'You will need everything anyone can give in the coming struggle,' she insisted.

'Where did you get this charm?' To humour her he began to take out the little pins which secured the hand to his wrist stump. 'From an old wise woman?'

She evaded answering him. 'It will work,' she said. 'I have been promised that.'

He shrugged and handed her the beautifully wrought silver thing. 'You must let me have it back soon,' he said, 'for it will not be long before I go to do battle with the Fhoi Myore.'

She nodded. 'Soon, Corum.' And she darted at him a

look of considerable affection so that again his heart was lightened and he was able to smile.

Then she took his silver hand into her small tent of skins, to the left of the altar, while Corum discussed the problems of the moment with Amergin, Ilbrec, Goffanon, Jhary-a-Conel, Morkyan of the Two Smiles and the other remaining Mabden war-knights.

By the time Medhbh had returned and given Corum back the metal hand, offering him a reassuring and significant glance, they had determined what their best course of action would be.

With Terhali's help, Sactric would conjure a vast illusion, to transform Craig Dôn into a form which the Fhoi Myore would not fear, but before that could be engineered, the Mabden must risk the few warriors they had left in a final attack upon the Cold Folk and their vassals.

'We take a considerable risk,' said Amergin, watching Corum strap the silver hand back upon his wrist, 'and we must be prepared for the possibility that none of us will survive. We might all be dead before Sactric and Terhali can keep their part of our bargain.'

And Corum looked at Medhbh and he saw that she loved him again and the prospect of dying saddened him then.

CHAPTER THREE

The Struggle Against Old Night

And now they went, for the last time, upon the Fhoi Myore, and they were proud in their ragged armour and they carried their shredded standards high. Chariots moaned as their wheels began to turn; horses stamped upon the ground and snorted and the booted feet of marching men began to thump like the beating of a martial drum. Pipes skirled, fifes wailed, tabors rattled, and all that remained of the Mabden strength poured out of the sanctuary of Craig Dôn to do battle with the Cold Folk.

And all that remained, perched upon the old stone altar, were a small black and white cat and a box of bronze and gold.

Corum led them, riding the Yellow Stallion, the moon-coloured sword Traitor in his hand of flesh, a round war-board upon his left arm, and two javelins in his silver hand (with which he also held the reins of the yellow steed). And Corum felt the power and the confidence of the horse he rode and he was glad. On one side of Corum rode the High King, the Archdruid Amergin, disdaining armour and clad in flowing robes of blue over which were draped furs of ermine and the skin of the winter doe, and on the other side of Corum rode the proud Queen Medhbh, all in stiff armour, her crown upon her shining helm, her red hair flowing free and mingling with the heavy furs of the bear and the wolf, her sling at her belt and her sword in her hand; she smiled once at Corum before he had ridden past the last stone circle and into the thickness of the mist, calling:

'Fhoi Myore! Fhoi Myore! Here is Corum come to destroy you!'

And the Yellow Stallion opened its ugly mouth and displayed discoloured teeth and from its curling lips there issued a peculiar noise that was like nothing but defiant, sardonic laughter, and then it leapt forward suddenly and it was plain its marigold-coloured eyes could see easily through the mist, it carried Corum so surely towards his enemies, as it had carried its old master Laegaire into the last and ninth of his fights, at Slieve Gullion.

'Hai, Fhoi Myore! You'll not hide for long in your mist!' Corum called, drawing his fur collar around his mouth to keep out as much of the cold as he could.

For a moment he saw a huge, dark shape looming close by, but then it had gone again, and then he heard the familiar creak of wicker, the shambling sounds of the Fhoi Myore's malformed beasts of burden, and then he heard soft laughter that was not Fhoi Myore laughter, and he turned and he saw what at first appeared to be a fire flickering, but it was the armour of Prince Gaynor the Damned, glowing crimson and yellow and then scarlet, and behind Gaynor rode a score of Pine Warriors, their pale green faces set, their green eyes glaring, their green bodies astride green horses. Corum turned to face them, hearing Ilbrec's voice shouting to Goffanon from another part of the field:

'Beware, Goffanon, it is Goim!'

But Corum could not see how Ilbrec and Goffanon fared against the horrid female Fhoi Myore, and he had no time to call out, for now Prince Gaynor came charging down, and he heard only the old, familiar note of the horn which Goffanan blew again to confuse the Ghoolegh and the Hounds of Kerenos.

The Arms of Chaos, the eight-arrowed sign, burned bright on Gaynor's breastplate as he charged, and the sword in his hand shifted its colours from gold to silver and then to sky blue, while Gaynor's bitter laughter sounded from behind his featureless helm and he sang out:

'Now I face you at last, Corum, for this is the time!'

And Corum raised his round shield and Gaynor's flickering sword bit hard into the silver rim and Corum struck with his own moon-coloured sword Traitor at Gaynor's helm and

Gaynor yelled as the blade almost pierced the metal.

Gaynor dragged his sword free and hesitated. 'You have a new sword, Corum?'

'Aye. It is called Traitor. Is it not fine, Gaynor?' Corum laughed, knowing his old enemy to be disconcerted.

'I do not think it is your destiny to defeat me in this fight, brother,' said Gaynor thoughtfully.

Elsewhere Medhbh was engaged with half a score of Ghoolegh, but was giving a good account of herself, Corum saw, before the mist obscured her again.

'Why call me "brother"?' Corum said.

'Because our fates are so closely linked. Because we are what we are . . .'

And Corum wondered again if the old woman's prophecy had referred to Gaynor as the one he must fear. Fear beauty, she had said, fear a harp, and fear a brother . . .

With a yell Corum urged his laughing horse at Gaynor, and Traitor struck again and seemed to pierce the armour protecting Gaynor's shoulder so that Gaynor shrieked and his armour burned an angry crimson. Thrice he struck back at Corum while the Vadhagh Prince tried to dislodge his sword from Gaynor's shoulder, but all three blows landed on Corum's shield and succeeded only in numbing Corum's arm.

'I like this not,' said Gaynor. 'I knew nothing of a sword called Traitor.' But then he seemed to pause and speak in a different, more hopeful tone. 'Would it kill me, do you think, Corum?'

Corum shrugged. 'You must ask Goffanon the Sidhi smith that question. He forged the blade.'

But Gaynor was already turning his horse about, for Mabden with brands had emerged from the mist and with fire were driving the Pine Warriors back, for that part of the warriors that was brother to the tree feared fire above all else. Gaynor called to his men to rally, to press the attack against the Mabden, and soon he was lost in the midst of the Pine Warriors, once more abdicating from a direct conflict with Corum, for Corum was the only mortal who could fill Gaynor the Damned with terror.

For an instant Corum found himself alone, knowing not where his enemies lurked or where his friends were, but hearing the sounds of battle all around him in the chilling mist.

Then from behind him he heard a small groaning noise which grew until it became a sort of bleat, and then a deep, melancholy honking, at once stupid and menacing. Corum remembered that voice and knew that Balahr sought him, remembering how Corum had once wounded him. And he heard the creaking of a great wicker battle-cart, and there came to his nostrils the stink of sickness, the odour of diseased flesh, and he controlled his wish to flee away from the source of that stink, and readied himself at last to face the Fhoi Myore. The Yellow Stallion reared once, its hooves lashing at the air, then became quiet and tense, watching the mist with its warm, intelligent eyes.

Corum saw a black shape approaching. It moved with lurching, unsteady gait as if two legs on one side were shorter than the others; large, blubbery lumps jutted from its body and its head lolled as if its neck had been snapped. Corum saw a red, toothless mouth, watery eyes set asymmetrically on the left side of its head, blue-green nostrils blowing shreds and scraps of leathery skin with every exhalation as, painfully, it dragged its master's chariot behind it. And in the chariot, steadying itself by means of one grotesque arm braced against the wicker wall, its body all covered in a kind of wiry, matted fur spotted with patches of something resembling the mould which grows on decaying food, with patches of bare skin bearing a form of flaking yellow eczema, stood Balahr, booming out his insensate anger.

Balahr's face was red, as if something had chewed it, and there were sores on it and pieces of raw flesh on it, and in places the bones showed through it, for Balahr, like his fellows, was slowly dying of a dreadful, rotting disease, the result of their inhabiting this alien plane for too long. And on Balahr's left cheek something opened and closed and it was Balahr's mouth, and, above the mouth and the eaten-away nose, there was a single huge lid of dead flesh covering Balahr's terrible, freezing eye, and from the eyelid there ran a wire secured to the flesh by a great hook, and the wire had been passed over Balahr's skull and under his armpit and the end of the wire was held in Balahr's hand, his two-fingered hand.

The honking became more agitated, the head turned, seeking out Corum, and Corum thought he heard his own name issue from Balahr's lips; he thought they formed the word 'Corum', but he guessed that this was his imagination.

Then, without Corum's urging, the Yellow Stallion leapt forward, even as Balahr began to move his hand to open his single eye. The horse jumped and it was on one side of the giant, immediately below it, and Corum was able to swing himself from his saddle and take hold of the side of the cart and drag himself up and plunge the first of his javelins deep into the rotting flesh of Balahr's groin.

Balahr grunted in surprise and began to feel around for the source of the pain. Corum drove the second javelin as hard as he could into Balahr's chest.

Balahr found the first javelin and plucked it out, but he plainly had not noticed the second. Again he began to tug at the wire which would open his lethal eye.

And Corum jumped and took hold of a handful of Balahr's wiry hair, clambering up the giant's thigh, almost losing his grip as the hair was wrenched free from the flesh and Balahr shook himself, just as Corum plunged his sword into the Fhoi Myore's back and clung on to the hilt, swinging, for a moment, free in the air.

Balahr snorted and honked, but kept his two-fingered hand upon the wire which would open his eye, slapping at his back with his other hand, and Corum managed to get another purchase in the hair and began to climb again.

Balahr swayed in the chariot; the beast which dragged the chariot seemed to interpret this as a signal to move so that suddenly Balahr was swaying and the chariot was moving and the Fhoi Myore was almost flung backwards from the platform but, with one awkward movement, was able to steady himself again.

And Corum scrambled higher up the back, choking on the stink of the diseased flesh, until he reached the wire at the point where it ran under Balahr's armpit. Then Corum raised his sword Traitor and he hacked at the wire. Once, twice, thrice, he hacked, while Balahr honked and swayed and blew out huge clouds of foul, misty breath, and then the wire was severed.

But with the wire broken Balahr had two hands free and he used them to find Corum, so that suddenly Corum was engulfed by a great, crushing fist and his arms were trapped so that he could not use his moon-coloured sword.

Balahr grunted then and lowered his head and Corum, looking down also, saw that the Yellow Stallion was there, lashing at Balahr's misshapen legs with its hooves.

The Fhoi Myore was not intelligent enough to concentrate on both Corum and the horse and it began to bend, groping for its new attacker, its grip on Corum weakening so that the Vadhagh Prince was able to struggle free, hacking at the fingers as he did so. One finger fell to the ground and sticky ichor began to ooze from the wound, and then Corum was falling, to land flat on his back, all the breath knocked from him. Painfully he got up and he saw that the Yellow Stallion stood near him and there was humour in its eyes; and Balahr's battle-cart was creaking and moving off into the mist again, its occupant honking in a strange, high tone which, at that moment, filled Corum with a feeling of deep sympathy for the creature.

He got back into the saddle, wincing as he realized to what extent he had been bruised by his fall, and at once the Yellow Stallion was galloping again, passing shadowy groups of fighting men, the monstrous shapes of the Fhoi Myore. Corum saw horns glinting high above him; he saw a face which resembled a wolf's, he saw white teeth, and he knew that this was the chief of the Fhoi Myore, Kerenos, howling like one of his own Hounds and striking about him with a huge, crude sword, striking at an attacker who sang a wild, beautiful song as he fought, whose golden hair shone like the sun, who rode a massive black horse which was clad in red and gilded leather and sea-ivory and pearls. It was Ilbrec, son of Manannan, on his horse Splendid Mane, his shining sword Retaliator in his hand, doing battle with Kerenos, as his Sidhi ancestors had done battle in the old times when they had answered the Mabden call for help and galloped to rid this world of Chaos and Old Night. And then Corum had gone past them, glimpsing Goim, with her hag's face and her filed teeth, snatching with clawed hands at the black-bearded dwarf Goffanon, who yelled at her as he whirled his axe, and hurled insults at the gigantic crone.

Corum wanted to stop, to aid his old comrades, but the Yellow Stallion bore him onwards to a place where Queen Medhbh stood over the corpse of her own horse and lashed out at half-a-dozen red-eared Hounds who surrounded her. Into these rode Corum, bending low in his saddle and slitting open the bellies of two of the beasts without pausing, calling out to the woman he loved:

'Climb up behind me, Medhbh! Hurry!'

Queen Medhbh did as he bid her and the Yellow Stallion did not seem to notice the extra weight at all but opened its mouth to laugh again at the Hounds snapping all around him.

Then all at once the mist was gone and they were in an oak-wood. Each oak flamed with fire which had no heat, a fire of intense brightness, illuminating the battle and making all those who fought lower their weapons and gape, and there was no snow to be seen anywhere.

And five monstrous figures, in five rudely-made chariots drawn by five grotesque beasts, covered their malformed heads and wailed in pain and fear.

For all he guessed the origin of the enchantment, Corum felt alarm growing within him, and he turned in his saddle and he held Medhbh close, and he was overwhelmed by a profound sense of misgiving.

Now the Fhoi Myore vassals milled about in confusion, looking to their leaders for guidance, but the Fhoi Myore themselves honked and groaned and shuddered, for the combination of oak-tree and fire was probably what they feared most upon this plane.

Goffanon came limping up, using his axe to help him walk. His body bled from a dozen long wounds he had got from Goim's claws, but that was not the reason his face was so grim.

'Well,' he growled, 'Sactric conjures no arbitrary glamour. Oh, how I fear that knowledge of his.'

And Corum could only nod his agreement.

CHAPTER FOUR

The Power of Craig Dôn

'Once such a strength of illusion is introduced into a world,' said Goffanon, 'then it is hard to be rid of it. It will cloud the Mabden minds for many millennia to come. I know that I am right.'

Queen Medhbh laughed at him. 'I think you relish gloomy thoughts, old smith. Amergin will help the Malibann and that will be an end to it. Our world will be rid of all her enemies!'

'There are subtler enemies,' said Goffanon, 'and the worst of all is that unreality which mars clear-sighted judgement of things as they are.'

But Medhbh shrugged and dismissed his words, pointing to where the Fhoi Myore were urging their chariots away from the conflict, seeking to escape the flaming oaks. 'There! Our enemies flee!'

Ilbrec came riding up, his face all flushed, his fair skin bearing the marks of the fight. He laughed. 'We did well, after all, to seek help on Ynys Scaith!'

But neither Corum nor Goffanon answered him and so Ilbrec rode on, leaning over in his saddle and chopping casually at the heads of Pine Warriors and Ghoolegh as he went by. None attacked him, for the Fhoi Myore vassals were too confused.

Then, as Medhbh dismounted from the Yellow Stallion and went to catch a horse she had observed nearby, Corum saw Prince Gaynor the Damned riding through the burning oak-wood towards him and, about thirty feet away, Prince Gaynor drew rein.

'What's this?' he asked. 'Who aids you, Corum?'

'It would be unwise to tell you, Gaynor the Damned, I think,' replied Corum.

He heard Gaynor sigh. 'Well, all you have done is to make another sanctuary for yourselves, like Craig Dôn. We shall wait on the edges of this place and you will begin to starve again. What have you gained?'

'I do not know, yet,' said Corum.

Prince Gaynor turned and began to ride away in the wake of the disappearing Fhoi Myore. And now the Ghoolegh, the Hounds of Kerenos, the Pine Warriors – all those vassals who still survived – began to stream after Prince Gaynor.

'What now?' said Goffanon. 'Shall we follow?'

'At a distance,' said Corum. His own men were beginning to regroup. Scarce a hundred remained. Among them were Amergin, the High King, and Jhary-a-Conel, who had a wounded side. His face was very pale and there was agony in his eyes. Corum went to him, inspecting the wound.

'I have put a salve on it,' said Amergin, 'But he needs better treatment than I can minister here . . .'

'It was Gaynor,' said Jhary-a-Conel. 'I did not see him in the mist, until too late.'

'I owe Gaynor much,' said Corum. 'Would you wait here or ride with us, after the Fhoi Myore?'

'If their end is to come, I would witness it,' said Jhary.

'So be it,' said Corum.

And they all began to follow the retreating Fhoi Myore.

So anxious were the Fhoi Myore and their followers to depart the burning oak-wood that they did not see Corum and the Mabden behind them. The only one who looked back and seemed evidently puzzled was Gaynor. Gaynor did not fear the oaks, he feared only Limbo.

Something brushed Corum's shoulder and then he felt a small body settle there. It was the black and white cat and Sactric's eyes stared out from its head.

'How far does this enchantment extend?' Corum asked the Malibann.

'As far as necessary,' Sactric told him. 'You will see.'

'Where is Craig Dôn? I did not know we had strayed so far from it,' Medhbh said.

But Sactric did not answer. He spread his borrowed wings and flew away again.

Amergin was staring hard at the burning oaks. He had a look of respect upon his pale features. 'Such a simple-seeming illusion,' he murmured, 'but what power it took to conceive it. I know now why you feared the Malibann, Goffanon.'

Goffanon merely grunted.

A little later the Sidhi dwarf said: 'I still cannot rid myself of the thought that it would be better for the Mabden to die now. Your descendants will suffer as a result of the allies you have used today.'

'I hope not, Goffanon,' said the Archdruid, but he frowned, considering the dwarf's words.

And then Corum saw something, a shadow behind the flaming oaks. He stared hard at it and it began to dawn on him what it was he saw.

Ahead, the Fhoi Myore had come to a halt. Their honkings and their boomings had become still more agitated. They lifted their diseased heads, calling to one another, and there was something pathetic and childlike about their voices.

Corum felt a wave of dizziness sweep through him as he noticed more of the tall shadows. He said:

'It is Craig Dôn. The Malibann have disguised it. The Fhoi Myore have entered the stone circles!'

And Jhary cried: 'My cat! Is Sactric still there?' And the little Companion to Heroes spurred his horse forward, heedlessly dashing towards where the Fhoi Myore gathered. Corum realized that the pain of the wound had affected his friend's mind and he shouted:

'Jhary! Sactric will protect himself!'

But Jhary did not hear Corum. Already he had reached the nearest group of Pine Warriors and passed them unhindered. Corum made to follow him, but the Yellow Stallion refused to move. Corum kicked his heels into the steed's flanks, but nothing he could do would make the Yellow Stallion take one step closer.

And now it seemed to Corum that the stone circles were whirling around him, and as they whirled the burning oak trees began to disappear, and the cold sky returned, and the white plain, and the mist, and he was half-blinded. They were still within the outer circle of monoliths, but the Fhoi Myore were at the very centre. And something seemed to be trying to pull Corum into that inner ring, and a powerful wind tugged at him, but the Yellow Stallion held its ground and Corum clung to the saddle, noticing that many of the Mabden had thrown themselves flat upon the frosty earth.

And Corum heard a terrible grunting and he saw that the Fhoi Myore were trying to burst free from the inner circle, but that the wind forced them back.

'Jhary!' Corum called, but the wind stole his voice. 'Jhary!'

Faster and faster the stones whirled and now only Corum remained in his saddle. Even Ilbrec kneeled beside Splendid Mane, close to where Goffanon stood, staring bleakly at the scene taking place at the centre of Craig Dôn.

Corum saw something crimson fling itself clear from the circle and he saw that it was Gaynor the Damned, fighting fiercely against the wind, moving with painful slowness towards the group of Mabden, sometimes falling down, but always managing to rise, his armour flickering with a thousand different colours.

Corum thought: *So you seek to escape your fate, Gaynor. Well, I shall not allow it. You must go to Limbo.*

And he drew his moon-coloured sword Traitor. And the sword pulsed like a live thing in his hand. And he made to block Gaynor's path.

But the wind still dragged at him and, unlike Prince Gaynor, Corum was not motivated by panic, so that when he dismounted from the Yellow Stallion to step in front of Gaynor he was almost knocked from his feet, but nonetheless he flung himself upon his old enemy, grappling clumsily with him.

Gaynor raised a metal fist and smashed it into Corum's face, at the same time wrenching Traitor from Corum's hand. He raised the sword to strike the Vadhagh Prince down, his armour glowing blue-black, while all around him the stones of Craig Dôn whirled faster.

Then Corum saw Goffanon come up behind Gaynor and seize him by the wrist, but Gaynor turned, breaking free of the Sidhi dwarf's grip and aiming at him the blow he had intended for Corum.

For the second time Traitor bit into Goffanon's flesh, and for the second time it remained there as Gaynor, still desperate, began to run, passing at last through the last circle.

Corum crawled to where Goffanon lay. The wound was a bad one. The Sidhi smith's blood rushed from the great gash Traitor had made and was sucked up by the hard earth. Corum tugged the moon-coloured blade from Goffanon's side and cradled the great head in his lap. Already the blood was draining from Goffanon's face. The Sidhi was dying. He could not last more than a few moments.

Goffanon said: 'The sword was well-named, Vadhagh. It has a fine edge, too.'

'Oh, Goffanon . . .' began Corum, but the dwarf shook his head.

'I am glad to die. My time on this plane was over. They have no place for the likes of us, Vadhagh. Not here. Not now. They know it not yet, but the Malibann disease will linger on this plane, long after the Malibann themselves have gone elsewhere. You should leave, if you can . . .'

'I cannot,' said Corum. 'The woman I love is here.'

'As for that . . .' Goffanon began to cough. Then his eyes glazed, then they closed, then his breathing stopped.

Slowly Corum stood up, oblivious of the great wind which still roared about him. He saw that the Fhoi Myore still struggled, but that few of their vassals could be seen.

Amergin came staggering through the wind and gripped Corum's arm. 'I saw Goffanon die. If we could get him to

Caer Llud when this is done, perhaps the Cauldron will be able to restore his life.'

Corum shook his head. 'He wished to die,' he said.

Amergin accepted this, returning his attention to the inner circle. 'The Fhoi Myore resist the vortex, but it has already taken most of their people back to Limbo.'

And Corum remembered Jhary and searched for him among the dim shapes and thought he saw him, his arms waving wildly, his face frightened and white, near the altar and then he was gone.

And then, one by one, the Fhoi Myore vanished and the wind no longer yelled through the monoliths, and the stone circles ceased to whirl round and round, and the Mabden were rising up and they were cheering and rushing forward towards the altar where still sat a small black and white cat and a box of bronze and gold.

Only Corum and Ilbrec held back, standing over the corpse of the Sidhi dwarf.

'He made a prophecy, Ilbrec,' said Corum. 'He advised us to leave this plane if we could, to go elsewhere. He thought our fates were no longer linked with the Mabden.'

'That could be,' said Ilbrec. 'Now that this is over I think I will return to the peace of the sea, to my father's kingdom. I can celebrate no victories with my old friend Goffanon not here to drink with me and sing the old Sidhi songs with me. Farewell, Corum.' He placed a giant hand upon Corum's shoulder. 'Or would you come with me?'

'I love Medhbh,' said Corum. 'That is why I must remain.'

Ilbrec got slowly into Splendid Mane's saddle and without further ceremony began to ride over the snow-covered plain, heading back into the west.

Only Corum saw him depart.

CHAPTER FIVE

The Return to Castle Owyn

They had come back to Caer Lludd to find the winter faded and a kind of spring in its place, and although there were many ruins to rebuild and many corpses to burn with due ceremony upon the stone pyres on the outskirts of the city, and although there remained, here and there, many signs of the Fhoi Myore occupation of the Mabden capital, they were still joyful.

Amergin went to the great tower where he had once been held prisoner under an enchantment (and from where Corum had rescued him), and he found the Cauldron and he found his Collar of Power and he displayed them to all the Mabden who had come with him back to Caer Lludd, he offered them as proof that the Fhoi Myore were gone forever from the land, that Old Night was surely banished.

And they honoured Corum as a great hero, who had saved their race. They made up songs concerning his three quests, his deeds and his courage; but Corum found that he could not smile, that he could feel no elation, only sadness, for he mourned for Jhary-a-Conel, banished to Limbo with the Fhoi Myore, and he mourned for the Sidhi dwarf Goffanon, slain by the sword called Traitor.

Soon after they had arrived at Caer Lludd, Amergin took the small black and white cat and the box of bronze and gold away with him to the top of his tower, and during the night there was a dry storm, and much lightning and thunder, but no rain, and eventually, in the morning, Amergin emerged from his tower without the box of bronze and gold, but holding the trembling body of the cat, and he told Corum that the bargain with the Malibann had

433

been completed. Corum took the cat, which no longer had Sactric's eyes, and kept it ever with him.

When the first celebrations were over, Corum went to Amergin and bade farewell to the High King, saying that he had it in mind to return to Caer Mahlod with those of the Tuha-na-Cremm Croich still alive, and that the woman he loved, Queen Medhbh, also wished this. So Amergin thanked Corum once more and said that soon he, too, would visit Caer Mahlod, for there were still many things they could fruitfully discuss, and Corum said that he looked forward with pleasure to Amergin's visit.

Then they left.

They rode back into the west and they saw that the west was green again, though the animals were slow in returning and the farms were deserted and there were nothing but corpses in the villages, and then they came to Caer Mahlod, the fortress-city on the conical hill, close to the oak grove, and not far from the sea, and they were there for several days before Medhbh woke one morning and leaned over Corum and stroked his head and said to him:

'You have changed, my love. You are so grim.'

'Forgive me,' he said. 'I love you, Medhbh.'

'I forgive you,' she told him. 'And I love you, Corum.' But there was a note of hesitation in her voice and her eyes looked away into a distance. 'I love you,' she said again. She kissed him.

A night or two later he lay again in bed and he awoke from a nightmare in which he had seen his own face all twisted with malice and he heard a harp playing somewhere beyond the walls of Caer Mahlod and he looked to wake Medhbh and tell her of it, but she was not in the bed and when he sought her he could find her nowhere. He asked her, in the morning, where she had been, but she told him that he must have awakened from one dream into another, that she had been at his side all night.

And the next night he woke up and he saw that she lay sleeping peacefully beside him, but he had a mind to get up (he did not know why) and put on all his armour, and to strap his sword, Traitor, around him. He went out of the castle, leading the Yellow Stallion, and he mounted the steed and turned its head towards the sea and he rode until he reached the cliff which had broken away, leaving an isolated peak on which stood the ruins of a place called by the Mabden Castle Owyn and by him Castle Erorn, where he had been born and where, until the coming of the old Mabden, he had been happy.

And Corum bent his head to the ear of the Yellow Stallion and said to that noble, ugly horse: 'You have great strength, horse of Laegaire, and you have great intelligence. Could you leap this gulf and take me to Castle Erorn?'

And the Yellow Stallion turned his warm, marigold-coloured eyes to look at Corum and there was not amusement there but concern, and the Yellow Stallion snorted and pawed the ground.

'Do this, Yellow Stallion,' said Corum, 'and I will free you to return to whence you came.'

The Yellow Stallion hesitated, then seemed to agree. He turned and trotted back towards Caer Mahlod, then turned again and began to gallop, faster and faster, until the gulf between the mainland and the promontory on which Castle Owyn stood was very close, and the spray was white in the moonlight and the sea boomed like the voice of a banished Fhoi Myore, and the Yellow Stallion tensed himself, then leapt, and his hooves came down squarely upon the rock on the other side; at last Corum had achieved his ambition. He dismounted.

Then the Yellow Stallion looked enquiringly at him and Corum said simply: 'You are free, upon the same conditions that Laegaire made.'

The Yellow Stallion nodded his head and turned and leapt again across the gulf and was gone into the darkness. And over the sound of the sea Corum thought he heard a voice calling to him from the battlements of Caer Mahlod. Was it Medhbh's voice that called?

He ignored the voice. He stood there and contemplated the old, worn walls of Castle Erorn, and he remembered

how the Mabden had killed his family and then maimed
him, taking away his hand and his eye, and he wondered,
for a moment, why he had served them so long and so
fully. It seemed ironic to him then that, in both cases, it
had been largely for the love of Mabden women. But
there was a difference between Rhalina and Queen
Medhbh that he could not understand, though he loved
them both, and they had loved him.

He heard a movement from within the ruined walls and
he stepped closer, wondering if he would see again the
youth with the face and limbs of gold whom he had seen
there once and who was called Dagdagh. He saw a
shadow move, glimpsed scarlet in the moonlight, called
out:

'Who's there?'

There was no reply.

He stepped closer until his hand touched the time-
smoothed carving of the portal, and he hesitated before
he went further, saying again:

'Who's there?'

And something hissed like a snake. And something
clicked. And something rattled. And Corum saw that the
body of a man was outlined against the light which
entered through a ruined window, and the man turned
and his face was revealed to Corum.

It was Corum's face. It was Calatin's changeling, his
Karach, smelling of brine. And the Karach smiled and
drew its sword.

'I greet you, brother,' said Corum. 'I knew in my bones
that the prophecy would be fulfilled tonight. I think that
that is why I came.'

The Karach said nothing, only smiled, and in the
distance now Corum heard the sweet, sinister tones of the
Dagdagh harp.

'But what,' said Corum, 'is the beauty I must fear?'

And he drew out his sword, Traitor.

'Do you know, changeling?' he asked.

But the changeling's smile merely broadened a little to
show white teeth the exact match of Corum's.

'I think I would have my robe back now,' said Corum. 'I know that I must fight you for it.'

And they came together, then, fighting, so their swords struck bright sparks in the gloom of the castle's interior. As Corum had guessed, they were perfectly balanced, skill for skill, strength for strength.

They fought all over the cracked floor of castle Erorn. They fought over slabs of broken masonry. They fought on half-fallen stairways. They fought for an hour, matching blow for blow, cunning for cunning, but now Corum understood that the changeling had one advantage: he was tireless.

The wearier Corum became the more energetic the changeling seemed to be. He did not speak (perhaps he could not speak) but his smile grew imperceptibly broader and increasingly mocking.

Corum fell back, depending more and more upon defensive swordplay. The changeling drove him out of the door of Castle Erorn, drove him to the very edge of the cliff, until Corum gathered his strength and lunged forward, taking the changeling by surprise and grazing his arm with Traitor.

The changeling did not seem to feel the wound, renewing his attack with vigour.

Then Corum's heel struck a rock and he stumbled backwards and fell, his sword flying from his hand, and he cried out in a miserable voice:

'This is unjust! This is unjust!'

And then the harp began to sound again and it seemed to sing a song with words. He thought it sang:

'*Ah, the world was ever so. How sad are heroes when their tasks are done . . .*'

As if savouring its victory, the changeling moved slowly forward, raising its sword.

Corum felt a tugging at his left wrist. It was his silver hand and it had come alive of its own volition. He saw the straps and the pins loosen, he saw the silver hand rise up and travel swiftly to where Traitor lay, glowing in the moonlight.

'I am mad,' said Corum. But he recalled how Medhbh had taken his hand away to put a charm upon it. He had forgotten, as, no doubt, had she.

Now the silver hand, which Corum had fashioned himself, took hold of the Sidhi-forged sword while the changeling looked wide-eyed at it and hissed, stumbling away from it, moaning.

And the silver hand drove the sword Traitor deep into the changeling's heart and the changeling yelled and fell and was dead.

Corum laughed.

'Farewell, brother! I was right to fear you, but you did not bring me my doom!'

The harp sounded louder now, coming from within the castle. Forgetful of his sword and his silver hand, Corum ran back into the castle, and there stood the Dagdagh, a youth all of gold, with sharp, beautiful features and deep, sardonic eyes, and he played upon a harp which seemed in some way to grow out of him and into him and was part of his body. Behind the Dagdagh, Corum saw another whom he recognized, and it was Gaynor.

Corum wished that he had not forgotten his sword. He said:

'How I hate you, Gaynor. You slew Goffanon.'

'Inadvertently. I have come to make peace with you, Corum.'

'Peace? You are my most terrible enemy and ever shall be!'

'Listen to the Dagdagh,' said Gaynor the Damned.

And the Dagdagh spoke – or rather he sang – and he said this to Corum:

'You are not welcome, mortal. Take your Name-robe from the changeling's corpse and leave this world. You were brought here for one purpose. Now that purpose is achieved you must go.'

'But I love Medhbh,' said Corum. 'I will not leave her!'

'You loved Rhalina and you see her in Medhbh.'

Gaynor said urgently: 'I speak without malice, Corum. Believe the Dagdagh. Come with me now. He has opened a door into a land where we can both know peace. It is true, Corum, I have been there briefly. Here is our chance to see an end to the eternal struggle.'

Corum shook his head. 'Perhaps you speak the truth, Gaynor. I see truth in the Dagdagh's eyes, too. But I must stay here. I love Medhbh.'

'I have spoken to Medhbh,' said the Dagdagh. 'She knows that it is wrong for you to remain in this world. You do not belong. Come, now, to the land where you and Gaynor will know contentment. It is a great reward I offer you, Eternal Champion. It is more than I could normally achieve.'

'I must stay,' said Corum.

The Dagdagh began to play upon his harp. The music was sweet and it was euphoric. It was the music of noble love, of selfless heroism. Corum smiled.

He bowed to the Dagdagh, thanking him for what he had offered, and he made a sign of farewell to Gaynor. Then he walked out of the old doorway of Castle Erorn and he saw that Medhbh was waiting for him on the other side. He smiled at her, lifting his right hand in greeting.

But she did not smile back. There was something in her own right hand which she now raised above her head and began to whirl. It was her sling. He looked at her in surprise. Did she seek to slay the Dagdagh, in whom she had put so much trust?

Something left the sling and struck him upon the forehead and he fell down, but he still lived, though his heart was in agony and his head was cracked. He felt the blood pour down his face.

And he saw that the Dagdagh loomed over him, looking down on him with an expression of sympathy. And Corum snarled at the Dagdagh.

'Fear a harp,' said the Dagdagh in his high, sweet voice, 'fear beauty,' and he glanced across the chasm to where Medhbh stood weeping, 'and fear a brother . . .'

'Your harp it was that turned Medhbh's heart against me,' said Corum. 'I was right to fear that. And I should have feared her beauty, for it is what has destroyed me. But I slew the brother, I slew the Karach.'

'No,' said the Dagdagh, and he picked up the tathlum which Medhbh had hurled. 'Here is your brother, Corum. His brain she mixed with lime to make the only thing which Fate would allow to slay you. She took the brain from under the mound, from the mound of Cremm Croich, and, on my instructions, she made it. Cremm Croich slays Corum Llaw Ereint. You did not have to die.'

'I could not deny her love.' Corum managed to rise to his feet and put his left hand to his cracked skull, feeling the blood flow over it. 'I love her still.'

'I spoke to her. I told her what I would offer you and what she must do if you refused that offer. You have no place here, Corum.'

'So say you!' Corum gathered his strength and he lunged at the Dagdagh, but the youth of gold made a sign and Corum's silver hand appeared, still clutching the moon-coloured sword Traitor.

And Corum heard Medhbh utter a shriek before the sword entered his heart at exactly the same spot it had entered the changeling's.

And he heard the Dagdagh say:

'Now this world is free of all sorcery and all demigods.'

Then Corum died.